CRAZY RAZOR

A NOVEL OF THE VIETNAM WAR

Dan —

From one struggling author to another. I'm just glad I don't need royalties to eat.

[signature]

8/14/20__

KENNETH LEVIN

ISBN: 1475143370
ISBN-13: 9781475143379
Library of Congress Control Number: 2012906340

CreateSpace, North Charleston, SC

Dedicated to LD

Author's Note

This is a war story. It's neither fiction nor nonfiction. It's a war story. The only real villain is the war.

It's impossible for me to write a story like this without lapsing into jargon and slang. Military jargon and post-adolescent American male slang. Words like cumshaw, jaygee, and gook mix with an alphabet soup of MACV, PCOD, LBFM, M-16, and AO. To those who were in the military and in Vietnam in the late 1960s, it was second nature, unambiguous. To those who were not, it may seem like an indecipherable foreign language. At the suggestions of readers of the many drafts of this book, I have tried to eliminate some of the jargon, or at least explain it in the text. But much remains. So I've added a glossary to this book to help and translate.

This book contains two major characters—each a protagonist or antagonist depending on your perspective. And the book has another dozen or so who are important to the story. Since many of the characters have military titles and foreign names, I've also added a list of characters to help you the reader.

And lastly, a word about the title of this book. Crazy Razor is a call sign. Radio communications in the military use call signs to identify a person or a combat unit. For example, a ship might be commanded by Captain Davey Jones. A call sign will be used to contact him or his ship. Rather than calling him "Captain Jones" or the ship "USS Constitution" on the radio, the assigned call sign is used. The call signs could be something along the lines of "Charger" or "Thunder" or even "Ditty Box." In this story, the call sign "Crazy Razor" was assigned to the senior US Navy advisor to the South Vietnamese Navy's River Assault Group Bravo. Crazy Razor was first the call sign for Lieutenant Gordon and then for his replacement, Lieutenant Coburn. Call signs for subordinates to the senior advisor would use a suffix: Crazy Razor Alpha for Chief Petty Officer Robinson or Crazy Razor Bravo for First Class Petty Officer Cruz.

In Vietnam, it was not unusual for call signs to be used during informal face-to-face communications. Often people were better known by their call signs than by their names or ranks.

"You can kill ten of my men for every one I kill of yours. But even at those odds, you will lose and I will win."

- Ho Chi Minh

THE RIVER

CHAPTER 1
SAIGON RIVER

The Saigon River is not one of the world's great rivers. It starts in Cambodia and about 140 miles later ends where it becomes just a tributary of a much bigger river southeast of Ho Chi Minh City. It's only a couple of hundred yards at its widest; a person can swim across it. Ships with drafts greater than thirty feet will go aground on its muddy bottom. Only shallow sampans can travel its full length. From a Huey helicopter, it looks like a brown intestine as it snakes from Cambodia southeast to the big southern Vietnamese metropolis.

In the late 1960s, as it had for centuries, the river supplied water to the Vietnamese for their cooking, their drinking, and their laundry. It irrigated their fields and sugar cane and rubber trees, watered their cattle and poultry, and cooled their industries. And it carried away all their wastes. The river was rich in nutrients, ranging from fish and crabs to microbes and bacteria. Vegetation, dead animals, and human corpses rotted in it. Until the Americans introduced defoliants to the riverbanks, the Saigon River was not polluted by man's chemicals.

People and goods traveled the river, downriver from Cambodia and upriver from Saigon. A bridge crossed it at Phu Cuong.

A muddy brown, the river stank of rot and sulfur as it flowed warm and languid. Many of the microscopic creatures that lived in it were phosphorescent. A boat's wake at night could glow a beautiful phantom silver. At dark a bowl of water allowed to boil dry looked as if it was filled with gems.

The Saigon River and its banks were a battlefield where men—and women and children—died. Not famous like Gettysburg, Waterloo, Dien Ben Phu, or Khe Sanh, but a battlefield nevertheless.

SELECTION

CHAPTER 2
NEWPORT, RHODE ISLAND

The commanding officer of the big guided missile cruiser USS DeKalb hung up the phone and leaned back in his desk chair, frowning at his scribbled notes. It was the first month of 1968, and his country was fighting a war in Vietnam. The war consumed men and material and money.

He had to get his ship ready for a deployment to the Mediterranean in a few months, and now he had another problem to solve before that could happen. Twenty-six years as a naval officer and nothing but challenges, problems to solve, sacrifices to make. No breaks, no easy times in his climb from ensign to captain.

His boss, a rear admiral, had told him that he was a strong candidate for selection to flag rank, which would be a real honor and vindication of all his efforts. And the cruiser's captain knew that the higher he climbed the ladder, the greater the load he would have to carry. But first, he had to deal with this new problem.

He picked up the handset and pressed the buzzer.

"Bridge. Petty Officer of the Watch BM2 Katoski," was the quick response.

"Ski, this is the captain. Is Mr. Coburn still up there?"

"Yes sir. He's out on the starboard bridge wing."

"What's our status, Ski?"

"Main engines secured. Tugs sent home. All lines over, doubling up now. Still waiting to shift to shore power. Phone lines hooked up, sir."

"As soon as we're on shore power and the generators secured, ask Mr. Coburn to come down to my cabin. Pipe the XO and weps boss to come to my cabin now, please."

"Aye, aye, Captain. Mr. Coburn to your cabin after the ship's secured. XO and weps to your cabin."

As the captain replaced the handset, the ship's loudspeakers came alive with the trilling of the bosun's pipe. "Now executive officer and weapons officer, your presence is requested in the captain's in-port cabin." Turning to the mound of neglected paperwork on his desk, the commanding officer sighed, picked up his pen, and started reading.

He had barely started on the paper pile when a knock on the cabin door interrupted him.

In walked the executive officer and weapons officer, both in heavy bridge coats, gloves, and scarves, with hats under their arms, faces red from the cold and noses running. "You wanted to see us, Skipper?"

"Yep, XO. Drop your coats and stuff on the couch. Grab a seat. Want some coffee?"

"I'd better pass unless you want me getting up every five minutes to pee," said the executive officer, a prematurely gray commander.

"Thanks, I'll have a cup, Captain," said the smiling weapons department head, a short, slim lieutenant commander.

After the captain ordered coffee for the weapons officer and himself from the ever-hovering steward, he turned his chair to face the two officers.

"Okay," he referred to his notes. "As soon as we got a working phone line, I came down here and let you two freeze on the bridge wings so I could call the Bureau of Personnel. We're short

8

three junior officers right now, and we lose the operations officer in the middle of the Med cruise. That means we'll be minus a department head and three junior officers. I asked the surface detailer where replacements are in the pipeline. He said that ops will be replaced by a guy who just started Destroyer School, so operations department will probably be gapped for at least a month or two. We can live with that since I have such a cracker-jack XO who can do anything with nothing."

"Captain, you *had* a superman XO who just quit. I want to go home to my mommy," grumbled the executive officer.

Without looking up from his notes, the captain said, "Tough shit, XO. You're stuck. Besides, your mother never loved you as much as we do." He went on, "The problem's with the JOs. Detailer says he can get us one out of Officer Candidate School with a stop for a basic ship handling school on the way here. But that's it. Everything else is getting sucked up by the Pacific and Vietnam."

The weapons officer stirred some sugar and milk into his coffee and thought out loud, "That still leaves us minus two junior officers, and that new fellow probably won't be carrying his load for at least six months or so. This could be a tough cruise with no one getting any sleep."

"You're right, Weps. But it gets worse. BUUPERS is going to cut orders this week for Clark Coburn to go in-countryin-country. Vietnam." ✓

The XO sat up out of his dejected slouch. "Captain, that means we'll be short another JO and we lose a qualified officer of the deck, an experienced OOD. What do they expect us to do, park the ship in the middle of the ocean when the officers of the deck collapse from fatigue?"

"Captain, Clark's our gunnery officer and guns division head," said the weapons officer. "I think we're scheduled for a lot of gunnery exercises as soon as we go on deployment. Will they yank him before that?"

"Yes, there's no way we're heading to the Med with Clark aboard. The whole Atlantic Fleet is getting raped. Everyone's

9

losing officers and not getting replacements. The surface detailer told me some Atlantic Fleet ships are going to be steaming with 60 percent of allotted officer complements, or worse."

"I want my mommy," groaned the XO.

"Don't we all," smiled the CO. "So here's the task for you two geniuses. First, XO, look at all the JOODs and pick out the best and accelerate their training. We need at least two more qualified officers of the deck ASAP. There's some good talent in the JO locker on this ship, so let's get them going.

"Second, figure out whom we can move into Clark's billet as gunnery officer and division officer. You got any likely candidates, Weps? If we need to rob the engineering or operations departments, let's do it."

The captain paused for a long moment and then in a more relaxed voice asked, "What's your opinion of Coburn? What's his background?"

The XO and Weps looked at each other. With a nod from the XO, Weps spoke. "Clark's a USNR out of OCS after graduating from some liberal arts college in the northeast. I think his family's from there. He's been doing a pretty good job. His division is well run and has few problems. Probably the best division in the weapons department, maybe the best on the ship. He has a real good chief and leading petty officers. How much of that division's performance is due to Clark or his senior enlisted? I don't know. I guess that doesn't matter since it's well run."

Weps paused and looked into his coffee cup and then continued, "Since his division is doing well and the guns and magazines are in good shape, I've been hands off and leaving well enough alone. I don't know if Coburn is exercising good delegating skills or simply taking advantage of his good chief and being lazy. But he is smart and has a good sense of humor. Looks like something out of a recruiting poster. Likable. Good ship handler. Lots of potential. But I think maybe an underachiever."

"My gut says he's always feeling out the situation to his own advantage," the XO said. "Trying to look good, trying to appear that he's on top of the situation, telling you what he thinks you want to hear instead of what you really need to know." The XO chuckled to himself. "I think I just described myself when I was a jaygee. He has a lot of unused potential and could make a real fine officer if he wants to make a career out of this."

The captain listened without expression and then made a quick nod. "That's sort of my take, too. He is an excellent ship handler, and I think he's the best OOD of the jaygees. I don't worry when he's on the bridge. He keeps me informed and has a good handle on the operations when we're underway." The captain paused then leaned back in his chair. "Doesn't he have some good-looking girlfriend I've met? She still around?"

"Yeah, Betsy whatshername. She's a fine looking young lady. They seem to be a number," answered the weapons officer.

"Okay, you two. Thanks for the background. Now get back to work and solve these problems for me. I've asked Coburn to come in as soon as he finishes topside."

Grabbing their coats, gloves, scarves, and hats, the two left, talking as they entered the passageway, starting on their problem solving.

* * *

US Naval Reserve Lieutenant (Junior Grade) Clark Coburn looked over the bridge wing at the thick nylon ropes holding the ship to the pier. The phone lines were connected, and the engineers had finished hooking up the ship to receive electricity, steam, and water from the navy base. After several weeks of running continuously, the ship's engines were now quiet, its boilers unlit.

He turned to the sailor standing beside him. "Looks like we're done up here, Katoski. Tell the tugs thanks. Then transfer the watch to the quarterdeck. I'm going below."

"Aye, aye, sir. The Captain requests you see him in his cabin as soon as you finish here, sir."

"He say what it was about?"

11

"No, sir. Just said for you to see him when the ship is secure."

Coburn nodded at the sailor, smiled, and shrugged his shoulders. Satisfied after another look over the side that everything was shipshape, he went down to the captain's cabin.

"Enter," replied the captain to the knock on his door. The commanding officer swiveled in his desk chair as the junior officer walked in. Coburn's face was red from the cold and wind, his bridge coat collar up in a vaguely dramatic manner. He looked like something out of central casting,.

"Throw your stuff on the couch, Clark, and take a seat. I'm going to have another cup of coffee. Want some?"

"Yes, thanks, Captain. Some hot coffee sounds pretty good right now."

"Makes you wish you were out of San Diego or Pearl Harbor, huh?" The captain turned to the ever-present steward. "Quezon, how about a hot cup of black coffee for me and a cup for Mr. Coburn, please?"

"Aye, aye, Captain. Mr. Coburn, you want cream and sugar?"

Coburn wanted cream and sugar. Navy coffee was strong and bitter. He never drank it unless it was buffered with cream and sugar. But the skipper was having his black. "No thanks, Quezon. Black, please."

"Everything go okay after I left the bridge, Clark?"

"Yes, sir. I had the tugs holding us against the pier to keep the wind from setting us off until we got all the lines over. We just secured the ship service generators. Nice to be back home in Newport."

"You got the duty this weekend?"

"No sir. Off the entire weekend. I intend to get some sleep."

"Going to see Betsy?"

"I hope so, sir. She's coming down from Providence this afternoon."

"What does she do up there?"

"Student, sir. She's a senior at Brown."

"Good. Say hello to her for me, please."

"Sure thing, Captain."

"Okay, Clark. I just got off the phone with the surface detailers' desk. They have you on the next slate for cutting orders. You won't be going with us to the Med."

Coburn kept a serious look on his face that did not reflect the buoyant feeling the last sentence gave him. He had not been looking forward to six months of dreary watch keeping, endless drills and exercises, tedious meals, boredom, and being at sea away from the familiar comforts of New England and Betsy.

"You're getting orders for in-country Vietnam." Coburn startled and then reset his serious mask. The captain didn't pause. "They have two jobs you can pick from. One, I take it, is a pretty good one, but you probably have to extend your time in the navy or augment out of the reserves to get that job. Go regular navy—USN—no more USNR. It's a career-building job."

He continued, "The other's not bad either, and you don't have to extend. The in-country jobs are for a year. But for that one, they'll send you home at your normal end of active duty date even though you'll have less than twelve months in-countryin-country. Here's the detailer's name and number. Phone him now; he's waiting for your call."

"Aye, aye, sir. I'll call him from the wardroom phone. Any chance I can stay with the ship and they send someone else?"

"Not a chance in hell. I tried that already. Needs of the navy means you are going. Let me know which job you take and the details of your schedule. Schools, leave. That stuff."

After a sip of coffee and a long pause, the captain asked, "You planning to stay in the navy or get out?"

Coburn hesitated and looked down at his shoes, thinking. He was over a year away from getting out and had not even thought about what to do. "I haven't made a decision about that yet, Captain. I like what I do and the ship and all. But I've been thinking about going to grad school, and my family would like me to come back to Hartford and get into the family business."

"What's that, Clark?"

"Insurance, Captain. Like everything else in Hartford. But that's sort of boring, at least to me."

"To me, too. I don't think you'll be bored in-countryin-country. Better call the detailer soon to catch him before lunch."

* * *

Coburn sat in the wardroom lounge while the stewards set starched white tablecloths and silverware for lunch, waiting for the detailer at the Bureau of Personnel to pick up.

"Lieutenant Commander Sperling."

"Good morning, sir. This is Lieutenant JG Clark Coburn on the DeKalb in Newport. My captain told me to call you about orders."

"Right. I was talking to your skipper this morning. Good man to work for, huh? I've got your card and info right here. Lemme see." Coburn could hear the rustling of paper. "Here we go. I've got two jobs for you. It's your pick. One's a plum. You'd be an advisor to the South Vietnamese Navy. It's important to get them up and running so they can stand on their own. High profile. You'll be relieving Arnie Gordon, who's done pretty well for himself. Bronze Star. Great fitness reports. Saw a lot of action, got a lot of good attention. Arnie's going to the Destroyer School executive officer course, and then he'll be XO on a tin can."

"Where is the job, sir?"

"Well, the unit's a River Assault Group with the Vietnamese navy. Headquarters in Nha Be. That's near Saigon. But the unit is usually on the Saigon River, upriver. Your American boss would be in Saigon, and you'd be part of the Military Assistance Command. It's twelve months in-countryin-country. Independent duty, no one looking over your shoulder. If you want that job, you'd have to extend your end of service date or make a decision to augment to the regular navy and stay in. Figure by the time we detach you from the DeKalb, thirty days' leave, four weeks of counterinsurgency school, two weeks of weapons and survival, six weeks of language training, and a week of SERE training, you'd have to extend at least four or five months."

"SERE, sir?"

"Yeah. Everyone going in-countryin-country and all the aviators have to go through the prisoner-of-war compound experience."

"Where's all that training, sir?"

"Most of it is at the Coronado amphib base outside San Diego, two weeks at Camp Pendleton with the jarhead marines, and a week at Hot Warner Springs for SERE. It's a good job."

"What's the other job, sir?"

"That one is the administrative officer at the base in Cat Lo. Basically the XO of the base's right-hand man. No training other than Pendleton and SERE. You'd probably spend about nine or ten months in-countryin-country, and then we'd ship you home as a civilian. It's a decent job, but not one for someone who wants to make a career of the navy. Location is pretty nice, near the in-country R&R center in Vung Tau. All US Navy except for a few Coast Guard types. Any questions?"

"Well...yes, a couple, sir. If I took the Cat Lo job and then later decided that I wanted to stay in the navy, would it hurt me?"

"No, not at all. It's just not as good a job as the advisor job."

"How did I get in the running for the advisor job?"

"We need a qualified OOD, division officer experience, and gunnery experience with decent fitness reports. Foreign language aptitude desired but not required. You fit all the areas. I need you to make a decision soon so we can start cutting your orders one way or the other. There are others waiting in line for that advisor job if you don't want it. I have to have a relief identified for Arnie Gordon ASAP."

"One final question, sir. Which one would *you* recommend?"

"If you want a career in the navy, take the advisor job. If you don't fuck it up, you'll be ahead of a lot of your peers."

Neither man said a word for nearly half a minute. Then Coburn said, "I'd like the advisor job, sir."

"Okay, I just penciled in your name. We'll start cutting your orders. You should get them in a few weeks and detach from the ship at the end of February to give you time for leave and schools. Good choice, Mr. Coburn."

"Thanks, sir. I'll let my skipper know. I'm pretty excited. Good-bye."

* * *

Betsy Cooke and Coburn sat with several DeKalb junior officers, young wives, and girlfriends at a large round table in The Datum, the casual officers club in Newport favored by the younger officers and their dates over the stuffy main club across the base. Pitchers of beer fueled the laughs, joking, and good-natured ribbing around the table. The young men were relaxed. Several had taken rejuvenating late-afternoon naps.

The DeKalb's weapons officer walked by their table with his very pregnant wife and another couple from one of the other ships in port. He stopped to say hello, his wife smiling broadly at the familiar faces.

"Honey, watch out for this band of pirates. How they latched on to these good-looking women is beyond me. Think I should buy them a pitcher or just let them die of thirst? They really don't deserve beer."

"Aw, c'mon, boss. We're just a bunch of penniless galley slaves. You can afford to buy us a pitcher," one of the more vocal junior officers called out over the din of the jukebox.

"Well, if he won't buy you a pitcher, I will." The pregnant wife signaled to the waitress, who came over a few minutes later with another pitcher of beer.

"Let's hear it for Mrs. Weps!" yelled Coburn, and the whole table started cheering and clapping.

"Thanks, Clark. David tells me you're getting orders soon. Good luck. We will certainly miss you."

"We won't!" piped two of the junior officers in unison as the table broke into laughter and the weapons officer and his wife waved goodbye and joined their friends across the room.

Betsy looked at Coburn with a frown. "Are you getting orders? When did this happen? Where are you going?"

"I just found out a few hours ago. I haven't had a chance to tell you yet."

"Clark, we've been together since three this afternoon. It's now nearly seven. What do you mean you haven't had a chance?"

"Well, you and I were sort of busy after you arrived."

"Clark, what's going on here? You can't talk to me? Where are you going?"

"Let's go outside. I can't talk about this here." He turned to the table. "Guys, be right back. Leave some beer for me. We going to Salas for clams and stuff?"

He put his arm around Betsy's shoulder as they walked out of The Datum. It was cold, and Betsy huddled near him. "Clark, what's happening?"

"Okay, the navy picked me to go in-country Vietnam as an advisor for the Vietnamese navy. I don't know when I leave the ship yet, and there's a whole lot of school on the West Coast before I go to Vietnam. I think I have to be there by mid-June or July or something like that. I'll be there for a year. I can't really tell you what I'll be doing because I don't really know."

"A year?"

"Yeah, a year in Vietnam and about three or four months before that on the West Coast."

Betsy shivered in the cold. She leaned heavily against Coburn. "I'm cold. We'd better go back in."

"You okay?"

"I don't know." She pressed her lips into a thin line, thinking. "No, I'm not. This is a shock. I wish you had said..."

"We were a little occupied, weren't we?"

"Clark, I don't like you talking like that. There are more important things. Let's go back in." She walked back to the table, Coburn following her.

Later that night in Betsy's Howard Johnson motel room, Coburn lay next to her; her head was on his arm. "I'm still sort of...I don't know...shocked, Clark," she said. "I know the navy has orders and all that, but still..."

"That's right. They order, and I go. That's my job. I'm a naval officer. They picked me ahead of a lot of others to do an important job." He paused for a few seconds, then lowered his voice. "I was offered a real good job, and I picked it. Maybe I'll stay in the navy. This job will be good for me."

"Will it be dangerous? I mean with all that fighting and that Khe Sanh battle."

"Hey, it's a war. War's dangerous. People get hurt, people get killed. But not me. It will happen to the other guy, the bad guy. Not me."

"I love you, Clark. Promise me it won't happen to you."

"Sure. Promise. The bad guys will never hurt me." He kissed her and cupped her bare breast.

She kissed him back and then pulled away. "What about us, Clark? What do we do?"

"What do you want to do?"

"I can't even think straight now. I don't know."

"Betsy, we have a couple of weeks before I leave the ship and then a couple of months on the West Coast before I go to Vietnam. You're graduating soon. Let's take this a step at a time. I don't want to lose you."

She lay there quietly, her back to Coburn, snuggled into a cocoon with his arm over her shoulder. "Have you told your parents, yet?"

"No. I'll do that tomorrow. I'll have to tone it down so my mother doesn't freak out."

CHAPTER 3
HANOI

The two men were seated across from each other, separated by the academic's desk, the winter sun warming the room. In front of each man sat a small glass cup of thick, caffeine-laden Vietnamese coffee floating on a layer of sweetened condensed milk. The professor and the colonel had become friends during the years since the French left Hanoi, working together on projects in engineering, economics and logistics—academic projects with practical applications. They respected each other's intellect. But Professor Cao Tri Thieu had as much trouble with Colonel Nguyen Sy Ong's pragmatism as Colonel Ong had with Professor Thieu's theories.

"Professor, tell me about..." he looked down at the file on his creased uniform trousers, "...this student Tran Vo. I have his grades here and read your comments and the comments of the other professors, but I want to know what kind of a person he is. It seems that you have mentored him and used him on several of our projects."

"Colonel, your people have been following Vo for years. I don't know what else I can add." He took a sip from the coffee and looked out the window, collecting his thoughts.

Familiar with his friend's thought processes, the soldier just sat and waited. After a few minutes, Professor Thieu turned to Colonel Ong and took a final drink of the coffee.

"Vo's very gifted academically. His grades show that, as do the comments from his teachers. He appears to have been born smart. Difficult concepts come easy to him. He's a civil engineering student but quickly grasped economics, operations analysis, transportation theory, logistics. He has been the main researcher and writer of many of the recent projects we have completed for you."

Colonel Ong smiled. "So he's doing a lot of the work you've taken credit for?"

"I am happy to admit that to be true. The best days for a teacher are the days you realize your student knows more than you do."

"Did he need a lot of supervision from you or the other professors? Did he work alone or in teams?"

"At first he worked with just me or one of the other professors, constantly coming back to us to check his work. That was a joke around here. Each time we checked his work, we were the ones learning something new. It finally got to the point where we'd give him a task and tell him to not show it to us until it was completely done. Rarely did we ever have to change a word." He looked directly into his friend's eyes. "I was hoping to have him join the faculty."

"Perhaps when he has finished his work with us, my friend," Colonel Ong said quietly with an overtone of cold firmness. "Did he always work alone? Did he ever work with a group or team?"

"After a short time, we put him charge of project teams. He did well, but I think he has little patience for the lazy and those not as smart as he is. I suspect that he personally made up for the shortcomings of his less talented colleagues to ensure the quality of the product."

"Good sense of responsibility. Would you call him a leader?"

"Leader? I don't know. His classmates and the junior students all seem to look up to him. A leader here at the university? Yes. A leader in your world, Colonel? I don't know."

"Personality. You know, what's he like?"

"Very polite, very respectful. But I don't know much more than that. He comes across to me as almost cold, but that just may be the face he wears here in the classroom."

"Decision maker?" Colonel Ong shifted forward in his chair, resting his chin on his steepled fingers.

"Yes. At least he's not afraid to recommend and defend a decision. If he recommends a decision, I am certain his recommendation is well thought out, logical, and backed by facts or substantial theory."

"Can he make decisions quickly? Under stress?"

"My soldier friend, I do not know the answer to that." Professor Thieu looked at the clock on the wall. "I told him to be here at 3:00. We have ten minutes left. Any more questions for me?"

"No, but I do want you in the room when I meet with him."

"What are you planning to do with Vo?"

Colonel Ong slid back in chair and relaxed. "Depending on my impressions of him, we may offer him a position of great importance in the army. He'd become part of a team that would utilize his brain that you have been training here at Hanoi Polytechnic. If he accepts, he leaves his academic life immediately and we put him in uniform."

"And if he doesn't accept this position?"

For a second the officer drilled the teacher with his eyes, then leaned back in his chair with a sad smile. "We put him in uniform and he will be sent to the infantry. We need leaders, smart soldiers. We're at war."

"Don't you think that staying here, he will be of better use to the nation and the people than getting killed in some sinkhole in the South?"

"We're at war; we need soldiers. He's been privileged to have attended this university when others have been sent to war. He's also going to be given a choice. He should feel honored. As so should you, my friend."

The conversation was interrupted by a knock on the door. The professor's secretary walked in and announced that Tran Vo was here for his 3:00 appointment. Professor Thieu looked at Colonel Ong, who nodded and closed the file on his lap. "Show him in, please," said Professor Thieu.

A tall, well-built young man walked in and looked around the familiar office.. In one of the two chairs across the desk sat an army officer dressed in an immaculate, tailored uniform wearing polished shoes. The officer looked about the same age as the professor. Neither of the older men stood up as introductions were made. Vo was told to sit in the chair next to the soldier.

Colonel Ong was struck by Vo's appearance. He had expected a pale, delicate scholar, but here sat a man who looked anything but that. The soldier thought that Vo must have had some large-boned ancestors, possibly from Mongolia. And this student did not look his age. His face and expression were that of someone older. The colonel broke the silence.

"How old are you, son?"

"Twenty-two, Colonel."

"You look older. Has anyone ever told you that before?"

"Yes, my mother. She calls me her old man-child."

"I can see that. Is your father alive?"

"Yes."

"What does your father do? Your mother?"

"My father works for the people's railroad, and my mother is a teacher."

"Do you have brothers or sisters?"

"Two brothers, Colonel."

"What do they do?"

"Both are in the People's Army."

"Where is your home?"

"My parents live in Ninh Binh, but I live here."

The colonel already knew the answers to all these questions. These answers and much more were in the closed file on his lap. He looked at Vo's face and hands. The professor was right. Vo was polite and respectful, but he might as well be wearing a mask. The colonel opened his file, intently looked at a page, shut the file, and turned his chair to face Vo.

"You joined the Thirty-Seventh Youth Brigade when you left secondary school. The brigade was mobilized, but you were not. Do you know why?"

"I was told that the nation needed good engineers for the future more than it needed a brigade member today. I was sent to Hanoi Polytechnic University, here."

"Would you have rather gone with the Youth Brigade?"

Vo's eyes flicked to his professor and then back to the colonel. "Yes, Colonel, I wanted to go with my friends."

"Why didn't you?"

"I did not think it was my choice. If the good of the people is better served by my studying engineering, then I see no choice but to study engineering."

"You have two brothers in the People's Army. Your family does not have to send another to war. Would you go to war if the nation asked you to?"

"Yes."

Colonel Ong looked long and hard at Vo's face. Like his answers, his face was without expression. A cold mask covering a deep intellect. After years of serving his country and evaluating the mettle of men, the officer sensed that the mask was also covering deep emotions. But he really didn't know. He opened his file again and glanced at another sheet of paper.

"Do you speak any languages besides Vietnamese?"

"Yes, French and English. I'm fluent in French. I can read, write and understand English well, but my spoken English is poor."

Colonel Ong stood up and walked over to the window, file in his hand. He looked out over the campus buildings and the sandbagged air raid shelters, then turned to the student and the teacher, his back-lit face in shadow.

23

"Tran Vo, your country now needs you and what you've learned. It's time to leave the university and your studies and projects and join your comrades in unification." Colonel Ong walked over to the desk and stood besides Professor Thieu's chair. He put his hands on the desk and leaned toward Vo.

"This has been a long war, and it will be even longer until we achieve victory. Heroes and glory will be made in battle. But there is much more to victory than fighting battles. In fact, we cannot even fight if we do not have the men to fight, the rations to eat, the fuel, the weapons, the ammunition, the communications. Getting all that to the soldier about to encounter the enemy is the biggest challenge the people face in this war. That part of the battle is without glory, without medals, without heroes. But it is a battle that must be won."

The soldier took a deep breath and paced back to the window, Vo's eyes following him, his face without expression. Professor Thieu just looked at Vo. Colonel Ong turned and walked back to his chair, sat down, and leaned close to Vo.

"The People's Army 557 Transportation Group is forming a unit of experts like you. They will all stop their academic lives and be sent to basic training. Because they are a select group, they must be both hardened and tested. Our trainers have been told to test these men both physically and mentally during their training. They will undergo the training of a combat infantryman. If they succeed, they will then be given specialized further training and sent in small groups to base areas, where they will put all that education and training to use. Do you understand what I'm saying, Vo?"

"Yes, Colonel."

"We need men who think strategically as well as tactically. More importantly, we need men who can implement the strategy. You can be one of those men, Vo." The Colonel looked at his friend. "Professor Thieu and your other teachers have convinced me you have these abilities."

He went on. "This will be dangerous, but that is the nature of war. You will be sent south, and you may die. If you live, you may not see home again for many years." He suddenly dropped his voice and asked almost paternally, "Do you have a sweetheart, Vo? A woman you like?"

For an instant Vo's face registered surprise at the question. But he showed no emotion as he answered, "I do have a woman friend."

"Where is she?"

"Hanoi. She lives in the same building I do. She lives with her mother and uncle."

"What does she do?"

"A student. A medical student."

"Tran Vo, do you have any questions?"

Vo was quiet for nearly a minute as both older men watched his face.

"Yes, Colonel. When would I leave to start training?"

"You will be picked up and transported to the basic and infantry training camp thirty days from now. That should be enough time to finish your work here, visit your home, and make your good-byes."

Professor Thieu opened his mouth for the first time since introducing Vo to the colonel. "Most of your projects here are complete. I'll pass those that are not to the faculty. You can leave the university at any time. Even tomorrow if you wish."

Vo didn't say anything. Finally Colonel Ong spoke up. "Vo, the people need you to do this."

"Yes, Colonel. I will do the best I can."

"I'm sure you will, Vo. Unless Professor Thieu has more for you, you can leave now. We will be contacting you shortly with orders and arrangements."

Vo stood, thanked the two men, and walked out of the office. The two friends looked at each other.

"Colonel, you didn't give him a choice."

"Professor, he didn't want a choice."

The thought of leaving the sterile university environment to do something different, exciting, even dangerous, elated Vo. Vo went downstairs to his cubicle and put on his coat and walked out into the winter afternoon sunshine. Hands in pockets, he walked back to his apartment building thinking that a beer would taste very good.

* * *

That evening Vo went to Ngoc's apartment. Ngoc's mother opened the door and smiled broadly as she ushered him in. The room smelled of garlic and fish sauce from the evening meal. Ngoc was sitting at the table across from her uncle. After exchanging pleasantries with Ngoc's mother and uncle, he asked Ngoc to take a walk with him.

Once they left the courtyard and started walking up the dark street, Ngoc put her arm in his and walked close. Vo could feel her breast against his arm. They walked arm in arm to Nhang's coffee shop and went inside. Vo ordered two small coffees. They sat across a small table.

"I'm leaving the university, Ngoc. I'm going into the army."

"Oh." Ngoc was stunned, speechless.

"Yes, they told me this afternoon."

"When do you go? Where will you go?"

"I have thirty days. I will take a day or two to turn things over to Professor Thieu. Then the time's pretty much my own. I will take a trip to Binh Ninh to say good-bye to my parents. I just sent them a letter."

"Where will you go? What will you do in the army?"

"I don't know. The only thing I know for sure is that I will start basic training in thirty days. After that, I really don't know."

"My mother and uncle will miss you. They like you."

"I will miss them, too. And I will miss you, Ngoc. More than anyone or anything."

"Me too." She stared at her coffee cup and then looked into his eyes. "Can I write you? Or even visit you?"

"I'm sure you can write. I don't know about visiting in training. I don't think we'll be able to see each other until after training is over. Maybe not even then."

Ngoc looked at Vo, and her eyes started to water. He reached over and wrapped his big hand around hers. She looked down at the table, and a tear rolled off her cheek onto the little saucer holding her coffee cup. Without looking up she said softly, "I knew this would happen. I knew you would have to go sometime. I knew the war would not end soon enough to keep you here with me." She looked up at Vo and squeezed his hand. "How are you? How do you feel about this?"

"Ngoc, I don't know how to say this to you, but I feel sort of free, happy. It's as if the suspense is finally over. Now I move on. I wanted to go with the Youth Brigade, but I was forbidden from doing so. Now I am finally going." He put his other hand on top of theirs.

"But Ngoc, the thought of leaving you and not seeing my parents for I don't know how long saddens me. I'm a mixture of happy and sad."

They walked back through the night to the apartment building. In his small room on his narrow bed, they held each other. Not sleeping. Saying nothing. Just holding each other as the air raid sirens sounded. Holding each other until the sun came up.

CHAPTER 4
NEWPORT, RHODE ISLAND

DeKalb was ready to deploy to the Mediterranean. In two hours the ship would get underway. The crew would not see Newport again for six months.

Coburn was in the captain's cabin, drinking black coffee as the captain reviewed Coburn's performance aboard DeKalb. A fitness report would be written later, the official performance review that would become a permanent part of Coburn's personnel file in the navy. The fitreps and the needs of the navy determined an officer's career. A good career required and produced good fitreps.

"Clark, I'm going to miss you, especially when I'm trying to sleep and we're underway. You're a fine ship handler. You stand an outstanding watch and manage the bridge team well," said the captain.

"Thank you, sir. I like driving this ship."

"It shows. You also led a division that is one of the best I have. Guns and magazines in good shape, squared-away sailors, no discipline problems. At least none that have made it to my attention." The skipper chuckled. Then he looked at Coburn and asked seriously, "Tell me how you ran that division."

"Captain, in Officer Candidate School, they beat into our heads to rely on our petty officers and chiefs, keep our boss informed, and use the chain of command both ways. Up and down the chain. I pretty much followed that advice. Sort of wound up with me working closely with Chief Graham. He filtered out the small problems so I could deal with the big ones. I tried to keep him from having to deal with...uh...excuse me sir, the chickenshit from above. It seemed to work, sir."

The captain looked at Coburn closely. "It worked well. But you won't always have a chief like Graham, and some chickenshit may need to work its way down to the sailors. You'll need to get your hands dirtier in the future, Clark. You've been very lucky. What do you do when your chief or leading petty officer gets sick, wounded, or killed?"

"Yes, sir, I realize that," Coburn said quickly.

"Okay, Clark. I've got a ship to get underway, and I'm sure you've got to get your gear off the ship unless you want it to visit Naples." The captain shook Coburn's hand. "Good luck, Clark. Send us a letter when you get in-countryin-country."

* * *

Coburn looked around his stateroom to make sure he had not forgotten anything. Lieutenant Mathew Geralds, the ship's assistant supply officer—referred to in the navy as a pork chop because of the shape of his supply corps collar insignia—and Coburn's roommate walked in.

"Looks like you're packed up and ready to go, Clark. Said goodbye to everyone?"

"The ones who count. Skipper, XO, Weps, gunnery chief, and now you. I'm going to load the car and then stand on the pier while you poor fools sail away. I'll toss off the last line."

"Going home?"

"Not yet. I'm going up to Providence and spend some time with Betsy. Then home. Then maybe back to Providence before I fly out to San Diego. I got a month to fuck around."

Coburn looked up at the wing of the bridge and saw the captain smiling and waving at him. He saluted the captain, who saluted back and then turned his attention to getting his ship safely to sea. Coburn walked through the groups of families and girlfriends on the pier—some crying, some waving—and got into his car.

He felt he was starting a new life, with all vestiges of the past simply ending. DeKalb's gunnery division's problems were no longer his. Someone else had to be on deck during watches at sea, not him. Family, friends, and Betsy were soon to be a continent away and then, in a few more months, on the other side of the world from him. He was setting out on an adventure, doing something he had never done before. He felt oddly freed of old ties and responsibilities. As far as Coburn was concerned, the slate would soon be clean.

* * *

Coburn arrived at Betsy's Providence apartment about the same time the DeKalb rendezvoused with its escorting destroyers. For three weeks he kept himself busy while she attended her classes and studied for exams. He haunted the university's library and student union, read a series of mindless novels, flirted with the occasional coed, or simply napped.

Betsy drove with him to Hartford to spend a long weekend at his parents' house. For the sake of his mother's feelings, they slept in separate bedrooms but took advantage of every opportunity for intimacy. With five days of his leave left before he had to report to Coronado, he put Betsy on the train back to Providence.

"Okay, Bets, you have a good trip. I'll call you when I get to Coronado. As soon as I know my schedule, maybe you'll fly out?"

"Let's hope so. I don't know what my schedule will be. Too bad you can't be here for my graduation, Clark. That would be nice."

"Hey, needs of the navy."

"I'm starting to hate that phrase," she said as she looked at him with that concerned look, which was becoming more and more common since the evening at The Datum. Double-meaning innuendos or evasive stock phrases seem to creep into his conversations with her, especially when she tried to talk about their future.

"Clark, I do love you," she waited a few seconds. "Thank your parents again for me. I really do appreciate their hospitality." She kissed him.

"Will do, Bets. They like you. You'd better get a seat." He handed her the small overnight bag and kissed her.

"Love ya, Clark."

"I love you, too, Bets."

* * *

Coburn sat with his father at the kitchen table as his mother collected the dirty dishes and loaded the dishwasher. He was mulling over whether to just lie around the house and watch TV or get together with a few of his college friends who had migrated to Hartford.

"Mom and I sure like Betsy. She's really a nice girl."

"She likes you two a lot and asked me to make sure that I give you her thanks again. She's started her job search. Graduates pretty soon."

"She mentioned that. Journalism and editing. Said she's lining up interviews in New York. That's the right place for that business. Hell of a long way from you, though."

"Dad, everything's a long way from Vietnam. Nothing's close to where I'll be."

By this time his mother had joined them at the table. "When you were born, your daddy was flying around Burma or somewhere, and I was about a mile from here living with Grandma and Grandpa."

"I found out I was a father nearly a month after you were born. I got a letter and photo of you and Mom in the hospital. Your mother looked great, but you looked like some skinny, ugly monkey. I figured either they got you mixed up with some other baby or that was one terrible joke your mother was trying to play on me."

"Oh, c'mon," Coburn's mother admonished. She looked at her son. "I thought you were adorable. You were certainly the cutest baby in the maternity ward. And look at you now." She turned to her husband. "Still think he's a monkey?"

"No, he turned out okay. The hospital probably straightened out the mix-up and gave you a cuter baby to take home."

Coburn took a sip of coffee. "Mom, were you worried about Dad? Back then?"

"I think worry was always in the back of my mind, but I kept it there. So many families were in the same boat during the war. Your other grandparents—Dad's parents—I know they were worried. A lot. But no one really talked about it."

"Did you know what Dad was doing?"

"He wrote as often as he could. Most of what he wrote frankly sounded boring. Picking up supplies here, flying them to there. Picking up more stuff there, flying it back to here. And playing poker when he wasn't flying. Sometimes things would be blacked out by the censor, but not much."

"That pretty much describes what I was doing," his father added. "It was sort of like that ship in *Mr. Roberts*, only instead of getting bored on a ship, I got bored flying a C-47 around the Western Pacific."

"Did you see much action, Dad?"

"Very, very little, and most of that was pure spectator sport at a distance. My biggest fear was the weather and pissing off my crew chief. I was afraid he might pee in the fuel tanks. And that the war might not end until you were grown up and had kids of your own."

His mother looked hard at her son. "Will there be much shooting where you're going, Clark?"

"I don't think so, Mom. It seems most of that stuff over there is a ground war, and I'm navy. I'll be on the water, in a helmet and flak jacket."

"What's your job over there, Clark?" asked his father. They had never talked about what Coburn would be doing in Vietnam.

"Advisor to the South Vietnamese Navy. Some amphibious or waterborne patrol stuff. I don't know much about it yet. Other than it's a plum of a job."

His mother's stare bore into him. His father lifted a quizzical eyebrow and shifted in his seat. After a few quiet moments, Coburn's father asked, "What you going to do for these next few days? Any plans?"

"Tonight I'm going to meet with some of my frat buddies who are in town. Then not much else except to get fat on Mom's cooking and your booze; I won't be getting much of that while I'm over there."

"Going to see Betsy before you leave?"

"I don't think so, Mom. I'll call her. Maybe she'll visit me in Coronado, depending on my schedule."

"What you going to do when you're done with all this?" asked his father.

"You mean after Vietnam?"

"Yes, after that."

"I've been thinking about that," Coburn said. "I like the navy, and if I do a decent job over there, I'll be ahead of my peer group, so maybe I can get some plum orders like graduate school or something where I don't have to go to sea so much."

"But a naval officer's career is a seagoing one, isn't it?"

"Yeah, I guess. Maybe use the GI bill for graduate school or something like that. Maybe look for a job. Maybe come back here. I don't know, but I'm thinking about all that."

"What about you and Betsy?"

"I like Betsy a lot. But can a relationship last for that long and at that distance?"

"Don't overestimate the distance and time, and don't underestimate Betsy," said his mother in a gentle maternal rebuke.

"Before I forget," Clark changed the conversation, "I'm going to leave my car with you guys, okay? Drive it as much as you want. Mom, you'll be a real babe in a convertible with the top down.

I'm gonna take a shower and get ready to meet the guys." He kissed his mother on the cheek and went upstairs.

Later that night Coburn was sitting next to a woman he had met an hour ago in the loud body exchange of a bar just outside Hartford. He was tipsy. So was she, and—judging by her knee rubbing against his thigh, her hand constantly on his forearm, and her breasts constantly bumping into his upper arm—interested in more than just talking at the bar. She wasn't bad looking, nothing to be ashamed of if his buddies saw him leaving with her. But Betsy was on his mind, and he was tired and not sure he wanted to go through the whole stork dance of getting her into bed and the guilty feelings afterward. Although it probably would be a very short dance. Maybe he'd just take her out to the car, but the Mustang was pretty cramped for anything other than a blow job.

Hell, it wasn't worth it. He'd just have another drink and go home.

* * *

Coburn seated himself in the first-class seat on the flight from Hartford to Chicago, from which he would change flights to San Diego. Although he could fly in civilian clothes, he wore his uniform. A month earlier the DeKalb's chief yeoman had handed him his orders and travel vouchers and advised, "Mr. Coburn, wear your uniform. The pukes at the airline ticket counters will give you a pity upgrade to the front of the plane if there's room. They figure you're goanna get killed or wounded. It salves their conscience."

The chief was right. Coburn was flying first class to San Diego all the way. Big seats, free booze, good-looking stews.

He had called Betsy the night before and talked for ten minutes, most of which was filled with awkward silences. He promised to write her with his mailing address in Coronado. She seemed restrained, almost remote. He figured she was getting her period.

37

His parents drove him to the airport and waited in the departure lounge with him until he boarded. For the most part, they sat in silence. He told them he doubted if he'd be able to make a trip back between the training and going to Vietnam and mumbled something about schedules, the needs of the navy, and the importance of his new job.

When it was time to board, he shook hands with his father, who told him to be careful. Coburn hugged and kissed his mother. She looked at him with wet eyes and grabbed her husband's arm, and the two of them watched him walk into the jet-way.

Window seat first class from Hartford to Chicago. Then another window seat first class on the long leg from Chicago to San Diego. He picked a steak from the little menu card the stewardess gave him. For airplane food it wasn't too bad. After a scotch on the rocks and a nap, he chatted about nothing with the businessman sitting next to him.

In the early San Diego evening, Coburn drove his rental car the short distance to the ferry landing and took the little ferry to Coronado. A quick drive from the ferry landing and he was at the gates of the navy's amphibious base. The gate guard saluted and directed him to the Bachelor Officers Quarters. A few minutes later, he was in his BOQ room. Not bad. Not bad at all. Nicely furnished. Television. Private bathroom. Air conditioned.

He changed into civvies and drove back into the small business section of Coronado to grab a quick meal and a beer at the Mexican Village. The chief yeoman had recommended that place as "a good spot for you young, swinging-dick officers." Again, the chief was right.

Tomorrow morning he'd report in and start his training.

CHAPTER 5
HANOI

Vo returned to the university the day after his meeting with Professor Thieu and Colonel Ong. His project files were gone, taken by his mentor and distributed to various faculty members. A small bag sitting on what had been his desk held his few belongings: slide rule, straightedge, pencils, pen, a bottle of ink, a glass, and a chipped cup and saucer. Next to the bag sat a note from Professor Thieu: "Please see me before you leave. I want to say good-bye."

After saying good-bye to various faculty members, secretaries, and a few students, Vo met with Professor Thieu. His teacher did not ask him to take a seat. Instead, he moved from behind his desk to grasp Vo's right hand in both of his. After a long and awkward pause, the older man let go of the young man's hand and looked at him, studying his face.

"Tran Vo, I do not know if I will ever see you again. Time does not stop. Death cannot be avoided." He waved his hand as if flicking away a mosquito. "Age, sickness, war. So I say good-bye to you."

"Professor, thank you for your guidance and advice. You are right; we don't know if we will ever meet again. No one knows. Good-bye, Professor Thieu. And thank you again."

Vo bowed his head in respect, then turned and walked out of the office. Professor Thieu stared at the closed door, shook his head, and sat heavily at his desk. War, he thought. I will never understand war. Why plant a seed and protect the sapling as it grows into a tree—only to chop the tree down and burn the wood in a fire that gives no warmth or light?

* * *

Vo and Ngoc sat across from each other in the coffee shop. Two days had passed since he left the university. A few hours ago, a People's Army messenger had delivered an envelope. It contained his orders.

Ngoc stirred the syrupy residue in the bottom of her cup. Vo looked at her, then reached across the small table and held her wrist. Ngoc raised her head, tilted a little to the side, and asked, "You haven't even left, and I am already missing you. What's your schedule now?"

Vo exhaled a long slow sigh and took his hand off her wrist and picked up his cup. He took a bitter sip and made a face. "I want to talk to you about that. I want to visit my parents and take some of my books and clothing to them. My orders say to just bring the clothes on my back and enough food and water for half a day."

"When will you go to your parents?"

"I'm really ready to go now. Probably tomorrow morning or the next day. My mother wants me to stay in Ninh Binh until I have to report to the army." Ngoc was looking into his eyes.

"But I want to spend as much time as I can with you," he added.

"Vo, you must spend as much time as you can with your parents, not me," Ngoc said without much conviction.

"Yes, but maybe you can come with me to Ninh Binh? At least for part of the time? You've never met my parents, Ngoc."

"I would like that very much, Vo. But do you think that's proper? I mean, we are not married..." Ngoc drifted off into an awkward silence. "Should we be?" she asked.

He smiled, his eyes met hers, and then he looked down at this coffee cup. "Ngoc, I'm going to war. I would very much like you to be my wife. But I do not want you to be my widow. I've been told that what I am going to do needs focus and determination. I can't be distracted. As much as I want to be by you."

"I will wait for you, Vo. As your wife or your friend or lover, I will wait for you."

"You may wait for an eternity, Ngoc."

"Yes, I know. I don't like it, but I know that." She straightened up in her chair and smiled. "And I want to go with you to Ninh Binh. At least for part of the time. Proper or not. I don't care."

They planned their trip over the empty coffee cups. Marriage was not discussed. The air raid sirens and loss of electricity ended their evening at the coffee shop. When the "all clear" sounded, they walked through the dark to Vo's small apartment.

* * *

Vo and Ngoc rode a *xyclo* to the train station: he with a cardboard carton of books and clothes on his lap, Ngoc with two small bags of their clothing. The station was in chaos. Rail lines had been bombed that morning, and only strategic freight would move after repairs were made. The stationmaster told them they were welcome to climb aboard the freight-laden cars and take their chances on not getting bombed or strafed. Or they could show some common sense and take one of the buses to Ninh Binh. Or just stay in Hanoi.

Another xyclo ride to the central bus station, and after two hours of waiting and another eight of the hard jostling of spring-flattened wheels on rutted roads, they were in Ninh Binh. They walked the three kilometers in the early night to Vo's family home.

Vo's mother hugged her big son, the top of her head barely reaching his chin. His father stood beside her, waiting for her to let go so he could greet his son. Ngoc stood quietly behind Vo, holding the clothing bags and the cardboard box. When Vo's mother relinquished her son to his father, she turned to Ngoc and smiled.

"And who is this pretty young woman, Vo? Don't tell me you had her carry this box all the way from Hanoi?"

Vo introduced Ngoc to his parents—his mother smiling warmly, his father smiling not so warmly with a raised eyebrow. They knew he had a girlfriend but not much else. Their reticent son had not told them how serious this relationship had become.

Ngoc blushed as Vo's mother wondered aloud about where she would sleep. Vo's declaration that Ngoc would sleep in his room raised his father's other eyebrow and wiped what little smile remained from his face. Vo's mother just continued to smile warmly and grabbed the cardboard box from Ngoc's hands.

For the next two weeks, Vo and Ngoc explored the town of Ninh Binh and the countryside around it. This was the longest time Vo had spent in his home since going off to secondary boarding school in Hanoi. For Ngoc, born and raised in Hanoi, the small town and rural surroundings were a revelation. Except for the occasional bombing and strafing of the railroad line, Ninh Binh seemed to be far away from war and air raid sirens and power outages.

Ngoc marveled at the rice paddies and the gentle power of the water buffaloes. Together they walked or biked, Ngoc riding Vo's mother's bike and Vo riding his father's. As they sat on a paddy dike after finishing a snack from Vo's backpack, Ngoc asked, "Is this what it will be like after the war?"

Vo looked at the conical hat of a rice farmer moving along the dike bordering the next paddy. "I don't know what it will be like. It may still look like this. The land may be the same. But the people will probably change. Some will be replaced. Some will be gone and never replaced. And even the survivors will change."

She put her head on his shoulder. In a few days, she would say goodbye to Vo and take the bus back to Hanoi. She didn't want to think about that but forced herself to do so. The more she thought about their separation, the more it hurt. But the more she hurt, the more she got used to the pain. She didn't hurt any less, she was just getting accustomed to a dull ache in her heart.

They spent their evenings with Vo's parents at dinner. Ngoc helped Vo's mother with the cooking and cleaning while Vo's father sat with his son talking about the railroad and the effects of the war on his job as the stationmaster. He never discussed Ngoc with his son. He was polite to her, even kindly. But he could not shake the awkwardness in having a young woman under his roof in the same room at night as his son. Vo's mother, on the other hand, treated Ngoc as a member of the family, a daughter.

Only after Vo's parents went to their bedroom did the young couple go to Vo's. They passionately made love in a charade of silence to avoid awakening the older couple. Early each morning they were dressed and out of the bedroom before Vo's parents awoke.

At the end of two weeks, Vo and Ngoc held hands at the bus station, waiting to put Ngoc aboard the Hanoi-bound bus. The night before, Vo's mother repeatedly told Ngoc she was always welcome in their home. That morning she gave Ngoc a package of rice, fish, and vegetables to eat on the bus ride north to Hanoi. Vo's father smiled at Ngoc genuinely. He silently shook her hand goodbye.

It was time for Ngoc to board the bus. She and Vo hugged. Fiercely. Ngoc smiled at him but couldn't say anything. Vo kissed her forehead and gently helped her up the first step into the bus. She sat by a window and looked down at him, her hand against the window as the bus pulled away. Ngoc cried bitterly all the way back to Hanoi.

* * *

Le sat in the bright winter sun in front of the farmhouse a few kilometers west of Ninh Binh. His boyhood friend Vo squatted on his haunches next to him. Le inhaled deeply on a cigarette and leaned back in his chair—a hand-pedaled wheelchair. Le's legs stopped at his knees. For the last three years, Vo had made it a point to see Le whenever he visited Ninh Binh.

Le shivered in the cool breeze, and Vo stood and wrapped a blanket around his friend's thin shoulders. Le nodded his thanks and took another drag on his cigarette.

"You're going off to camp in few days, and then they're going to try to make you an officer, Tran Vo?"

Vo smiled and shook his head. "That's what my orders say. Whether they succeed in making me a soldier first and then an officer...we'll see how good they are at magic."

"Then what?"

"I join a special logistics group. And go south, I guess. I don't really know."

Le snorted a laugh and tobacco smoke from his nostrils. "I hope you'll have a much longer career than I did. I must have the shortest military career in history." Le took the cigarette stub out of his mouth, snuffed the ashes out with his forefinger and thumb, then stripped the paper off the stub, catching the tobacco in the palm of his hand. "Pass me that tin, Vo."

Vo removed the cap from a small tobacco tin and held the dented tin in front of his friend, who carefully brushed the tobacco shreds from his palm into the tin. Vo put the metal container back on the makeshift table. Two ducks watched him, hoping for some food to fall to the ground during the transaction.

"They sent me south, too. As an infantry soldier. All puffed up after basic training and indoctrination. Ready to gloriously become a hero. Even a dead one." Le smiled. "So I went south for about thirty kilometers from the train station. And then the fucking world exploded."

Le shut his eyes. "First the explosions. I saw them before I heard them. Like big, burning, black-and-orange blossoms. The hot air squeezing my chest and stomach like a vice. Then the noise. You can't imagine the noise, Vo. I still hear the noise. Then the heat and the smell and the ground shaking. Then more and more. We jumped out of the train, and I stood there like an idiot. I had no idea what to do. Where to go. The only noise was this terrible rushing of air and wind in my ears." He opened his eyes. "They had bombed the front part of the train. Everyone was running, and I just stood there."

"No one was in charge?" Vo asked.

"I don't know. I think I was too deaf and dazed to know if anyone was giving me orders. I didn't know what to do. Then I started running toward the front of the train. I don't know why. Maybe I thought I could help..."

Vo waited for Le to resume. Le had shut his eyes again.

"Then I saw the orange-and-black blossom again, and the heat and the stink, and then the noise, and that's all I remember until I was in some truck being taken to a hospital. Then it became all black and filled with terrible dreams and smells and ringing in my head, and I was in the hospital. Pain, dreams, pain, dreams. I don't know how long. Finally they give me this fine contraption." Le patted his hand-pedaled wheelchair. "They taught me how to use it and how to take a shit and wipe my ass and sent me back to my mother's house here. A disabled veteran of the great battle of the American war that was over for me about an hour after I went off to fight it."

"Do you still have pain and bad dreams, Le?"

"The only pain is in my ass from sitting on it all the time. But my wounds are healed. Alcohol helps. The dreams are always there. I'm afraid to go to sleep because of them. I can even smell the dreams. Alcohol helps there, too." Le looked at his friend. "It would have been better if I had died in the bombing. If I could find the jerk who put me on the stretcher to save my life, I would shoot him. He probably got a medal for that."

"Le, as far as I'm concerned, whoever he is saved your life, and he deserves a medal. I'm glad you're alive and my friend."

"Too many of our friends are gone, and more will follow them, never to come back. Vo, you be careful. For me. You come back and see me."

* * *

Vo was waiting for the bus back to Hanoi. He had no baggage, just a small parcel of food for the day. He had said goodbye to his parents in the morning and walked to the bus station alone.

After Ngoc's return to Hanoi and his visit with Le, Vo spent the days walking the countryside and the evenings talking with his parents. Neither of them understood why he had to go to war. His father could get him a job on the railroad; they needed people badly, and his father could get him an exemption from military service. Since two of his brothers were already in the military, he should have been exempted from the draft. So why had he volunteered? Couldn't he change his mind? Did he have to go?

Vo's parents feared that they might never see their children again. Three young men sent to the military to never return. When he left the house, the tears in his mother's eyes said it all.

Vo wondered if he'd ever see them again.

He boarded the bus and took a window seat. For reasons he could not explain, he felt that he would never see this country-side, his parents, Ngoc, or Le again. He did not try to hide from the feeling but instead embraced it. It was oddly reassuring and liberating to consider himself already dead.

After nearly nine hours on the bus, he was standing at the Hanoi bus station where his orders told him he'd be picked up. He looked around and saw a group of young men, without baggage, talking and joking. He joined them, all new recruits waiting for the army transportation. An hour later two green trucks pulled up, and four men in the green uniforms and pith helmets of the People's Army disembarked in front of the young men. One carried a megaphone and clipboard with papers; the other three had bamboo canes.

The three with canes stood behind the group of forty young men. The soldier with the conical megaphone stood by the lead truck and addressed the group as Class 8-68. He called out forty names. All were present.

The soldier then told them to line up by height in five rows of eight men each. The three soldiers with canes immediately came alive, herding the young men into the ranks. The megaphone then called them to attention, and the cane wielders again went into action, poking the men into an erect military posture.

After another roll call, the men were told to turn right. Two of the soldiers with canes climbed into the back of the trucks. The megaphone barked for Class 8-68 to board the trucks smartly and sit down. No talking. With cane prods and shouts from the soldiers, the recruits climbed into the truck beds and were seated in less than thirty seconds. The trucks rumbled out of the station.

They rode through the night. When one recruit said something, he was smacked on the back of his neck and barked at to be silent. They pulled up to Basic Training Camp in Kinh Mon. Vo could see an antiaircraft battery at each side of the gate, the gunners sitting on the sandbags watching uninterestedly as the trucks came to a stop. Two sentries moved the concertina wire from the front of the gate, then slid the metal gate open. They waved the trucks into the dark camp. The bus came to a stop before half a dozen thatch-roofed huts with woven bamboo walls. With the cane soldiers herding, Vo and the other recruits ran off the trucks and stood at attention with two other ranks of recruits in front of the huts.

PREPARATION

CHAPTER 6
CORONADO, CALIFORNIA

It was a typical US Navy classroom—clean, functional, well lit, well equipped, and comfortable, with forced air heating and cooling and acoustic ceiling tile. Outside the second-floor windows, the sands of the beach and training area reflected brilliant yellow in the southern California sunshine. Two dozen uniformed students stood around the rear of the classroom, drinking coffee and chatting. A few knew one another. Most did not.

Coburn looked around the room. Twenty-four of them. All navy. Twelve enlisted men: two second-class petty officers, three firsts, five chiefs, a single senior chief, and a youngish-looking master chief. From the rate badges on their sleeves, he knew that all were operating ratings—radiomen, gunner's mates, boatswains, enginemen, machinist mates, and a lone hospital corpsman. No logistical types, no storekeepers or cooks, no pencil pushers. For a navy crying about shortages of experienced sailors, this was an impressive group of talent in one room. The DeKalb's CO and XO would kill to get their hands on just one of these guys.

The other twelve in the room, including Coburn, were all commissioned officers. He counted just one other jaygee besides himself, eight lieutenants wearing their silver railroad track rank bars, and two lieutenant commanders. All were surface line officers. No hot-shot jet jocks, submariners, special warfare UDT or SEALS, supply corps pork chops, or intelligence spooks. After talking to the other jaygee, Coburn figured out he was the junior officer in the room, probably the one with the least time in the navy. Being the "baby" wasn't bad. It showed he was picked for this job even though he did not have the rank or the experience of the other officers. His talents were obviously recognized by the detailers.

All two dozen men—ranging in age from Coburn at twenty-four to the master chief and one of the lieutenant commanders in their late thirties—were ordered to be advisors to the navy of South Vietnam, the SVN. This was the first day of a thirteen-week training course in counter- insurgency, weapons, land operations, language, survival, escape, and evasion. Sixteen of the men came from ships on the East Coast; the rest were from the Pacific. At 0800 the commanding officer of the school walked in, and the future advisors took their seats at the gray metal desks.

Their training began.

The school's CO welcomed them and laid out the schedule for the next three months. Ten of the weeks would be spent in the classrooms for counterinsurgency and language instruction. The other three weeks would be in the field running around Camp Pendleton—the sprawling USMC base an hour north— the nearby beach of North Island, and the scrub desert of Hot Warner Springs for the infamous week of SERE training. SERE exposed the students to grimly realistic survival and evasion as well as resistance to interrogation and the rare escape from a prison compound.

The CO introduced a middle-aged Vietnamese man wearing a suit and tie as the director of the school's language and cultural training. Finally, the instructors for the first four weeks were introduced: an army major, three navy lieutenants, and a navy diver chief.

Coburn focused on the three lieutenants. They were all about the same age, had just returned from advisor duty in-country, and wore three rows of ribbons signifying a lot of action in combat. Each had the red, blue, and white ribbon of a Bronze Star medal, and two had Purple Hearts. Coburn's solitary National Defense medal ribbon—the ubiquitous "I was alive in '65" medal for being in the military during the not-so-cold war—made him feel self-conscious. He was the only uniformed person in the room with just one award on his left breast. But his year in-country would take care that.

The army major and the four navy instructors all wore identical, black-faced, luminous-dial, olive-drab wristwatches with nylon cloth bands.

After half a morning of welcome and introductions, they climbed aboard a gray navy bus and toured the base with one of the lieutenant instructors pointing out the base exchange, commissary, swimming pool, officers' club, chiefs' club, enlisted club, library, and the training beaches and gymnasium.

All the officer students walked across the parking lot to the officers' club for lunch. They sat together and talked about where they were from and where they were headed in-country. Coburn and the other jaygee were the only ones going to River Assault Groups. Except for the senior lieutenant commander, who was going to an advisor job in the headquarters in Saigon, the rest were sprinkled up and down the South Vietnamese coast.

The afternoon started with a talk by a Judge Advocate General commander—a uniformed attorney—from the naval district's legal office and his yeoman. They handed out generic wills, power of attorney forms, next-of-kin notifications, and government insurance beneficiary designations forms. The lawyer looked around the room.

"Gentlemen, you're starting training to go into a combat zone for a year. We all hope you'll return in one piece. I know it's 'the other guy' who gets hurt, but you just might be that other guy. I strongly recommend you get your personal affairs in order.

In fact, do it now. It's your choice; you don't have to. But you're stupid if you don't." He then went through the documents.

Coburn toyed with putting Betsy down as his beneficiary. He mused that she'd be all sad and upset at his death, and then she gets a cool $10,000, which should really make her miss him. But then he filled in his father's name on the forms and handed them to the yeoman.

They boarded the bus again and motored to the base sickbay, where all two dozen went through a half hour assembly line of fluid samples, probing, and poking. Then a shorter line of shots. Back on the bus to the gymnasium, where they were issued jungle fatigues, floppy jungle hat, two pairs of the new leather-and-nylon jungle boots, olive-drab underwear and T-shirts, socks, and a black-faced, luminescent, olive-drab wristwatch with an olive-drab nylon strap.

On the bus ride back to the classroom, Coburn shared a seat with the instructor who had been their guide. The instructor noticed the watch box on the top of the pile of gear in Coburn's lap. He smiled and pointed with his chin at the box.

"You be sure to wear that all the time here. Thursday night at the Mexican Village is the night all the WESTPAC widows show up, and if they see that on your wrist, your probability of scoring goes way up."

Coburn laughed. "They put out just because you're wearing a green watch?"

"Well, you may have to throw a little bullshit into the mix, but yeah, that's the myth. The story is that around Coronado, they know it means in-country, and you are either going to die or you just came back from nearly dying. Sort of gets their female hormones percolating for pity sex."

"I have no problem with that," laughed Coburn as he took off the watch his parents gave him when he graduated high school and replaced it with the government-issue Timex.

Classes started in earnest the next day.

* * *

The counterinsurgency training was mostly classroom lectures with a sprinkling of guest lecturers and an occasional field trip to another part of the base. The day started at 0800 and ended at 1700 with the entire class changing into their jungle fatigues and boots and exercising and running on the beach under the tutelage of the diver chief. Evenings, weekends, and holidays were free time, although they all had homework: reading assignments and papers, and several were assigned research reports to present to the rest of the class.

Much of the history and culture of Vietnam was presented by the army major, who wore the insignia of an intelligence specialist. Coburn found the information interesting; he knew little of Vietnam other than the names Dien Bien Phu and Ho Chi Minh. The major's lectures were entertaining as well as informative as he added tales of his own experiences. As much as he tried to hide it, a sad skepticism and lack of conviction came through as he dryly recited the canned description of why the United States was involved: domino theory, Gulf of Tonkin, saving a democracy, stopping terrorism, invitation by the South Vietnamese to be there, and winning the hearts and mind of the people.

During one coffee break, the major asked Coburn how he thought the lectures were going. Coburn said he enjoyed them and was learning a lot, but then he hesitated. As if reading his thoughts, the major spoke before Coburn could resume. "The people in charge of that country are corrupt. The rest have been fighting all their lives. They don't trust the government. They don't know what peace is. They want their children to be safe and healthy. But...I simply don't know what we can do to give them that. As military professionals, I mean."

He then returned to the podium and went through a careful and well-thought-out analysis and comparison of the siege of the French garrisons at Dien Bien Phu, the marines' defense under siege at Khe Sanh, and the recent fighting during Tet. He made no mention of "the enemy shot his wad," "strategic victory," or "light at the end of the tunnel."

His last lectures were delivered at the end of the second week. He talked about the culture of the Vietnamese, their ethnocentric nature, their stoicism. He warned the class not to underestimate their counterparts, and more importantly the enemy.

"I don't know how many KIA the VC and NVA suffered in Tet and Khe Sanh, but they just kept on fighting, never stopped." He pointed at the class. "You have a tough job on your hands advising your counterparts how to defeat an enemy like that."

* * *

The weekend was starting. In the O Club, Coburn sat with Doug Vernon, the other jaygee. Unlike Coburn, Vernon was a graduate of the Naval Academy and had had his heart set on making a career of the navy since his junior year in high school. Also unlike Coburn, Vernon was short and stocky, not handsome but not bad looking either. The two had become friends.

"Whatcha have planned for this weekend, Doug? Hanging around or what?" Coburn asked.

"I'll be around. I have to do my research report on Tuesday, so I gotta work on finishing that up. Maybe catch some rays if it's warm enough. I dunno. You?"

"Not sure. Met this nurse at the Mexican Village last night with a great pickup line. Put on a face like I was going to cry, put a waver in my voice, looked her in the eye, and said 'I feel so terrible about Martin Luther King getting...' and then pretended to be choked up with sadness. Put her hormone pumps on high. Now she covets my body and my jungle combat watch. Maybe I'll let her wear it while I take off her clothes and do a reconnaissance of her body. I'm not sure I want to invest the time and money, although I am getting horny enough to reconsider my investment strategy."

"I thought you had a steady girlfriend in Rhode Island or someplace."

Coburn dropped the bravado from his voice. "I don't know where that's going, Doug. I really miss her, but with the distance and my going in-country...it's sort of cooling off. I don't know what I'm going to do about her. Hell, she's three thousand miles away. And in a few months, she'll be even farther. I don't want to sound altruistic, but I really think it would be best for her if she moved on. Y'know, we break it off. I really felt guilty flirting with that nurse." Coburn seemed lost in his thoughts, staring into his beer. "Might be better for me, too."

Vernon nodded. Then said, "Hey, Clark, don't you also have to give your report on Monday or Tuesday? You ready?"

"I will be. I can do those things pretty fast and can bullshit enough on my feet to get away with it. Besides, what are they going to do to me if I fuck it up? Send me to Vietnam for a year?"

"Clark, I wish I had your talent, brains and looks—and bullshit. Some of us poor bastards have to work at this stuff. And we're never getting laid."

"Doug, your problem is that you have a conscience. Get rid of it, life gets a whole lot easier."

"After that soliloquy you just delivered, you're giving me that advice?"

The two of them laughed and drank their beers.

"Okay if I join you two good timers?" Marty Lender, one of the instructors, was standing at their table, a soft drink in his hand. He was pulling out a chair to sit down.

"Sure thing, Lieutenant," said Vernon.

"Hey, call me Marty. Leave the rank in the classroom." Lender sat down and leaned back in his chair. "How you like the program so far?"

Coburn scrutinized the rows of ribbons on Lerner's chest as he replied, "I'm finding it real interesting and a real education. I didn't know much about the place."

"Or the people," added Vernon.

"But I'm not sure how I use all this stuff in-country on the job," said Coburn. "You've been there. You think we'll be able to apply this newfound knowledge?"

Lender laughed and shook his head. "Y'know, I really don't know. When I went over there in late sixty-six, we weren't given much of this. We just got the language training, SERE, and weapons, and off we went. So much of what I did there was in reaction to what was happening. I really didn't have much choice other than to react. If I had known more about the people, like you guys are getting—sure, it would have helped and been useful. But so little of it was initiating, and so much was just reacting, reacting, reacting."

"It looks like you did a pretty good job of reacting." Coburn pointed at Lender's ribbons with his glass. "That's a lot of fruit salad."

"It's hard not to come back with three rows or more. Whether you earn it or not. Somebody shoots at you, and you shoot back, and the next thing you know your boss or counterpart has written you up for an award. Stay in-country long enough and not fuck up, and you come back with a couple of rows."

"I think you're being modest, Marty," said Vernon.

"That has to be good for the old career, doesn't it?" asked Coburn. "It does say something about doing okay in an environment that most ship drivers don't get into."

Marty shifted in his chair, a little uneasy. "You do get experience that others don't get. That's for sure. And if you can believe the lying cocksucker detailer who cut your orders to be an advisor, it means you're a front-runner. You do get a leg up on your next set of orders or two. But does this mean that I'll make flag or even captain or get scrambled eggs on my visor? I think that a whole lot more than surviving a year on the rivers will decide that."

"Yeah, performance dictates selection in this man's navy." Vernon looked at his watch. "You two want to get some chow?"

Lender drained his soft drink. "Sure, I'm up for it."

Coburn thought for a minute. "Nah, you two go without me. I want to call a nurse I met. I think my watch turns her on."

Lender laughed. "You know why? All these women around here are used to the aviators from North Island and Miramar. Those assholes all wear those watches with the real big dials and all the buttons. And you know the story about fliers and their wristwatches."

Vernon laughed, "Sure do. It's the inverse proportion aviator wristwatch theory. They wear those big watches to compensate for their little dicks."

"Hmmm, think I can trade this one in for a child-sized version?" asked Coburn. "So when that nurse sees my little olive-drab micro watch, she knows I'm hung like a horse?"

Vernon and Lender walked into the O club dining room as Coburn went back to his room to call whatshername-the-nurse and take a shower.

* * *

The next two weeks focused on the role of the advisor and the mission of the naval advisor in the Military Assistance Command Vietnam or MACV.

Tactics and the dynamics of the advisor and the South Vietnamese counterpart team were taught with real-life examples from the three navy instructors' recent experience. Rounding out the rest of the time were guest lectures from a SEAL master chief, an EOD team chief, and a visit to the base engine shop for a demonstration of the venerable GM 671 diesel engine, which powered most South Vietnamese navy vessels.

Coburn spent occasional evenings with the nurse. Every Sunday morning he'd call his parents collect, a habit from his college days. His parents would ask how he was, which he always answered with "fine"; they'd chat a little about family and friends, and then they'd hang up until the next Sunday morning.

Betsy sent several letters the first week—long, newsy letters, telling him about her job interviews and classes, always ending that she missed him and worried about him. He avoided responding to the first few letters. When he did, he wrote about how physically rough and mentally challenging it was preparing to go into harm's way. He told her he wanted to write more but that he had little opportunity since he was so focused and busy, portraying the training as all consuming.

Letters from Betsy would pile up on his desk as he avoided writing her. Soon her letters dropped to twice a week, and then weekly, and finally she only wrote back after receiving a letter from him.

CHAPTER 7
KINH MON

The men stood silent in the moonlit night beneath a camou-flaged net canopy. Vo was in the second row, nervous and curious. He could hear his clothes rustling as he breathed. A figure walked to the front of the recruits and stopped.

The man was wearing the olive-drab uniform of a noncommissioned officer, perfectly ironed and pleated, immaculately clean. On his feet were sandals of truck tire tread held on with straps of inner tube strips, and on his head an olive-drab pith helmet with a red star centered on the crown. He carried a carved wooden cane like a swagger stick in his right hand. His left arm was missing, the empty sleeve of his uniform neatly folded and sewed in place. He looked at the recruits, moving his eyes but not his head.

With a nod from the one-armed man, one of the soldiers walked to the front row and faced the first recruit. The one-armed NCO walked behind the soldier, who ordered each recruit to say his name. The one-armed soldier inspected them in silence, looking at their faces. Vo noticed a nearly imperceptible nod when he said his name.

The one-armed man returned to the front of the rank.

"I am Senior Instructor Pham. It is my responsibility to produce soldiers, men who will fight and in all likelihood die. I am in charge of you. I am all you have. You have no mother, no father, no sister, no brother, no wife, no friends. I repeat: I am all you have. You will follow my orders. If you do so satisfactorily, you will leave here as soldiers and fight and die. If you do not follow my orders satisfactorily, you will stay here until you do. Only then will you leave here as soldiers and die. Believe me when I tell you that you will rather fight and die than to stay with me. You will refer to me as 'Senior Instructor,' not 'sir,' not 'Mr. Pham.' You will not salute me.

"Your training begins now, not in the morning. Now." Pham turned to the soldier who had led him through the inspection and gave him orders to start indoctrination. For the rest of the night, the men were herded in strict formation from huts to tents to huts.

The men were given physical examinations and then marched double time to the quartermaster's tent. There they were issued rucksacks, canteens, rudimentary mess kits, entrenching shovels, dark-green ponchos, olive-green uniform shirts and trousers, soft cloth caps, rubber-tire-soled sandals, underwear, black-and-white scarves, soap, razors, and toothbrushes. The size of the uniforms and sandals seemed to be at the discretion of the soldiers behind the counters, who piled up a mound of clothing and footwear for each recruit.

A young-looking recruit standing next to Vo could barely see above the top of the pile in his arms. "Do they expect me to fight a war with a shovel? Where's my rifle? How do we win a war..." His complaining was cut short by an NCO who barked for silence, poked the man to the front of the ranks with his cane, and ordered him to duckwalk around the quartermaster's tent, balancing the mound of his newly issued gear in his arms. Several others giggled at the sight and soon joined him in the gear-laden duckwalk.

Vo was no longer nervous. He was observing everything. As his nature, he was absorbing and learning. The men were double-timed back to the bamboo huts.

With Senior Instructor Pham watching silently, one of the NCOs handed out cloth sacks and ordered the recruits to take off their civilian clothes and put them into the sacks along with any personnel items they had—including rings, keys, money, wristwatches, religious items, and photos. The only items they could keep were eyeglasses. Vo did not remember seeing any bespectacled recruits. The men stripped in the dark night.

The NCO barked, "Tie your sack securely. Remember your number. If you ever finish training, it will be returned to you. Pass your package to the left. You four," he pointed at the far left edge of the rank, "collect all the packages and put them into that box." He pointed at a large wooden crate. "Be quick!"

Under the NCO's instructions, the men put on their uniforms. Vo's shirt was tight across his shoulders, but his trousers fit well. Many of the others were in uniforms too large, others too small. With the NCO pretending to not notice, a quick exchange of shirts and trousers and sandals between the men resulted in a better-dressed recruit company.

They were shown how to pack their rucksacks. When they finished, another NCO read from a list, assigning the recruits to the huts. Each hut held eighteen recruits. Candles illuminated the interiors. Blank postcards and pencil stubs were handed out.

"You have fifteen minutes until lights out. The first thing you will do is to write home that you are fine. Senior Instructor will read every card before it leaves here. If you want to complain or cry to Uncle Ho, your card will not be sent. You will send one letter each week as long as you are here.

"After you have written your letter, you will remove and stow your uniform, go to the latrine and wash area, and then lie on your mat, where you will stay until reveille. You do not have much time, so get some sleep instead of crying for your mother's tit."

Vo guessed that it must be about 0400. He was hungry and tired. On the card he scribbled a quick note to his parents telling them that he was well and would write once a week and asked them to share his letters with Ngoc. He took off his uniform, walked out to the latrine area, and washed in a bucket of cold well water. He dried himself with the black-and-white scarf and lay down on his bamboo mat. Vo was in a deep sleep before the candles were snuffed out.

* * *

At 0500 one of the instructors, followed by another banging his cane against a garbage can lid, ordered them off their sleeping mats.

"You have ten minutes to shit and shave if you have anything to shave and dress and stow your gear." Recruits stood up and in their sleep-deprived daze scrambled to follow his orders.

Ten minutes later the entire company was in rank and uniformed, with gear stowed. The senior instructor walked through the lines, looking at each man and tapping a missed button or non-centered belt with his carved cane. A sloppily dressed recruit was ordered to squat on his haunches and was sent on a waddling duckwalk. After the senior instructor finished inspecting the men, he inspected each hut. When finding anything not to his satisfaction, he nodded to the NCO walking with him, who loudly demanded to know the name of the recruit responsible for the mess. Ten recruits who had failed inspection were painfully duckwalking the perimeter of the drill ground in the dark.

"You are slobs and will probably kill yourselves because your rifle will be dirty and not fire or because you get a splinter and it gets infected by the dirt on your skin because you are too lazy to wash. This slovenly behavior will hurt your comrades more than you will hurt yourself. Your comrades don't have the time to button your shirts or get your gear squared away or wipe your filthy ass. All return to rank." With the urging of the ever-present instructors' canes, the duckwalkers painfully straightened their legs and took their places in the company. The senior instructor continued.

"Improperly stowed gear is now on the floor of your hut. If that gear is yours, when I tell you to, you will stow it correctly.

For the rest of you, why didn't you help your comrades stow their gear? You obviously knew how. Why did you not help your comrades? While they properly stow their gear, you will take the duckwalk. And you will duckwalk until all the gear is properly stowed." He paused for a few seconds. "Re-stow gear! Remaining trainees, duckwalk!"

After a few minutes, Vo's knees started to ache. In a deep knee bend, he waddled, the only sound being the shuffling of feet and the heavy breathing and occasional grunt from a less stoic trainee.

Vo understood what the instructors were doing—beating down the individual and encouraging the collective group. Those who did things best and fast would not be recognized for their achievements. Finishing first meant only that you did not stop to help others less adept. It was more important to get the entire group of comrades to the finish line then to have a few stars leading the pack and stragglers limping behind. This made sense to Vo. He would do everything he could to help his comrades. On the third time around the parade ground, the senior instructor called everyone back into ranks and attention.

"Did you like that?" Silence. "I asked you a question and expect an answer. Did you like that?"

The trainees responded raggedly. "Yes, sir!"

"Don't address me as 'sir,' you idiots. I am not an officer, I work for a living. Now try that again. I want you to speak as one."

"Yes, Senior Instructor!" was the ragged reply.

"Again, you idiots. Speak as one. Did you like that?"

In unison, the recruits shouted, "Yes, Senior Instructor!"

The senior instructor looked to the NCO at his side and nodded. The NCO ordered the entire company to take their mess kits and form up outside in their ranks. It was dawn. He marched them to a large tent covered with a camouflage net. Then he formed the group into a single file and ordered the first thirty-six to enter.

Inside the tent, at a steaming cauldron, stood an army cook with a ladle. Next to the cauldron were several large insulated jugs with spigots at their base. Six high tables were in the center of the tent. Each recruit received a large bowl of rice and a cup of hot tea. They stood at the tables and ate, six men to a table. As soon as they finished, they were replaced by the next group of thirty-six.

Vo was in the third group. He was surprised by the generous portion of rice in his mess kit.

"This would feed my entire family for days," marveled a trainee through a mouthful of rice. He looked around to see if anyone heard him. The nearest NCO seemed to ignore the talk.

"Hey, good clothes, good water, and food. Army life isn't so bad, huh?" said another.

Sensing that the silence rules were relaxed in the mess tent, Vo asked where the two were from. Both were peasants from the far northwest provinces. One was seventeen, the other nineteen. Conscription was inevitable, but both had felt enlisting was the right thing to do. When they asked what Vo had been doing before induction, he said only that he was a student in Hanoi and like them had enlisted.

The men were called to order and told they had ten minutes to wash and stow their mess kits, use the latrine, and line up back on the drill field in rank. They were to be silent.

The trainee next to Vo fumbled with his mess kit and ruck-sack. Silently reaching over, Vo showed him that the spoon had slid under the bowl and would not let the lid shut. With a smile and nod, the young trainee repacked his mess kit and put it back into his rucksack. As Vo turned to go out to the drill field, he saw that the senior instructor was looking at him. How long had he been there? What had he seen?

The rest of the morning was filled with close order drill and physical training. They ran an obstacle course, and Vo and several others who could have easily finished the course ahead of others ran near the end of the pack to help stragglers get over hurdles and climb walls.

At each stand easy, the men chatted among themselves. Two thirds seemed to be from the rural areas or fishing villages. The rest were from in and around Hanoi. The majority were conscripts. A few were married. Terms of service were indefinite for all. Their accepted destiny was the army until they died or the war ended.

The midday meal was a substantial one: three bowls of rice for each man, some vegetables, and a bit of meat. Again they ate standing up at the round tables in the mess tent. Afterward, on the drill field, they sat on the ground as one of the senior NCOs lectured on the organization of the army. Much time and effort was spent on the three-man cell. Each battalion was divided into three infantry companies, which were each divided into three platoons made up of three squads of nine men each. Each squad was divided into cells of three.

The cell was the nucleus of the fighting army, the soldiers' support and family. Each man cared for the other two in his cell. They were there to help one another. Vo suspected that the three men were there to keep one another in line. Later in the week, the recruits would be organized into a company of platoons, squads, and cells.

The lecturing NCO finished up by ordering the men to grow vegetables in the tilled area behind the huts. Quick-growing morning glory vines and tapioca roots would be harvested every five days and delivered to the mess tent.

The trainees were marched around the base as the NCOs counted cadence and chanted various marching songs. The senior instructor joined them as they filed into the quartermaster's tent and were handed new AK-47 assault rifles. They marched back to the drill field, holding the rifles across their chests.

The one-armed sergeant major addressed the recruits. "From now on you will never be separated from your rifle. You will take care of your rifle, clean it, learn how to repair it, and most importantly, you will learn how to kill with it. You will also wear your rucksacks at all times unless you are told to do otherwise." With the one-armed man watching, one of the senior NCOs started the recruits' weapons training. The recruits paid rapt attention.

Back at the huts, they were instructed to clean their gear and get ready for the evening meal. Vo and a few others made sure that the men in their vicinity put their gear in order. They were all tired, having had less than an hour's sleep in the last day and half. Some of the men from around Hanoi were exhausted from the physical training, marching, and the morning duckwalk. Most of the men from the rural areas seemed to be in much better condition.

They were called into ranks in the late afternoon sun. The senior instructor again made his inspection of the men. Two were ordered to duckwalk around the drill field. He then went into the huts and came out five minutes later.

"Who has position number seven-three? Step forward!" No one moved.

"Number seven-three must not be listening to me. So I will ask again for number seven-three to step forward!" A young man, one of the smallest in the company, sheepishly walked to the front of the ranks. His rifle looked bigger than he was. The senior instructor did not look at him. "Numbers five-three, six-three, eight-three, and nine-three, step forward!" With alacrity four men ran to the front and stood next to the small man.

"You four did not help your comrade. Your positions are right next to him. His mistakes in combat could kill your entire company because you didn't bother to see if he needed help and instruction. You will die anyway, but at least die fighting the enemy and not because you ignored your comrades! He is your responsibility, and you are his. You four duckwalk!"

The four started their painful waddle. The one-armed man looked hard at the miscreant and poked him in the chest with his carved cane. "You would have killed your company if you were in battle. When your four comrades return from their journey around the field, you will join them for another lap and then go with them and stow your gear in the proper manner!" The little man's knees were visibly shaking. "Until then the dead company you killed will stand here at attention. Do you think they would rather eat or stand at attention?"

No answer.

"You are deaf?"

"No, Senior Instructor."

"Then answer me!" the senior instructor shouted into the man's face, their noses nearly touching.

In a quavering voice the trainee replied, "Eat, Senior Instructor."

The company stood at rigid attention for nearly twenty minutes as the five trainees finished their duckwalk and went into the hut and squared away number seven-three's gear. The company was marched to the mess tent and ate the same meal as lunch. Number seven-three walked among the trainees, apologizing.

They were all exhausted, and some fell asleep as they stood leaning on their elbows at the round table, food still in their mess kits. Vo chatted with a few of the trainees nearby. They wondered in low tones if they were done for the day, or did Old One-Arm have more tortures in store for them? They didn't have long to wait before they'd find out.

The senior instructor loudly ordered the supervising NCO to take roll and then march them all to the classroom. After a fifteen-minute march with the NCO counting cadence, the men were sent into a nondescript building and told to stand in front of bare wooden benches arranged in five half-circle rows around a wood platform; a rudimentary amphitheater.

They were called to attention as a soldier in a uniform, every bit as crisp as the senior instructor's, mounted the low wooden stage. His uniform shirt had four pockets, unlike the two of the trainees, NCOs, and the senior instructor. Four-pocket shirts were worn only by officers. The senior instructor followed him onto the stage and stood next to him. The officer smiled, took off his pith helmet, and laid it on top of a small rostrum. A nod to the senior instructor was followed by Old One-Arm ordering the men to take their seats.

"Welcome, comrades. I am the training battalion's political officer. You will see much of me during your training. The instructors in my Military Party Committee and I will be working closely with Senior Instructor Pham and his men to turn you into soldiers. Soldiers who will liberate the South from the American invaders and reunify our country. The battle is a long one, a protracted one. Many of you will die." He paused and scanned the men. Despite their fatigue, they were all attentive, staring at him.

"Rest assured, victory will happen. It is your destiny." He paused, looking at his feet, then looked up and continued.

"Your training is much more than learning tactics and how to clean and shoot a weapon. This training is the first step of loyalty and sacrifice to the people of Vietnam. We will discuss this much more in the weeks ahead, and you will be critical of yourself and your comrades and your superiors. Constructively.

"Your country is proud of you. The people are proud of you. You will not let them down." He put on his pith helmet and nodded to the senior instructor, who called the trainees to attention as the political officer walked off the stage and out of the classroom.

Old One-Arm motioned with his carved cane to one of his ever-present assistants. The soldier handed a pile of cards to the nearest trainee and told him to give each of his comrades a card. The men were ordered to sit again.

"On this card is the Code of Discipline. You will keep this card with you at all times. It is as important as your rifle. You will memorize this code. If you violate this code, you will be punished, severely punished."

Vo read the card:

CODE OF DISCIPLINE

1. I will obey the orders from my superiors under all circumstances.
2. I will never take anything from the people, not even a needle or thread.
3. I will not put group property to my own use.
4. I will return that which is borrowed and make restitution for things damaged.
5. I will be polite to People, respect, and love them.
6. I will be fair and just in buying and selling.
7. When staying in people's houses, I will treat them as I would treat my own house.
8. I will follow the slogan: <u>ALL THINGS OF THE PEOPLE AND FOR THE PEOPLE.</u>
9. I will keep unit secrets absolutely and will never disclose information, even to closest friends and relatives.
10. I will encourage the people to struggle and support the Revolution.
11. I will be alert to spies and will report all suspicious persons to my superiors.
12. I will remain close to the people and maintain their affection and love.

The senior instructor ordered them to attention and to read the code out loud. As the trainees read the code, he and the NCOs recited the words from memory.

"You will now go back to your huts and stow your gear. Taps will be in one hour. Spend your time memorizing and understanding this code. It will be very difficult for you to do so if all of you are duckwalking because you did not help a comrade."

He walked off the stage, and the supervising NCO marched them back to their huts. They stowed their gear, studied, went to the latrine, washed up, and fell into a deep and exhausted sleep. Their first full day of training had ended.

* * *

For the next five days, the company continued its basic indoctrination to soldiering and the army. No time was set aside for physical training because all the time was dedicated to physical training. From reveille to taps, they wore their rucksacks, which were filled with varying weights of bricks. The days were filled with weapons training, close-order drills, marches of increasing distances, lectures, and, in the evening, self-criticism sessions led by someone from the Military Party Committee.

Each evening the senior instructor inspected the huts, gear, and trainees before they were allowed to sleep. He found fewer and fewer transgressions of his military order.

Just before lights out on the evening of the sixth day, he announced that basic indoctrination was over and the next day would be a light-duty day of morning, afternoon, and evening musters, meals, and laundry. No classes, no exercise, no marching. The day after that would begin the next phase of basic training, when they would learn their military skills.

Vo looked around at the men in his hut. They had grown close, watching out for one another. They all smiled.

* * *

The next morning's reveille was an hour later than normal. No NCOs banging garbage can lids screaming at them to get out off their sleeping mats. Although the huts were squared away and the men clean and properly uniformed and armed, the muster in ranks was just a roll call followed by the morning meal. They were given a luxurious thirty minutes to eat.

After mess gear was put away, the senior NCO told them all to remain at ease but pay attention. He read off the names of seven of them, including Vo, and instructed them to meet with the senior instructor in his small hut near the mess tent in five minutes.

Vo felt a knot in his stomach. He looked around and found most of the men near him staring at him.

"Why are you going to see Old One-Arm, Vo?" asked one in a quiet voice. "What's happening? You in trouble?"

"I don't know, but I will find out in a few minutes."

Vo got up, went to the latrine and wash buckets, and with the six others, walked to the hut by the mess tent. Vo knew these other men. In their early to mid twenties, they were all older than the average trainee in the company. Two were in his hut. Nervously looking at one another, they stood outside the door. One looked at Vo and motioned with his head to the door. Vo knocked soundly two times.

"Enter!"

With Vo in the lead, they filed in and stood at attention before a table at which the senior instructor sat. None of the trainees had ever been in this inner sanctum. The room was bare except for the table and chair, a cot, and a footlocker at the end of the cot. On the wall hung photograph portraits of Ho Chi Minh and General Giap and a large framed copy of the Code of Discipline. The only window was in the back wall. The room was spotless, sterile, cold.

Without referring to the papers in front of him, the senior instructor looked directly at each man and recited his name. He told them to stand easy but pay attention. The seven relaxed, but only slightly. All were visibly nervous.

"When we fought the French, we could always identify their officers. Not by their behavior or action in combat, but by their uniforms. Their officers were of the privileged class and dressed like toy soldiers. The Americans are not much better, but they've learned a thing or two. They wear the same uniforms as their men when fighting. But they're encumbered with badges of rank. The Southern puppets are following the Americans, but their officers are spoiled and privileged, worse than both the French and Americans. If you can spot one in combat, it will not be because of his actions. He will be the one whose uniform is tailored and boots shined, by some poor soldier, and probably taking cover behind his boot-shining servant."

Old One-Arm stood up and slowly paced back and forth as he spoke, carved cane held like a swagger stick.

"Our officers and soldiers wear the same uniform with a minor difference—the number of pockets. Sometimes, not even that. You cannot distinguish a Vietnamese officer from an enlisted soldier by his uniform. So how does the soldier know who is an officer and who is not? How does he know who is leading, giving orders?" He slammed the carved cane down on the table, startling the seven men. "By his actions!"

"You seven are candidates to become officers. I have been given orders to evaluate you during training. With my recommendation and the recommendation of the political officer, you will be sent to officer training, and upon completion commissioned as an officer." He sat down. "I believe you all are aware that you are candidates?"

The seven men answered "Yes, Senior Instructor."

"I will follow the orders I have been given. Without question. But I do not believe in making officers this way. Officers should be selected by their actions, not by some remote general's decision to send some untested snot to officer training before he has been tested as a soldier. Still, the political officer and I have been given the authority—and the responsibility—to deny you this privilege if either of us decides that you do not have the ability to act as an officer leading men in combat."

He looked at each one in silence, then in a quiet voice, continued.

"I have no idea at this time if any of you have the potential to be officers. But I will at the end of pre-infiltration training. Since I cannot observe you in combat, I will observe you in my own hell."

The senior instructor went on to describe the remaining weeks of training until he would make his recommendations for commissioning. Starting the next morning, the company was to be divided into three platoons, and each platoon into three squads, and each squad into three cells of three men each. The seven recruits in front of him would be assigned to lead the company.

Supervised by the NCOs, they would lead all drills, physical fitness exercises, meals, marching, mustering, and roll calls. One of the seven would be given command of the company, three would be platoon leaders, and three would be assistant platoon leaders.

"I have made my assignments based on my observations and the reports of your instructors. I do not care if you're some general's nephew or your father's the ambassador to the Soviets or you got here by sucking Uncle Ho's dick." One of the candidates smiled at the last comment. The senior instructor walked over to him.

"You think this is funny, Ky? You think you will have fun finding out if you can lead men or follow? Why are you smiling, Ky?"

"No, Senior Instructor."

"Then why are you smiling, Ky?"

"No reason, Senior Instructor."

"So you want to be an officer, and you smile for no reason like a fucking imbecile. But I don't think you're an imbecile, Ky. So you must be smiling because you think I'm funny. You think I'm a clown, Ky?"

"No, Senior Instructor."

"Are you smiling because you like me and you're a homosexual and think I am too?"

"No, Senior Instructor."

"So, you don't think I'm funny, and you don't like me, and you're not an imbecile. Then let's see how long you will smile." He walked back to the footlocker.

"Come here, Mr. Smiley." Ky walked to the footlocker.

The senior instructor told Ky to do a deep knee bend and stay in the squat position. He ordered Vo and Ninh, two tall and husky men, to pick up the footlocker and put it on Ky's shoulders. Vo estimated that the footlocker weighed over fifty kilograms. With Ky straining to maintain his balance, the senior instructor continued talking to the men, telling them their assignments.

Vo was assigned to lead the second platoon, Ninh would command the company, and Ky would be Vo's assistant platoon leader.

"You seven will have not only authority over your men but also responsibility for your men. If one of your men loses his cap, you are responsible. If one of your men smiles like Ky here, you will get to carry my footlocker. If one of your men makes a mistake or has an accident or malingers, you are responsible. And if they do well, then they deserve the credit and you are responsible for their not doing better. Do you understand what I am telling you?"

The seven men responded in unison, including Ky through gritted teeth.

"Consider yourselves in combat. You do not eat until your men are fed, you do not sleep until your men are asleep, you do not bleed until your men's wounds are bandaged, and you do not die until they do. Being an officer is a privilege, but that does not mean you deserve any privileges. There is no job or task that your men do that you will not do. You must know what they are being asked to do. And we will start that now."

From the footlocker tottering on Ky's shoulders, Old One-Arm pulled out three soup ladles and four canteen cups. He slammed the footlocker lid shut, nearly knocking Ky to the floor.

"Every light-duty day is the day that the latrine pit is cleaned. The honey buckets are removed and emptied into the fertilizer pit, and the latrine pit scraped clean of piss and shit. As leaders of the company and platoons, you will ensure this is carried out. You will inspect the results and report to me that the latrine pit is ready for inspection.

"There are shovels and brooms and buckets by the latrine for this cleaning. But because you seven are candidates and privileged, you will be the first in the company to clean the latrines. I do not want you to have to use heavy shovels and buckets and get blisters on your soft hands. So you will use these." He pointed to the ladles and canteen cups. He pointed at two other candidates.

"Take my footlocker off Mr. Smiley. Ky, stand up and join your comrades; they'll need your assistance and smiling demeanor."

The seven walked out the door, each armed with ladle or cup. The senior instructor and an NCO followed. When they reached the latrine, he ordered them to begin, and for them to wash, put on clean uniforms and report to him when it was ready for inspection. He left them under the supervision of the NCO.

Ninh, Vo, and the others briefly conferred, and then Ninh asked permission from the NCO to allow them to take off their uniforms. Ninh took charge and assigned tasks to everyone, saving the most disgusting for himself—climbing into the pit and scraping. They'd rotate until everyone had served his time in the pit.

It was hot, and the metal roof of the structure that sheltered the latrine turned the pit into an oven. Vo was as physically miserable as he had ever been in his life. He wanted to wipe the sweat out of his eyes but didn't dare because of the filth on his hands and arms. The men worked silently, not complaining. Ky was filling the honey buckets with the canteen cups passed from the pit. As he handed a brimming cup to Ky, Vo caught his eye and smiled at him.

"Better not let anyone see that smile, Vo. He'll say you're a real idiot for smiling while you're covered with shit and piss."

Vo chuckled. This was miserable. Insanely miserable. But the seven comrades toiled on, drawn closer by the absurdity of it all. Occasionally one of the other trainees came by but was told by the NCO to use the latrine behind the mess tent. At one time Vo looked up and saw the men marching to the midday meal. The thought of food and eating made him gag. Ninh vomited, but not until scrambling to a honey bucket so that his comrades would not have to clean up his vomit.

After five hours, they decided that the latrine was ready for inspection. They went to the wash buckets and well and first washed the ladles and canteen cups, scrubbing them until they gleamed in the sun. Then they washed themselves from hair to toes, the NCO standing by with soap and clothes that miraculously appeared from a pack he was carrying. They checked one another, smelled one another although their olfactory senses had long since been overpowered. Then they decided unanimously to wash themselves again. The NCO, out of smelling range, smiled and nodded his head. Finally, carrying their uniforms and cleaning equipment, they marched naked back to the huts and put on clean uniforms. Vo inspected Ninh, and then Ninh inspected the rest.

In two columns of three each, from tallest to shortest with Ninh counting cadence at their side, they marched back to the latrine and inspected it again. Then Ninh marched them to the door to the senior instructor's quarters. Ninh knocked twice, and the door opened immediately. Out stepped Old One-Arm, wearing his pith helmet.

"Latrine ready for inspection, Senior Instructor," announced Ninh, standing in front of the men, all at attention.

Without a word, Old One-Arm started walking to the latrine. Ninh looked at Vo with raised eyebrows. Should they follow him or stay here? Vo nodded in the direction of the latrine, and Ninh ordered them to face left and forward march, following the senior instructor.

They stood at attention while the senior instructor inspected their work. After ten minutes he came out into the sunshine.

"Satisfactory. Now you have to motivate your men to do the same."

"Permission to speak, Senior Instructor." It was Ninh.

"Speak!"

"Give us the opportunity to prove ourselves, Senior Instructor, and we will."

"Bullshit. Don't try sucking my dick, Ninh." Old One-Arm looked at Ky, who had a stern expression on his face, a smile being the farthest thing from his mind. "Continue your light-duty day. Tomorrow you start in earnest."

* * *

The company assembled in front of the huts for the morning muster and inspection. After a day of light duty, all appeared refreshed, almost happy at the prospects of the training ahead of them—training without the tedium of the indoctrination week they had just finished.

Vo was excited about the opportunity to lead a third of these men. He was confident, not anxious. To his surprise, he had slept well. Perhaps the five hours of scooping shit had been good for him. He smiled to himself and looked over at Ky, who gave him the briefest of smiles back.

The senior instructor walked to the front of the ranks. He told them that their intensive training as soldiers started immediately; indoctrination was over. Trainees had been selected to act as company commander, platoon leaders, and assistant platoon leaders. They would be leading the marching, drilling, administration, and day-to-day activity of the company, including discipline. He and his staff would be constantly supervising but would interfere only for incompetence and safety. The names of the seven men and their positions were called out and the men ordered front and center.

An NCO arranged the seven chosen leaders directly in front of the senior instructor, facing the ranks. The leaders of the first platoon were put to Ninh's right, Vo and Ky put in front of Ninh, and the third platoon's leaders to Ninh's left. The NCO pulled a list from his pocket.

The recruits were being assigned to platoons and reassigned to huts. When they heard their names and platoon assignments, they double-timed to form ranks in front of their platoon leaders.

Vo noticed that the second platoon, his platoon, was being populated by some men whom he thought were weak—complainers, men out for themselves. When all the men were assigned, the second platoon was filled with the shortest, skinniest, and sloppiest. Vo thought that the senior instructor was one wily character. These assignments must be because he was trying to break Vo and Ky. Or because he thought Vo and Ky could shape these men into soldiers. Or both. Never mind, the objective was clear: turn these men—and himself—into soldiers.

At the morning meal, Vo and Ky discussed how to proceed. The first step was to pick the three best to be squad leaders. Then to set up the three-man cells, putting the weakest under the best squad leader and the best under the weakest squad leader.

Vo had a platoon roster that the NCO had given to him. Setting up the cells took the most time. They put the best with the worst and average in each cell. Now it was time to lead.

CHAPTER 8
CAMP PENDLETON, CALIFORNIA

Coburn and his classmates spent the next two weeks running around Camp Pendleton, the marine base outside of Oceanside, north of San Diego. The navy sent them there for weapons familiarization and land operations taught by the United States Marine Corps.

Without exception, the two dozen students were products of the high-technology, oceangoing navy. They were accustomed to large machinery, sophisticated weapon systems, and electronics. Heated and air conditioned living spaces complete with hot showers, mattresses, sick bays, and kitchens producing three hot meals a day provided cramped comfort and blueberry pancakes. Operating in the ocean, the only time they sailed in confined waters was entering and leaving a port.

In less than ten weeks, these same two dozen would be in-country, operating on rivers a few meters deep and canals barely wider than their boats. The weapons at their disposal would be pistols, rifles, and machine guns. Instead of a suite of high-speed transmitters and receivers, their communications would be by portable radios, flares, smoke, hand signals, and shouting. Radar would be useless, and a handheld compass would be their major navigation tool. Ponderous and formal fleet communications protocols would be replaced by the simpler army and marine radio procedures. Their sick bay would be a small pack worn on their web gear and a medevac helicopter. If lucky they'd sleep on an air mattress, and breakfast would be C-rations, fish, and rice.

Most importantly, the border between water and land would be erased in-country. The new advisors were as likely to be crossing the river and canal banks and humping through the inland paddies and jungle as they would to be operating afloat.

The marines had to train these seagoing men for this new environment. And they had only two weeks to do it.

Coburn was suffering from the remnants of a hangover and a lack of sleep when he boarded the bus for the ride to Pendleton.

The day before, he had written a letter to Betsy, telling her he loved her but worried about their future. For her sake, he thought it best that she "see other people." He didn't want to hurt Betsy, and he didn't like the haunting guilt he felt. Hoping to not shut the door completely, he tried to leave it open ended and vague. After dropping the letter in the BOQ mail slot, he walked to the O club, drank a beer and a shot, and called the nurse.

He left the nurse's bed at about 0630, threw on his clothes, and grabbed a cup of coffee but refused the scrambled eggs and bacon, convinced he'd vomit if he got any of that got close to his nostrils.

With a "See ya maybe next weekend?" he gave her a dry kiss on the lips and drove to the BOQ. He grabbed a cold Coke from the vending machine and guzzled it down before showering and shaving. No khaki for a week, he thought as he got dressed in jungle fatigues and packed a duffel with shaving gear and clothing. He liked the loose and comfortable fit of the fatigues. No need to pin on rank or even name tags since the collars had embroidered black bars, and "US NAVY" and "COBURN" were embroidered in black across the top of his breast pockets. He liked the jungle boots even more. Lightweight and comfortable, and he didn't have to shine them. Satisfied with his mirrored image, he locked his room and walked into the brilliant San Diego morning sun. Donning his shit-hot aviator sunglasses, he walked the short distance to the bus and took the seat next to his friend Doug Vernon.

"Clark, you are the same color as your uniform. You look like shit."

"Feel like it. Excess alcohol and—I think—either pizza or pussy."

"Excess pizza, that's a problem. Excess pussy? Impossible. That's like having too much money."

"Doug, my man, you do have a point there, but she wouldn't let me sleep. Kept on begging for another go-around with Mr. Happy. Or was that a dream in an alcohol haze? I was afraid I'd have to refuse her, or worse, deal with a limp weenie, but fortunately I think I vaguely responded as the officer and gentleman that President Johnson said I am. Even got that in writing."

"Yeah, I got the officer and gentleman letter. But I don't remember him writing anything in there about pussy."

"Look on the back of your commission. It's in real tiny fine print just below where it says US Government Printing Office. How was your weekend, Doug?"

"Not bad. I got up the nerve and called that girl I dated a few times in high school and Annapolis and then off and on since then. Lives in DC now. She seemed glad to hear from me. I thought she had a boyfriend or got married or something, but she certainly didn't sound like that."

"Doug, and here I thought you were some monk celibate who had forsaken all enjoyment except Froot Loops. Well done, well done, lad. What you going to do about this?"

"Shit, I dunno, Clark. You know that week we have after SERE and having to report to Travis? I was thinking of asking her if she wanted to visit. But in typical brave warrior fashion, I'm afraid she'll say no."

"It's a good thing we aren't at Pendleton yet because I'd ask the fucking grunts to use you for a target to save on paper. Ask her to visit you, dummy. She'll probably say yes. And if she says no, that's her loss. Go for it. Shit, if you don't, I'll ask her to come out and spend the week with me. Unless she's fat and ugly, of course."

"Fat and ugly she ain't. To the contrary, Mr. Coburn."

"So?"

"You have fortified my courage. I told her I'd call Friday and will broach the subject at that time."

"Don't pussy out on me, Doug."

The two young officers were seated behind the senior officer in the class, Lieutenant Commander James Theodore. Theodore shared the seat with Marty Lender, the instructor. He turned in his seat, laughing.

"Y'know, you two swinging dicks are killing us old, married guys," said Theodore. "Are either of you two aware that there may be other things in the world besides sex?"

Coburn and Vernon looked at each other with straight faces. Coburn then said innocently, "There are, sir? Really? I don't think we knew about that. Like what?"

Vernon butted in. "Sleep? That must be one, huh, sir?"

"I give up on you two," said the senior officer. "I noticed that both of you two are going to River Assault Groups. I'm sure you are both aware that the South Vietnamese have a new law that no woman is allowed within a hundred miles of those groups."

"Tell me you're joking, sir. Otherwise Clark and I are going to have to join the Viet Cong."

Lender broke in. "We're almost there." The bus pulled up to the entrance of Camp Pendleton a few minutes later.

"Sir," Coburn asked Theodore. "Should we do a John Wayne and run off the bus charging and yelling like the marines in *The Sands of Iwo Jima*?"

"No, for the next two weeks try to act like naval officers. I know that's a lot to ask of you two, but try."

"Aye, aye, sir," both young officers replied in unison.

The future advisors were welcomed by a first lieutenant, a gunnery sergeant, and a sergeant. They were shown their bunks in the barracks, where they dropped off their duffels.

After a brief look around the sparse barracks, Coburn asked Vernon, "Doug, is this place a shit hole or am I still hungover?"

"It's not the Hilton. It's not even the BOQ. I guess we're living like grunts for a while. I don't think we get room service at this hotel."

The next four and a half days consisted of, among other things, eating in the field. They were shown how to use the little can openers that came in the C-rations cartons and how to turn an empty fruit cocktail can into a field stove fueled by little blue heat tablets. Every lunch was a lunch of C-rations, which produced a barter market of nonsmokers trading their little packs of cigarettes for the smokers' peanut butter, which soon became known as asshole putty due to its constipating effects. Breakfast and dinner were served in the marines' mess. Warm, calorie-laden, and tasteless.

They fired, stripped, and cleaned rifles, shotguns, and pistols. They each threw a single grenade under careful supervision of a sergeant who stood inches away, ready to grab the grenade if the thrower froze. The M-79 grenade launcher soon became a favorite due to its simplicity and accuracy. At every live firing and demonstration, the first lieutenant, gunnery sergeant, and sergeant patrolled the firing line with spent .45 cartridges stuck in their ears for sound protection, watching for safety violations and reaching in and adjusting the positions of the navy men. Coburn thought the cartridges sticking out of their ears made them look like Frankenstein's monster.

For most of them, this was a novel experience, certainly nothing like what they had done on the destroyers, cruisers, and amphibious ships they had sailed. A grudging respect grew for the skills with which the grunts wielded their tools of war and their comfort in the sparse and nearly hostile environment they trained in. The marines showed a lot of patience in dealing with the squids. The grunts probably considered it charity. Shitty duty, but charitable all the same.

Sometimes the marines' patience wore thin. The gunnery sergeant started a lecture before a live firing with "There are no dumb questions. You got a question, ask it!" After finishing his spiel, he looked around the classroom and asked if anyone had any questions. One of the sailors, a young engineman, raised his hand and asked the only question.

"Gunny, I heard that if you put your helmet over a grenade and sit on it, it will contain the explosion. That true?"

"Sailor, you just made a liar out of me. I just said there are no stupid questions, and you just asked one. What will happen is that the grenade will go off and shove that helmet up your stupid asshole, turn the helmet to shrapnel and kill all your buddies within fifteen yards of your dumb ass. Any more questions?"

There were none.

Some of the weapons were only demonstrated by the marines and not given to the students to fire. When the gunny showed them the M-60 machine gun, which was all black plastic and steel, he looked slowly around the two dozen, smiled, and simply said, "Mattel. It's swell." But as he demonstrated, the M-60 was a very lethal toy.

They watched recoilless rifle firings, mortars, illumination, and night firings. And on the last afternoon of the first week, they had a lecture and demonstration of field first aid by a navy senior chief hospital corpsman. The good-natured joking and whining stopped after that.

The bus ride back to Coronado that Friday evening was a quiet one. They were all tired, and their ears were ringing from the weapons firing. Their fatigues were dirty and smelled of sweat and cordite. Theodore got up from his seat behind the driver and strolled down the aisle, chatting casually with his crew of students. He stopped by the seat shared by Coburn and Vernon. "How you two doing? What'd you think about that first week of being in the army?"

Vernon answered first. "Sir, I'm glad I'm in the navy. I have decided that shitting in the woods without a sink nearby is not my favorite activity. But I'm glad I'm going to Vietnam with this week's training under my belt, that's for sure."

"That field first aid was a real eye-opener for me, sir," added Coburn. "Especially after the gunny told us about the corpsman pissing on the guts of one of his men before the medevac got to him."

"Yes, I heard that one loud and clear, too. We're all going to be in for a very interesting and different twelve months in-country."

Coburn walked with the other officers to the BOQ, went up to his room, and found a letter from Betsy in the mail slot. He tossed it on his desk, stripped off his fatigues, took a long, hot shower, put on some civvies, and went to the O Club for a beer and a steak with French fries. By 2100 he was deep asleep between clean white sheets, the unopened letter from Betsy still on his desk.

He slept the dreamless sleep of a dead man, waking up in the late morning disoriented, not sure where he was. That would sometimes happen on the DeKalb when they finally reached port after several weeks of sleepless watch keeping and too much caffeine. He stretched and stayed in bed for a while, thinking about what he had to do. Get the dirty laundry taken care of. Maybe hit the beach and collect some rays. He sat up on the bed's edge and looked at the envelope on the desk. He wasn't up for it; he'd read it later.

He ran into Vernon and one of the other classmates at the BOQ laundry room.

"Hey, Clark, I took your advice to the lovelorn and called Jean, that girl I told you about. Made the big invite to come out for the week between SERE and the trip to Travis."

"Yeah, so? What'd she say?"

"What she said was that she'd 'love to,' and as soon as she gets to work on Monday, she's going to look at her schedule and start planning the trip, is what she said. Jean is obviously deeply in love with yours truly. How could she not be, huh?"

"No shit. Are you going to introduce her to me, or are you afraid she'll see me, forget about you, and start sending me her used panties to use for tea?"

"No fear, she won't send you her skivvies. She doesn't wear any."

"My type of woman, Doug. Bravo zulu, young man, bravo zulu."

"You going to bring out your girl? Whatshername, Betty?"

"Betsy. I don't think so. Depends what's going on around here. It would be nice to see Betsy again, but I sort of broke up with her last weekend. I just got a letter from her, which I haven't even opened yet." Coburn's voice was uncharacteristically flat and soft.

"Probably don't want to send Betsy a photo of me in your reply, or she'll fall head over heels for me," said Vernon after pretending to ponder, trying to lighten the atmosphere.

The other officer in the laundry room finished folding his laundry and laughed at the two of them. "When you two Romeos get done looking at yourselves in the mirror, you might want to sign up for the detailer's visit. Lieutenant Commander Theodore told me he found out this morning that the surface JO detailer is making a West Coast and WESTPAC tour and will be here the first few days of our language training. There's a signup sheet in the lobby on the bulletin board." After loading his laundry into the washer, Coburn went down to the lobby and signed up to meet with Lieutenant Commander Sperling, the surface junior officer detailer.

The next day, after spending the night with the nurse from the Mexican Village and calling his parents in the morning, Coburn finally opened Betsy's letter. It was dated six days earlier, before she had received his letter.

Dear Clark:

I haven't heard from you—they must still have you running around doing whatever you are doing. I want to tell you about what's happening here. I had a second and then a third interview with Newsweek, *and much to my delight they offered me a job in the New York editorial office! I sent them my acceptance about a minute after I read the offer letter. That's where I was hoping to land, but I frankly didn't think I was competitive enough to get picked. I'm so excited and happy about this. It's like a dream coming true. I start the Monday after graduation.*

You've written that you can't say much about your schedule, but will you be able to be at my graduation? From what I remember, you finish your training somewhere about that time. It would mean a lot to me if you're there, Clark.

Clark, I do miss you and want to talk to you. Isn't there a telephone number where I can call you? Or can you call me? Call collect if you need to.

Please write or call soon, Clark. Tell me how you are and as much as you can about what you're doing. Remember I love you very much.

With love,
Betsy

Coburn looked at the calendar on his course schedule outline. Betsy's graduation was in the week between finishing SERE and the trip to Travis to board the plane to Vietnam. He put Betsy's letter back into the envelope and decided that he'd write her back next week, or maybe the week after that.

* * *

The next day the two dozen were back on the bus to Pendleton for five days of land operations—an activity foreign to seagoing sailors. Coburn was sitting next to Lender.

"Have a good weekend, Clark?"

"Not bad, sir. Slept a lot, recharged my batteries. Looking forward to another week of Boy Scout camp at Camp Pendleton with the grunts."

"You won't see much of the marines this week. This is all our show. The school's teaching this week."

"Teaching what? I saw the schedule, and it looks like the stuff I did when I was a kid playing war. Or playing with my green toy soldiers in the sand box. I always wanted to be a machine gun man."

Lender chuckled. "Yeah, I liked the guy with the bazooka myself. Hopefully this will be a lot more useful and serious than playing soldier."

The bus pulled into Camp Pendleton and dropped them off at the same barracks they had used the week before. They piled off the bus, dropped their duffels on the same bunks they had left Friday morning, and then mustered in the building that was used as a classroom. Lender and another of the instructors laid out the schedule for the week: land navigation, booby trap and mine detection and defusing, ambushes, and then an overnight exercise. They would be issued obsolete M-1 and M-14 rifles with plugged muzzles and clips of .30-caliber blank ammunition.

Lender added a final word. "Gentlemen, we have tried to make this training as realistic as possible. I know we're all seagoing types, and this is new to probably all of you. It may seem like game playing, but I suggest you all take it seriously."

* * *

They used their sheath knives as probes in a minefield buried on a stretch of dirt-and-gravel road. Crawling on hands and knees, they slowly pushed the blades of their knives into the dirt, finding the mines and marking their locations.

Coburn was in charge of the first team. He found the minesweeping boring, and the hardscrabble of the road hurt his knees. His team—all enlisted men—were doing exactly as they had been instructed, but Coburn grew impatient. He sped up his knife thrusts into the ground in front of him. Lender was standing behind the group, watching.

"Better go slower, Mr. Coburn," said Lender.

Coburn was sweating and irritable and impatient. There was another ten meters of road in front of him. Yeah, sure, slower. As if it makes a shit of difference if sticking this fucking knife straight down or at an angle. As if a fast knife is going to detonate some toy mine in this stupid game. He took a breath and slid his knife into the dirt at a shallow angle. Nothing. He tried again a foot or so to the left. Nothing. Impatiently, he stabbed the ground with his knife a foot further to the left and was startled by the sharp crack of the training detonator. Involuntarily he jumped up and took a step, and another detonator went off.

"Mr. Coburn, you've detonated two mines," said Lender. "If these were not blanks, you would have only detonated one, unless your dead body fell on the other one. Your reward for having identified two mines and killing yourself and most of your team in the process is that you get to start over in the next lane with group three." Blushing, Coburn self-consciously giggled and walked back to the start of the minefield.

* * *

They studied booby traps. How to spot them, how to avoid them, how to set them. Coburn's lack of patience and the feeling that this was all kids' stuff grew worse. He found the exercises tedious. Besides, he was an officer and worked with his brains, not on his hands and knees trying to find trip wires or discover a punji stick pit. Wouldn't the enlisted guys or the Vietnamese be doing this stuff in-country? Weren't they more suited to this? Lesser mentalities handle tedious work better.

* * *

One morning Lender was changing into a clean set of jungle fatigues while Coburn lay in his bunk. Lender had a large, purple scar on his right thigh.

"You get that over there?" asked Coburn, looking at the scar.

"Yes. Ambush."

"Looks pretty bad. You okay?"

Lender smiled. "It looks a lot worse than it is. I'm fine. Doc told me that if you have to get shot, the fat part of your chubby legs is not a bad place. Lots of meat, not much in the way of nerves or bone. A big, fat ass is not a bad place either. But it's certainly better to not get shot."

"Hurt much?"

"Not sure what 'much' means. Bullet passed clean through. It hurt, but I'm still here, so I'm not complaining."

"That send you home?"

"Nah. Cleaned me up, bandaged me up, gave me some shots for infection, and then put me on light duty helping the boss. I was back with my counterpart in two weeks. I think if I was near the end of my tour they might have just said, 'send the asshole home'."

"Well, you got a Purple Heart out of it."

"Listen, Clark, a Purple Heart is a medal no one wants to get. Unless you're nuts. It really doesn't mean much in the overall scheme of things. But if you do get it and show it when you board the Coronado Ferry, they'll let you ride the ferry for free—after you pay full fare."

Coburn laughed and stood up. It had rained last night, and the air was a little cooler. Today they were going to break into two teams for land navigation combined with ambushes. The teams would be pitted against each other—one trying to get from point A to point B and the other trying to ambush them on the way. Then the roles would be reversed.

They worked throughout the morning setting and trying to detect ambushes. One of the problems was that the scrub vegetation of Camp Pendleton offered few hiding places for a team of a dozen men. Bushes, trees, and ditches were in high demand at each ambush site.

The last exercise of the day found Coburn's team as the ambushers. They had gone out ahead of the other team and picked a spot for the ambush. Lender stood watching, saying nothing but nodding his head in approval at the ambush site selection and how the booby trap trip lines were being set. When all was in order, the team leader, Theodore, gave final instructions and told his team to get into hiding places down the road from the trip wires.

Most of the team and Lender got behind whatever they could find, lying on their bellies in the brown mud from last night's rain. Coburn looked around and to his delight and satisfaction found a large, green bush beneath a tree. The ground was fairly dry. The bush was lush. He could hide in there, out of the mud, and never be seen. A little surprised that no one else had found this plum ambush spot, he crouched down into the bush and found that he had an unobstructed view of the killing zone. Coburn waited and relaxed, enjoying himself.

About ten minutes later, Coburn could see Vernon. He was acting as point, leading the other team. Vernon stopped and gave a hand signal to point out the trip wire he had spotted. Each member of the team silently signaled the trip wire to the man behind him. Vernon then stopped again, about five meters from Coburn's bush, and pointed out another trip wire, the last before the killing zone.

The plan was to open fire when a booby trap went off or, if no booby trap tripped, when the man acting as point was at or past the second booby trap. A rifle cracked a few meters to Coburn's left, and then all the ambushers opened up. Coburn stood up, firing his M-1 and shouting, "We got you, we got you!"

The instructor who had been working with the ambushed team looked at Coburn and started to laugh. "Yeah, you got us. But you got poison oak."

Coburn had been hiding in a luxuriant growth of the toxic and rash-producing plant.

The two teams combined back into one and ate their C-rations as the staff instructors led discussions on what went right, what went wrong, and lessons learned. Then they explained the next and final exercise.

The instructors were soon joined by several more driving up from Coronado. Students and instructors were to be adversaries. The assignment was to plan defenses and attacks that were to occur at dawn. Lender would stay with the students as a silent observer.

Once the staff was out of earshot, Theodore met with the senior enlisted student and laid out a plan. Theodore would send out Vernon and two of the enlisted students to identify the staff location. After they returned, an attack plan would be developed.

Coburn tried not to show his disappointment in not being picked to lead the reconnaissance. Just as well, he consoled himself. Better to rest. He lay on the ground and shut his eyes, trying to get some sleep. His arms and the back of his neck started itching.

Around 2200 Vernon and his group returned. Coburn got up and walked over to the huddle by the fire, where Theodore was drawing in the dirt with a stick. Vernon and the two enlisted men were filthy and scratched. Noticing Coburn at the edge of the firelight, Vernon flashed a broad smile and a thumbs-up. Coburn smiled back and nodded his head.

Theodore mustered the students and laid out the plan as Lender stood silently by. The staff was camped at the base of a hill and had set up defenses on the downward slope. They were obviously not expecting an attack from the uphill side since it would take the attackers several hours in the dark moving through rough terrain to get into position. A virtual impossibility.

Theodore directed the students into two groups. Half would cross the rough terrain and climb into position above the staff's camp and wait until 0500. They left immediately to get into position.

At 0500, the other half would make a frontal assault on the staff camp, directly into their defenses. As the staff moved to meet the frontal assault, the students on the hillside above them would attack from their rear.

Coburn was put in the frontal assault group and made point. Theodore put his hand on Coburn's shoulder. "You get to lead the suicide squad. I'm sure they've set up trip wires on the path. So as soon as one goes off, assume you're still alive and start shooting and yelling like crazy. You lead the charge."

At 0400, Coburn led the "suicide squad" to the staff's camp location. After half an hour, they could see the campfire about a hundred meters away. They hunkered down. Coburn kept on checking the luminous dial of his olive-drab watch. At a minute before 0500, he stood up and felt a tap on his shoulder. It was the officer in charge of frontal assault group. "Okay, Clark, let's go do it."

Coburn started walking toward the campfire, then broke into a jog. He could hear the others crashing through the bush behind him. His shin hit a trip wire, and a pop was followed by a small illumination flare.

This is it!

Coburn started running, shooting his M-1 and yelling at the top of his lungs. More trip wires went off with rifle like cracks, all drowned out by the shooting and yelling of the suicide squad.

He ran into the staff's camp. Several illumination flares were floating beneath their little parachutes above the camp. Lender was standing beside Theodore and the master chief—all filthy and scratched but with wide smiles on their dirty faces. After a few seconds, all the yelling and shooting stopped as the rest of the squad followed Coburn into the camp.

Everyone, staff and students, gathered in a circle around Lender, Theodore, and the master chief. Coburn, for no explicable reason, felt elated, happy. He felt like giggling and couldn't keep a smile off his face. Excited, full of life, awake, aware.

Vernon walked up and Coburn wrapped a filthy arm around his friend's shoulder and gave him a hug.

An instructor popped another illumination flare. Lender looked around the circle of navy men. "Gentlemen, the students have never successfully ambushed the staff before. You're the first class to do so. Attacking from the rear with the diversion from the front was great." The sky was lightening to dawn. "Let's pack up and get aboard that bus and go to Coronado. This is the end of your counterinsurgency course. You're off to language training and SERE. Well done to you all."

* * *

The two dozen students and four instructors who walked off the bus two hours later were filthy. A crate of oranges and tomatoes was waiting for them in the parking lot. They started eating the tomatoes and peeling the oranges with their dirty hands. Then they walked back to their quarters for showers, shaves, and sleep.

Vernon caught up with Coburn and walked beside him, munching a tomato. "We're back in the classroom on Monday. By my calculations, we're halfway through this training if you don't count SERE."

"Yep, eight weeks and we get aboard the big bird to Vietnam. Man, I'm tired, and I stink. I hope the base pork chop ordered enough hot water to clean my body."

"What you doing this weekend, Clark? Gonna see Florence Nightingale?"

"Yeah, probably. I've gotta reply to a letter from Betsy, too. What you doin'?"

"Shit, shower, shave, and sleep in that order. Maybe go to Disneyland, never been there. Want to go with me?"

"Never been there either. I might."

The two junior officers went to their rooms.

The itching woke up Coburn early the next morning. By 0800 he was at sick bay being examined by the duty corpsman.

"Yes, sir, you have a case of poison oak. Been walking around Pendleton recently?" Coburn glumly confirmed the obvious. The corpsman started painting Coburn with cotton balls soaked in a milky liquid. The itching eased as the liquid dried to a white crust.

"There's not much to do other than give you some calamine lotion to ease the itching and some Benadryl if it gets real bad. Use cold, wet compresses, too. It'll get worse for a couple of days, and then it'll get better. It looks like it's just your arms, face, and the back of your neck. Good thing you didn't try to take a leak in that stuff." Coburn tried to smile. "And sir, try not to scratch or pick the scabs. You risk infection then. If you itch, use the calamine lotion. If it doesn't get better in two weeks, come back in, and we'll have the doctor look at you or send you to Balboa Hospital."

Coburn took the bag that contained two big bottles of calamine lotion, a small vial of pills, and a box of cotton, thanked the corpsman, and walked over to the O club for breakfast. He walked up to a table occupied by four of his classmates, one of which was Vernon. Vernon started the comments.

"Man, I'm not going to Disneyland with you. You'd scare all the little kiddies." The rest soon joined in.

"Clark, what's wrong with your face? You got zits?"

"Nah, some LBFM in Olangapo probably sat on his face trying to snatch up some pesos balanced on his nose," said one officer whose last duty station was a ship that had stopped in the Philippines after weeks in the Tonkin Gulf.

"LBFM?" asked another of his classmates.

"Yeah, one of those Filipina little brown fucking machine," answered another.

"Maybe you ought to sit somewhere else. Those cooties might be contagious."

"Geez Clark, bad enough you died three times in Pendleton, but now you caught leprosy."

Coburn wearily waved off the zingers and asked, "Three times? What do you mean I got killed three times?"

"Two land mines, and then weren't you the guy leading the charge that tripped all those booby traps? Hell, you probably died about a dozen times. Amazing you're still here."

Coburn smiled and slumped down into a vacant chair. Keeping the smile on his face, he picked up the menu. The kidding slowly fizzled out as the conversation turned to families, girlfriends, and the remaining seven weeks of training.

They had heard all the scuttlebutt about the language course and SERE training. The former was eight hours a day in the classroom and then evening language labs five days a week for six weeks. It was as much an introduction to Vietnamese culture as it was language training. From day one nobody spoke English in the class.

SERE had become mythology since those who went through it were not supposed to talk about it. But they all knew the basics: beach survival, land survival, evasion, escape, and then the last day in a brutal POW compound. Coburn was anxious about SERE. All the classroom time and running around Pendleton playing toy soldier was fine, and his innate intelligence would pull him through, as it always did. But what good was charm when some interrogator is knocking you around the room, locking you into claustrophobic steel boxes, or screaming in your face trying to get you to sign confessions and become a traitor? Coburn's anxiety was palatable every time he thought about SERE. He'd hyperventilate and feel his heart pound. Then he would calm himself down by telling himself he'd find some way around it. As he always did.

* * *

He sat down at the desk in the BOQ room and reread Betsy's letter. It was postmarked two weeks ago.

How to handle Betsy? Wait another week to reply? He went into the bathroom and put on some more calamine lotion. His handsome features were now covered with white patches of dried lotion. The hairs on his forearms were stiff with the dried crust. And he was itching. Maybe take one of the pills? No one else gets this crud. Why him?

Back at the desk, Coburn thought for a few minutes, then pulled out some paper and an envelope.

Hi Bets,

I just read your letter. We were out in the field for two weeks. I was just released from sick bay this morning but should be okay. The training has us on the go. No breaks until we're done. Preparing for combat in a dirty war is important to survival.

By now you've read my last letter. I know it's a jumbled mess of words—I had a terrible time writing it. With this separation and my career going one way and yours starting, I just don't know how it will work for us. It's really not fair for you. I wish it were otherwise, but I don't see how. I feel bad and sorry about it all.

That's wonderful news about Newsweek. *They certainly picked the right girl for the job, whatever the job is. I'm glad you're excited about it. I was just thinking how different it would be to work in an office in Manhattan with no one shooting at you, blissfully unaware of the fighting that's going on. I doubt if I'll ever find out.*

My schedule is still up in the air, especially the time between course completion and when I have to get on the plane to Saigon. I'm out here until I get on the plane. I really would have liked to see you graduate. But in light of the situation, it's better that I'm not there.

I wish I could write more, but I've got to run. And I'm stumbling over my thoughts and words.

Clark

He reread the letter and nodded with satisfaction. An odd, unexplained feeling of relief and—for want of a better word— freedom came over Coburn. He felt good.

He dropped it in the mailbox in the lobby as he and Vernon left for Disneyland.

CHAPTER 9
KINH MON

Ninh, Vo, and Ky, along with the first and third platoon leaders, found the road to leadership strewn with boulders and ditches and an occasional poisonous snake. The first day was a shambles, with the NCOs interrupting with shouts and swearing. After the first week, the seven men were sleep deprived and exceptionally hard on themselves at the self-criticism sessions. Surprisingly, though, the criticism from the other trainees was muted. Vo took this as an encouraging sign.

Each day got incrementally better—fewer mistakes, less interrupting by the NCOs—at least where second platoon was concerned. Still the burden of responsibility was a heavy one.

Ninh had the hardest job. An echelon away from the rank and file, he had the most responsibility and the most authority but had to observe the chain of command and work through his subordinates. After one particularly miserable day of nothing but problems, including the entire company missing a meal and a lecture from the political officer because the trucks to take them back from a training exercise were sent to the wrong pickup point, Ninh shook his head and confided to Vo, ignoring the presence of an NCO.

"Being privileged is no privilege. Old One-Arm threatened to make me sleep in the latrine pit."

"What went wrong with the trucks, Ninh?"

"I checked to make sure I had the right time and place for the pickup. I did. But the clerk in the transportation pool got it wrong. I was too busy to double check. Shit, my fault."

The NCO stood near them, obviously listening. That didn't stop the men from talking.

"Ninh, you need some help. You're the company commander, but you're doing it all by yourself. I'm the platoon leader, but I work with Ky. We're always covering for each other. Why don't you set up a staff of one or two?"

"I've been thinking of that. In fact, your platoon and first platoon each have one more soldier than third platoon. I can take one from you and the first."

"Sure, two extra pairs of hands should certainly help. I've got a good fellow who's smart and hard working. Not the best physical specimen, but I don't think you need that attribute. Do you want me to assign him to your new staff?"

Ninh smiled and then chuckled. "Vo, you're not going to send me second platoon's biggest fuckup, are you?"

"I hadn't thought of that, but it's not a bad idea."

The NCO moved away as the men prepared for lights out and sleep. The next morning two men were assigned to be Ninh's staff. The man Vo sent was a short, skinny seventeen-year-old, but he was smart and eager, one of Vo and Ky's best. The fellow from first platoon was their worst. The first platoon leader and assistant leader were glad to be rid of him. Lazy and dumb.

* * *

The seven potential officer candidates were university-educated men. Every summer they had undergone two weeks of rudimentary military training. As such, they were a step ahead of the other recruits.

The company of 108 men started to coalesce as the training progressed. They went through extensive small arms familiarization, firing their new AK-47 assault rifles and various rocket and grenade launchers, and training with Russian and Chinese grenades. The NCO at the firing range insisted that they do hours upon hours of dry firing. Aiming the unloaded assault rifles, pulling the trigger, and yelling "bang, bang." When they did live firing, the NCO reminded them that bullets that missed their targets were wasted.

"We're not Americans who can afford to shoot thousands of bullets to kill one person. And never, ever, leave a weapon on the field."

The bayonet and hand-to-hand combat training sobered them all to the reality that they may have to look the enemy in the eyes and smell his breath.

Field sanitation inspired some ribald comments, usually focused at the slobs in the squads. First aid was combined with squad and platoon tactics. Sappers fired live explosives, mines, and booby traps, and then the men practiced with inert but realistic-looking devices. Larger weapons, radio communications, and vehicles were demonstrated. Those selected to operate crew-served weapons, radios, and vehicles would be trained when they reached their battalions. It was all very serious. The men knew they were not playing games.

They marched longer and longer distances, carrying increasing numbers of bricks in their rucksacks. Increased appetites accompanied their improved physical fitness. Despite the seven bowls of rice supplemented with their own vegetables and occasional pieces of meat and fish, the company was always hungry. The fat became lean and hard. The lean became skinny and hard.

The men in second platoon responded well to the training. Morale was high, although complaining continued about the lack of women, liquor, entertainment, and mother's cooking, as well as the shortages of sleep and food. Complaining was the soldier's inherent right.

Nearly all of the second platoon, except for Vo and Ky and a few others, were from the rural areas. Vo realized that the conditions these men had in the army, as harsh as they may be, were better than what their villages and hamlets had to offer. They had regular and ample meals, medical care, less boredom and, most importantly, camaraderie.

He could also see that the Vietnamese culture's values of fatalism and group loyalty were at work. These soldiers-to-be took it as their destiny to be here, and their three-man cells had become their immediate families within the larger families of their squads, platoons, and even the company. Vo felt the same way. He was destined to be here and have these men in his care.

* * *

There were still problems with the platoon. Most were minor, such as the two in the first squad who always seemed to be late despite the best efforts of their squad and cell mates to help them. Or the man who, no matter how hard he tried, could not keep food or dirt off his uniform. Another couldn't keep in step. But these were all good men, loyal to their comrades, willing to do whatever was called of them. A petty theft turned out to be just a misplaced belt. A few things were lost or broken.

But two problems were not minor.

One man suffered a malarial relapse. When cogent, he fought going to sick call for fear he'd be put into the hospital and separated from the platoon, maybe even held back. His condition grew worse, and he was carried to the medical station in the middle of the night. A week later the man died. His comrades wept.

That evening the senior instructor called Ninh, Vo, and Ky into his hut.

"A man in your company," he said to Ninh, "and in your platoon," to Vo and Ky, "has died. He is dead, and the enemy did not have to shoot one bullet. Why did you let that man die? He was your responsibility. He is now dead, so you killed him. You have killed a loyal soldier, a comrade. Why?"

Ninh spoke first. "Senior Instructor, it is my fault. He should have been taken to the medical station earlier. That may have saved his life. I take full responsibility."

"Senior Instructor," said Vo, "Comrade Ninh could not have known that the man was sick. The squad leader and the man's cell tried several times to take him to the medical center, but he refused and made them promise not to tell me or Comrade Ky. He was afraid he would be separated from the platoon if he went to the hospital. I am responsible. He was a valued member of my platoon. When I did find out he was sick and heard of his fears of going to the hospital, I made the decision that he could rest in the barracks until the malaria went back into remission. That is my mistake and my responsibility, Senior Instructor."

"And you, Ky?" The senior instructor pointed his carved cane at the assistant platoon leader.

"Senior Instructor, I was the one who suggested to Comrade Vo that we let him rest in the barracks. It was my idea. This is my fault."

"Did you know the man had had malaria?"

"No," said Vo.

"Were you instructed in the treatment of malaria in field first aid?"

"Yes, Senior Instructor."

"What did you learn from field first aid?"

"To let the patient rest, especially if a relapse. Wet cloths if hot, blankets if chilled. Let the relapse pass. If necessary, make the man comfortable and leave him. If possible, take him with you."

"You are at a training base with a staffed medical center. Are you in the field? Do you consider this base the field, Vo?"

"No, Senior Instructor."

"Carry on. Dismissed."

The three men walked out of the sterile hut. They were shaken and felt terrible. The senior instructor had not shouted at them or berated them. He had just sat listening and asking questions. They did not know how much longer they would be leading the company or the second platoon. Becoming an officer looked doubtful.

"Vo, Ky, I don't know what he's going to do. But until it's done, we carry on as he ordered. There's not much more we can do than follow his orders as best we can. Agreed?"

Vo and Ky nodded in agreement. Vo thought that if it was his destiny to not be an officer, then that was his destiny. But "carry on" meant to continue doing what they were doing. Perhaps he was destined to be an officer. Perhaps he was not. In the meantime, he would do the best he could.

The other major problem was not as serious as a man's death, but a serious problem just the same.

A tough, streetwise eighteen-year-old from Hanoi was the problem. He boasted about leaving school as soon as he could and supporting a lifestyle that the others could not even imagine by stealing, fencing, smuggling, and pimping. The only reason he was in uniform, he claimed, was because he had bribed the wrong person. He had connections and would not be in the army for long. If they didn't get him out of this low-life organization, he'd just leave, hide in Hanoi for a while, and then go back to "business."

He shirked his duties, despite his two cellmates trying to get him to do his share. His performance was marginal at best, bringing down both his cell and squad. The squad leader would get a verbal commitment to do better and then watch him continue to slack off. One night his cellmates caught him trying to sneak out of the camp, obviously deserting, although he claimed to be sleepwalking. Another night he was found asleep on watch by the roving sentry, whom he first tried to bribe to keep his mouth shut and then threatened to beat if he told. The sentry did his duty and reported the incident to the squad leader. Vo decided that enough was enough.

"Ky, let's take care of this asshole."

"Should we go to Ninh?"

"Not yet. If we were in the field in combat and we had a character like this in our platoon, we'd have to handle it by ourselves, on the spot. We're preparing for that, so let's act that way. We'll tell Ninh after."

"I agree, Vo. We'll probably get ourselves in trouble with Old One-Arm again and maybe even get kicked out of the candidate program, but what the hell, we're probably kicked out already."

The two men talked for a while and then told the man's squad leader that they wanted to see the miscreant by the latrines just before lights out. The next morning they told Ninh what they had done in the latrine shack.

While the company ate their morning meal, the three walked over to the senior instructor's door and knocked.

"Enter!" The trio walked in and stood in front of the table at attention.

"You three again. Why are you here spoiling my morning?"

Ninh spoke first. "Senior Instructor, last night one of the second platoon's members was sent to the medical center and is now in the hospital."

"Yes, I received a report of that earlier this morning." He tapped a piece of paper in front of him. "What happened?"

Vo spoke up. "He suffered several fractures and bruises. Also possible infections from ingesting sewage from the latrine pit."

"Are you saying a fall into a one-meter-deep latrine pit broke his bones?" An incredulous expression was on the senior instructor's usually expressionless face.

"No, Senior Instructor." It was Vo again. "I beat him."

"And I pushed him into the pit, Senior Instructor. After he tried to hit Comrade Vo with a shovel," said Ky.

The one-armed man was speechless. He looked at the three of them for a silent minute. This hospitalized character was someone he, the political officer, and the NCOs had had their eyes on since the very first day. A troublemaker, a tough bully, a criminal. Desertion was expected, or a fight with his squad mates that would put them all in the stockade. But this?

"You three, stand easy. Tell me what happened." He pulled out a ballpoint pen and a sheet of paper. "Everything."

107

Ninh looked at Vo, who relayed the history of the man's poor performance and detrimental impact on the squad and, in particular, his cell that had to cover for him. He described the attempted desertion, sleeping on watch, the attempted bribe, and the threats.

"Comrade Ky and I met with him at lights out yesterday behind the barracks. We told him that his behavior was dangerous and that it undermined the morale and cohesiveness of the entire platoon, and unless he changed his ways immediately, we would charge him with violation of the code and request disciplinary action. He said for us to do just that because he had influential friends who were working to get him out of the army, and he'd never spend a day in the stockade.

"I replied that I didn't care who his friends were and what they may be doing and that we were going to take him to see Comrade Ninh and then you to charge him. Comrade Ky grabbed his arm to escort him, and he grabbed the latrine shovel and lifted it to hit Comrade Ky. I kicked him in the groin and then hit him with my fists until he fell down. He lay there conscious but not moving at first, and then got to his feet, using the shovel as a cane. When I reached for his arm, he lifted the shovel to hit me, and Comrade Ky pushed him into the latrine pit. He stopped resisting."

The senior instructor's face had hardened into its normal mask. "So you broke his bones?"

"According to the medical center, Senior Instructor, I fractured his jaw, nose, and cheekbones."

Ky broke in. "It could also have been a result of the fall into the pit, Senior Instructor."

"Ky, you are still the idiot. I'd have you squat with my foot-locker on your shoulders again, but that's too good for you. Go on, Vo."

"Yes, Senior Instructor. Comrade Ky and I dragged him from the pit, rolled him to the water buckets, and washed him down as best we could. The duty NCO drove by in the sentry truck, asked what we were doing, helped us load him into the back of the truck, and drove us to the medical center. The injured man told the medic that we and two others had attacked him for no reason and told him to have us arrested. The duty NCO drove us back to the barracks. This morning he told us the man was in the hospital."

"Ninh, I want a report of this in writing to me by the evening meal. Leave nothing out."

"Yes, Senior Instructor."

"Do any of you have anything else to tell me?"

"I do, Senior Instructor." Vo's voice even surprised himself. But he knew this one-armed veteran wanted no charades or pretenses. Old One-Arm had to make decisions about him and his two comrades and needed to know what they would do when bullets were being shot and men were bleeding and dying.

"If I had someone acting like that while I was in enemy territory and under fire, his actions would be as dangerous to me and my men and our mission as the Americans or their Southern puppet. If I had spare people and somewhere to take him to, I would send that person there under arrest. But I doubt very much if I would have spare people or a regimental headquarters nearby. So I would kill him."

Ninh added, "Comrade Vo speaks for both Comrade Ky and myself, Senior Instructor. We have discussed this at length. We agree with one another."

The senior instructor stared coldly at the three men. "So you would do the enemy's job and kill your own man? Save them a bullet and waste a man of your own?"

Ninh answered for all of them. "Yes, Senior Instructor."

"Do you realize that this answer of yours may have consequences for you three, severe consequences?"

Again Ninh. "Yes, Senior Instructor."

"Do you have anything else to say?"

"Yes, Senior Instructor." It was Ky this time. "We were ordered to lead the company and the platoons. We were ordered to act as if we are in combat. In combat we would have shot him rather than have his behavior kill our comrades and divert our mission."

"Ky, so what would you recommend we do with this individual?"

"Do not discharge him. That is what he wants, Senior Instructor. That would only put a criminal on the streets of Hanoi. He should be put in the stockade and kept there. I respectfully recommend charging him with violation of the Code of Discipline, assaulting persons in senior positions, sleeping on guard duty, dereliction of duty and...uh...whatever the regulation is for being an asshole."

The corner of Old One-Arm's mouth twitched. Despite himself he burst out laughing. Vo, Ninh, and Ky had never seen him smile, much less laugh. They hadn't thought it possible. The three men remained stone faced.

Finally composed and his mask put back in place, the senior instructor told the men to carry on and reminded Ninh that the report of the incident was due before the evening meal. They left the room not believing what they had seen. The old fart was human. Sort of. Maybe.

Vo and Ninh spent the rest of the day writing the report while Ky covered their duties.

* * *

Infiltration was the last phase of training. Ninh led the company in field exercises and demonstrations. The fieldwork involved a lot of camouflage and concealment, land navigation, signals and communications, coordinated movements, and ambush. Self-criticism and critique sessions became more philosophical, centered on group dynamics rather than any particular individual's shortcomings.

The ever-present instructor NCOs and the senior instructor appeared to have softened a bit—less shouting and less correcting, and criticism when given was often in private and constructive.

One day in the middle of the last week the senior instructor was absent from the field training. He was in conference with the political officer.

On the table were seven files, each labeled with the name of one of the seven officer candidates leading the company and the platoons. The two combat veterans had gone over each file in detail, discussing their opinions and recommendations. Their work was complete. Now they sat relaxing for a couple of minutes, sipping tea, smoking cigarettes.

As career military men, they were more comfortable using rank instead of names or position when talking between just themselves. The political officer exhaled and watched the smoke tendrils climb up to the thatched roof.

"Sergeant Major, like you, I've been skeptical about selecting officers before they start training. The military academy is one thing. You get enough time to really wring out the best, although some of the worst still do make it. But this?" The officer took a sip of his tea. "This experiment has surprised me. I feel the five who have made it will make good leaders. The two who didn't can get another chance if their actions as soldiers show them to be officer material."

The senior instructor stubbed out his cigarette. "Major, I tried to create stress—mental, physical, and emotional. I made sure they were sleep deprived and often hungry. These weeks in a training base are certainly not combat, but I feel we have a good indication of how these men would perform in combat. And more important, how they're committed to their mission and orders, whatever those may be." The senior instructor tapped the lip of his teacup with his carved cane. "But I still don't like it. I hope we have not accomplished something that will set a precedent for the higher-ups."

"Who knows, Sergeant Major? We've done our job, and I think we've done it well. Senior Colonel Ong's insistence on placing the three economists or logisticians or whatever those men are called in this experiment really had me wondering. But when the commander of the Transportation Group says 'do it', I do it. They did well."

"Yes sir, they did. I really tried to make them fail. I loaded that platoon with the weakest trainees, and that platoon had its problems, but in the end they did the best. They lost only two men—the death and that hooligan in the stockade—no defections."

"Let's go over our recommendations one more time and then call it a night. They leave in two days."

They went through each file and summarized their thoughts. The first platoon leader and assistant leader were not recommended for commissions and instead would be regular infantrymen. That platoon had two defections and was plagued with malingerers. Its performance and morale, while satisfactory, was lower than the other two platoons. The senior instructor in particular did not like that at every chance the first platoon had tried to send its worst performers or toughest assignments to another platoon or the company staff.

The two leaders of the third platoon, in contrast, were recommended for commissions. The platoon had performed well and had only one defector. The leader and assistant leader were always willing to work with the other platoon leaders and company commander, sharing the load for the good of the entire company. Morale was solid. Leadership was sound, if not especially creative. And they were adaptive.

Vo and Ky were recommended without reservation or much discussion. They had been given the worst material to work with, yet their platoon performed the best. Both were creative, adaptive, and charismatic leaders, putting the welfare of their platoon ahead of their own. The political officer and the senior instructor remarked that Vo was a tough person to read, showing little emotion but obviously a deep thinker and smart. The political officer especially liked their handling of—as he called him— "the Hanoi Gangster." The death of the soldier from malaria was tragic, but both the political officer and the senior instructor said that they would have probably acted the same. But the death would catch the eye of the commander of the Transportation Group when he read their recommendations.

Ninh was also recommended without much discussion. His performance from the very beginning was solid. The weak leadership of the first platoon forced him to spend an inordinate amount of energy and time to bring it up to a satisfactory level of performance and morale, but he did it and did it well.

Ninh, Vo, and Ky were the three whom Senior Colonel Ong insisted go through the rigors of the program and be evaluated for commissioning as officers. While Ninh, Vo, and Ky knew that they had similar academic backgrounds, none of them knew that the other two had also been picked by Senior Colonel Ong.

They would meet the commander of the Transportation Group again in two days.

* * *

On the drill field in front of their huts, the company was called to attention. Without preamble, the senior instructor informed them that their training was over and they were to return to their huts, pack their rucksacks, and return to the drill field in fifteen minutes ready to march south. Candidates Ninh, Vo, and Ky were to report to the camp commander's office immediately after packing their rucksacks.

As they packed, many of the men hugged one another and shook hands, and a few cried. Ninh made it a point to shake hands with every man in the company. Vo and Ky stood in the middle of a crowd of their platoon, shaking hands, hugging. One of the squad leaders shook hands with Vo.

"Comrade Vo, I feel proud. So proud. I couldn't even sing the national anthem. It gagged in my throat. I was crying. The pride of this day will follow me to the end of my life."

Vo looked around at the barracks huts, the latrine, and the line of water buckets. "The only way they'll get me back here is if I lose an arm and they give me a carved cane." he said to Ky.

* * *

Seated around a table in the base commander's conference room were Senior Colonel Nguyen Sy Ong, the political officer, and Senior Instructor Pham. They had been discussing the three candidates for Ong's program. Ong was pleased but not surprised that they had done well. A lot of research and vetting had gone into their selection.

But he was concerned about the handling of the malaria death. Like the other two combat veterans, he admitted that he probably would have done the same as these three had. But the three young men had made that decision without ever having been in enemy territory away from medical care and short of people to carry a stretcher.

The clerk knocked on the door, stuck his head in, and announced that the three candidates had just arrived. Ong told the clerk to keep them in the outer office until he came for them.

Ong looked at the two men. "Major, Sergeant Major, your efforts in preparing these men for what lies ahead of them is noted and much appreciated. I will let your superiors know. Now I'll give you a few minutes to meet with those three youngsters in the outer office, and then I'll bring them in here to talk to me. Goodbye and thank you."

Ninh, Vo, and Ky jumped out of their chairs, came to attention, and saluted the political officer and the senior instructor as they walked into the outer office. The political officer smiled and told them to stand at ease. He shook hands with each man and congratulated him for doing well. Old One-Arm just stood by, saying nothing. The officer said good-bye, wished them luck, and left.

With a gesture of his carved cane, Senior Instructor Pham looked at the three with a scowl and said, "I've stuck my ass out for you three. Don't make a fool out of me. Stay here until you're called." He left.

When Senior Colonel Ong opened the door to the conference room, the three young men simultaneously jumped up from their seats and stood at attention. Ninh saluted.

"Soldiers Ninh, Vo, and Ky reporting as ordered, Senior Colonel."

They were waved into the room and told to take seats at the table.

The senior officer lit a cigarette. He did not offer the pack to the three young candidates. Puffing on the cigarette and looking at the ceiling rafters as he exhaled, he walked around the table, then sat down opposite them, stubbing out the cigarette in an ashtray filled with butts.

"Now it starts for you three."

He looked at the candidates. Ninh—handsome, self confident, capable. Ky—quick, witty, likeable. Vo—physically imposing, intense, unfathomable. All were well educated, loyal, charismatic, and intelligent. The flower of Vietnamese youth. The leaders of the future Vietnam. If they lived long enough.

"You have done well these previous three months. Very well. Seven possible officer candidates were in your training company. Two will not be officers. Two will go on to officer training and serve as infantry officers. You will join these two tomorrow morning to start officer training, but it is your destiny to serve in a more important and far more difficult assignment for the people of Vietnam. You will be waging a war with no glory and many dangers. You will be waging a war that may take fifteen or twenty years to win before victory is ours. But victory will be ours. Victory is our fate, have no doubt."

Ong leaned back and smiled. He visibly relaxed, bent forward, and put his elbows on the table.

"I spoke to each of you a few months ago. You volunteered for a role that took you out of academia and civil service. Were any of you aware that your two comrades here were also volunteers for my project?"

Ninh spoke first. "I was not, Senior Colonel. When I was given my enlistment orders, your staff told me to not talk about my recruitment or your conversation with me. If asked, I was to say I was a volunteer recruit. Which is what I did. I did find it interesting that Comrades Vo and Ky had similar academic backgrounds and interests as I but thought it just coincidence."

"Same for me, Senior Colonel," said Ky. "Coincidence, but a happy coincidence as far as I was concerned."

Vo nodded in agreement.

"Well, now you know. And my plans are for you to work together in the future." The three candidates looked at one another and could not keep the smiles off their faces, even Vo.

"Tomorrow you will start officer training. Transportation will be waiting for you after we finish here. Get a good night's sleep. Your training will be part of the normal officer candidate syllabus, but the last weeks will be spent at my headquarters in Hanoi. After training, you will be given three days of leave to visit family and friends before you start your assignment. Now I have some questions for you. Perhaps I can learn some lessons to better train those who will follow you."

He asked about the training methods used, the fieldwork, and the transition from the senior instructor and his staff running the company to the candidates taking on leadership. The questioning turned into more of a roundtable discussion, with Ong making brief notes in a file before him.

He noted that the three were members of the Lao Dong, or Communist Party, and had joined the Labor Youth Groups and Youth Brigades when younger. He asked them how that had influenced them in training.

"Frankly, Senior Colonel, I didn't think of my affiliations at all during the training," said Ky.

Vo added, "Yes, sir, it was just natural, second nature. I didn't put much conscious effort, if any, into my affiliations. They are what I am."

"In my opinion, sir, that's the way it should be. A natural part of you," added Ninh.

"You are correct, that is the way it should be," replied the senior officer.

"One last question, and then we can finish. The death of the man in the second platoon. I have been thoroughly briefed on what happened, your actions in particular. I have read both the reports from you and the hospital. My question: what would have prevented another man from dying like that?" He was staring at Vo.

Without hesitating Vo looked directly into the older man's eyes and answered. "Sir, if a man is known to have suffered malaria or have a medical problem, he should be evaluated as to how his medical condition, even if dormant, may affect the mission of his unit in combat and enemy territory. If a man falls ill and cannot function, his unit has lost a man and not to enemy fire. If the man needs to be carried to an aid station—if there is an aid station—the unit loses two more men as stretcher bearers. If he needs medical attention immediately—if there is a medic in the unit—the unit then loses a fourth person, the medic. I respectfully suggest that if the probability of the man being incapacitated is significant, then that man should not be assigned to an operational unit but rather assigned to a position where if he does fall ill the combat efficiency of his unit will not be degraded. Make him a clerk in a headquarters or a staff driver or an anti-aircraft missile or gun crew member around Hanoi." Vo spoke forcefully but quietly, and Ong studied his face and body language for any sign of emotion, of which there were none.

Vo continued. "If the decision is made to assign the man to a combat unit, or any unit for that matter, his superiors should be made aware of not only the man's condition but the treatment for it. And either provide the man's superiors with the means to treat the incapacitation or be resigned to his possible unfortunate death."

Ninh was about to say something when Ong cut him off with a small wave of his hand. "Thank you for your thoughts, Comrade Vo. I am done here. I will see you in a few weeks in Hanoi. Your truck will be here in a few minutes. Do you have any comments or questions?"

Ky looked quickly at Vo and Ninh, then at Ong. "Well...uh... sir, yes I do, if I may and it's not too impertinent of me. How did Senior Instructor Pham lose his left arm?"

"Did you ask him, Comrade Ky?"

"No, sir. I was afraid to do that. It just didn't seem right."

Ong chuckled. "There are many of us who are afraid of Sergeant Major Pham. He's a forceful personality, isn't he?" He lit another cigarette.

"Sergeant Major Pham was working with a forward artillery observer team in Con Thien, fighting the American marines and a company of Southerners. An incoming explosion shredded his left arm and wounded him with shrapnel in many places. It killed all of the squad with him but one. He dragged that survivor over a kilometer to the safety of his company. Then he had to be physically restrained from going back to retrieve the bodies of the others. At the medical aid station, his arm was amputated and most of the shrapnel removed. We got him back to the group hospital and treated him for infection. Two months later he was in Hanoi fighting his discharge and demanding to be sent back to his battalion.

"After many meetings, it was decided that his invaluable experience and leadership skills could be utilized in headquarters, but he fought that, saying a desk job was worse than being discharged and sitting around all day drinking *cafe sua* and learning to eat with the same hand that wipes his ass. He was offered and grudgingly accepted the position of senior instructor of basic training, where you met him. He's been very effective, but at least once a month General Giap gets a letter from Pham requesting a return to his battalion."

Their transportation was waiting. They saluted, said goodbye, tossed their bags into the truck bed, and climbed in.

* * *

"Dear Ngoc," Vo wrote. "I should be able to write more now that basic training is finished. I've been relocated with four of my comrades to the officer training command. A few more weeks and I will be done with all this training and will have a few days to see you and my family. Your letters are wonderful to read and have helped my morale, but they have increased my desire to see you again. I truly miss you, and I love you." He added his new address, closed the envelope, and dropped it in the outbox for the censors to read and edit before it was sent to the post office.

Ninh, Vo, and Ky were united with third platoon's leaders at the officer training school. After a short welcome by the senior instructor—this time an army captain—the thirty candidates were given physicals, issued new uniforms—with four-pocket shirts—and class schedules. Their barracks was similar to where they had lived in basic training, but the latrine and water buckets were replaced by plumbed bathroom and showers.

Of the thirty officer candidates, twenty-five had come from front-line battalions. These men had served in combat, and their actions were recognized by their commanders as signs of leadership. The other five—Ninh, Vo, Ky and the two third platoon leaders—were not combat tested. But that seemed to make no difference to the veterans. They were all in the same boat, training to take command and, more importantly, to lead.

In his short time in the military Vo had become convinced that leadership was much like an inherent talent. If someone had musical talent, it would take little to bring out that talent and create wonderful music. If the talent was not there, no matter how many lessons and years of practice, the best you could expect was a technically sound imitation of someone else's creation.

Same for leadership, he thought. A man had it within him to be a leader. If he didn't, no amount of officer training, uniform decoration, or imitating a leader's actions would make that person a leader.

The thirty men formed a platoon. One man and two others were appointed as platoon leader and his support staff. The remaining twenty-seven were broken down into three squads and each squad into three cells of three men. Vo, Ninh, and Ky were in the same cell in the first squad, and Vo was assigned the duties of squad leader. Vo knew it was no coincidence that the three of them were in the same cell. Senior Colonel Ong had a very long reach.

The days were long and full. Training was more physically arduous than basic training. And far more academically challenging. Company tactics, logistics, intelligence gathering and interpretation, interrogation, administration, artillery observation, covert movement, advanced first aid, insertion, ambush, explosive ordnance handling, and psychological operations were taught through field exercises, hands-on practical training, and demonstrations followed by live firing exercises. But the best training came from the combat veterans themselves as they helped one another and the five products of Old One-Arm.

Extensive political indoctrination, self-criticism sessions, and presentations on strategic goals and missions filled the rest of the time. The candidates often went without sleep for a day and a half or more when night field exercises were being conducted. Bone tired, they were asleep as soon as they lay down on their bamboo mats. There were no light-duty days and very little "stand easy" time. Vo still managed to write his parents and Ngoc.

Despite the grueling schedule and exhaustion, morale was high. Vo found the training challenging and interesting, almost enjoyable. The veterans told him it was also realistic.

Officer training school finally came to an end as the men marched back—tired, hungry, and dirty—from a night of insertion and evasion exercises. The senior instructor captain was waiting for them as they filed into the barracks. He announced that the afternoon of the next day was officer commissioning. All thirty men would become second lieutenants. He handed an envelope with orders to each man. They were to use the rest of the time cleaning their gear, resting, and getting ready to leave immediately after receiving their commission.

Twenty-seven of the men were given three days' leave and then were to report for transportation to front-line units. Vo, Ninh, and Ky were ordered to report directly to the commander of the Transportation Group's Hanoi headquarters. No leave for the three of them.

That night, their first free time in four weeks, Vo finished his preparations for the next day's travel to Hanoi and wrote letters to Ngoc and his parents. Tomorrow he would be commissioned an officer.

CHAPTER 10
CORONADO, CALIFORNIA

On the first day of Vietnamese language school, the two dozen advisors were joined by another thirty officers and enlisted men—Swift boat crews, PBR patrol boat crews, Naval Forces Vietnam staffers, UDT, SEAL and Explosive Ordnance Demolition team members. Most would be taking a two-week course in Vietnamese. Only the advisors, NAVFORV staff, and a lone SEAL would be taking the full six weeks of language training. The students were welcomed by the middle-aged Vietnamese director of training they had met the first day of counterinsurgency school. After a few perfunctory remarks, he introduced the language teachers—nine Vietnamese men and women. Three of the five women wore silk *ao dais*, the Vietnamese high-necked, tight-bodice dress slit from the ankle to the waist with silk trousers and high heels. The men and the oldest and youngest of the women wore Western garb. Coburn was taken by the grace of the women in their ao dais. Delicate, slender, nearly birdlike.

The students were assigned by rank into nine sections. After two days of basic instruction and testing, they were reassigned into nine classes based on teachers' recommendations and test-predicted aptitude for the language. Teaching teams were also assigned based on class skill level. No language other than Vietnamese was spoken during the classes. Students were assigned homework and frequently tested, usually orally.

After reassignment, Coburn found himself in the highest-level section along with the SEAL, the two senior officers in the class, and two lieutenants, one of whom was an ex-USMC aviator who had attended divinity school using the GI Bill and returned to military service as a navy Protestant chaplain. Vernon was in a lower-level section.

Coburn liked the top-level section. The SEAL, a first class petty officer, would be good for war stories. Coburn was going to enjoy language training.

His section was taught by four of the Vietnamese women. They were patient, thorough, and demanding of the correct pronunciation, especially the subtle raising and lowering of pitch as dictated by the little lines and squiggles that punctuated the words. Words spelled identically could have very different meanings depending on whether the speaker raised, dropped, or clipped the intonation of the word.

Culture was taught as much as language. Considerable time was spent on the proper etiquette and customs of Vietnam. This included the importance of saving face, presenting novel concepts, constructive criticism, and preserving the Vietnamese's rice bowl. Food, interpersonal relations, and emotional reactions were all covered in depth.

Coburn and the SEAL traded silent, raised-eyebrow glances when told that it was normal for Vietnamese men to hold hands and cry, as well as giggle when embarrassed or faced with a serious problem.

* * *

During the first week of language school, the surface junior officer detailer Lieutenant Commander Sperling arrived. He set up a temporary office in the BOQ's VIP suite. Coburn arrived punctually for his late-afternoon appointment.

Sperling was tall and skinny. The room smelled of cigarette smoke. Two empty coffee carafes sat on a table next to a cup and saucer. He wore a command-at-sea pin beneath his three rows of ribbons, signifying that he had served as the commanding officer of a commissioned US Navy ship.

Coburn quickly sized up Sperling. High achiever, probably a dedicated workaholic, early command. Wedding ring, Naval Academy ring. Smoker, coffee drinker. Lots of nervous energy. Little time to spare—don't waste his time, get to the point, make an impression, and then leave. Later, run into him at the O club to reinforce the impression.

The detailer was standing, leaning over the desk and supporting his full weight with his arms, studying a file. It was the end of a long day. He flipped the file face down on the desk, turned to Coburn, put out his hand, and pointed to a seat. "Mr. Coburn, Harry Sperling. Nice to finally meet you in the flesh. Have a seat. Want some coffee? Cigarette?" His speech was rapid and staccato with a faint twang. Midwest? Not-so-deep South?

"No thanks, sir. I'm fine. Had too much coffee trying to keep alert in language class this afternoon."

"Okay, let's get to it. I've reviewed your files, dream sheet, and record. You've got a good, solid start for a nice career. OOD of a deep draft ship, solid fitreps, and you're going to get a year in-country in a good job that should count as joint staff duty since you'll be under MACV—that's the big military advisory command—and with the army. Good start for a jaygee. Unless you really fuck up, you should be putting on railroad tracks about half way through your tour. So let me ask you a question or two, and then it's your turn."

"Sure, fire away, sir."

"What's your plan regarding a career? You want to stay in as a surface officer, transfer to a restricted line designator like engineering duty or intel, leave, leave and stay in the reserves, what?"

Coburn had expected this question. Obviously, the good jobs would go to the guys who stayed in driving ships. Up until three months ago, he had no idea if he wanted to stay in, and driving ships was occasionally fun, with lots of boredom and sleep-deprived drudgery combined with separation from land and family. But he liked being an officer, and he wanted the good jobs a career offered. He had rehearsed his answer. And all this stuff was at least a year or more in the future. Things could change. He could always figure out how to make this work for him.

"Sir, I'm seriously considering a career driving ships. There's no way I want to sell insurance. I like the navy, I like what I'm doing, and I'd like a command. The navy's been good to me, and where else can I get responsibility like this so soon?"

Sperling nodded. "Okay, Mr. Coburn. You're not even in-country yet, but I've got to start on the slate for the next fiscal year's moves in about six months. That will include you. Advisor jobs are considered arduous duty, and assuming you do okay and are qualified, you will get priority treatment. That can be a big leg up for you."

Coburn kept a serious face and nodded, waiting for Sperling to continue.

"It's probably too soon for you to have considered it much, but have you given any thoughts on where you'd like to go after Vietnam? No guarantees on any of this, and everything's subject to change."

Again Coburn had expected the question and had prepared a response. There was no way he would have accepted the advisor job if he was not going to have his choice of plum assignments afterward. Maybe assistant surface officer detailer in DC assigning people he liked or who had kissed his ass to good jobs and assholes to miserable ones. Technical advisor to Hollywood. ROTC instructor at UCLA or University of Florida. Recruiter in Hawaii. Or aide to some flag officer in some nice place.

"You're correct, sir, I haven't thought much past getting through Vietnam alive. But I want to take a long-term view about my career. What job is going to be best for my career, meet the needs of the navy best? That sort of view. I eventually want command at sea."

"You're doing well, but you're not ready for command yet. You need to go to sea as a department head, get an XO job, and screen for command. I'm thinking we send you to the department head course at Destroyer School, department head on a tin can, then postgraduate school to get a graduate degree, then XO, then CO. Or maybe graduate school first and then Destroyer School. You're going to have to be a good performer to get promoted. And a top performer to get the XO and CO jobs. The pyramid narrows down rapidly as you go up."

Sperling had just described a twelve-year post-Vietnam scenario of three or four years of schools interlaced with eight to nine years of seagoing.

"Any chance of getting command at sea earlier, sir? As a lieutenant or lieutenant commander?"

"There's always a chance. Get yourself a couple of medals for valor and recommendations for accelerated promotion fitness reports and show a combination of leadership and ship handling, and sure, you could get an early command." Coburn was looking at Sperling's command pin. Like many naval officers, Coburn aspired to command. He was making it obvious. Or he could be one of the slickest bullshitters Sperling had to deal with.

"Okay, sir, that's clear enough."

"Good. Now it's your turn. Any questions?"

"Yes, sir, lots of questions. Do you have the time for me?"

"Sure, shoot."

"When will you be sending me orders? I know this is early."

"Nope, not too early. I think the first thing we need to do is get you screened for PG school. I see you put your curriculum choices on your dream sheet here: management, operations research, and math. As soon as I get back to the office, I'll make sure your file is in front of the postgraduate board. They make their choices strictly off academic background. It's up to me to see if the class openings fit your schedule. If so, we'll probably send you to PG school. That board meets in five months, so we should know if you're on the list in about six or seven months. That would be the earliest I could pencil you in on the new slate."

Coburn let himself smile.

Sperling continued. "Based on this conversation, I'll also put your file in for selection to Destroyer School. I'll do that right away, and we should know pretty quickly on that one. But I'll hold all assignments until we see what happens with grad school. And your fitreps."

"Are there any other opportunities for me besides grad school or Destroyer School?"

"Sure. You want to go back to sea on some staff or take another division officer job, I've got plenty of those. But I wouldn't recommend going that route; you don't need that. If you want some do-nothing shore job, we can probably find that, but then you might as well get out of the navy. And frankly, with the shortages we're facing, I might have a tough time selling you to become naval attaché at some skivvy house in Paris."

Coburn laughed.

"Face it, Mr. Coburn, you come back with a Medal of Honor and Ho Chi Minh's corpse, you'll probably wind up working in the White House or for the Secretary of Defense. You come back with a lousy fitrep, and you'll be happy as security officer in Adak, Alaska, or chief engineer on a sailboat."

"Aye, aye, sir. Don't think I want either of those jobs." Coburn put on his serious face and asked another rehearsed question. "Can you give me a quick review of my fitness reports? Where I need improvement, what to do. That kind of stuff?"

This kid really is a slick one, thought Sperling. He took out a sheet of paper that had a summary of the two years of fitness reports, all from the CO of the DeKalb. Sperling went through the summary in some detail, pointing out that each of his fitreps was better than the preceding one. He was always recommended for promotion but not accelerated promotion and was usually ranked two or three out of the eleven division officers on the ship. The reports were good. With room to get better.

"We still have to get your skipper's last fitness report on you from the DeKalb. You'll also be getting a very important fitness report at the end of your in-country tour. It will be reporting your performance in a combat zone, working with both the other military services like the flyboys, grunts, and army pukes, as well as dealing with a foreign navy. You're getting a once-in-a-career time to shine. And an opportunity to fuck it up, too." Sperling smiled and gave Coburn a soft punch to his shoulder. "You'll do fine."

"I hope so, sir." Although the DeKalb's skipper had not ranked him as the number-one division officer, had not recommended him for early promotion when he had recommended others, and had not given him the highest grade possible in leadership, Coburn kept a smile on his face. He had a good report card, but he didn't have the best report card. He'd do whatever he had to do to make his next fitness reports the best fitness reports.

The meeting ended with handshakes and thanks. Coburn went to his room and changed into civvies and debated on whether to try to suck up to Sperling at the bar or spend an evening with the nurse. After finding out she had to work that evening, he decided he'd put on the bib and knee pads and go to the club for dinner. For sure Sperling would be there.

Coburn knocked on Vernon's door, and together they walked over to the club and grabbed a table. Sperling walked in an hour later with the CO of the school. The detailer smiled and waved at the two junior officers, stopped and chatted by a table where four others were eating, and walked into the bar.

"There's the man with the keys to our future," said Vernon. "Seems like a pretty decent guy. Straight shooter, huh?"

"Yeah, I guess. How'd your meeting go with Sperling?"

"Pretty well. We went through my options and my dream sheet. He found out this morning that I'm on the selection list for lieutenant. I might be wearing railroad tracks by the time I get to Vietnam. That ought to help with my counterpart, whoever that turns out to be."

"No shit. Well congratulations, Doug." Coburn smiled and shook his friend's hand.

"Thanks, Clark. It's all a matter of time. Not much else. But I will enjoy your saluting me and calling me 'sir.' No more Doug to you. From now on it's Mister Doug."

"I guess I'm just going to get a court martial for insubordination, you chickenshit ass kisser." They both laughed. "What'd he say about your orders after Nam?"

Vernon leaned forward excitedly. "No promises, but he says I might be up for an XO's job or even a CO spot!"

"You're shitting me. Don't you need to have a department head tour under your belt first?"

"On the Sarsfield I fleeted up to weps for a year and a few months when my boss wound up getting sick, and then he got a permanent change of station without a relief. So I had the job. According to Sperling, a year of that counts as a weps department head job. He says I have the tickets, and unless I wind up getting caught with General Giap's dick in my mouth, I have a good chance of getting XO or CO of a minesweeper or maybe a destroyer escort or LST. How'd your meeting go?"

"Offered me PG school and a blow job. I told him I like the navy. But nothing definite. Too early for him to say much."

They paid the check and went into the bar. Sperling was nursing a beer in a circle of junior officers, mainly lieutenants from their class but several other lieutenants, jaygees, and a lone ensign from nearby ships. The school CO had left. Vernon and Coburn shook hands with Sperling, who called them by their first names. He congratulated Vernon on his promotion and offered to buy him a drink. Vernon thanked him but declined, saying if he had a drink in midweek, he'd fall asleep in class, and he was having enough trouble in school as it was.

The easy camaraderie between Vernon and the detailer was obvious. Coburn thought of intruding and making some witty comment but then held off.

* * *

Language training was easy for Coburn. He had an ear for languages. Despite doing the bare minimum required in assignments and homework, he led the class. The women teachers enjoyed him, sometimes even flirting with him. He spent evenings working in the obligatory language lab and hanging out with Vernon or the nurse.

Language lab consisted of donning earphones and responding into a microphone to taped questions. Their own voices were then played back to them, followed by the proper taped response. One of the teachers was always present, sitting at the back of the lab with earphones and microphone, listening to the students' responses. Occasionally the teacher would break in and correct the student's pronunciation or come to the student's station and work face to face.

Ba—or Misses—Hung was in the back of the room as Coburn and several others were listening and responding into their microphones. Her nickname among the students was Ba Sung Dai Lin, or Madame Heavy Machine Gun, for her stern demeanor, staccato speech, and the high level of performance she demanded. Ba Hung was slender and had exotically pretty features. She always wore her long hair in a tight bun. The severe hairstyle, brisk no-nonsense manner, and stern expression masked her beauty from the students.

Her voice was in Coburn's earphones. "Trung Uy Coburn. Toi la shiquan haiquan My. Sin lap lai." She had asked him to repeat a phrase that identified him as an American naval officer. He did so and continued his lesson. Occasional clicks in his earphones told him that she was listening, but she did not interrupt again.

One night he walked alone through the parking lot to the BOQ. The click of heels made him turn around. Ba Hung was walking toward him, car keys in hand. She smiled at him. "Good evening, Lieutenant Coburn." The only trace of her accent was the staccato rhythm of her speech.

"Chao Ba. Speaking English tonight?"

She laughed, something Coburn had never witnessed before. He looked at her. She looked so different smiling. She was beautiful.

"No, my work day is over. I don't have to be your teacher now. Lovely night tonight, isn't it?"

"Yes, indeed, Ba Hung."

"You seem to have recovered from that rash you had."

He felt himself blush. "Thankfully, yes. Please tell me they have no poison oak in Vietnam."

"I don't think so. At least I've never seen anyone with what you suffered from. You do look much better." She unlocked the Volkswagen and hesitated a bit. "You need a ride?"

"No, I'm just going to the BOQ. But thanks for the offer."

"See you tomorrow in class, Trung Uy." She got into the beetle, started the engine, and looked at him as he walked by the car. A few seconds later, she drove by him, smiling and waving her hand.

Back in his room, Coburn called the nurse, and they made plans to see each other the next evening and the weekend. An unanswered letter from Betsy sat on his desk.

Betsy had written that she was sad and had long sensed that they were going their separate ways, drifting apart. She seemed reconciled and perhaps a little relieved at the prospect.

Coburn didn't know if he would reply. He didn't want to throw salt in her wounds. But maybe there were no wounds? What would he write? What to say? He'd think about all that later.

He lay in bed a while, enjoying his usual array of sensuous thoughts and fantasies before drifting asleep. Ba Hung came drifting into his thoughts. He was surprised by that but did nothing to stop it.

The next day when Ba Hung entered the classroom, Coburn noticed she looked and acted as she always did—brisk, demanding, all business, intense. At one time when the students were practicing conversation with her, she slightly bent her head forward and stared at Coburn as he went through his spiel. She had never looked at him that way before. Later the students were paired up for role-playing, Coburn with the SEAL. Ba Hung walked around the classroom, eavesdropping on the pairs of men and occasionally correcting their pronunciation. She stood next to Coburn's chair while he and the SEAL pretended to be waiter and diner.

She stood still, listening, arms folded across her breasts, expressionless, and then bent forward to read the SEAL's notes. When she did so, Coburn felt the pressure of her thigh against his arm. He edged away from the contact, but a second later the pressure followed him. Her close presence lasted a few seconds, and then she moved on to listen to another pair of students. Coburn had an erection, and his heart was pounding. He really didn't know what to do.

* * *

It was Saturday evening after the end of the second week of language school. Coburn and the nurse were dining in the seafood restaurant at the San Diego terminus of the Coronado Ferry. They sat on the patio overlooking the lights of Coronado and North Island across San Diego Bay. They were talking about how many more weeks he'd be in Coronado before he would have to leave for Travis Air Force Base and fly to Vietnam.

He was very at ease with her. She was fun, not bad looking, and seemed to have no great desire for a commitment from him. At least not yet. Never can tell with women. In the meantime, he intended to just enjoy being with her. If she started to get clingy, he had a thousand excuses to not see her. But she seemed to be fine with the status quo. At least so far.

SERE training came up. She asked, "Isn't that where they put you in a POW compound and torture you?"

He made a sour face. "That's what I heard. Y'know, I'm less anxious about going to Vietnam than I am about that."

"I heard from one of the fliers that they starve you for a few days, get you so tired you're dopey, and then throw you into some jail or something," she said.

"That sounds about right. I wish I could avoid it. Or go hide when the torturing starts. Not big on starving or staying awake all the time either."

She laughed and took a drink of her wine. They had had cocktails before dinner and were at the bottom of a bottle of chardonnay. "Why don't you just take some food and a couple of tranquillizers? That would work."

"Sure, I just show up with a grill and a couple of steaks and go to sick bay and ask for a couple of feel-good pills."

Again she laughed. "No, really. Hide a couple of candy bars or jerky in your hat or something, and how hard would it be to sneak in two or three Valiums? I can get those for you. You have to get your own Hershey bars."

"Maybe not a bad idea. How about you come with so I don't get too cold sleeping in the woods?" He drained his glass. "Want some dessert?"

Before she could answer, a couple walked up to their table. The woman said, "Chao Trung Uy," then nodded at the nurse and said, "Good evening."

It took several seconds before Coburn recognized Ba Hung. She was holding the hand of a handsome Asian man with graying hair. Her usual ao dai was replaced by a silk blouse and straight skirt. Her long black hair was freed from its severe bun and hung straight and thick to her shoulders. She was smiling broadly.

"You didn't recognize me out of the classroom and the ao dai, did you?" Ba Hung laughed.

He stood up, flustered. "No, I sure did not, Ba Hung. You look so different."

The language instructor introduced her husband, Ong Hung, and Coburn introduced Kelly. Ba Hung and her husband had just finished dinner and were on their way out when she spotted Coburn.

Kelly invited them to join them for coffee or a drink.

"That would be nice." Ba Hung's husband pulled a chair out for her, and she sat down next to Coburn and across from the nurse.

Ong Hung waved the waitress over and ordered a cognac for himself and looked around the table. The other three thought a cognac sounded good, and soon four snifters of golden-brown liquid were delivered.

Ba Hung asked Kelly what she did and listened intently to the description of working in an emergency room. Coburn asked Ong Hung—who asked to be called Andy—what line of work he was in.

Andy said he was the chairman of the Asian language department at the Defense Language Institute in Monterey. Every Friday, either he or his wife made the drive between San Diego and Monterey and the return trip on Sunday. Coburn asked how Andy wound up there.

After graduating college in 1953, Ba Hung's future husband left Hanoi for France and a doctorate in linguistics. Seeking postdoctoral work and a chance to improve his English, he came to the United States nearly ten years ago.

As Ong Hung talked, Coburn felt Ba Hung's knee brush against his leg. He did not move his leg away. She pressed her knee lightly on his. He looked at her, but she was focused on her husband. Coburn stole a glance at Kelly, who seemed equally enthralled with Andy's narrative.

In the course of the conversation, Kelly asked the couple how it was being separated during the week.

"We're used to it now. Andy's opportunity to be department chair coincided with an offer for me to work here. We decided to take both offers and try this commuting for a while. It's been three years so far. But it's fine. It does get a little confusing when I go looking for my hairbrush or slippers and they're in Monterey." She moved her knee away, shifted in her chair, crossed her legs, and ran the toe of her shoe along Coburn's calf. "How long have you two known each other?"

"Oh, I think I met Clark the first or second week he was in Coronado. When he came here for his schools. That had to be, what, about two months ago?"

"Yep, that's about right," said Coburn, his voice uncharacteristically hoarse. He looked at Ba Hung, who gave him the same penetrating stare she had flashed at him in the classroom the day before.

When the two couples prepared to leave the table, Coburn made an excuse of looking on the floor for his keys before he stood up so his erection could subside. The men shook hands in the parking lot before helping the women into the cars.

Back at the nurse's apartment, Coburn and Kelly snuggled on the couch, a little too intoxicated to move to the bedroom.

"She's a very pretty woman. I thought you said those teachers were all tough hard-asses. She certainly didn't act or look that way," said the nurse.

"At school she sure doesn't act or look like she did tonight. Her nickname is Madame Heavy Machine Gun. Husband seemed like a cool guy, huh?"

* * *

Class went on. The students in the highest-level sections were carrying on conversations with less and less correcting from the teachers. Outwardly, Ba Hung treated Coburn the way she did his classmates. But occasionally as she passed out reading material or collected their written work, her body would brush against his. Coburn found her exciting but intimidating. He decided to remain passive. If she wanted to flirt with him, he'd let it happen and enjoy the attention. If she wanted more, she'd have to initiate it. He didn't want to play games with a cock tease.

One evening at the end of the next-to-last week of language training, the three highest sections gathered in the conference room. All the instructors were there, including Ba Hung in her ao dai and her hair in a tight bun. On the table was a veritable feast of Vietnamese food prepared by several of the instructors.

The director of training explained in Vietnamese that this was an opportunity to try the foods of Vietnam. As advisors, they would be exposed to many foods and tastes, some of which they may not like. While their counterparts could understand someone trying a food and not liking it, they would not understand and would probably be offended by someone not even trying the food, not taking a taste. He also warned them that finishing food you did not like quickly to get it off your plate could very well be misinterpreted by your host that you not only like the food but wanted more, and they'd pile some more into your bowl.

One of the male instructors then gave a brief lesson on the use of chopsticks and identified the dishes on the table. Beef broth with noodles, bean sprouts, thin slices of beef and slices of pepper. Thin and delicate fried egg rolls filled with vegetables and shrimp. A thick corn and chicken soup. Steamed rice. Marinated and grilled slices of pork, chicken, and beef. Fish sauce for dipping. Tea. Chilled tofu cubes in a sweet syrup. Cold vermicelli rice noodles. Pickles. Thick, dark coffee and condensed milk. Braised fish with scallions. Stir-fried vegetables. Lettuce leaves for wrapping. And a red sauce that he warned was only for those who liked their food very spicy. The students were invited to try the food, and then they'd talk about what they liked and didn't like.

Theodore and Coburn were standing at one corner of the conference table with the SEAL, all three of them trying to eat and speak in Vietnamese, thoroughly enjoying the experience. Theodore was especially clumsy with his chopsticks and grabbed an errant piece of grilled pork with his fingers, dipped it into the spicy sauce, and wrapped it in a lettuce leaf with some rice noodles and pickled cucumbers and carrots. As he took a bite, Ba Hung walked up to him waving an extended finger and with a smile said in Vietnamese he should not use his fingers. Even children did not eat with their fingers. With a mouthful, the senior student replied that he just couldn't wait; it was all so delicious.

She turned to the SEAL and Coburn and asked them if they liked the food. Both nodded, unable to speak because of full mouths. Ba Hung asked the SEAL, who had had several in-country deployments under his belt, if he had tried Vietnamese food before. He swallowed his mouthful and said he loved the cuisine and was hoping that someday a Vietnamese restaurant would open in San Diego.

Coburn asked Ba Hung if she made this kind of food for herself and, pointedly, her husband. She smiled with her mouth but not her eyes at Coburn, waved her hand at the feast in front of them, and said that, yes, she did cook traditional Vietnamese food but nothing this grand and certainly not this much. She stared at him intently for a few seconds and then moved to talk to the other students around the table.

"My imagination, Mr. Coburn, or was she pissed at you or something?" asked the SEAL. "That look she gave you."

"I don't think so. I think it's just her Dragon Lady intimidation instincts. Look, she seems to be giving the stare to Mr. Vernon now."

"No, that's not the same one she shot at you. You probably insinuated that she didn't know how to cook or something."

"Yeah, that must be it. This food is pretty tasty, huh?"

At the end of the exercise, the director of training went through each dish and led a short discussion on what the students liked and what they didn't. There was very little they didn't like. The biggest complaints seemed to be the lack of expertise in using chopsticks to get slippery foods from the bowl to the mouth, the smell of the fish sauce, tofu's lack of flavor, and the need to calibrate the heat of the hot sauce. The instructors started clearing the dishes, and several of the students helped. Coburn found himself stacking dirty dishes next to Ba Hung. Her breast brushed against his arm as she turned to get more dishes.

After a few minutes, she walked up to Coburn with a cardboard box of condiments, serving ladles, a wok, and long cooking chopsticks. In English she quietly said, "Will you please carry these to my car? I'll get my briefcase and papers."

He followed her out to her Volkswagen in the parking lot. She opened the front hood and bent over next to Coburn as they placed the box and briefcase into the trunk. They were out of sight and earshot of the others.

"Did you like that food?" she asked softly in English.

"Very much."

"Please come to my house for dinner Saturday."

Surprised, he was at a temporary loss for words. "Sure, I'd like that. Can I bring anything? What kind of wine do you and Andy like?"

"My husband will be at a conference in Washington, DC."

"Oh, uh, well, should I bring anything?"

"No, just yourself. Say seven o'clock." She told him the address and gave him driving directions, got in the car, and loudly in Vietnamese thanked him for his help and said goodnight.

Later that night Coburn was at Kelly's house. She nonchalantly gave him a small envelope with half a dozen Valium pills inside. He laughed a false laugh, thanking her but saying he doubted if he'd need them. After all, it was less than twenty-four hours in the prison compound. He could stand on his head for that long.

As they snuggled on her couch, she asked what he wanted to do for the next Saturday. Dinner out? Cook here?

"Aw, shit, hon, that night's no good for me. We've a mandatory intercultural exercise that night. We're supposed to try Vietnamese traditional food and display proper table manners. That last part will be tough for a bunch of slobs."

"Can you bring a guest? Like me?"

"No, it's just for the students."

"Will you be by afterwards?"

"I don't think so. It's starting pretty late, and knowing those teachers, it will go on for a while. I'll probably just go back to the BOQ and hit the rack." He noticed the little pout on her face. "But if plans change, I'll call you, okay?"

* * *

Ba Hung lived in an upscale apartment complex overlooking the Pacific. She must be making some decent money, thought Coburn as he locked his rental car and took the flowers and a bottle of wine into the lobby and rang her bell. The inner door unlocked with a click. He decided to take the stairs instead of the elevator. He wanted a few more seconds to calm down.

Coburn was surprised at how nervous he had been for the last twenty-four hours. Before leaving the base, he had a beer to try to settle himself down. When it came to women, he imagined he was always in control, the master manipulating emotions and passions of others to suit himself. If nothing else, he was never this excited. He had never even fantasized about a liaison with an exotic woman who must be ten years his senior.

The door to her apartment was ajar. He knocked, said hello in Vietnamese, and walked in. She came out of the kitchen, hair down, a green silk blouse and blue jeans covered by an apron. "No Vietnamese language is necessary tonight, Trung Uy. We're out of the classroom, yes?"

He awkwardly held out the flowers and wine.

"I told you to just bring yourself." She took the flowers. "Put the wine on the counter. I'll put these in some water. Hand me that knife next to the stove." He did as she ordered.

"Should I open the wine? Want a glass, Ba Hung?" he asked.

"If you want some, go ahead. But this meal is better with beer."

Coburn took his hand off the wine bottle. "Smells good. What is it?"

"Corn soup, yellow rice, crab. Take that ladle and fill those two soup bowls from that pot and put them on the table. There's beer in the refrigerator. 33, Vietnamese beer. Pour two glasses. I'll take out the platters from the oven. Light the candles; there are some matches over there." She pointed with her elbow.

As in her teaching, everything was organized. Glasses and bottle opener on the kitchen counter next to the refrigerator. Ladle and soup bowls next to the saucepan on the stove top. The small, round dining table was laid out in military precision.

She surveyed the table. Satisfied, she ordered Coburn to a chair and went back into the kitchen to take off her apron. She turned off the kitchen and dining room lights and sat down. Coburn noticed her green jade bracelet and a thin gold necklace that, with her silk green blouse, contrasted beautifully with her pale, near white, olive skin.

She picked up her glass of beer, held it out toward Coburn, and said, "Welcome."

He clicked her glass with his. "Thanks for inviting me. This is really special, Ba Hung." He took a large gulp of beer. The evening seemed surreal to him, as if he were a spectator watching himself in a movie or a play.

"Ba Hung, I know you yelled at Thieu Ta Theodore for using his fingers, but I don't think I'll be able to eat this delicious-looking crab with chopsticks."

She laughed and then reached over and deftly shelled the crab with her own chopsticks, putting chunks of the meat and sautéed roe on his plate.

"There, Trung Uy. Just remember I won't be there in Vietnam, so you'd better practice with those chopsticks."

She used the Vietnamese for his military rank. This was much too informal an occasion for her to be calling him by his rank. And for him to be calling her the equivalent of Madame Hung.

"This food is wonderful." He took another gulp of beer. "My first name is Clark. What should I call you?"

She put her slender and well-manicured right hand over his. "I know your first name, Trung Uy. I'm more comfortable with Trung Uy and Ba Hung." She squeezed his hand.

"Uh...sure." He was confused. Had he been misreading what he thought were obvious flirtations? Here he was, sitting at a candlelight dinner with some sexy woman who was coming on to him, and she was insisting on his calling her Misses, and she was calling him by his rank? Was she mind-fucking him? He drained his glass. She went into the kitchen and opened another bottle.

The beer settled Coburn down. Ba Hung asked where Coburn was from and what he had studied in college. He found out from

139

her that she was from Saigon, met her husband in France where she was an undergraduate, and married in Saigon nine years ago. She relaxed with her second glass of beer. Coburn tried to gain some control by asking more questions, pretending to be interested in her answers. There was no handholding, no knees rubbing under the table. But she seemed happy and comfortable, enjoying his company.

In reply to one of his questions, she said she liked the United States very much, certainly the availability of creature comforts. Her husband would never willingly return to his home in Hanoi, and the two of them felt the political situation in the South was simply too precarious. So for now, as long as they could, they'd stay in the United States.

But she did find Americans to be crude and unsophisticated. They could take lessons from the French. Coburn just nodded his head to this comment and thought she sounded like a snob.

Together they stacked the dishes in the sink, and then she told him to take the two brandy snifters that were on the counter and put them on the coffee table in the living room. After turning out the kitchen lights, she followed him, carrying a bottle of cognac. Sliding glass doors to the balcony were open to the warm spring ocean breeze. He walked out and rested his elbows on the railing. She walked up behind him a minute later with the two snifters of cognac. After clicking glasses, he took a sip.

"I'd better watch this stuff. It's pretty potent, and I'm not sure how it'll mix with beer and crab."

Ba Hung stood silently next to him, close but not touching. She sipped her brandy, staring at the black Pacific. He found the silence awkward but decided he'd be better off just keeping his mouth shut and drinking her husband's cognac.

"So, one more week of class with us, then a week of survival school, and then how much time until you have to be in Vietnam?"

Relieved that she had finally broken the silence, he replied, "I've got a week to get from here to Travis Air Force Base up by San Francisco."

Both snifters had been refilled with cognac, although Coburn hadn't noticed her doing so. Typical of her. Efficient, graceful, perfect, never spilling a drop or clanging a bottle against a glass. He envisioned a cat walking on a mantelpiece. He didn't like cats; he liked dogs.

"And you will stay in the military, Trung Uy?"

"If I can get the right set of orders after Vietnam, maybe."

She silently nodded. He felt irritated, almost losing patience, and stole a glance at his illuminated watch dial. It was nearly 10:30. This was going nowhere. Time to retreat, cut his losses, go back to the BOQ, and maybe call the nurse.

He turned to her to say he was calling it a night. But before he could say anything, she turned away from him walked into the living room and put her snifter on the coaster. She walked back to him, staring at him in that bent-forward way she had looked at him in the classroom, took the snifter from his hand, turned, and put it on the other coaster. To his surprise, he had been holding his breath, He exhaled slowly as she walked back to him.

Ba Hung stood before him on the balcony, the top of her head just reaching to his chin. She tilted her head up and put her hands on his hips and drew herself against him. The faint smell of her perfume penetrated the smell of the ocean. Without thinking, he grabbed her silk-covered shoulders and kissed her, a long lover's kiss. She opened her mouth and played her tongue against his, wrapping her arms around him and pressing him against her. Coburn felt her thighs against his. He moved his hands down her back to her waist and then her rear, which was small, round, and hard. She pushed back to arm's length and led him to her bedroom. The bed covers were turned back.

At the bedside she pulled his polo shirt out of his pants and up to his shoulders. He bent over, and she pulled the shirt the rest of the way off. She kissed him again. Coburn found the smooth and cool silk of her blouse on his bare chest uniquely exciting. He reached for the pearl buttons of her blouse. She leaned back to give him room, but his thick and nervous fingers fumbled with the little buttons on the thin green silk. Her nimble, manicured fingers came to his aid.

They moved onto the bed, and she opened the silk blouse and slid it off her shoulders. She wore no bra. As they kissed he held her narrow but muscular shoulders and then moved his hands down the arch of her back. Her tongue sought his, and she brushed, then pressed, her hard nipples against his chest. Coburn kicked off his loafers, undid his belt, and stepped out of his khaki trousers and boxers.

He kissed her perfectly formed breasts and a little mole beneath her collarbone. Lying between her jeans-covered legs, Coburn put his mouth over her breast, circling her nipple with his tongue and then holding her nipple with his teeth and then lips. She arched her back, subtly moving her breasts to meet his lips and tongue and teeth. She moved so he could kiss her stomach and the line of her ribs and her chest and shoulders and neck. Her back was arched and her knees bent, her hips moving back and forth.

With his lips moving from breast to breast, he fumbled with her belt. Again her hands pushed his away, unbuckled her belt, and unbuttoned her jeans. She lifted her hips and slid the blue denim down the violin curves of her hips and thighs and off her shapely legs. She pushed her blue-and-white panties to her thighs, and his trembling hands rolled them down and past her small feet. She spread her legs wide as he kissed her mouth, nervous, excited, not convinced this was anything but a dream. Her hand reached between her legs and guided him into her.

She was like nothing he could have imagined. Warm, oiled silk. Soft rose petals covered with summer dew. Where did these thoughts come from?

Eyes closed, undulating and holding him in her, she moved her hips and body imperceptibly as she kissed him. A low, quiet violin note came from deep in her throat. He asked her if she was okay, and she opened her eyes and looked at him with the stare from the classroom and nodded her head. He came, violently and completely. He came. But she kept him hard.

He was on his back and she mounted him, then slowly began sliding him in and out of her. He came again, and she still kept him hard. She leaned back against his knees with him still inside her, smiled, and then leaned forward, letting her hair brush against his face and down his bare chest. She lifted herself off him and lay down on her side.

Coburn lay behind her, spooning her body into his, his arm across her narrow waist, her firm, round, beautiful buttocks against his hip bones. He felt he should say something but instead just lay there, holding onto her. He kept on thinking this wasn't really happening to him—he'd wake and be disappointed that this had just been a wet dream.

"Trung Uy, it's late. Now you must go."

He kissed the back of her neck. Still on their sides, she slid him into her from behind. Her right hand reached behind and stroked him from his back to his thighs. Her movements and warmth and moist smoothness brought him to a draining climax.

Lying on his back, he watched her pad to the bathroom then come out a short time later wearing a terry cloth bathrobe. He sat up on the edge of the bed and put a hand out to her. She stayed out of reach. "You must go now."

"I can stay if you want. I've nothing doing tomorrow."

"Trung Uy, you can study tomorrow or go to the zoo. You need to go now." Her voice was firm, definite.

Coburn dressed slowly, not sure whether to do as she said or just grab her and start kissing her. Get that robe off and back onto the bed. Fuck her brains out and then just go to sleep. She could make him some of that thick coffee with condensed milk. Shit, why did he have to leave? He put on his shoes and stood up. She and stood at the bedroom door. All the lights were on.

"Do I still call you Ba Hung?"

"Yes, Trung Uy, you still call me Ba Hung." She was not smiling but seemed to be studying him.

"When will I see you again, Ba Hung?" He emphasized "Ba Hung."

"You'll see me Monday in class."

"Sure, but when will I see you again like...well you know."

"You will see me Monday in class and then Tuesday, Wednesday, Thursday, and Friday in class."

"Got it." He walked to the front door. She stood next to him. "Thanks for the wonderful dinner and the even better dessert, Ba Hung." He debated kissing her goodnight but decided for whatever weird reason she might have that she'd probably knee him in the balls, so he just walked out. She shut the door behind him.

It was only 11:45 on a Saturday night. That was a wonderful piece of ass. He had never experienced an evening like that before. Should he go to the BOQ or maybe stick his face in the Mexican Village? Mexican Village would be busy now, but he'd have to buy some skank a drink or two. He was tired, drained.

He drove to the BOQ, went up to his room, showered, and got in bed, tossing and turning until 2:00 in the morning before he fell asleep. Thinking of Ba Hung.

He woke up late Sunday morning a little hung over. After calling his parents, he called Kelly and told her what a lousy time he had last night and should have blown it off, gone AWOL, and seen her. He'd see her in the evening.

The unanswered letter from Betsy sat on his desk. Maybe he'd scribble something back to her. Maybe not.

* * *

The last week of language training was devoted mainly to role-playing, oral reports, and testing. Ba Hung treated Coburn as she did all the other students in the classroom. Professional, tough, stern, demanding. The SEAL, who was often Coburn's role-playing partner, remarked that Ba Hung was an excellent teacher, probably the best of the staff. Coburn agreed.

He watched Ba Hung, looking for that special stare she'd sent his way in the past, waiting to see if she'd brush by or press an arm or leg against his when she was standing near his chair. But none of that happened. He hung around the parking lot before and after class, hoping to run into her. The one time she did walk by, she gave him a sterile nod and smile and said, "Chao Trung Uy Coburn," and walked on. Didn't she enjoy that evening? Was that some kind of sick trick she was playing on him?

The final day of class ended at noon with a brief graduation ceremony and the director of training handing out certificates of completion. With little fanfare, the director announced the honor student, the student with the highest grade—Lieutenant (Junior Grade) Coburn. With a chorus of "attaboy," "way to go," and "teacher's pet," he accepted the honor student certificate.

As they left the auditorium, the language staff lined up inside the doorway and shook hands with each student. Coburn was behind Theodore, Vernon, and the SEAL as they filed out. He watched Ba Hung shake their hands and congratulate them, smiling. She acted the same exact way when he took her hand. He stood around a few minutes more and watched her say good-bye to some of the other students. Shit, she treated them exactly as she had treated him. But that evening in her apartment—didn't that count for something?

* * *

It was a typically quiet Sunday night at the Mexican Village. Coburn and the nurse were eating the special combination plate dinner. He was uncharacteristically quiet, distracted. She sensed he was worried about the SERE training that would start the next day. To distract him she talked about their plans for the week-long trip up the coast to Travis.

Coburn was anxious about the infamous survival course. He knew his anxiety wasn't rational. Thousands had taken the course, and all the graduates he knew seemed none the worse for doing so. But what if he didn't do well? What if he started crying like a baby, begging not to be hit, selling his soul for a cookie, or going nuts in some claustrophobic box for all his classmates to see? The shame and humiliation of going from cool and in total control to a sniveling slave of some prison guard made him start to hyperventilate.

The only thing that seemed to distract him from these anxious thoughts was his bruised and bleeding ego, courtesy of the evil Ba Hung. The more he thought about how she used him to get herself off and then unceremoniously dumped him, the more upset he became. He needed to take control, get one more time with her. He should stay in San Diego the week between SERE and Travis and camp out at her apartment during the day and jump her bones at night. The bitch.

Looking up from his dinner plate, he realized that Kelly had stopped talking and was looking quizzically at him.

"You okay, Clark?"

"Uh, yeah, sure. Excuse me. Be right back."

Coburn went to the bathroom, upset at himself for being upset. He stood at the urinal, looking at the scribbles on the blackboard mounted in front of him. Typical navy graffiti, mostly about which part of the navy community does what better—inner service rivalries and a lot of ribaldry.

He had to settle himself down. The Valium will take care of SERE, he thought. If I need it, I have it. That thought calmed him down immediately. He looked at the blackboard, zippered up, and used his hand to erase some of the scribbling and create a clean spot. With the stub of chalk he wrote that for a great blow job call the language school staff number and ask for Ba Hung.

Back at the table, he gave Kelly a kiss and sat down. He felt much better. They talked about what to do on the ride up the coast.

* * *

Several aviators and Swift boat crews joined the two dozen future advisors. They were all in their olive-drab jungle uniforms, field jackets, and jungle boots. That and identification were all they were allowed to bring with them. In the brief classroom introduction, they were told that food, medicines, alcohol, and tobacco were prohibited and to toss whatever they had with them into a garbage can on the way out. Coburn walked out of the room with three Valium wrapped in tinfoil in his hat sweatband and two packages of peanuts in his socks.

They spent the first day and night on beach survival. They rigged fishing lines and hunted for crabs and sea urchins and driftwood to burn. They scavenged very little food. At dawn after a night of trying to stay warm and giving up on being able to sleep, Coburn ate a bag of his forbidden peanuts, burying the wrapper in the sand. They boarded buses for the trip to Hot Warner Springs for the rest of the training. The men were quiet during the ride, trying to doze off.

At Hot Warner Springs, they mustered in a classroom, where they were lectured by a civilian—an ex-POW who had survived over two years of Japanese captivity in World War II. He emphasized the importance to their survival of maintaining the chain of command and leadership. He gave the example of the Turkish Army POWs in Korea as proof. Unlike the other forces in Korea, all the Turks who were captured survived and made it home. He also presented the Geneva Convention on the treatment of prisoners but with the caveat that the North Vietnamese did not appear to be abiding by it.

They then started two days and nights of supervised land survival and evasion training. Hot Warner Springs was essentially scrubland with little wildlife to catch and little edible vegetation. But the area had a few flowing streams, and several water trailers were provided. Dehydration was a serious threat in this high desert.

At the end of the first day the SERE instructors brought several rabbits and demonstrated how to kill and clean and cook them. Coburn wondered if there were rabbits in Vietnam. The instructors provided a bag of rice. The students killed, cleaned, and cooked the rabbits with the rice and the few edible wild greens they gathered in large drums on open fires. Each man got a canteen cup full of the hot stew. Coburn, like most of them, burned his mouth in his haste to eat but eventually cleaned his cup. Within an hour, about half the students, including Coburn, had diarrhea.

They had been taught survival first aid and knew the remedy for loose bowels. Charcoal. The men took the blackened remains of the cooking fire and ate it. By morning they were a very motley-looking group. They were dirty and unshaven, with a ring of black charcoal around their mouths and sunken eyes. But the diarrhea had stopped.

The next day was more of the same but with no rabbits or rice to sustain them. They crawled through an evasion course with instructors walking through the course and sending students back to the start if their evasive techniques were poor enough that they'd be captured. Despite the assurance of no snakes on the course, one student jumped up out of his concealment when he found himself face to face with a rattlesnake.

Tired and hungry and getting more and more anxious, Coburn thought about the approaching final evasion and prison compound. Another thirty hours and he'd be done with it. Hell, he could tap dance for thirty hours, so why was he so scared?

Coburn took a big swallow of water from his canteen and told Vernon, who was resting against a tree, that his bowels were acting up and he'd better go find a bush to crap in. Behind some foliage away from the group, he bent down. He took the remaining bag of peanuts from his sock and ate the contents. Taking the three little foil packages out of his hat, he put two in his socks, opened the third one, and swallowed the little pill with a swig from his canteen. The piece of foil and the peanut wrapper went into a small hole he dug with his boot heel.

About a half an hour later, Coburn felt himself calming down. He was still hungry, but he also had a sense of well-being. Along with Vernon, who was now a full lieutenant, a jaygee flier, and four enlisted men, they were on the final land navigation exercise before the evasion and prison compound. With Vernon in the group, Coburn was not senior or in charge, and that suited him fine. He'd just tag along, and if something got fucked up, it wouldn't be his problem. Hell, we're almost done with all this school bullshit.

At the final predawn briefing, they were given their instructions. Unlike most of the previous days, they would not be in teams. As individuals they had to evade from the starting point through a heavily patrolled wooded area to a flagpole in a clearing. If they successfully evaded the patrolling guards and made it to the flagpole, they'd be given a peanut butter sandwich and a glass of milk and could rest until the siren went off. At that time they'd be taken to the POW compound.

If they were captured before they could get to the flagpole, they were sent directly to the compound. If they were not captured but did not make it to the flagpole before the siren went off, they were to stand up, walk directly to the clearing, and then be sent to the compound.

Once in the compound, they could attempt to escape. If they escaped and could evade the patrolling guards, they were to go to the flagpole, where the guards would give them another glass of milk, a peanut butter sandwich, and an hour's rest before sending them back to the prisoner compound.

If they saw an escape opportunity but it would involve physical danger such as strangling a guard or bludgeoning the guard with a rock, they were to say, "I have an escape." The guard would listen to the escape plan and decide if the prisoner could indeed leave the compound and try to evade to the flagpole, or be overcome and face the consequences.

The tranquilizer had erased Coburn's anxieties and replaced them with a mild sense of well-being. The lack of food and sleep compounded the effect, making him lightheaded and dull. He was well aware of what was happening to him and was adopting the super cautious and careful attitude of someone who has too much to drink and knows he's impaired but drives his car home anyway. Creeping in the right lane, fifteen miles per hour slower than everyone else.

Dawn broke, and the field instructors gave the signal to start. Coburn rushed into the woods, crouched, and froze. Telling himself to just be careful, he hid in some low foliage. Listening to the sounds of other students crashing through the bush, he waited the few seconds until it was silent. Getting ready to move forward, Coburn heard footsteps crossing behind him and froze in place. Probably one of the guards. When it was quiet, he peered around him and crawled, then ran, another hundred meters to another clump of bushes and vines. Again he froze and listened. Nothing. Coburn repeated his scooting and freezing four more times. The last time as he froze in position, he could hear footsteps behind him and in front of him. Peering through the leaves, he saw a person in a Soviet bloc uniform carefully and quietly walking through the brush. The man stopped for a second, raised his left arm straight up, and held it there. Another guard silently walked up to the first.

With a few hand gestures, they quickly took a few steps, reached down, and pulled a student to his feet by his field jacket collar. They hit him on the side of the head and yelled at him to walk directly to the flagpole and report that he'd been captured. Coburn didn't move. He just stayed in position. He could see the flagpole above the tree line. He was about a hundred meters away from the clearing. His heart started pounding.

Coburn lay there until the siren went off. As soon as he stood up, he felt two hands grab his shoulders and push him to the ground. He fell and saw a pair of shiny leather boots in his face. Strong hands grabbed his collar and hoisted him back to his feet.

"What, you were going to lie there until the war was over, you shit?" the owner of the boots yelled in his face. "You deaf? I asked you a question, you idiot." He was shoved from behind and another voice said quietly, "Answer him."

"Coburn, Clark. Lieutenant Junior Grade, US Navy, 708311."

"That's not an answer," yelled the man in front and hit Coburn with a cupped fist on the side of his head, ringing his ears and stunning him. Again the quiet voice from behind repeated. "Answer him."

"Coburn, Clark. Lieutenant Junior Grade, US Navy, 708311"

Another cupped fist. "Take him to the clearing."

Coburn was pushed from behind to the flagpole. He was the last of the students.

"Here's your missing hero. He has wasted my time, and you all will suffer for it," bellowed the owner of the shined boots to the other prisoners. They were herded into the compound and put into ranks with shoves and smacks before a wooden building with a low porch. The commandant walked out onto the porch and stood with legs apart, hands on his hips. "Who's in charge of this?"

The students looked around, and then Lieutenant Commander Theodore stepped forward, giving his name, rank, and serial number. The commandant ordered a guard to bring him into the building. In a few minutes, yells, thuds, and slaps could be heard coming from the open doorway. The prisoners stood in their ranks looking around and started to talk, trying to figure out who was next in the chain of command. They were silenced by yelling and smacks. Several more students were taken away to different parts of the compound.

Being the junior officer in the class, Coburn was not going to worry about ever being the senior officer. And there was no way in hell he'd step up for it, either. He'd just ride this one out until it was over.

The men were told that they smelled and to strip to make sure they were not tic and lice infested. A shock of alarm went through Coburn. He had to get the pills out of his socks. They all undressed. When Coburn took off his socks he palmed the pills. Feigning a cough, he put the two little foil packs between his cheeks and gums. He winced as the foil reacted with one of his fillings.

Coburn was surprised to see that he had several blood-engorged ticks on his waistline. Several guards walked up and down the ranks, looking at the naked men and pushing through their clothes with bamboo canes. They stopped at one pile, conferred a minute, and then grabbed the naked owner of the pile and put him into a metal box about a meter high with an air slit and slammed the lid. They drummed on the box with their canes and then went back to inspecting the clothing piles and the naked men. The sun was high in the cloudless sky, and the heat was suffocating.

"Give these pigs a bath, I can't stand the smell. Put their clothes on, I can't stand the sight," yelled an unseen voice.

Two guards turned on a hose, and the men were sprayed with ice-cold water. The man in the metal box was hauled out and dumped on the ground and sprayed. The hoses stopped, and one of the naked men stepped forward and turned to the others.

"I'm Lieutenant Commander Kent. Unless otherwise directed by someone senior to me, I'm the acting officer in charge. Get dressed."

Immediately two of the guards grabbed Kent and put him in the metal box. Another officer stepped forward and mimicked Kent's proclamation, and he was dragged off to another part of the compound. Three more officers stepped forward, and each was taken away. But the next was not. Coburn didn't know any of these volunteers and was glad to see the attrition stop before it got down to him.

As he dressed, Coburn put one of the pills back into his sock and palmed the other, removing the foil as he pretended to be untying a knot in a bootlace. Rubbing his mouth, he popped the pill into his mouth and swallowed it. The bit of foil went into his sock.

The acting senior officer was demanding that the guards give the prisoners water and food. A burly guard dragged him up into the commandant's office. But the water spigots that the two bath hoses were connected to were unguarded and left trickling. The prisoners started stealing and guzzling water behind the guards' backs.

Coburn was in a haze, carefully keeping a low profile. He made no attempt to escape or take a leadership role as the prisoners were assigned cleanup duties or brought in for interrogation. At dusk, he snuck the last pill into his mouth and swallowed.

Standing with a rake as part of a work group in the cold dark, Coburn felt calm, detached, as if asleep with his eyes open.

Despite having guzzled water at every opportunity, his mouth felt full of cotton, his throat dry. Two guards walked up to him, grabbed him, and dragged him into the commandant's office.

A guard he had never seen before sat at the desk. "Mr. Coburn Clark, you sign this, please." He shoved a piece of paper and a pen in front of him. "It's a simple agreement. You agree to answer some questions, and we will give your men something to eat and drink and let them get some rest."

"Coburn, Clark. Lieutenant Junior Grade, US Navy, 708311," he slurred.

"Come on now, Mr. Clark, we already know the answers to the questions we want to ask you, so you will not be telling me anything new."

"Coburn, Clark. Lieutenant Junior Grade, US Navy, 708311."

After another five minutes of cajoling, another guard stepped forward, said he was out of patience, and hit Coburn with a cupped fist, ringing his ears. This time Coburn didn't even bother to give his name, rank, and serial number but just sat there in a drugged stupor. The gentle guard put a glass of water in front of him and told him to drink. Coburn just sat there, staring at the glass.

"Enough of this shit," yelled the impatient guard, and Coburn felt himself being dragged out of the chair, onto the porch, and across the compound to the metal box. He was made to crouch inside, and the lid slammed shut.

The box was cold, and Coburn shivered at first, but after a while he stopped, almost dozing off. At some time he urinated, soaking his trousers and socks. He had no idea how long he had been in the box when he heard the lid being opened and two guards hoisted him out onto his feet. He was unsteady, wobbly. They pushed him roughly to the courtyard in front of the commandant's office, where all the students stood in rank, with Theodore at the head. Coburn stood next to Vernon. He was still in a mellow, tranquilized daze.

The commandant came out to the porch and directed Theodore to have his men do an about-face. They did so, and there at the top of a flagpole waved the flag of the United States of America, illuminated by a spotlight. "The Star Spangled Banner" blared out of an unseen speaker. Spontaneously, all the men sang the national anthem, many of them crying. When the music stopped, the commandant said, "Welcome to America."

As the sun came up, the men were served milk and hot oatmeal from a large, steaming pot.

The thirteen weeks of advisor training had come to an end.

CHAPTER 11
HANOI

Vo, Ninh, and Ky stood before Senior Colonel Ong's desk at the Transportation Group headquarters. Rising from his desk chair, he waved them to seats at the conference table and sat himself opposite them. Maps were strewn across the table. A tough-looking female clerk in uniform brought in four small glass cups of intensely bitter coffee floating on thick, sweet condensed milk.

The map nearest Vo was labeled with a southern province name and marked with grid lines. It was extremely detailed, far more so than the maps they had used in the field exercises. It was marked with the seal of the Corps of Engineers and a date stamp from the Map Division, Library of Congress. This was an American map. He looked up and saw Senior Colonel Ong looking at him.

"Yes, Lieutenant Vo, this map is American. Don't be so surprised. They have the best training, the best weapons, the best equipment, the best food. So why shouldn't they also produce the best maps? And why shouldn't we use them? Especially since they are so readily available." Ninh and Ky looked at the maps near them, and Vo translated the seal and the date stamp to them.

"Sir, they even have the names of places and things in both Vietnamese and English," exclaimed Ky.

"Yes, Lieutenant, they do. I'm sure they did not mean to be so accommodating to the people." They all sipped their cafe sua.

"Let's get started," the senior officer said and drained his cup.

Without being beckoned, the clerk appeared, cleared away the empty cups, rolled up the maps, and laid them neatly on the conference table in some order indecipherable to the three young officers. She carried out the cups and some papers from the senior officer's outbox and closed the door.

"Lieutenants, we are destined to reunite Vietnam. It will not happen tomorrow. But it will happen. Our strategic plans look more than twelve years ahead. And even that may not be enough time. But it will happen. That is our fate, the people's destiny."

Ong paused for a moment. "The Americans will not have the stomach for this fight. Their political climate at home will eventually make them leave. Their puppets, the Southerners, will be worn down, and corruption will rot them from within. No matter what the Americans, Australians, and Koreans do to help the Southerners fight and rule, they will fall. Your mission is a strategic one."

He pushed back his chair and walked to his desk, took three folders, and gave them to the three men.

"Here is a historical synopsis of six victories and failures in warfare. Napoleon in Czarist Russia, the Germans in the Soviet Union during the Great Patriotic War, the American General Patton in mainland Europe in 1944 and 1945, the Americans in the Pacific from 1942 to 1945, the British in Malaya, and the Chinese and Americans in Korea in 1951. You will read this and discuss the lessons to be learned. I want you to focus on one major issue—the logistics required to fight a war over a great distance.

"Napoleon and the Germans were defeated as much by lack of supplies as they were by the spirit of the Russian proletariat. The Americans used far more troops to move fuel and equipment and ammunition and men than actually faced the enemy. They spent their treasure wisely."

"The effects of your labors," he poked a finger at each of them, "will be part of a system that will support a liberation army at great distances, but also over a long period of time—years, decades—as long as it takes."

The clerk again appeared without being summoned and pinned several of the maps onto a bulletin board. The maps covered the area from the Cambodian border to the southeast edge of Saigon. Through the middle of the maps snaked the Saigon River. The clerk stood beside the bulletin board with a pointer. Without looking at the maps, Ong outlined their mission.

"The area that Sergeant Nguyet is outlining with her pointer will be your area of responsibility. Essentially the Saigon River and the bordering land, from the Cambodian border into Saigon. A rudimentary and limited supply line has been created by some of my people and the National Liberation Front from Cambodia down the Saigon River and from the Mekong Delta and Saigon up the river."

Sergeant Nguyet moved her pointer as the senior officer talked.

"The river can be an effective means of moving large amounts of material, especially in this area. Movement by land is difficult but feasible by trucks on these roads parallel to the river. And as you can see, this is the shortest path to Saigon from any of our land borders."

Vo recognized the locations of several large American and Southerner bases in the area. "Sir, may I ask a question?" Ong nodded. "There is a large American and Southern force presence in the area, and given the proximity to Saigon, there must be air and artillery support available within minutes. A truck convoy or barge loaded with war material would be easily detected and destroyed."

Ong interrupted him. "You are correct, Lieutenant Vo. That is a problem, a major problem. And I expect you and your two comrades here to move material in a manner that will not allow it to be destroyed. That is your mission, and your fate."

"Yes, sir." Vo realized the enormousness of what he was being asked to do.

"In order to fight, to liberate, we need men, weapons, communications, equipment, fuel, food, money, and medicines. Some we can get from the land, some from the people, and some from the enemy. And some must come from outside, from our friends and allies.

"Lieutenants, listen carefully. You are directed to be the representatives of the People's Army of Vietnam and the National Liberation Front in the Phu Cuong area. This may be a more difficult task for you than moving vital materials." Sergeant Nguyet put her pointer on the town of Phu Cuong where the Saigon River made a sharp turn before flowing under a concrete highway bridge.

"This area is between the NLF units that are responsible for Saigon and the units operating to the northwest of this bridge. Lack of coordination and arguments over areas of responsibility and priorities of operations and supplies have cost us lives. Our NLF comrades have the same goal as we do—reunification under a people's government. But our NLF comrades can also be stubborn and look at the People's Army as interlopers."

He leaned on his elbows, hands steepled in front of him. "I expect you to show initiative and turn this around. You will go on operations with them. You will live with them. You will fight alongside them. This is as much a job for a soldier and an officer as it is for a logistician.

"Lastly, I want you to keep forever in your mind that this is independent duty. You will report to me administratively, and the NLF and People's Army regiment across the border will help and support your efforts. But you are essentially on your own. Communications will be slow and unreliable at best. When you leave here in two weeks, you will have your orders and all the briefing we can give you. After that, I expect you to act accordingly. If you have to ask for permission or how to do something, by the time you get the answer—if you ever do—it will be too late. I am expecting you to act decisively for the good of the people."

Sergeant Nguyet left the room, shutting the door behind her. The senior officer went on to describe what the next two weeks would entail. They were expected to be at headquarters from 0800 to 1900 every day but Sunday for briefings and study. They would apply their own experience and education and the information presented to them to problems posed to them during the two weeks. They would give presentations of their solutions and recommendations to selected senior staff officers and occasionally to Ong. They would spend the last day reviewing their orders with the group commander.

"A few final words, Lieutenants, and then you can start reading your files. First, this is classified. You will not discuss this outside of this building, not even among yourselves. No notes will be taken; you must commit everything to memory. I do not want the enemy finding documents on your body." He gave each man a cold, piercing stare, which they answered with silent nods.

"You have been assigned an office for your work here. Lectures and all discussions will be conducted in that office and nowhere else. I do not want you in uniform. You will be provided a small allowance to purchase civilian clothes to wear. After you finish for the day, your time is your own." His formality relaxed a bit. "I know you are all from this area, so I suggest you take advantage of that. It will be a long time before you return." He smiled. Vo immediately thought of Ngoc. She didn't even know he was in Hanoi.

"Sir," said Vo. "May we write letters or visit family and friends?"

"Yes. But you are to not discuss any part of what goes on here nor your mission. You may tell them your departure date but not your destination. Letters will be reviewed by one of my staff officers." He leaned back in his chair.

"We're done for this morning. Each morning, check in with Sergeant Nguyet, and each evening check out with her. Tell her where you will be at all times. When we finish now, see her for your clothing allowance and work room location." Ky's expression caught the senior colonel's eye. "Something wrong, Lieutenant Ky?"

Startled, Ky blushed. "No sir."

"Then why the odd look?"

Ky smiled. "Sir, no offense to Sergeant Nguyet, but she reminds me of Senior Instructor Pham. I don't mean she looks like him, I mean..."

Ong laughed. "Lieutenant, I know exactly what you mean. If it's any comfort, your feelings are shared by many. Now, you three get to your duties."

* * *

The gray predawn light outside Ngoc's open apartment window woke up Vo. After several months of military training, he was accustomed to early morning wake-ups. Ngoc had her back nestled against him. A sheet and her body kept him warm in the chill of early morning. He lay there, his arm draped over her waist—enjoying the intimacy, the privacy, and her. All of which would be difficult, if not impossible, to recapture in a dozen days. He kissed her shoulder, gently, trying not to wake her but hoping she would awaken. Ngoc moved her buttocks closer to him but did not open her eyes. Vo became excited and hard.

Ngoc moved harder against him and put his hand on her breast. She turned to face him, her eyes still closed, and kissed him hard. He pushed her onto her back and kissed the line from her ear down her neck to her chest and nipples, causing her to arch her back and breathe deeply through her nostrils. "Oh, Vo, I love you so much. I love you too much."

"I'm glad you do, Ngoc. I love you. You're so much a part of me."

Ngoc opened her eyes and smiled at him. She moved her arms up his back and spread her long, slim legs. Putting his weight on his elbows, Vo moved over her and then into her. They made slow, silent love as the day grew lighter.

The evening before, Ngoc had answered a knock on her door to find Vo standing there, smiling.

"Want to go for coffee, Ngoc?"

Stunned, she stood there staring at him, unable to answer, unable to move. Then, as tears welled up in her eyes, she stepped out into the hallway, put her arms around him, and hugged him, her head on his chest.

"Vo. What are you doing here? I...I knew you were coming to Hanoi, but I...I..." she kissed him, never releasing her bear hug hold on him. "I don't want to go for coffee. I want to just stand here like this."

He laughed and untangled his arms and wrapped them around her.

"Fine, Ngoc. But I think we'd better move into your apartment instead of blocking the hallway."

She laughed, grabbed his hand, and led him to her small table and chairs. They talked over tea, Ngoc either holding his hand or stroking his forearm or rubbing his shoulders.

She asked about his training and what he would be doing next. He described Senior Instructor Pham and his two comrades, Ninh and Ky. Apologizing, Vo said he could not tell her more, except that after the next week, he had three days' leave and then would leave Hanoi. He didn't know when he would be back after that.

Her face grew sad as she listened. She looked at the tabletop somberly, kneading Vo's hand. Then she looked up and smiled at him.

"But you are here now. And with me. Will I see you again before you go?"

"You will see me so much that you will be tired of seeing me, Ngoc."

"Impossible. Will you visit your parents during those three days before you have to leave?"

"Yes, I am planning on spending those days with them. I would very much like you to be with me."

"Classes will not be in session that whole week. Yes, please take me with you. I like your parents very much, Vo."

"Good. They like you, too."

It was getting late, and Vo felt awkward. He wanted to stay, but he was not sure. Would it be too presumptuous? Too forward? She answered the questions for him.

"When do you have to be back?"

"I have to report to headquarters at 8:00."

She smiled, stood up, and pressed his head against her breasts.

* * *

While they waited for Sergeant Nguyet to bring them a package of reading material, Ky looked over at Vo.

"What?" Vo asked.

"Nothing."

Ninh said, "Nothing? Ky, it's never 'nothing' with you. What's up?"

"Since you ask, Ninh. Have you noticed that we don't see much of our good Comrade Vo these days? We've been here in Hanoi a week, and I see him here with us. I see him at about 7:00 each morning before we walk over here. But I don't see him at other times. Just wondering if our good comrade has been corrupted by some Hanoi beauty and he will defect, leaving us to win victory by ourselves."

Vo said, straight faced, "Defect? You know, I hadn't thought of that. What a wonderful idea. Thanks, Ky. I'll be sure to tell Transportation Group Commander Ong that you recommended I do so."

Ninh joined in. "That is a good idea. I'll join you, Vo."

Ky laughed.

"Wait a second," Ninh resumed. "I just figured out what Ky's trying to do. He's trying to get rid of us. Do you know why?"

Vo shook his head. "No I don't. Now why would our good Comrade Ky want to get rid of his two best cell mates?"

"He's in love with Sergeant Nguyet and wants to get rid of the competition. He gets us out of the way and then convinces Senior Colonel Ong that Sergeant Nguyet should take our place. She weighs about as much as the two of us put together. Then he and she can have a honeymoon on the banks of the beautiful Saigon River until the war is over."

"Of course, Ninh, he and she and that pointer she uses on the map. She can whip him with that when he doesn't perform properly."

"Tell me, Ky," demanded Ninh. "What's she like? Is it true she wears lace underpants and bra? You keep on talking in your sleep about her. She must be a real demon when you give her the full Lieutenant Ky love bullet."

Vo added, "I hear she collects miniatures, so she must really like you, Ky."

Sergeant Nguyet walked in before Ky could defend himself. She passed out the three packets of briefing material and noticed that Ninh was smiling broadly, Vo had on his usual stone face, and Ky was staring at the desk, blushing brilliantly. Odd bunch, these three. Senior Colonel Ong likes them—but why?

As he opened his packet, Vo turned to his two friends. "Tomorrow's our day off. My friend Ngoc has asked me to invite you two for a picnic lunch at the Lake of the Rosewood Sword. Since the bombing stopped, it's not a bad place. We'll bring the food; you two can bring some beer or something."

"Thanks, Vo. I'd like to go very much," answered Ninh.

"Me too. I'd like to meet Ngoc," said Ky.

"She'd like to meet you, too. I've told her about you two." Vo paused and made a serious face as he scratched his chin. "But I don't know, Ky, she might be too attracted to you."

"Does she like tiny, little miniatures?" asked Ninh.

"I don't think so. But she's in medical school, and maybe she can provide a few more centimeters with some enhancement surgery. She can probably do that tomorrow. She's smart and is always looking for a challenge. I'll bring a sharp knife and sewing needle."

"It's inevitable that she will find my charms overwhelming and immediately ask me to seduce her," said Ky. "I'm sorry, Vo, but that's what happens to me all the time. It's a curse being this charming and handsome, but I bear it."

"That explains why Sergeant Nguyet keeps on making eyes at you," teased Ninh.

"Don't worry, Ky, Ngoc and Sergeant Nguyet are very good girlfriends, and so Ngoc invited her, too."

"Vo, you are kidding me, now. Aren't you? Sergeant Nguyet's not going to be there, is she?"

"Comrades, I think we'd better get to work," said Vo as he and Ninh started to read the briefing material. Ky realized he was not going to get an answer and, yes, they had work to do.

* * *

The next day Ninh and Ky met Vo and Ngoc at the lake. The park was crowded with women with children, older couples, and young men in uniform enjoying the bombing halt and sunshine.

The three young officers and the medical student ate the cold foods Ngoc had prepared and drank the beers that Ninh and Ky had brought. Ngoc immediately liked Ninh and Ky, although she thought them very different personalities. For that matter, neither was like Vo. But they were obviously devoted to and enjoyed one another. She laughed at the tales of Senior Instructor Pham and Sergeant Nguyet, whom Ninh kept on referring to as Ky's fiancé.

A youth with a guitar and a young girl were sitting on the grass not far from them. Ninh said he hoped the fighting would end before the young guitar player was old enough for conscription into the People's Army.

"I hope the fighting ends before you three have to leave," said Ngoc somberly.

"So do we, Ngoc," said Ky. "But our destiny is victory and unification, and I don't think that will happen in a week and a half."

"Still, I want this fighting to end. I know that sounds selfish. But it's how I feel."

In a surprisingly husky-throated voice, the girl sang as the boy played the guitar. Seated on Ngoc's blanket, the three men and the one woman listened, not talking. Vo reached over and held Ngoc's hand.

At dusk Ninh and Ky took a xyclo back to the officers' quarters, and Vo and Ninh walked to her apartment.

"I like your friends, Vo. They're really nice."

"They're more than friends, Ngoc. They're family, comrades. The three of us together are far more than just three lieutenants." He was silent as they walked several blocks. "And they liked you, Ngoc. Very much. I could tell."

"That's nice to hear. And I understand what you say about your camaraderie. But I'm partial to just one of the trio."

Vo smiled and shook his head. "I knew it. I knew you'd fall for Ky. Now I'm left with Sergeant Nguyet." She laughed and playfully hit his chest, then tightly wrapped her arm around his, her head on his shoulder.

* * *

It was their last day at headquarters. In three more days they would finally start the journey south. They reported to Sergeant Nguyet, who told them that transportation was waiting to take them to the military medical clinic. There they would be examined by a dentist and have their teeth x-rayed. She added coldly that that was necessary for body identification. When they returned an hour later, she said that Senior Colonel Ong would be seeing them in five minutes. They took seats in the outer office as she worked through a pile of papers on her desk. She looked at them.

"Lieutenants, you should know that Senior Colonel Ong will be promoted to brigadier general the first of January. We have just received word from the People's Army General Staff."

"That's good news, Sergeant Nguyet," said Ky. "Should we congratulate him? Is that proper?"

"I think it appropriate, Lieutenant, but be very military in your bearing when you do so."

A few minutes later, Sergeant Nguyet showed them into Ong's office. He was sitting at his conference table and motioned them to seats. Unlike other visits, the table was bare except for three thick envelopes.

"Your last day, Lieutenants. Now it all begins. This will be your final briefing. It will be short. When you leave here, Sergeant Nguyet will provide you with identification, transportation passes, and money. The morning after your three days' leave, you will report directly to the transportation section at 0700. I will not see you again before you go south.

"First off, your transportation. I was hoping to send you by an allied merchant vessel to Sihanoukville and then overland to the northeast to your insertion point near Loc Ninh. Unfortunately, the Americans seem to have cultivated a new friend in Cambodia, and that route is closed to both our men and material. It's too risky.

"So you will instead go west into Cambodia and down the Truong Son Strategic Supply Route to your insertion point. You will be met by Transportation Group liaison officers at each way station. They have my instructions to move you as fast as possible. If you cover twenty-five kilometers in a day, that will be a lot. It will take you several weeks, maybe months, until Loc Ninh. Lieutenants, be patient in your travel. It is more important to our mission that you be there than to be there quickly. The route is dangerous, and haste and impatience may get you and your comrades killed. Any questions?"

There were none. They had gone over the transportation to the south many times during these two weeks.

"Secondly, you have obviously developed a camaraderie and spirit between you, a band of brothers, so to speak. A trio of equals. Very good implementation of our people's doctrine. But

I must have someone in charge—an older brother, one who's a little more equal than the other two." He looked directly at Vo.

"Lieutenant Vo, you are in charge." Ong didn't ask if there were any questions.

Vo nodded, his face expressionless. Ong looked at him a bit longer. The other two glanced at Vo, both with smiles on their faces. Typical, thought Ong. And good. Egos could be toxic in a combat unit.

"Lastly, and I know you have been briefed extensively, you will be carrying money. American dollars, US Military Payment Certificates, Southern piasters, French francs. You will need this to lubricate your mission. In the South, bribes are the grease of government—from the local hamlet to the presidential palace. If one of you dies, the survivors must take his money. You will need it. Any questions?" As he expected, there were none.

"Good. Lieutenants, you have been selected and trained well for a vital mission for the people of your nation. Victory and reunification are your destiny." He stood up. "Please see Sergeant Nguyet now. Good bye."

The three young men stood up and snapped to attention. "Sir, Sergeant Nguyet has informed us that you are being promoted to general rank. Please accept our congratulations," said Vo.

"The passage of time, Lieutenant Vo, simply the passage of time."

IN TRANSIT

CHAPTER 12
CORONADO, CALIFORNIA

Coburn fell into a deep, drugged sleep as soon as he sat down next to Vernon in the navy bus taking them back to Coronado after SERE. He felt someone nudging him.

Vernon said, "Hey, you okay? We're almost at the base."

Disoriented, Coburn looked around, not sure where he was. He shook his head clear and rubbed his face with his palms, then stretched. "Thanks, Doug. My mouth feels like cotton, and it tastes as if you took a shit in it while I was sleeping."

"I did."

Theodore got up from his front seat and held onto the grab bar in the swaying bus.

"Listen up! Wake up! For all you advisors, our orders are ready at the admin office. If you want to get out of here before Monday, you need to pick them up no later than 1800 today. I suggest you go to your quarters, shit, shower, shave, and get in the uniform of the day and check out. Then go back and sleep. I don't want any one of you getting on the road until you've had some sleep."

A marine guard waved the bus into the base.

"What you doing, Doug? When you leaving?"

"I'll pick up my orders today but won't check out until tomorrow. My girlfriend will be flying in early tomorrow morning."

"Girlfriend? You mean that girl from your adolescent, pimple-dorky days?"

"The very same. I'm bringing her back to the base, and we'll grab some brunch or something at the O club. Wanna join us? 0930 or 1000 or so?"

"Sure, why not? Do me a favor. If you don't see me by 1000, throw a hand grenade into my room."

"Hand grenade, aye. You've been sleeping like you're drugged or something."

* * *

The O club's dining room was full with the Saturday breakfast crowd.

Coburn walked in. He felt much better. After picking up his orders, he fell asleep on top of the covers in his dirty jungle fatigues, finally waking after fifteen hours of sleep. He picked off two blood-engorged tics, took a long hot shower, shaved in the shower, and then scrubbed his body and hair all over again. Unlike at sea, there were no water hours in the Q. He put on civilian clothes.

Vernon was waving at him from the far corner of the room. Theodore was eating at a nearby table, with an attractive woman and two boys who looked to be around eight and ten years old. A couple other classmates were also eating. Coburn waved back at Vern but walked over to Theodore to say hello. The wife and kids had driven down from Long Beach and were helping Dad pack up his BOQ room.

Vernon stood up as Coburn approached the table. "Well, Sleeping Beauty, I almost had the pin pulled on the grenade." A good-looking young woman sat across the table. "Jean, I want you to meet Clark Coburn. Clark, Jean Miller."

"Hi, Jean. Doug's told me about you."

Jean smiled and looked at Vernon. "He did, did he?"

172

"Yep, and I don't believe a word he said about you and the football team, or that the Cub Scout troop has a restraining order keeping you a hundred yards away from their campground."

She laughed. "Well, Clark, at least I can trust what he says to be the truth. All those stories are true."

"Can I join you two?"

"No," said Vernon, pointing at the seat next to Jean.

"I'm starved. The last thing I ate was a bowl of oatmeal about a month ago," said Coburn.

"I couldn't wait," said Vernon. "Went over to the Mexican Village last night and ate two of the enchilada *grande* platters. Waitress looks at me and says, 'Just got back from SERE, huh?' But I'm hungry all over again."

Jean looked at the two of them. "Isn't the navy famous for its food? You mean they don't feed you two?"

"Well, chow's not bad as a rule. But somehow the brass has figured out that survival is synonymous with starvation," said Vernon.

"Amen to that, Doug. I'm going to carry a survival pack wherever I go filled with Oreos, fried chicken, and butter pecan ice cream. Just in case I get captured."

Over grapefruits, plates of eggs Benedict, mounds of toast and endless cups of coffee, the three sat and chatted for nearly two hours, often breaking out into loud laughter. Coburn found himself stealing glances at Jean.

She was cute and sexy, not classically pretty, with large blue eyes and a turned-up nose. Her smile came easily and lit up her face. Full lips. Dark brown hair, straight and full. Buxom, broad shouldered, but not husky or fat. Muscled, athletic, tanned. He wondered what her breasts were like. What she would be like in bed? He moved his knee toward her as far as he could, but there was no contact, not even the accidental brush. She laughed as easily as she smiled. The meal was moving much too fast for Coburn. He wanted to be near her.

"So what are your plans? You two going straight up to San Francisco?"

Vernon answered. "No, we're going to wander up the coast. Jean's never been out here before. We'll hit the zoo and Sea World and Disneyland, Hearst Castle, all the good stuff."

"I also want to see some more of this navy Doug's so in love with."

"Sure, we'll drive around and visit a base or two. We'll spend a night in Monterey or Carmel. Visit the PG school."

Coburn said, "PG school, huh? Detailer says he's put my name in for screening. Might be my orders after this tour."

"What's PG school?" asked Jean.

Vernon answered. "Naval Post Graduate School, in Monterrey. Navy graduate work. This dummy has suckered the detailer into thinking he can pass remedial counting, much less grad school."

"I can't help it if the navy is perceptive enough to recognize my genius-like prowess. It's my burden. Sometimes I wish I were just barely illiterate like you, Doug. What's it like?"

"Well, I sort of like it, Clark. By the way, what's illiterate mean?"

"You two better stop it. Every time I take a drink of coffee you make me laugh, and it'll come out my nose."

"Wow," said Coburn. "That would be so cool. Boogers and coffee. C'mon, Jean, do it. I'll give you a dollar."

"Man, I knew you were the girl for me," Vernon added. "But I didn't realize just how really perfect you are. Who else has a girlfriend who can shoot coffee-snot out of her nose?"

Jean had her napkin against her mouth, trying to hold back the coffee and laughter as her face turned red. She finally controlled herself and quit laughing long enough to swallow her coffee.

"I almost won a dollar just then." She took a deep sigh. "What's your plan, Clark?"

"I'm out of here after this. Throw the bags in the rental car and turn it in, and then my friend will pick me up. We're going to drive up the coast in her car. Maybe up to the wine country for a free hangover. San Francisco the last two days. She'll drop me off at Travis late Saturday since we're flying out very early Sunday morning."

He looked at Jean and let his eyes move down to her chest. Then he turned to Vernon.

"Want to meet in Monterey?" Coburn asked. "When are you going to be there?"

"Let's see. Right now we're looking at getting in early Wednesday and staying there that night. Want to get together for dinner?"

"Sure, there's a place there that Marty Lender told me about that is supposed to be a once-in-a-lifetime gourmet meal. Gallatin's. After what we've been eating during SERE and running around Pendleton, we owe it to ourselves, buddy."

"I'll make reservations for four at 1900 when I get in Monterey. Gallatin's, right? That'll be fun," said Vernon.

They talked a little more, and then Coburn said he had to get going. Together they walked out of the O club, and Vernon reached out his hand and said they'd see him soon in Monterey. After he shook hands, Coburn turned to Jean, who smiled and gave him a hug. He briefly held her tight, pressing her into his chest. As he said goodbye to her, his hand, as if by accident, brushed against her breast. Her smile didn't change when she turned away and grabbed Vernon's arm as they walked to his car.

Coburn thought that in nearly every way, Jean Miller was the opposite of Ba Hung.

* * *

Coburn and Kelly walked into Gallatin's restaurant Wednesday evening. For the first time in a long time, Coburn was in a coat and tie. He spotted Vernon similarly attired at a table for four with Jean Miller. The restaurant was plush, quiet, elegant.

Vernon and Jean stood up as the couple threaded their way through the dining room. Jean gave Coburn a welcoming hug but instead of wrapping her arms around him, held him by his arms so only their cheeks touched. Vernon kissed the nurse on her cheek. The two men shook hands, and Vernon introduced the two women.

"Jean, I'd like to introduce Kelly Meredith. Kelly, Jean Miller." Both women were dressed in fashionable summer dresses with heels, and sweaters on their shoulders to ward off the Monterey fog-induced chill. Coburn told Jean that she looked nice.

The four immediately started chatting comfortably and ordered drinks from the tuxedoed waiter, who put the leather-bound menus in front of them, took the linen napkins from the silver napkin rings, and draped them across the women's laps. He recommended the house specialty of mushrooms in cream as a starter, chateaubriand with roasted vegetables, and then the crepes suzette or peach melba for dessert. As he left to place the drink order, the four decided that they were all hungry and the recommendations sounded perfect. They didn't bother to read the menus.

The meal was perfect. A bottle of recommended wine was followed by a second. Brandy and coffee followed the dessert. As Vernon told a funny story of waking up his ship's skipper to come and look at a strange light that turned out to be a rising moon, Kelly affectionately covered Coburn's hand with her own. He shot a quick glance at Jean to see if she reacted. Jean was laughing, her head back, her hand on Vernon's forearm.

"Doug, come next week I don't think we're going to be eating like this, surrounded by such pulchritude."

"Clark, I think you and I are in for a year of fish heads, rice, and Tums for the tummy."

Kelly laughed. "Jean, let's you and I send them CARE packages every week with this same meal. We'll ask the waiter for the recipes. I'll make the roasted vegetables, you make everything else."

"Good luck with that. My cooking, along with a week or two of sitting in some mail pile, will require the navy to buy them their own personal stomach pumps."

"Sounds like your cooking is as good as mine. Forget that idea." Kelly looked at Vernon and Coburn. "Looks like you two are stuck with the fish heads. But I'll send you lots of Tums."

"Thanks, you two are real sisters of mercy," said Coburn. "Fortunately for the time being, I am pleasantly stuffed. But I think I may have a wee bit of a headache tomorrow morning."

They all felt the same way.

"You don't have to drive a long way, do you?" asked Vernon.

"No, we're just down the road in Pacific Grove at the Butterfly Lodge. We'll go to Napa Valley in the morning. Where you staying?"

"Carmel. We'll go up to San Francisco Friday afternoon."

They walked out of the restaurant into the Monterey fog. The two women were holding the young officers' arms, leaning against them. Jean shivered a bit in the cold, and Vernon took off his suit jacket and put it over her shoulders.

"Thanks, honey, you're a real gentleman," said Jean as she put her head on Vernon's shoulder. "This is so beautiful. I want to come back here again." She looked at Kelly. "Let's plan that. When these two come back, let's re-create this evening."

Kelly smiled and nodded. "Great idea. Give me your address and phone number. Let's make sure we keep in touch."

Coburn had a smile on his face, but the last thing he wanted was for this nurse to plan his future—and do so with Jean.

Both women dove into their purses and began scribbling their numbers and addresses on scraps of paper. Vernon and Coburn shook hands and said they'd see each other at Travis early Sunday morning. The women hugged each other's dates, Jean still keeping Coburn away from her body with a sturdy grip on his arms.

Coburn suggested that he and Kelly walk around the Naval Post Graduate School grounds to let the food settle and his head clear before driving to Pacific Grove. They walked arm in arm past the library, where students could be seen studying at the long wooden tables. They walked on the green before the big administration building, an old *grand dame* of a hotel that the navy had converted.

"Clark, they're really a nice couple. Real fun, seem very happy with each other. I can see why."

"Yeah, Doug's a good guy."

"Cute couple. Jean's a sweetie, too. I think she's very attractive."

"Think so? I guess. A little too chunky for me," said Clark in an uninterested voice.

Kelly stopped and stood in front of Coburn. She put her hands around his waist and drew him to her. "I love you, Clark."

"I love you, Kelly," Coburn answered and kissed her. Why did he say that? Too much to drink? Did he really like her? Or was he just trying to make her feel good?

* * *

Kelly sat on the bed while Coburn talked to his parents from the hotel room atop Nob Hill in San Francisco. In a few hours they would drive across the Bay Bridge and out to a motel in Fairfield near Travis AFB. Early Sunday she'd drop him off at the departure terminal.

He hung up the phone and looked at her. "What's wrong?" he asked.

"Clark, you told them about driving up the coast, dinner with Doug and Jean in Monterey, wine tasting, sight seeing...and you never mentioned that I was with you. That's what's wrong."

As was happening more and more frequently during the trip, Kelly was irritating him, but he kept her from seeing that. Great, just what he needed when trying to get underway with no attachments. Now she was pissed that he hadn't mention her to his parents, who still didn't understand why he hadn't come home to visit them and kept on asking what was happening with Betsy. Shit.

"I guess it did sound that way, but my mom was crying, and I was trying to get her mind off my leaving by giving her the travelogue. Hell, they knew weeks ago that you were traveling with me," He reached out and held her. "I guess I didn't say your name this call, but they mentioned you a couple of times. Want to meet you when I come back."

She looked at him skeptically, then relaxed and smiled.

Later that night they were in the Fairfield motel room, lying in bed. He wanted to catch a few hours' sleep before she drove him to the air base. She raised herself on an elbow and traced her finger down his jawbone and throat and let her hand come to rest on his chest.

"What's next for us, Clark? You and me?"

How did he answer that? If he screwed it up, she'd kick him out, and he'd wind up standing outside naked trying to get a taxi to the air base. That would make a funny story. She caught his smile.

"What's so funny, Clark? I say something funny?"

"No, no, hon. It's just your question. It's exactly what I was thinking. The problem is I don't know what's next for us. In a couple of hours I get on that plane, and then it's zip for a year. I don't even have an address yet for you to write to." He thought about what to say next. "What do you want to happen?"

"Clark, I love you. I do want a future with you. But if that's not going to happen, then I want to know that and move on with my life."

Coburn momentarily toyed with the opportunity to take her offer to let her move on with her life, but he didn't want to have to deal with the tears. Instead he said, "Well, you and I want the same thing." He kissed her breast.

CHAPTER 13
BINH NINH

Vo and Ngoc walked hand in hand in the rural sunshine. They had spent most of the two previous days with Vo's parents around a table never empty of food. Much to the benefit of whoever happened to be at the table, when Vo's mother was anxious, she cooked.

Her youngest son was going off to war, following his two brothers. The three boys were dedicated, intelligent, patriotic. She was proud of them. But she hated their going into harm's way. Vo's father felt exactly the same way. Vo's young woman was even more strident.

Ngoc made no attempt to hide her hatred for this war. But she knew that Vo had to do his duty. Not only for his country and his people, but for himself. Still, her dream was that a truce would be announced and rare peace would return to Vietnam. The cessation of the bombing of the North by the Americans had to be a harbinger, a sign of progress, to end this war.

The two young lovers walked back to the house. Soon they had to catch the bus back to Hanoi. Travel was much easier since the bombing halt, but the trains were still dedicated to military transport. Civilian travel was easier by bus.

Vo and Ngoc took a seat at the head of the table, and his mother put a plate of sweet rice cakes and cups of tea in front of them. Vo pushed a piece of paper across the table to his father and gave a duplicate to Ngoc.

"Here's how you can send me letters," Vo said. "The most reliable way. Send the letters to this address at the Transportation Group in Hanoi. You can hand carry them if you want to, which is probably faster than by post. They'll send your letters on to me.

"Whatever you send me will be read by a censor, and the same for what I send you. But ignore the censor's eyes. I'm sure you will have no military or state secrets to send, and neither will I. The censors don't care if you send someone your love or ask about someone's health and happiness."

"Who's this Sergeant Nguyet that we're supposed to send the letters attention to?" asked his father.

Ngoc giggled. "You mean Lieutenant Ky's fiancé?"

Vo's father gave her a raised-eyebrow, questioning look.

"Sergeant Nguyet is the administrative wizard at the Transportation Group headquarters," said Vo. "The sergeant is a very capable woman. She's sort of...imposing, I guess is the word I would use. And intimidating. But she gets the job done. She insisted that all correspondence to and from me go through her."

"Well, okay, Vo. But then who's Lieutenant Ky, and are they getting married?" asked his father. Ngoc burst out laughing, and Vo chuckled.

"Lieutenant Ky is my comrade whom I will be working with, along with another good friend, Lieutenant Ninh. We have been teasing Ky about Sergeant Nguyet since he's half her size, and despite his rank, afraid of her. For that matter, Ninh and I are pretty careful around Sergeant Nguyet." Vo smiled. "But there's no one I would trust more than her when it comes to communications."

Vo's parents waited with them at the bus stop. As the bus pulled up, his mother hugged Vo tightly as his father hugged

Ngoc. Then his mother turned to Ngoc, hugged her, and kissed her on her cheek as Vo's father hugged him.

"Don't worry, I'll be safe. I'll be back," said Vo as he followed Ngoc up onto the bus.

* * *

Despite the bombing halt, Hanoi was still blacked out at night. Vo and Ngoc walked quietly arm in arm from the bus terminal to her apartment. They spent the night, sleepless, making love in Ngoc's small bed. In the morning she walked with him to the Transportation Group headquarters.

In front of the guarded gate, Vo turned to Ngoc and hugged her. "I love you, Ngoc. I love you."

"Oh, Vo, I love you, too. You haven't even left, and my heart's breaking. I miss you already." Her voice was calm, soft, and steady but her eyes were filled with tears that ran down her face. "I will write you. And I will look after your parents, Vo."

"They want you to visit as much as you can. You're like a daughter to them."

She smiled, but still, tears rolled down her cheeks. "When I bring the letters here, maybe I'll be able to actually meet the infamous Sergeant Nguyet."

Vo smiled. "Maybe so. I have to go now. I love you, Ngoc."

"I have to go to class, too. I love you, Vo."

They both turned, and without looking back, Ngoc walked down the street and turned the corner as Vo presented his papers. As the sentry checked his clipboard, Ninh and then Ky walked up. The three warmly greeted one another and walked together to the transportation section. Waiting for them as they entered the transportation office was Sergeant Nguyet.

"Good morning, Lieutenants."

Vo nodded at her. "Sergeant Nguyet, good morning. We didn't expect to see you again."

"General Ong wants to make sure your travel orders are executed smartly, sir."

Within fifteen minutes they were processed. Sergeant Nguyet followed them out of the building. She held out three bracelets, simple bands of brass.

"Lieutenants, the staff wishes you to have these, to remember us. They're made out of the casings of spent artillery shells. Please be careful, and we wish you success."

Surprised, the three men looked at one another and took the bracelets, and Ky said, "Thank you, Sergeant. This is very unexpected. It would be impossible to forget you and your assistance."

Sergeant Nguyet opened both passenger-side doors of the waiting colonial-era Citroen sedan, snapped stiffly to attention, and saluted. The lieutenants saluted back and got in the car, and the driver eased out of the driveway on the way to a staging area outside of Hanoi.

* * *

After a series of gates and sentries, the Citroen dropped the three young officers at a nondescript building in the middle of a rail and truck yard. Sandbagged anti-aircraft missile and gun batteries surrounded the marshaling yard. Dug-out, reinforced air raid shelters as well as several one-person shelters—little more than garbage cans buried in the pavement with perforated cement lids—lined each truck lane and cargo-handling area. Reinforced concrete vehicle sheds lined the railroad tracks. Firefighting trucks and equipment were parked inside several of the sheds. The men walked through the open door of the building.

A harried army captain looked up from a pile of papers at the sound of the three pairs of tire-soled sandals walking toward him. "Ah, General Ong's three musketeers, right on time." He stubbed out what little that was left of his cigarette and immediately lit another. "Have a seat. You're priority personnel, and I have to get you to Vinh safely. The general's administrative NCO has called me several times the last few days to make sure I do my job." He shook his head as he leaned back in his chair and deeply inhaled.

"What's so funny?" he asked, looking at Ky.

"Captain, I'm assuming the NCO is Sergeant Nguyet? We spent the last few weeks at group headquarters and saw her every day. She's sort of...un..."

The captain finished Ky's sentence. "A bitch. A fucking bitch. I'm trying to move tons of supplies and hundreds of soldiers in and out of here each day, and she calls to nag me and remind me that the general wants this or the general wants that. Shit, I know what the fuck the general wants. I have my orders from him. She makes me want to go back down south. She's worse than the Americans. At least with them, I could shoot back." The captain stopped himself, shook his head, and smiled, then leaned forward in his seat.

"Even though the bombing has ceased, I still don't like moving a lot of vehicles during daylight. And I really don't want to move you three in daylight if I don't have to. There's a small convoy I'm sending to Vinh that will leave just before dusk. You'll be on it. With luck we'll have you in Vinh by dawn. The Vinh transportation manager will send you west from there."

He looked at the clock on the wall behind him. "You have eight hours until you load up. Be back here at 1600. Get some rest. There are bunks and a latrine in the back. A mess hall is in the next building. Eat and sleep; you'll need it. You can leave your gear here."

The three stretched out on cots, and within minutes all were sound asleep. None of them had slept in the last day and a half, having spent their time with their lovers.

Vo was the first to wake, groggy but unable to sleep due to the noise of the trucks and loading equipment. He used the latrine and splashed cold water on his face, then walked into the busy office. The captain nodded to Vo but kept silent with his ear to the telephone as he scribbled notes. Vo studied a detailed map on the wall. It covered both the People's Republic of Vietnam and South Vietnam as well as portions of China, Cambodia, Laos, and Thailand. Like the maps in General Ong's office, this one was American, produced by the Corps of Engineers and issued by the United States Library of Congress.

With his forefinger, Vo traced the route from Hanoi to Vinh and then tried to imagine what the route would be from there. Due west into Laos? Southwest across the demilitarized zone and into South Vietnam? Certainly into the Truong Son Mountains no matter what route they followed. Using his fingers as dividers, he tried to scale off the distance from Hanoi to the Saigon River northwest of Saigon.

"Figure about 1,300 kilometers to Saigon, Lieutenant Vo," said the captain, who was watching him. "Tonight's ride will be the easiest. Unless the Americans decide that the bombing halt is over."

"How long, how many days do you think, Captain?"

"I don't know where you are going. For good reason. I only know where your next stop will be—Vinh. That's how it will be for you. The only destination known at each way stop is the next stop for you three. But figure that after tonight, you might average twenty-five kilometers a day, give or take."

Vo nodded. He quickly calculated in his mind. A thousand kilometers from Vinh to the area of operations. That meant forty days of travel. If they traveled four days and then rested one, that would mean the journey would take about fifty days. They'd get there in the last days of summer, perhaps later. Maybe by then a truce would be reached and the war would be over. He was starting to think like Ngoc. A grim smile and shake of his head brought him back to the reality of the long battle ahead.

A few hours later, they checked their gear—BA 70 dry rations, two full canteens, mess kit, hammock, flashlight, waterproof sheet, message pads, backpack, K9 pistol in a hip holster, and money belts under their green uniforms. The captain shook hands with all three, wished them luck, and watched them climb up into the canopied back of a rumbling Russian GAZ truck. Two enlisted soldiers in the cab would share the driving.

The truck bed was full with sacks of rice and cartons of bandages and medicinal supplies. Ky looked around as he settled himself onto a rice sack.

"At least they didn't put us with the ammunition or fuel."

With the grinding of gears, the truck moved off and took the middle position in a convoy with four other trucks. As the sun went down, they left the marshaling yard and started down the road to Vinh.

The trucks rumbled through the blackness. They could only see the dim headlight slits and the glowing cigarette ash of the driver of the truck behind them. Every hour on the hour they pulled over for a pee break and to switch drivers. At about midnight, one of the drivers handed them a thermos of hot tea. Although none of them was hungry, they split the contents of a dry BA ration and sipped the bitter, hot tea.

They rode in silence for another three hours. A sterile white light suddenly bathed the convoy. The trucks pulled off the road, and all the drivers left the cabs, running for cover in a roadside ditch.

Not knowing what to do, Vo, Ninh, and Ky jumped out of the truck and ran after the drivers. Ky had his pistol drawn as they stumbled into the ditch. They could hear the drone of an airplane as a two-kilometer-long string of flares floated over the road.

Shadows were sharp, the trucks crisply outlined by the flare light. Vo could see clearly the faces of his comrades and the ten drivers, all huddled in the ditch. He nudged Ky's shoulder. Ky looked at him, smiling sheepishly and obviously embarrassed for brandishing his pistol like an American World War II cinema hero.

Holstering his gun, Ky asked, "What the fuck is this?"

"Reconnaissance, I guess," answered Ninh. "Probably taking pictures and counting traffic on the road."

The lead driver and convoy commander, a grizzled sergeant, was crouched next to Ninh. "Yes, sir. Taking our pictures. Fucking Americans. If they were going to bomb us, they'd have done so already. Two months ago they'd have attacked, strafed the trucks. I don't trust those fuckers with their bombing halts. Bullshit."

"What do they have up there?" asked Vo.

"Don't know, sir. I'm guessing one plane taking photos and two escorts. That's what we usually see during the day. Probably from the fucking aircraft carriers. Uncle Ho needs to join us in this ditch." Vo could see the sergeant's crooked smile, unlit cigarette hanging from his lip. "How are we going to beat these fuckers with a bunch of broken-down trucks?"

Vo didn't answer.

When the flares died out, the sergeant collected the drivers and told them that he was going to take an alternate route by going first west and then turning south, paralleling the road they were on. It would take them three hours longer, but if the Americans came back to bomb the road, they could bomb some other convoy, not theirs.

A few kilometers down the road, the convoy turned west. From the dim light of the truck behind them, Vo could see that the road was unpaved, rutted, and strewn with rocks. The convoy's speed dropped as the trucks bucked hard, jarring the cargo, drivers, and General Ong's three musketeers.

The trucks turned south onto a washboard road that was even rougher. They could hear glass clinking against glass in the medical supplies as the bone-rattling ride worsened. Ninh tried to wedge some of the smaller boxes between the rice sacks to cushion the jolts to the vials and bottles but kept losing his balance, nearly falling out of the truck.

"Next break, let's try to move some of this stuff around. I'm afraid we're going to lose some valuable medicine or something," he shouted above the creaking of the truck body, rumbling of the engine, grinding of the gears, and squealing of the brakes.

They finally pulled over to switch drivers and take a break. Vo, Ky, and Ninh were bruised and battered. The sergeant in charge of the convoy walked up to them as they stood alongside the truck, stretching and getting ready to rearrange the cargo.

"Lieutenant Vo, sir. We're not going to make Vinh before sunrise. We'll probably have another four hours to go when the sun comes up. Do you want to pull over and hide the trucks under tree cover at dawn and wait for night, or keep going?"

"What's in the rest of these trucks, Sergeant? Anything critical that needs to go to Vinh as soon as possible?"

"Sir, everything's critical. We're carrying food, medical supplies, spare engine parts, tires, fuel, and ammunition. But my orders are specific—the most critical cargo is you three."

"This route we're taking, any chance of reconnaissance flights?"

"You'll have to ask the Americans that one, sir. Probably not as much chance as if we stayed on the main road. But I don't know."

Vo looked at Ky and Ninh, who were standing near him. Ky had a swelling on his cheek that was turning blue. They both nodded at Vo. They trusted in whatever he decided.

Vo turned to the sergeant. "Okay, Sergeant, let's continue on until the sky starts to lighten. We'll reevaluate where we are and make our decision at that time. If we're still four hours out of Vinh, we'll pull over and hide the trucks, get some sleep, and continue at dusk." The sergeant nodded, and Vo asked, "Do you know this area well? I don't know where we are."

"Yes, sir. Been up and down this shit pile of a road many times."

"You know good places to pull over and keep the trucks out of sight?"

"Yes, sir, plenty of them. I won't let us get too far away from any good rest spots."

"Good, Sergeant. Let's get going."

The convoy started up again, moving southeast to Vinh. Vo, Ninh, and Ky hung onto the canopy braces, their arms and legs absorbing the shock of the ride. After less than an hour, the convoy stopped in the middle of the road, engines idling. The sergeant's faced appeared at the back of their truck.

"Lieutenant Vo, I think our decision is made for us. Second truck just lost a tire. Torn to shreds. I recommend we transfer its cargo to the other trucks, leave the second truck drivers to repair the tire, and bivouac a few kilometers down this road in a grove of trees just east of this road."

Vo stuck his head out the back of the canopy and looked to the east. The sky was just starting to lighten. Dawn was less than an hour away. "I agree, Sergeant. Let's start moving the cargo out of that truck."

For the next half hour, the three officers and the ten drivers carried the heavy crates of engine parts and ammunition cases from the disabled truck and loaded them into the other four. Vo conferred with Ky and Ninh and decided that rather than risk getting crushed by shifting heavy cargo, they would each ride in the cab of one of the first three trucks.

The four trucks moved on. As the sun rose, they turned onto a small dirt path and then parked under the sparse branches of a grove of trees. The sun revealed a rural landscape with prominent hills and no dwellings.

Half a kilometer to the east was what must have been another grove of trees but was now mostly shattered tree trunks and ragged stumps, the ground pocked with craters and littered with the skeletons of burned-out trucks.

"That's ominous," said Ninh, as he sat on his haunches poking a small fire that the drivers had started to brew tea.

"How do the Americans target something like that?" wondered Ky. "Out of all the places and potential targets, to pick the one spot that's a temporary truck park? They couldn't have had a spotter on the ground this far north, could they?"

Ninh shook his head. "I don't know. Maybe they had a forward air control airplane that saw the trucks? Maybe they have some sophisticated electronics that somehow can identify these things. It is ominous indeed."

"Probably used heat detection," volunteered Vo. "It's pretty cool here. Hot truck engines maybe give off enough heat that the American pilots can pick up an infrared signal. I'll send our thoughts back to group headquarters in my first report."

The drivers and officers ate and slept near the trucks. They might as well have been on the moon. No birds, no other people, the only sound the wind and their talking and snoring. In the middle of the afternoon, they were awakened by the engine noise of the now-repaired truck rejoining them. As soon as the truck was parked and the engine shut off, both drivers fell sound asleep in the cab.

At dusk Vo, Ninh, and Ky climbed into the back of the now-empty, repaired truck, and the convoy continued its slow pace southeast to Vinh. The ride in the lighter truck was even rougher and more jarring than before. Ky smiled at his two comrades. "So, this leg of the trip is the easiest, huh? I can't wait for what's next."

"You're just missing Sergeant Nguyet," chided Ninh. "If she were here, you could nestle in her ample bosom and not feel a bump."

"Say what you will, but right now that sounds pretty appealing to me," answered Ky.

"Remember what the captain said about her before we left?" asked Vo. "He'd rather fight the Americans again than deal with her."

Ky put on a superior air. "Well, of course, he doesn't have my natural charms and animal magnetism for the women. He's just overcompensating for not being the stud that I am. I feel sorry for him. And you two. You'll never know what it feels like to be a sex idol. Poor guys."

Vo laughed and Ninh replied, "I understand you've been getting a lot of sex these days. With your right hand. Or is it your left? You know if you masturbate too much, you'll get a bruise on your cheek. Proven medical fact."

Vo turned on his flashlight and pointed it at Ky's face. "Ninh, isn't that a bruise on Lieutenant Ky's cheek? A very big bruise?"

"So it is, Vo. I think maybe we need to have Lieutenant Ky castrated. He's wasting too much of his energy. Give me your knife."

"You two think that you can cut off my balls with a knife? You are dealing with a man of steel. Unless you have a cutting torch in your backpack, forget about it. Why humiliate yourselves?" said Ky. "I'm indestructible. Know why the Americans didn't bomb us? Because once they heard that Lieutenant Ky the Indestructible was in the convoy, they knew it would be a waste of time and bombs."

"Vo," said Ninh. "I'm getting a distinct smell of bullshit in this truck."

"Yes, I've noticed it too, Ninh. It's been with us since we left Hanoi. Think we stepped in something?"

"No, Vo, I checked our boots. But I didn't check Lieutenant Ky's underpants."

"You'd probably like that, you homosexuals," said Ky. "It's going to be tough being the only real man on a long journey like this."

The long ride took its toll on drivers, passengers, and trucks. As the sky lightened in the east, they stopped at a small village to shift drivers and pee. The sergeant came back to their truck and told them that they were less than an hour away from their destination outside Vinh. He pointed to the silent village. "That's Kim Lien. Birthplace of Uncle Ho."

The convoy moved on. As they entered the outskirts of Vinh, the dawn's sunshine revealed a devastated landscape. Shells of buildings, rubble, bomb craters. Women, old men, and children were picking through the debris, pausing only to look at the passing trucks. All the roads were cratered, forcing the convoy to weave like a snake around the meter deep holes. The only other vehicles on the road were military. No bicycles, no taxis, no xyclos. Few civilians were seen. Stray dogs ran in small packs. The air stank.

Nearly forty hours after leaving Hanoi, the convoy dropped the three officers at a sandbagged corrugated iron building in the middle of what had been an intermodal cargo transfer yard. Wrecked cranes and ripped-up rail tracks, as well as more burned-out trucks, were piled in heaps around the yard. Crews were filling craters with debris.

They walked into the sandbagged building. Kerosene lanterns cast deep shadows around the inside and filled the air with fumes. The room was jammed with desks at which sat civilians wading through desktops of paper.

A major stepped out of a corner shadow, smoking a cigarette. "You three get something to eat. There's a mess hall, next building to your right as you leave this one. They also have BA rations and good water. Load up. Be back here in an hour ready to move. We have your transportation ready."

"Yes, sir," said Vo. "We'll travel during daylight?"

"Yes, but it will be overcast and misty. You'll be safe. As safe as you can be in war. Get some food; you'll need it. Back here at 0700."

At 0700 a Russian-made jeep was idling outside the major's office, a corporal at the wheel. Vo got into the seat next to the driver, and Ky and Ninh climbed into the back seats. The driver nodded to Vo and without further word gunned the engine and drove out of the cargo yard and onto the cratered road that had brought them to Vinh. They were the only vehicle on the road, but progress was slow due to the surface condition. The ride was bumpy but better than the trucks.

"Corporal, are we going to be part of a convoy?" asked Vo.

"No, sir. The convoy will leave later, when it's dark. The major is trying to make up some of your lost time. Besides, with this fog and cloud cover, we might as well be driving at night."

"Where we going?"

"Due west to the mountains, then head south. Then southwest into Laos, and I'll drop you off." The driver looked at Vo. "Good thing you brought your field jacket, sir. This ride gets cold."

"How long?"

"We've got this GAZ 67B," the driver tapped his hand on the dashboard, "so we should make good time. It's about 190 kilometers, so about ten to twelve hours driving time plus a few rest stops. I'm scheduled to get you there at 2300 tonight."

The jeep picked up speed as the road, while still rough, had fewer bomb craters. There were fewer bombed-out buildings, less rubble, but little sign of life. The occasional hill tribe village was quiet, with a child or woman stopping to look at the camouflage painted vehicle as it passed. No smiles, no waves.

As they entered the foothills of the Truong Son Mountains, the road became steep. Then abruptly the surface changed to nothing but bomb craters. The corporal pulled over. "Sir, I recommend we take a break and eat something."

"You're the driver," said Vo. "It's your call."

The corporal parked the jeep next to what had been a mature pine tree but was now just a shattered trunk.

"What happened here?" Vo waved his hand at the pocked roadside and unrecognizable pieces of metal.

"A convoy was bombed in the middle of the night. Eleven trucks. Two were carrying ammunition and explosives. One with medical supplies and food. The rest were loaded with a Youth Brigade, nurses, and two doctors to set up a hospital. The Americans bombed in the dark, no flares, no spotter aircraft. But they were very accurate." The corporal looked around, scratching his left forearm. Vo could see the beginning of a wide, red scar at the cuff of the corporal's sleeve.

"You were here?" asked Vo.

"Yes, sir. I was driving the last truck, the one with the food and medical supplies."

Ninh asked, "How bad?"

"Sir, it was terrible. Terrible." He looked at the ground and then started to gather some brush to make a fire for tea and to heat some rations.

The three officers and the driver ate in silence. Then they stretched out, trying to nap before getting back into the jeep.

Ky looked at the corporal, who was collecting the field kit teapot and spreading the burned-out ashes with his boots. "Did you get hurt in that bombing, Corporal?" Ky was pointing at the man's forearm.

"Yes, sir." He smiled a sad smile and shook his head. "But I was the luckiest of the lucky, sir. The trucks with the ammunition exploded. What few were alive after the bombs went off were killed then."

"How many died, Corporal?" asked Ky in a quiet voice.

The driver said nothing for a while. Then he looked at Ky, Ninh and Vo who were staring intently at him.

"It's easier to say how many didn't die, sir. Three of us lived. Me, my alternate driver, and one of the Youth Brigade girls who was riding in our cab. The only thing that saved us was that we were the last truck. It caught on fire, but we were able to get out of it in time."

"Everyone else died?" asked Ninh.

"Yes, sir—eighteen drivers, the two doctors, all the nurses and all the Youth Brigade but one. I think it was about fifty-five or sixty."

"Fuck," said Ky, more to himself than to the others.

* * *

The Russian jeep rode into the mountains, then turned south parallel to the mountain spine and the Laotian border. Little more than a dirt path, the road snaked through the hilly terrain. Just before dark, they stopped to eat again and this time slept for almost an hour before returning to the road.

Vo offered to share the driving, but the corporal politely declined. This was his job, his responsibility. A responsibility that was not to be delegated, even to an officer.

The corporal pulled off the road. Leaving the engine idling, he turned to the three shadows in the moonless night.

"This is the Mu Gia Gap. It runs between two high ranges. The Americans have halted bombing on this side, but the other side is Laos. They have not halted on that side. The Royal Laotian Army may also be on patrol. But it has been quiet. From here on we are in greater danger. Our stop is just fifteen kilometers past the gap. We should be there in an hour."

"What do you do then, Corporal? Go on with us?" asked Ninh.

"No, sir. I'll, rest and refuel, and then I have passengers to take back to Vinh."

"Let's go, Corporal," said Vo. The driver put the jeep in gear, and they rumbled through the black night down the path between the high walls of the gap. Gravel laid down by Youth Brigade road workers smoothed out the ride.

They were in Laos. A kilometer out of the Mu Gia Gap, they caught up with a slow-moving truck and jeep convoy carrying troops and supplies.

"This is the convoy that left the night before we did," said the driver. "I can't get around them unless they pull off. I suggest we follow them into the way stop." Vo nodded his approval as they fell into line behind the last truck. A soldier waved at them from the back of the truck. The corporal waved back.

The road was surprisingly smooth, and the slower speeds reduced the jarring bumps of the last fourteen hours. Drowsy, Vo let his eyes close, his body swaying with the jeep's motions. Ky was asleep, and Ninh still awake.

From the black sky, a red, silent ribbon of fire sprayed down before them, followed immediately by the thunder of impact and then a horrible whirring noise. A truck in the front of the convoy burst into flame, turned violently, and then fell on its side. Like a dragon's tongue, another red ribbon flamed down from a different direction, flowing for what seemed like minutes but was only a few seconds. The red tongue lashed the trucks at the front of the convoy. Gusts of hot wind rolled over them. The smell of cordite filled the air. They could taste it, bitter on their tongues.

The corporal jerked the jeep off the road and into the trees as fast and as far as he could. All four leaped out, ran into the trees, and fell onto their stomachs, their hands covering the backs of their heads, their faces buried into the soggy, decaying vegetation and dirt. Vo heard the impact and terrible humming again and looked up.

The first three trucks were on fire. The smell of melting and burning metal mixed with the acrid odor of cordite and the skunk stench of burning rubber. And the terrible smell of burning flesh. The other vehicles had pulled off the road. What sounded like firecrackers came from the burning trucks.

Vo could also hear insects buzzing by. Then he realized the sound was the rifle ammunition the troops carried cooking off as the fire burned the soldiers' bodies. Pushing his face harder into the ground and gritting his teeth, Vo thought how ironic it would be to die from a dead comrade's bullet.

They lay like that for a quarter of an hour. Other than the crackling of the fire, it was quiet. No one moved. Vo looked around and got up.

"Ky, Ninh, let's go."

The other two and the driver followed Vo to the flaming trucks. As they got close, the smell of burning diesel fuel overpowered their senses. Then Vo smelled the sickly odor that reminded him of burned duck feathers. Men were burning. Hopefully, dead men. A group of soldiers was running towards them. They were part of the convoy. Wide-eyed, scared, in shock.

"You men," Vo pointed at the first four to arrive. "Search for wounded. Take a muster and let me know how many are missing. Ky, grab that next group and see what's the condition of the other vehicles and get them ready to move."

Vo turned to Ninh. "Figure out if we can get the other trucks and our jeep around these three wrecks or do we have to clear them off the road. Corporal!" Vo yelled for the driver. To his surprise, he was standing right beside him.

"Yes, sir."

"You've been through this before. If we move will we be hit again?"

"I don't know sir. That was a gunship. They can stay up there for a long time, but I think that if they were still there, they'd have kept shooting. But I don't know."

"Okay, we'll assume he's gone. Figure out who's this convoy commander and tell him to get ready to move out. Lieutenant Ky's up there somewhere. Work with him."

A few minutes later a soldier came up to Vo. "Sir, we've got four badly burned. I think one is hopeless. Our medic's with them."

"How many are dead?"

"I don't know if dead or missing, but we had a total of fifty-three men, including drivers. Besides the four wounded, there are thirty-seven in good condition. At least physically."

"That's twelve dead or missing," said Vo. "How many men were in those three trucks?"

"Six in the first one, five in each in the other two."

"Including drivers?"

"Yes, sir."

"Load the four injured on the first operational truck in line." Vo looked at the three burning trucks. They were crematoriums. There would be no remains to collect.

Ninh ran up to him. "We can get the trucks and the jeep around these. We don't have to move them."

"Ninh, it seems like those trucks had sixteen men in them. We have four wounded and twelve missing or dead. Those twelve must be in the fires. If not, they're on their own. Let's get moving. Let the wrecks burn themselves out."

Ky and the corporal marshaled the remaining trucks and jeeps into order. The corporal ran back to Vo.

"Lieutenant Ky says we're ready to move. The injured are in the first truck. He will stay with that truck as convoy commander. Whenever you're ready, sir, he says we can move."

"Tell him to start. You stay there. I'll pick you up. We'll be the last vehicle."

"One request, sir. That GAZ jeep is the best vehicle we have. Don't break it, please."

Vo smiled briefly, slapped the driver on the back, and ran back with Ninh to get the jeep.

The damaged convoy rolled into the way stop at 2100. The way stop was more than what the name implied. It was a network of camouflaged paths and parking areas, all separated by hundreds of meters and defended by mobile antiaircraft batteries, some armed with missiles. Vo could see no buildings other than dug-out and sandbagged bunkers, one of which sported several antennae. He was surprised by the number of what he assumed to be civilian laborers and young women and men Youth Brigade members. Although it was nearly midnight, the way station was busy with activity.

As the corporal turned off the engine and they wearily climbed out of the jeep, a man in his early thirties walked up to them. He wore a light-colored shirt and dark trousers, sandals made from inner tube rubber and tire tread, and a light, non-descript jacket. He nodded to the driver, who nodded back. They obviously knew each other. The man looked at the three officers. "Vo?"

"That's me, sir."

"Drop the 'sir.' Rank doesn't mean shit here." He looked at the other two. "Ky? Ninh?"

"I'm Ninh."

"I'm Ky."

"Three out of three. That's good," said the man with a tight-lipped grin that was more of a grimace. "I'm the head of this Binh Tram. I have the responsibility to get you to the next Binh Tram south." He did not offer his hand or his name.

He turned to the corporal. "Get some food and sleep. Your passengers are ready to go at 0400. You need to be on the other side of the Mu Gia Pass before dawn. We'll get this jeep refueled. It need any repairs?"

"No, best vehicle we have." The corporal was about to walk away when Vo grabbed him by the arm. Vo took the corporal's hand.

"Thank you, Corporal. You did well." Then Ky and Ninh shook the driver's hand, and he turned and walked away.

Vo turned to the nameless head of the Binh Tram. "That young man did a good job. He deserves recognition."

The head of the Binh Tram made his grin-grimace again and snapped, "Fuck that. He did his job. Like most of these people here. Let that knowledge be enough recognition for him."

Vo stared at him. He made a mental note to be sure to include the corporal in his first report back to Transportation Group headquarters. This grumpy asshole standing in front of him wasn't worth arguing with.

"Sorry about that," apologized the man. "I'm going on about two days without sleep and am fucking hungry. Too short tempered and irritable."

Vo just nodded. The man pointed to a path.

"There's a clearing up that path that's level and dry. Rig your hammocks there and get something to eat. I'll be up there in a few minutes. Don't go to sleep yet."

The three went up the path and found the clearing. Several others had also rigged their hammocks and had small fires going. A forest canopy of leaves shielded the firelight.

"I almost punched that motherfucker," said Ninh. "I don't care if he is sleep deprived and missing his breast feeding. The asshole."

"Think we'll get like that?" asked Ky.

"Probably," answered Ninh.

Half an hour later, the Binh Tram leader appeared and sat on his haunches by their fire. Ky offered him some tea and a share of their rations warming on the small fire. The man accepted the offer and ate with his fingers directly out of the mess kit, sharing Ky's canteen cup of tea. He looked at Vo.

"What happened at the pass?"

Vo described the gunship's attack dispassionately and in detail, with Ky and Ninh adding to the narration. The casualty count was twelve dead or missing—but probably dead. Four were burned, and one of those was probably not going to survive. Thirty-seven men okay, three trucks and their cargo destroyed.

"That's a casualty rate of over thirty percent. We can't sustain that," said Vo.

The Binh Tram leader sighed. "Sometimes the casualty rate is one hundred percent. You're right. We cannot survive casualty rates that high. But do you know how many die or get injured due to bombing and the gunships on this trail?"

Vo shook his head. The man looked at Ninh and Ky, who also shook their heads.

"Two percent. That's right, two percent. Malaria kills five to ten times that much. Dysentery and foot infections take a greater toll than the Americans' expensive bombs and bullets. But the bombings have a great impact, greater than the loss of lives. They disrupt our logistics. They force us to live like this."

He waved his hand at the crude encampment. "We live and fight on a few tons of fuel, ammunition, and food a day. They disrupt the trail. And if we don't repair the trail quickly, the traffic backs up, and then they can bomb and kill much more than two percent."

Ninh asked, "How could they so accurately target the convoy? It was dark, overcast, misty."

The man shrugged. "Ask them after the war. Technology? Who knows? Spotters? We know there are Americans with the Laotians as well as their mercenaries. I'm sure there are some of my own staff who are quite happy to sell movement schedules and routes for a bottle of Remy Martell cognac."

"I'm sorry about leaving the twelve missing," apologized Vo. "The only option to moving on was to wait for the trucks to stop burning and sift through the ashes."

"No, you did the right thing. We'll send a patrol out later and take a look." He sipped his tea and stared into the fire.

"This is the first time I've sat on my ass in two days," he added. "Get some sleep. I'm going to do the same. I can't get you out before dawn. If the weather's foggy, we'll get you out during the day. Otherwise it's dusk tomorrow."

He looked at Ky and patted his shoulder. "Thanks for the tea and food." Then he stiffly got up and walked down the path.

Two hours later Vo was awakened from a sound sleep by someone tugging his hammock. He groggily looked around and saw a young man in a pith helmet. It was early morning, the day gray and foggy. "Get up. You need to get going. Be at the main bunker in fifteen minutes."

Vo rolled out of his hammock and woke Ky and Ninh. They had filled a thermos with hot tea before going to sleep, and Vo poured cups for the three of them and ate some cold rice and bits of dried fish left over from previous meals. They packed their gear and walked down the path to the bunker. The head of the Binh Tram was standing by the entrance, a pile of supplies at his feet. He waved at them as they approached.

"This shitty weather is good for us. With luck we can get you to the next Binh Tram in two days, maybe less." He pointed at the pith-helmeted man who had awakened Vo. "There is your guide. Unless the road washes out or the Americans get lucky, you'll be riding all the way. Enjoy it; you'll be on foot after that."

He pointed at the supplies at his feet. "This is for you. More rations and an extra canteen each. Also a change of clothes and some salt."

Vo, Ninh, and Ky loaded their backpacks with the canteen, rations, and clothes. They wrapped long linen tubes of rice bandolier style around their shoulders and waists. The guide led them up a narrow rutted dirt road to a flat space where three trucks were parked, loaded with cargo and young members of a Youth Brigade.

The guide pointed at one of the trucks. "We ride in the back of that one." He smiled. "Nothing explosive in there."

The trucks twisted and bounced through the fog, heading south. Occasionally they'd pass a group of workers or youths filling a bomb crater or rigging camouflage. The sky above the tree canopy was completely overcast, and the fog turned into a chilling drizzle. After four hours, they reached a stream where three young women waded with poles, probing the bottom before waving the trucks across. The trail climbed steeply, the truck tires spitting gravel behind them.

The small convoy stopped at the peak where the road led through an area that was completely denuded of foliage and pockmarked with bomb craters. They sat silently at the edge of the barren area while the guide listened and then scanned the sky with his binoculars. Satisfied that there were no aircraft nearby and that the overcast and mist were still thick, he gave orders to cross the area and wind down the other side of the mountain.

Mid afternoon the fog lifted, and the cloud cover broke. They were near another stream. The guide ordered them off the road, and the three trucks dispersed to separate level areas with heavy forest cover. Everyone disembarked. The Youth Brigade members immediately started preparations for a meal.

The guide said to Vo, "The youths will do the cooking. But you need to give them some of your food. They'll make a communal meal." He smiled. "Very ideologically appropriate."

Vo asked, "How much farther?"

"We've made good time." He looked up at the sky. "I don't think it will cloud over before dark, so we'll stay here for a few hours until it's dark and then move on. With luck, we might get there by dawn tomorrow. I don't want to move during daylight, so if not dawn tomorrow, we'll sit it out when the sun comes up and move on when it goes down. At worst, maybe another thirty hours."

"Ever experience ambushes on these runs? This terrain looks as if it would be perfect for that."

"Not often. We're all armed, and the Laotians are not looking for a fight, at least not with us. Sometimes the Americans and Southerners seem to gather up some hill tribes or Cambodian mercenaries and try something, but we usually hear about that beforehand and just take another path. I think the Americans are happier dropping bombs."

"I'm going to wash up there," said Vo to Ky and Ninh, pointing at the fast-running stream.

"Careful with that water," cautioned the guide. "If you want to fill your canteens, boil it first or use purification tablets if you have some. Okay to wash, though."

After a cold-water wash in the stream and a meal of rice, dried fish, and bits of vegetables, most of which Vo did not recognize, they sat on the ground near their hammocks. A few Youth Brigade women—probably in their late teens—were in their hammocks nearby. One was lazily singing in a surprisingly smoky-throated voice. It was warm and humid, but not uncomfortable.

"Before we get in our hammocks and try to rest, I want to discuss our 'lessons learned' with you," said Vo. "We should send back reports to Transportation Group of our progress. But equally important, we need to send our identification of problems and recommendations. I think we get a day's rest at the next Binh Tram, and I am planning to write the first report then."

"Good. I was thinking the same thing," said Ninh. "I suggest the report be a strategic planning tool, not an inspection deficiency report. General Ong charged us to think strategically, to think in the long term."

Ky nodded. "I agree. Despite the bombing halt and the wishes of our parents and friends, we cannot count on peace in the near future. We're in a prolonged struggle, and the three of us may never see its end. Transportation Group needs sound recommendations from us."

"Let's put our thoughts together at the next Binh Tram and send a report out before we leave there," said Vo. "I'm going to try to sleep."

Ninh slapped at his neck. "Fucking mosquitoes."

They dozed off to the young woman's singing.

CHAPTER 14
TRAVIS AIR FORCE BASE, CALIFORNIA

After a tearful goodbye kiss from Kelly, Coburn grabbed his duffel bag and a book, *In Cold Blood*, from the back seat, smiled at the nurse, and waved goodbye. "Drive safe, hon. I'll write as soon as I can." He walked into the terminal, not looking back. She sat in the car, watching him until he was out of sight.

Check-in went quickly. In the officers lounge he found Theodore and a few of his other classmates. Vernon wasn't there yet. Coburn settled himself down in a chair, opened his valise, and took out a blank piece of paper and an envelope he had already stamped and addressed to Betsy. Using his book as a writing surface, he wrote her a letter.

Dear Bets:

I want to drop you a line before I get on the plane. This is it, off to Vietnam.

I hope graduation was nice. And I hope you enjoy your job and NYC. You have to be pretty excited.

I don't have an address yet but as soon as I can, I'll write you a letter and let you know what it is. If you don't mind, I would like to keep in touch.

It looks as if we're getting ready to board the plane, so I'll sign off. You take good care of yourself. Don't worry, I'll be safe,
Clark

He found a mailbox, went to the bathroom, and ran into Vernon as he walked back into the now-crowded lounge. Over in the corner sat four South Vietnamese Army officers. To Coburn they looked like sixth-grade military school cadets.

It was time to board the chartered stretched DC-8 for the long flight west.

The plane was boarded from rear to front. The lower-ranked enlisted got on first, then the non-commissioned officers, and finally the officers, with the most senior in the front seats. Coburn took his aisle seat and looked at the stewardesses. One wasn't too shabby, but this wasn't the time or place to flirt.

A quiet mixture of excitement, liberation, and happy anticipation came over Coburn as the plane lifted off. This was the start of an adventure. All problems and commitments were behind him. He didn't have to deal with those. Ahead of him was a future with welcome challenges. He knew he'd do well.

Coburn had no illusions that his life up to this point was one of underachieving, bullshitting, and selfish good times. He had lived a life of not worrying about consequences that could, at worst, embarrass but not much else. But now he was going to war, the real deal. All his talents, intelligence, and potential would be used and tested. He had no doubt that this war was his crucible.

In the darkened cabin, Coburn read his book, ate the meals and snacks, napped, and stretched his legs at the four stops across the Pacific. The cockpit announced that they were making their approach to Ton Son Nhut just as he finished *In Cold Blood*. He gave the book to his seat partner with his recommendation that it was a good read. The view out the cabin window was black. If there was a city down there, the lights must have been turned off.

206

The plane landed and taxied to the terminal. The flight attendants opened the cabin doors and wet, hot air smelling of jet exhaust, rot, soot, and sweat replaced the sterile air conditioning.

He was in-country.

CHAPTER 15
LAOS

Report Number 1-68 Detachment A of Recommendations to Commander, Transportation Group:

1. *American air attacks outside People's Republic of Vietnam limits transportation of personnel and supplies disproportionate to the physical destruction caused. Based on our observations of the last five days, precautionary measures to avoid air attacks limits transportation of cargo on the Truong Son trail to approximately fifteen tons per day. While this appears to be enough to maintain the current low level of activity, it is not enough to allow any escalation.*

2. *The American air attacks have the capability to detect concentrations of vehicles in any visibility. While intelligence gathered from local indigenous hill tribes and even espionage or agents within the network of Binh Trams is undoubtedly used in the targeting process, the quick reaction and accuracy leads us to conclude that the Americans are utilizing sophisticated technology.*

3. *We respectfully recommend that an analysis of non-visual targeting technology be conducted by Transportation Group. Specifically, it is our opinion that the Americans can detect heat generated by vehicle engines, or infrared radiation.*

4. *We also respectfully recommend that vehicles be dispersed as far as possible when parked. This should reduce the heat signatures of engines that have not yet cooled.*

5. *We further respectfully recommend that consideration be given to the placing of decoy heat generators along a "phantom" trail. Charcoal burners or other flameless methods may simulate a truck parking area and deflect targeting away from actual truck parking areas. Placing the decoys near unfriendly villages may also have a psychological benefit if these villages are subsequently bombed or strafed.*

Submitted:
Transportation Group Detachment A-South

Vo debated with Ky and Ninh on whether to send two copies of the report to the Transportation Group by two separate courier pouches to ensure that at least one copy would make it through. Ky's argument prevailed that two copies sent separately would double the chances that the report would be captured, so just the original was sent. Vo kept no copy for the same reasons.

They did discuss writing a commendation for their corporal driver from Vinh to the first Binh Tram. But they did not know the driver's name, only his rank. So no commendation was sent.

They did add a paragraph six to the report:

6. *Finally, we respectfully request encryption directions to preserve the security of future reports.*

* * *

The small convoy rolled into the Binh Tram just before dawn. They were south of the Demilitarized Zone. Directly east lay what the Americans and their puppets called "I Corps" and Danang. This Binh Tram was busy with trucks, porters pushing bicycles, and troops, as well as Youth Brigade and civilian laborers working on the trail. The southbound truck traffic stopped at this point. Trucks appeared to be heading east as well as returning north. It was warmer and more humid than the previous Binh Trams.

As soon as they arrived, their guide for the next leg of the trip met them. They would leave at dusk the next day. A whole day of rest with no travel seemed luxurious.

After a meal and then a bath in the nearby stream, which was more like a small river, the three finalized a report to the Transportation Group and handed it to a courier. They fell asleep in their hammocks next to those of half a dozen young men and women of the Youth Brigade. In the late morning, the Youth Brigade members sat in a circle listening to a man Vo assumed to be the Binh Tram's political officer. Vo, Ky, and Ninh contributed rice and canned rations to a communal lunch.

Four of the young women walked over and introduced themselves to Vo. Ky and Ninh joined them. The four, all under twenty years old, were from the Hanoi area and had joined the Youth Brigade a year and a half ago. One, in fact, had gone to the same school as did Ky. She and Ky discussed several of the teachers they had in common.

The young women were thin, too thin. Their hands were rough, scabbed, scarred, and their nails were cracked. They were pale, their hair cropped short and shapeless. Their tire-tread-sandal-shod feet were covered with insect bites and circular scabs and scars that Vo realized were probably from leeches. The same scabs and scars were visible on their legs and arms. But they were smiling, apparently happy, chatting with Ky.

Ninh was standing between Ky and Vo, looking at the foot of one of the women. A wide, jagged scar ran from her left ankle up her leg to her calf. When he looked up, she was looking directly at him.

"What happened there?" he asked, pointing at the scar.

"We were repairing one of the vehicle bridges submerged in the stream when the rope holding it broke. My foot and leg fell under the bridge. I should have known better than to be so close."

"The bridge was underwater? A bombing?"

The girls laughed. "No, not a bombing," said the girl with the scarred leg. "We sink the bridges to hide them, so that they cannot be seen by an airplane. Some we raise at night and then put across the stream. After the trucks go over, we move it and sink it again. Some we build so that the bridge surface is a quarter of a meter beneath the water. Then the trucks just drive across. They get their tires wet, but that's all."

"So, your corps does bridge work?" asked Ninh.

Again the girls laughed. "Yes, bridge work, road repair, road grading. Whatever we have to do. We even forage for food."

Another added, "We can't let the trucks or the porters bunch up. That invites the bombing and the gunships."

Vo, Ninh and Ky exchanged knowing glances. These women were younger than Ngoc, doing rough and dirty labor and living in shit. What drove them?

Ninh asked the question aloud. "Did you know you would be doing this kind of work when you joined the brigade?"

The quietest of the four responded. "I was so young, we were all so young when we volunteered. We didn't know anything about what we would be doing other than whatever it was, it needed to be done. Our patriotism was…" she searched for the right word, "like a fever…no…an inspiration…I don't know what it was like. But it was so strong. We went willingly."

"You are doing a very important job for the people," said Ninh earnestly. "Please keep that in mind when you are tired and hungry."

"We never forget that. But we do get discouraged and depressed."

Another added, "Discouragement and sadness can be like very contagious and deadly diseases. Fortunately, we have one another. When some of us are down, the others bring them back up."

She looked at the other women. "We have to get back to the medical clinic." She turned to Ninh. "A new aid station for the Binh Tram. We get many wounded here." The young women smiled and went up a path leading into the thick forest.

Ninh climbed back into his hammock. He gave a dry cough. "I'm tired, ready to nap again. Wake me if it's time to eat or Sergeant Nguyet comes by to see Ky. I want to watch that."

My dearest Ngoc:

We have a day's rest and a long way to go on our journey. I hope you're feeling well and your studies are interesting. I'm fine and doing well. You are always in my thoughts. I miss and love you very much.

Please tell my parents that I am fine. And please give my respect to your mother and uncle.

Thinking of you and loving you.

Vo

Vo reread his note to Ngoc and considered ripping it up. He wanted to write to her about how much he loved her, how much he wanted to make love to her. And how different his life had become since leaving her. But while he was comfortable with his emotions, he was awkward in writing them, even to someone he loved. He sighed, folded the note, and stuck it in his backpack to send with the next report.

* * *

The air grew warmer and more humid as they traveled on their way south. Higher altitudes offered little relief. During the days they slept.

At night they traveled. Sometimes they walked, often in the company of troops or bicycle porters. Occasionally they rode crammed into the back of a rattling GAZ truck with troops, Youth Brigade members, or cargo.

The forest floor often shook, followed by a low rumbling. The first time they had experienced that, their guide told them it was an American bombing raid elsewhere on the trail, probably fifty kilometers or more away. They'd passed through bombed areas, all trees and bushes bare of foliage, three-meter-deep craters twenty meters across in neat rows. Several times they saw the red ribbon of a gunship but never as close as they had at the Mu Gia Gap. And once they heard small arms fire to the west. A parallel trail was being ambushed.

It was their third full day's rest since they had left Vinh fifteen days ago. The forest had turned into thick jungle. They didn't even bother to swat mosquitoes or the other unidentifiable bloodsuckers. They took their canvas boots out of their backpacks and gave them to some Youth Brigade women. The boots were of no use to Vo and his comrades. Wearing the rubber tire sandals let their feet dry out.

Dry rations were gone, so Vo and Ky scavenged with some of the youths in the nearby stream, while Ninh hung the hammocks and started a cooking fire. In the mountains they had found red ginseng, which the youths boiled into a broth, but here they were in the wet forest jungle. One of the youths pointed out cassava and tapioca root, and another found crabs under submerged rocks and even scraped moss and fungus off rocks. Vo and Ky, both from the city, had little ability to recognize what was edible and what was not, but they were learning.

All three had lost weight. Vo and Ninh were huskier, more muscled, than most men their age. Now they were slim, not gaunt, but spare. The reduced rations, the appetite-sapping heat and humidity, and the physical exertion of trekking were taking their toll.

Ninh was constantly fatigued and had developed a hacking dry cough. But he never complained, never failed to carry more than his load of responsibilities, physical chores, and weight.

Vo and Ky followed the youths up the path to where the hammocks were strung. Crabs and some water greens were wrapped in Ky's shirt.

Ky grabbed Vo's arm. "Vo, I'm worried about Ninh. He doesn't look good, and that cough is getting worse."

"Yes, me too. But what do we do about it? He's not complaining, he keeps up, he's carrying his load. More than his load. We just keep on moving south, Ky. The three of us."

"Sure. But I'm going to ask any of the Youth Brigade if they have any remedies for that cough. You know, some boiled potion like they did with the red ginseng."

They walked a few meters more when Ky grimaced and yelped. "Fuck, fucking ants. Fucking ants." He swatted at his left leg, knocking off the large jungle ants. "Fuck, that hurts."

One of the young women had run back to see what the problem was. She took off her conical straw hat and started scooping ants into it. Vo asked her what she was doing as Ky ran back to the stream to bathe his foot in the cold water.

"We collect the ant venom. It's an antidote for snakebite. Don't worry about your friend; the bites hurt, but he'll be okay."

"Snakebite?" asked Vo.

"Yes. They are not aggressive, but if you put your hand or foot near one, it will bite you." She pointed at his feet. "When you wear these sandals, your feet are vulnerable."

Vo shook his head in amazement. Bombs, gunships, ambushes, mosquitoes, ants, skin diseases, leeches, coughs, and now snakes.

* * *

Three nights later they approached a small river crossing in a truck and found a line of vehicles backed up. A bridge had torn away from its moorings, and a dozen Youth Brigade workers were in the water and on the bank wrestling the bridge back into place. They were working by moonlight. The guide, Vo, Ky, and Ninh climbed out of the truck and moved off the path and under cover.

Vo heard the engine of an airplane above them. The night was erased instantly by a sterile, white, shadowless glow. The trucks were outlined in detail, and he could see the workers in the river hurrying to the shore and cover.

The driver of the truck they had been riding in threw it into reverse and sped backward up the trail and then backed it into the jungle. More flares illuminated the other trucks and the trail. Vo could see the other drivers running to their trucks to back them out of the brilliant white light.

An orange ball of fire appeared where the trail met the river, followed by a deafening whoosh and then the scream of a jet airplane. Another ball and another, and another. Each seemed to suck the breath from their lungs. The air was scalding hot and smelled of gasoline. Vo, Ninh, and Ky were lying on the jungle floor, hands protecting their heads, faces buried in the rotting vegetation. It was quiet. Or were they deaf? Then four more orange balls in rapid succession bracketed the river. Vo raised his head and could see vegetation burning, and then the truck nearest the river exploded. It was quiet again except for the ringing in their ears. They could smell the searing hot smoke of burning wood and petroleum as well as feel it. Pieces of metal, wood, and dirt fell out of the sky.

The guide jumped up. "We've got to get out of here. Those fucking bastards will be back. To admire their handiwork."

He led them back to their truck, which was already turned around on the trail, and for the first time in nearly three weeks, they traveled north. The guide directed the driver to a side trail, and they pulled off into a space between two large trees.

"We've got to wait here. That's the only crossing narrow enough. Let's wait and see what the damage is and if it can be repaired."

"If not?" asked Vo. "What's our alternative?"

"We go west about two days, and it's shallow enough to drive across. Or we forsake the truck and swim across. But then we walk from there. It will take us more than five days to get to the next way station if we don't have the truck."

"Okay, we'll assess the damage, and then I'll make the decision," said Vo, thinking out loud.

The guide looked at Vo and said in a whisper, "No, you're my responsibility. I make the decision."

Vo stared at him. This fellow knew the jungle and the trail, he knew the pitfalls. Vo did not. He'd listen to this man's expertise and his recommendation, but if he did not agree with this man's decision, he would not follow it. Vo kept silent. This was not the time or place for a power struggle.

They sat silently in the dark for fifteen minutes, then they heard a jet engine above them. It made a pass, dropping flares. Then it circled and made another pass, then a third pass. Then it flew off. Ninh asked the guide, "Reconnaissance?"

"Yes, taking pictures. We probably have at least an hour to take a look. I think they're done for the night."

The four of them walked down the path. All the trucks except for the one nearest the crossing were unscathed. Surprisingly, no one was killed, but several were burned, and one man must have inhaled flames and would probably soon die. As they approached the river to check on the bridge, a Youth Brigade woman stopped them. They could go no farther. There was an unexploded bomb at the near river edge.

"Take care of it," said the guide to the woman. "We've got to get this trail open again."

"We'll be ready to clear the bomb in a few minutes. Everyone must get clear." She looked at the trucks. "They're far enough back; no need to move them."

Vo, Ky, and Ninh exchanged questioning looks. "They have explosive ordnance technicians here?" asked Ky incredulously.

"They must have. She said they're disarming that bomb in a few minutes, didn't she?" Ninh looked around. "Who's trained to do that? Some of these drivers or bike porters? I think those troopers over there are just infantry."

Pointing at the woman who had warned them about the bomb, the guide answered their questions. "She will."

"You mean the Youth Brigade is trained in explosive ordnance disposal?" asked Ninh.

"I wouldn't call it training," answered the guide. "We have to get repairs done as soon as possible to keep traffic moving. You saw what just happened if you don't. It didn't take long for the Youth Brigade to realize the problem and set up Dare to Die teams. They clear the bombs."

"What do they know about disarming fuses?" asked Vo.

"Nothing. They disarm the bomb in place. They blow it up. A while back a few of the more daring tried to take the bombs and shells apart to salvage the explosives and the casings. They dared and they died. Now, the safest and quickest way is to blow up the bomb."

"You have explosives for that?" asked Vo.

"Yes, usually courtesy of the US Army. Their C-4 and fuses are excellent and safe. We have captured quite a bit from the Southerners, and some makes it back to the Binh Trams. The Claymore mines are also good sources of explosives. And we always have the ammunition we transport as well as the grenades of our troopers. We have to move back." The four of them walked up the path to where their truck was parked. It was dawn.

The guide tended to the truck and driver while Vo, Ninh, and Ky squatted a few meters away and marveled at what was happening. Necessity and expediency produced results, even by the most crude of methods. They startled at the sudden whoosh of the explosion and the familiar petroleum smell of napalm.

"Let's take a look," said Ky.

At the river's edge, a shallow crater where the bomb had rested was being filled in with gravel from the river bottom by some of the human cargo—troops heading south. In the river, more troops and several of the Youth Brigade tugged and pushed the bridge back into place. One of them, the woman who had attended the same school as Ky, smiled at him and waved. On the opposite bank more youths foraged for crabs, cassava, and fungi. In midstream, two young men harvested stunned fish.

Ninh stood between Ky and Vo on the riverbank. "Look at this. We are going to win this war. How could anyone defeat this?"

They strung their hammocks near their truck and settled in, hoping to sleep away the hot and humid day and then to get moving again at dark. The woman who had waved at Ky from the river and several other young women and men hung their hammocks from nearby trees. She came over and chatted with Ky while Vo cleaned his pistol and Ninh fell into an exhausted sleep after a fit of coughing.

Within a short time, all were asleep except for Ky and the woman who talked in low voices. Then they stood up and walked farther into the trees.

* * *

It had been thirty days since they left Vinh. The trail was bombed twice more, but the bombs damaged the jungle, not the gravel road or the travelers. Their diet was rice with whatever they could find or were given. Cassava, wild turnips, bamboo shoots, crab, and once after an American bomb exploded in a river, fresh fish. As they went farther and farther south, more captured rations—American C-rations, Southerner army rations, and even South Korean rations—trickled into the diet. The weather was hotter and more humid the farther they traveled, offering no respite in altitude or darkness of night.

They had traveled with a dozen different guides, each handing the trio off to another guide at each way stop. The three young officers saw more and more wounded soldiers being evacuated from the east. Some lying on bamboo stretchers, some lying in the back of trucks, and some hobbling on their own. The way stations smelled of the sickly sweet stench of rotting flesh and death.

At least once a week, Vo conferred with Ninh and Ky and sent a report to the Transportation Group in Hanoi. He had not received—or expected—a reply or acknowledgment of receipt. Letters home were often put in the courier pouch along with the report. Their morale was high despite their surroundings and physical condition. But they were anxious to be done with the journey.

All three were suffering from dysentery. Frequent watery stools interspersed with constipation, cramps, stomach pains. They forced water to fight dehydration but often found themselves, especially during the heat of the day, dizzy and lightheaded. The dysentery was taking its toll, making them too tired and weak to climb out of their hammocks and causing them to soil themselves.

Once a Laotian guide gave them bitter sour tea made from a local flower and citrus fruit. It tasted terrible but seemed to calm their innards. The guide handed them a bag of the petals and fruit as he passed them to the next guide at the way stop. Slowly, Vo and Ky recovered but still could only tolerate boiled water, the tea, and rice.

Ninh was uncomplaining but suffering. His diarrhea and stomach pains stopped, but his fatigue and cough worsened. Despite that, he dragged himself out of his hammock and kept up. But at every rest stop and when riding in a truck, he fell into a restless sleep.

An army medic whose company had just joined them looked at Ninh. He felt his forehead. Ninh had a high fever. When he tried to sit up so the medic could examine him better, he complained that his joints ached and couldn't move, and then he vomited the tea and rice he had eaten half an hour before. Vo told the medic that they were all suffering from dysentery. The medic shook his head. Ninh had more than dysentery. He had malaria.

Before they got to the next way stop—a Binh Tram with a field hospital—Ninh became delirious, violently shivering and then sweating profusely. When they reached the way stop, Vo and Ky carried Ninh to a sheltered area, rigged his hammock, and put him in it. Ninh was conscious, awake but dazed. He shut his eyes and immediately fell into a deep sleep. The medic asked two Youth Brigade women who had helped build the field hospital to look at Ninh.

They brought clean cloths and boiled water. While they stood there, Ninh's body went rigid, then he started shivering again. The women undressed him and wiped him down with the cloths and water.

"He has malaria. We will help take care of him, but there's little we can do other than let it pass," said one of the women to Vo.

"How long will that be?"

"If he gets better, we will know in two or three days."

"If he gets better? What do you mean? Why won't he get better?"

"I don't know how sick your friend is. Some people do not get better. They die. Malaria is..." She just let her words hang there as she looked at Ninh, now quiet in his hammock.

The guide and another man whom Vo assumed would be their new guide walked up to them. The stranger said he would be responsible for their next leg of the journey.

"You were supposed to move out at dusk." The guide looked at Ninh. "We do not want to move you at this time. We will stay here until he recovers and is ready to travel."

Vo looked at Ky and then back at the two guides. "Okay, we'll stay here for a while. How far are we from the next way stop?"

"One day by foot. We will be crossing into Cambodia."

Vo turned to the women. "Should we take him to the hospital? You have one here, right?"

"He's comfortable here. There's little that can be done for him in the hospital that we cannot do. Let's keep him here."

Worried and dejected, Vo sat down next to Ky and leaned against a tree. Their comrade, their friend, lay in his hammock a few meters away. Ky reached out and held Vo's hand.

They both thought of the man they had been responsible for in basic training. The man who had died from malaria.

* * *

The hospital was a hospital in name only. It was in a jungle clearing halfway between two parallel gravel paths of the Truong Son trail. The surgery was a subterranean dirt floor and dirt wall vault, two and a half meters deep, roughly three meters square—little more than a ditch. A bamboo frame supported wood planks—the operating table. One kerosene lamp that had been converted to a candleholder hung from the ceiling, which was made of layers of thick logs. A steep, narrow ramp led up to the jungle clearing, providing the only ventilation. Above the surgery was a thatched hut that served as the dormitory for the nurses and doctor and the hospital ward for the wounded and sick.

The smell of pus, blood, feces, and rotting flesh made Vo gag. He could see that Ky was trying to breathe only through his mouth. They were in the thatched hut. Ten lower versions of the operating table held patients. Another six were in hammocks. Limbs were missing, and bandages were soaked with blood. One patient appeared perfectly fine except for his labored breathing and the dried blood trails from his ears and nostrils.

The Binh Tram commander introduced them to the doctor, a small, bird-like woman who brushed her hair off her forehead and looked at them with weary eyes. Vo stared at what he thought was lacquer or paint on the front of her shirt and then realized it was blood. He looked up to see her staring at him.

"I'm busy here. These men are from the last two nights' bombing. I expect more to arrive today." She took off her rubber gloves and gave them to a woman Vo assumed to be a nurse. The nurse took the gloves and started washing them in a bucket.

The doctor sighed, brushed back her hair again, and said, "So, you are that special detachment moving south. And one of you is sick. I can see it's not you two. What's wrong with him?"

"Malaria and dysentery," answered Vo.

"Everybody gets malaria and dysentery. Why are you here?"

The Binh Tram commander spoke up. "They have to make a decision to leave him here, take him with, or wait until he recovers or..."

"Dies." Vo finished the commander's sentence. "We've been here a week and must move south as soon as possible."

"How long has he been sick?" asked the doctor.

"About two or three weeks, I think. We only found out he had malaria when we arrived," Ky replied.

"Coughing?"

Vo answered this time. "Yes, that started at least a month ago."

"Joint pain?"

"Yes, but I don't remember when it started."

"Sweats, fever, hallucinations?"

"Just when we got here."

"Loose bowels, vomiting?"

"I don't know when that started. We've all had dysentery.""

"Convulsions?"

"Shortly after the fevers started."

"How's he now?"

"Very weak but clearheaded when he wakes up. Until he starts shivering or sweating."

"Anything else?"

"He's losing his hair. His urine is black."

The doctor's mask of a face cracked into a frown. "Has he been given anything?"

"A tea our previous guide gave us of some flower petals and a dried, sour fruit."

Ky added, "And a black worm from one of the youth corps."

"I had better take a look at him. Bring him here." The doctor turned and went to the bed of the man who looked fine but had labored breathing and dried blood trails on his face.

"Doctor," Vo said to her back. "I don't think we should move him. Can you come to him?"

The doctor turned on her heel and glared at Vo. "No, I cannot. You and he," she jabbed a finger at Ky, "can carry him here. There's no privilege in my hospital. These men are badly wounded, and some are dying, or hadn't you noticed?" She turned away in disgust.

An hour later, Vo and Ky carried Ninh on a bamboo stretcher and laid it down in the sun outside the thatched hut hospital ward. Ninh lay quietly, his eyes shut. Vo and Ky, with the help of the Youth Brigade woman, had cleaned him up. The doctor came up from the underground surgery.

She glared angrily at Vo and barked, "Take him out of the sun, you idiot. Bring him inside."

Obediently, Vo and Ky picked up the stretcher and put Ninh in the middle of the ward. Vo noticed that the bed of the man who had looked unscathed was empty.

Putting her hand on Ninh's forehead, the doctor asked in a gentle tone if he could hear her.

"Of course, I can hear you," said Ninh as he opened his eyes. His eyes had become a ghostly white. She pushed his eyelids back with her fingers and looked at each eye closely. She noted his pale skin and nearly purple lips.

"Does your head ache?"

"Not right now, but yes."

She palpated his stomach and chest. With the aid of a nurse, she rolled Ninh on his side and thumped his lower back several times with her small hands.

"What's your name?"

"Call me Ninh."

"Ninh, do you know where you are?"

"On the Truong Son trail."

"How long have you been at this Binh Tram?"

"Two days, I think."

"Who are these two?" She pointed at Vo and Ky.

"Two bums. Vo and Ky. Don't trust them."

She smiled. "Put him on that bed there." She pointed at the empty bed. Vo and Ky helped the nurse put Ninh on the wooden slats of the bed.

"Vo and Ky, come with me." She started to walk out of the hut.

"Doctor," said Ninh. "Please, I'm part of this team. Tell me what you are going to tell my comrades."

She looked at Vo and Ky, who both nodded. "Very well, we'll talk here."

She stood by Ninh and bent over and put her hand on his forehead, not as much to see if he had a fever as to give him a gentle human touch.

"Ninh, you have malaria that, combined with dysentery and some of those infections on your feet and legs, has become critical. Your kidneys are failing, and your spleen and liver are damaged. I am frankly surprised that you do not appear to have brain damage, but that may be just a matter of time. There's nothing I can do for you here other than to keep you hydrated and nourished. You are too ill to travel. In your condition medical evacuation to the north would probably kill you faster than the malaria."

"I am dying?"

She looked at Ninh in silence for nearly a minute. "I intend to keep you here. You are young, and your body may be able to fight the malaria long enough to repair what is not permanently damaged and grow stronger. Or it may be too late and you will die. Right now you are between fever and convulsions, but they will return shortly. If you do survive, you may be brain damaged. Cognitively impaired."

"What do you think will happen, doctor?"

"Ninh, as a physician, I think it is most likely that you will die within a week. The probability of your survival without permanent impairment is very small." She looked out the hut door at two just-arrived stretchers of wounded men. The wounded were being triaged by one of the nurses at the entrance to the surgery.

Vo spoke first. "Thank you, Doctor. You'll need to take care of them." He pointed at the new arrivals. "Is it okay if we stay here for a few minutes more?"

"Yes, of course. But stay out of the way." She walked over to the surgery ramp.

Ninh was the first to speak once she was out of the hut. "Shit, you two fuckups are headed for disaster without me to save your asses."

Ky held Ninh's hand and couldn't think of anything to say. Vo just stared at Ninh.

Again, Ninh broke the silence. "Let's talk while I'm still conscious and before those fucking shakes hit me again. This seems to be a pretty easy decision for you, Vo. In fact, the good doctor has made it for you."

"I'll tell the Binh Tram commander to get us a guide and get us out of here as soon as possible. I have your money belt in my backpack, so that's taken care of. We can't stay here any longer, Ninh."

"You and Ky have stayed too long already. Give my pistol to the Binh Tram commander; he'll have a good use for it." Ninh touched the brass bracelet on his wrist. "I'll keep this as a reminder of Ky's fiancée. You two better get moving."

Ky squeezed Ninh's hand. "We will see you before we go."

"Shit, I'm starting to feel cold again." Ninh started shivering. He looked terrible. A nurse came up, looked at Ninh, grabbed a stained blanket, and put it on him.

As Vo turned to walk out of the hut, his eyes met those of the man in the bed next to Ninh's. His eyes were sunken, questioning. The man had no right arm, and both his legs were nothing but bandaged stubs. His bandages were stained the red brown of dried blood. Vo thought of his friend Le in Ninh Binh. Fucking war. Terrible fucking war.

Report Number 4-68 Detachment A of Detachment Personnel
Detachment A member A-2 is unfit for travel and will remain at Binh Tram. Members A-1 and A-3 continuing as ordered.
Submitted:
Transportation Group Detachment A-South

* * *

They crossed into Cambodia.

Much of the forest and jungle cover had been denuded by the American bombs. Foraging for food consisted mainly of gathering what they named air-raid vegetables, which were the hardy mosses and fungi scraped off rocks, the only living things to survive napalm and high explosives.

They were in a truck convoy of troops and supplies moving down a gravel trail in an area scarred by craters. At about 0400, the blinding light of flares directly overhead illuminated the convoy and the line of bicycle porters behind them. Before their truck could turn off the path, Vo and Ky had already jumped out and were running into what little cover there was, throwing themselves down on their stomachs, burying their faces in the dirt, and covering their heads with their backpacks.

The ground erupted around them, bouncing up into their faces and bruising their lips and bloodying their noses. The concussion squeezed the breath out of them. Vo felt his heart throbbing, beating loudly in his ears. His body trembled. All he could do was squeeze his eyes shut even tighter and clench his teeth until he thought they would shatter. His ears rang so loudly that he was deaf to all else. The explosions were muffled, felt more than heard through the ringing. Each explosion sent out a wave of superheated air and concussion. The now-familiar smell of cordite, burning diesel fuel, and hot metal filled their nostrils when they lifted their faces out of the dirt to breathe. The air was thick with acrid dust and smoke.

Things fell around them and on top of them. Dirt, gravel, hot chunks of what had been a bicycle chain, and little pieces of GAZ trucks. And pieces of bodies. Some easily recognized. A head and shoulder. A leg. A chunk of a torso. And other objects that only a butcher or a surgeon would know.

The bombing stopped. The flares burned out. The noise of the explosions ceased but not the ringing and terrible heart pounding in their ears.

Vo tried to stand but found himself too dizzy and fell. His eyes wouldn't focus. He crawled over to Ky, who was on all fours. Ky had blood running from his nose, and his lips were cut. His face was covered with embedded dirt. Trying to clear his vision, Ky shook his head like a dog. He shouted in Vo's ear, "Vo, your nose is bleeding, and you have a cut on your forehead. You okay?"

Ky's hearing must have been as bad as his own. Vo could hear, but everything was muffled, drowned out by the ringing. He shouted back in Ky's ear, "Your nose and lips are bleeding. I think I'm okay. Give me a few minutes."

Slowly the two got up. Vo's head ached with a pain he had never felt before. They stumbled back to the trail. Several fires illuminated the scene. Four of the six trucks were destroyed, the other two damaged but still on their wheels and not burning. Body parts, broken bicycles, and supplies were scattered everywhere. Troops, porters, and drivers who could walk were being herded to the side by an infantry officer.

Vo tried to focus his eyes on what first looked like a black, smoldering, fallen tree limb. After a few seconds he realized it was the body of a man, burned to a crisp.

* * *

A day and a half after the air strike, Vo was still a little deaf, and his head still ached. But his heart had stopped throbbing, and his body had quit trembling.

My dearest Ngoc:

I cannot tell you how much I wish you were in my arms right now. At home. There's nothing in my life here that is of tenderness, love, and passion other than my cherished memories of you. I'm so grateful I have them.

A few days ago I met a doctor, a woman, who treats the sick and wounded among us. I could not help but compare her to you. Perhaps when your medical studies are over, Vietnam will be united and you will only have to treat sick, not wounded people.

I hope you are well and enjoying your studies. Other than missing you so, I am fine. And sad at the losses that war creates.

Please write when you can. As of yet I have not received any letters, but I think I am probably traveling faster than they are. Soon they will catch up to me.

Thinking of you and loving you.

Vo

"What are you writing, Vo?" asked Ky. They were waiting for sunset to move down the trail. It had been five days since they left Ninh at the hospital, four days since they entered Cambodia.

"A letter to Ngoc."

"Telling her about Ninh?"

"I want to, but the censors will cut it out. I also don't want her to worry about my health and safety any more than she's worrying now."

"So what are you writing about?"

"Here." Vo handed the letter to Ky, who read it and handed it back.

"Nice letter. Thanks for sharing it with me. It must be nice to have someone like Ngoc—I mean to feel that way about someone."

Vo smiled and shook his head. "I don't know if it's nice or not, Ky. I love Ngoc, but given where you and I are and what we are doing, would I—and she—be better off never having met, never having fallen in love?"

"I can't say. I just don't know. I don't have anyone like Ngoc in my life, and I don't know if that's better or not." He sighed. "Ninh, the bombings..." Ky's voice trailed off as he picked at a scab on his ankle.

Without looking up he asked, "Do you think you will die fighting this war, Vo? Do you think you will die before you ever see your parents, or Ngoc, or Hanoi again?"

"Probably. Yes. You?"

"Yes."

Vo put his letter to Ngoc in his backpack. He'd send it with his next report to Transportation Group. Ky asked Vo for a sheet of paper and started writing a letter to his parents.

When Ky finished Vo asked, "No girlfriend, Ky?"

"Not really. Several good female friends, but nothing like Ngoc. My mother was trying to arrange a marriage, but I told her to stop, I'd find my own wife. Besides, I'm saving myself for the beautiful Sergeant Nguyet, who will be waiting for me when I return in triumphant glory." For the first time in months, the two men burst out laughing.

After a few minutes of silence, Ky asked Vo, "Should we write Ninh's parents?"

"No. We don't know if Ninh is dead or alive. What would we tell them? That we left him in some hut in Laos?" Ky nodded in agreement. They continued packing their backpacks.

A woman walked up to them, carrying a canvas pouch. "Vo?" she asked. Ky pointed at Vo.

"Vo, I'm a medical aide at this Binh Tram. Your guide asked me to check on you." She looked at Ky. "And you."

Ky snapped back, "We're fine. Why don't you check on somebody who needs your skills and energy?" He was sitting on the ground, his back against a shattered tree trunk.

She looked down at Ky's feet and what she could see of his legs. "Your infections need my energy."

She squatted in front of Ky, took off his sandals, and rolled his pants legs up to his thighs. For the next fifteen minutes, she drained and cleaned the pus out of infected bites, scratches, and cuts. She checked the soles of his feet, roughly scraping the skin with her thumbnail. Then she did the same to Vo.

She looked at their chests, arms, and eyes and into their mouths. Then she asked if they had headaches, coughs, or joint pains. She asked about the color of their urine and the consistency of their stools. She washed her hands from a canteen on her hip and packed her canvas bag.

"Both of you are fighting dysentery, as all of us are. But you seem to be doing okay. Boil everything you drink, or if you have any, use purification tablets or bleach. Unfortunately, you won't find either on the trail. When you're not marching, take off your sandals and pants and expose your legs and feet to the air and sun. Given the part of the world we're in, you two are about as healthy as can be expected." Without waiting for questions, she turned and walked away.

"Wonderful," said Ky. "Now when we get blown up, everyone will remark how healthy our pieces are."

"The way she was rubbing your feet, I think she likes you."

* * *

It was dusk. Their guide came to tell them that they'd be leaving soon. The next two days would be on foot since the truck trail had been accurately targeted by the Americans. Until they could relocate the truck trail, bicycle porters would carry the loads.

They were near the border, and the foot trail would snake in and out of Cambodia and Vietnam. It was the safest path through this area, but by no means was it safe.

Vo and Ky walked alongside the guide. The going was slow and sometimes steep. The guide mentioned that during the rains, they would slide down the hills on their packs and have to take their sandals off to climb up the hills. Fortunately, this was not the rainy season.

Vo saw a smile at Ky's face. "What are you smiling at?"

"I was just remembering what Ninh said after the Youth Brigade exploded that bomb at the river's edge."

"What did he say?"

"You and I were with him, looking at the repair work on that bridge. He said something like, 'Look at this. We are going to win this war. How could anyone defeat this?' Don't you remember?"

"Yes, I do. It reminded me of what we studied at the Transportation Group the last week. There was a line from the American president, Kennedy, that stuck in my mind. Kennedy knew what Ninh knew. But still he sent their men and airplanes to fight us."

"You're a better student than I am, Vo. What did Kennedy say?"

"That we—the National Liberation Front and the army—are 'seeking victory by eroding and exhausting the enemy instead of engaging him.' I think the American president was prescient. But he and his followers have chosen to ignore his wise words."

* * *

Their path turned to the southwest, following the curve of the Cambodian border. The weather was hotter but less humid, and the terrain flattened out with small rolling hills. Although much of the travel was on foot, they made good time, often traveling with just a guide. A few times, depending on the guide, they even traveled during daylight. Several times they encountered porters and guides heading north with goods that had entered Cambodia through the port of Sihanoukville.

Their new guide told them that he would be their last. He would be with them for a week and take them southeast into Vietnam, where the National Liberation Front would meet them.

Vo and Ky were asleep in their hammocks when the plane flew over the large Binh Tram. The loud droning woke them up, and they immediately dived out of their hammocks and scrambled into a foxhole.

It was a propeller-driven plane, not the screaming jets of the fighter bombers or the invisible and silent high-altitude bombers they had encountered before. The plane had multiple engines; it was not a reconnaissance or forward air controller airplane. After half an hour, they crawled out of their foxhole. Their guide walked toward them in the dark. He held his hand over his lips, signaling them not to speak. Then he motioned them to follow him.

After about three hundred meters in silence, he stopped and pointed to a shrub in the middle of a clearing, his hand still signaling to be quiet. He marked the shrub's location on a map he unfolded from his pocket. They walked another hundred meters, and there was a similar shrub, this time in the middle of a path. Another hundred meters, and underneath a tree was another shrub, but this time on its side, not rooted in the ground. They could hear other shrub hunters walking through the darkness.

The guide turned on his flashlight and pointed it at the shrub on its side. Vo and Ky reached over and touched it. It was metal. Green painted metal. With metal leaves, a single metal trunk, metal branches, and a pointed metal spear instead of roots. The fake shrub was half a meter high.

The guide led them back to the Binh Tram commander's camouflaged operations center, an underground room with a timber-reinforced roof, not unlike the hospital surgery of Laos.

Inside was a candlelit table with a large scale map of the area. The operations center was crowded. One man was plotting the positions of the fake shrubs from the reports of the others.

"What was that?" asked Vo. The Binh Tram commander was standing behind them.

"That is the Americans' latest technology," said the commander. "We've been seeing them for several months now. They fly a path that they hope will intersect our supply trails, cross them at right angles. If you don't look closely or if they fall into heavy vegetation, you would think they're real."

"I certainly did until I touched one," said Ky. "How do they work? What do they do?"

"I'm not sure," replied the commander. "But we do know they attract the bombers. We've sent several to Transportation Group for analysis. Nothing back yet. What I think, and what we've learned from bitter experience, is that they are listening devices. They pick up sounds and transmit them to the Americans who must analyze what they're hearing, and if they think it's a concentration of trucks or troops, they send in bombers or mercenaries. I'm sure they're doing the same across the border."

"How sensitive are these things?" asked Vo. "Can they hear us walking around and talking, or does it have to be something louder like a truck engine?"

"Again, we don't know. We think each sensor has limited range, maybe only fifty meters. From what has happened to us, I assume it takes truck engines for them to call in a strike. But one time after they dropped these things, we were bombed with no vehicle traffic moving, but a large concentration of bicycle porters and troops were in the area."

"So what do you do?" asked Vo.

"Stay quiet as much as we can. Identify the sensor locations and move around them. Travel where the sensors are not." He put a finger on the map. "You can see they started dropping these here and then flew to the northeast. We'll shift our trail to the west, behind where they dropped the sensors." His finger drew an arc on the map.

* * *

The guide led Vo and Ky around the Cambodian border town of Satum and into Vietnam. The three dressed as local peasants in loose shirts, floppy black trousers, and tire-soled sandals. Their pistols and food were in the cloth satchels that replaced their backpacks, their water in plastic bottles instead of canteens. Conical straw hats shaded their faces. Both Vo and Ky had sizeable amounts of South Vietnamese piasters in their pockets to use as bribes if their counterfeit identification cards were questioned. A local official with nothing better to do and in need of money might wonder why three healthy young men were not in the army. They really didn't have a good answer to that question other than a bribe.

From the border they headed south along the east side of a large reservoir and then along the northern bank of the Saigon River to the little village of Bau Sinh, just west of the Michelin Rubber Plantation.

The guide took them to a farmer's ramshackle house. The farmer greeted the guide warmly, and his wife immediately started putting a meal together of rice and fish and vegetables for the travelers.

After eating, Vo and Key walked to the river, discussing the next report to the Transportation Group. They had seen many sampans on the river in their journey and were familiar with the puttering sound of the little engines. But now they heard a deeper, diesel-throated rumbling coming upriver. They moved back into the bushes and watched. A string of large, slow, gray craft glided by, some bristling with guns. The yellow and red flag of the South fluttered from their masts. On one of the boats, sitting on the roof under a canopy were two large men. One very pale, one very dark, almost black. Music from a radio could be heard over the engine noise.

Tomorrow they would meet their National Liberation Front counterpart. Their long journey from Hanoi to the South was over.

* * *

Report Number 6-69 Detachment A of Recommendations to Com-mander, Transportation Group:

Detachment A is in position and commencing operations. The follow-ing recommendations and comments are respectfully submitted.

1. *American sensors are air dropped perpendicular to logistics routes. The sensors are believed to be able to receive and transmit ambient noise from within a fifty-meter radius. After analysis of collected information, Americans appear to be able to target the logistics routes and even base camp areas. In addition, we assume that this collected information is used for further intelligence analysis by the Americans and Southern forces.*

    a. *It is respectfully recommended that examination and analysis of these sensors be expedited and countermea-sures developed.*

    b. *It is further respectfully recommended that electronic jam-ming of wide radio frequency bands be conducted to adul-terate whatever signals are being sent.*

    c. *It is also further respectfully recommended that a tactic be developed to covertly relocate dropped sensors to other sound sources—such as a village or enemy base—which may result in American air attacks on these targets.*

    d. *It is also further respectfully recommended that recordings of vehicle engines be used near sensors in either neutral or enemy areas as a decoy for American air attacks.*

2. *Considerable amounts of vehicle cargo space are allocated to fuel transportation. It is respectfully recommended that fuel-carrying pipelines be installed along the logistics routes, freeing vehicles for other cargo and allowing an increase in fuel supplies.*

3. *Observations of vehicles reveal that two types of fuel are required: diesel and gasoline. It is respectfully recommended that all gaso-line-powered vehicles be replaced with diesel-powered vehicles. Die-sel fuel is less flammable and less likely to explode than gasoline.*

4. *Observations over the last six weeks reveal that an individual can carry approximately twenty kilograms twenty kilometers in a*

day, a bicycle-equipped porter can move two hundred kilograms in the same time period and distance, and a GAZ truck can move six thousand kilograms one hundred kilometers in a day. This means that when a truck can be used, the truck takes the place of 1,500 individuals with backpacks or 150 bicycle-equipped porters. It is therefore respectfully recommended that improving all possible logistics routes to be vehicle capable be given highest priority. It is also respectfully recommended that as many trucks as possible be procured for this purpose.

5. *It is respectfully recommended that insect repellent, antiseptics, mosquito netting, and water purification tablets be issued to all Transportation Group units in the field.*

Submitted:
Transportation Group Detachment A-South

IN-COUNTRY

CHAPTER 16
TAN SAN NHUT, SAIGON

The Saigon night was black, hot, damp, and sulfurous.

Coburn walked off the plane, across the hundred yards of hot asphalt, and into the terminal. His khaki uniform was already soaked with sweat. Small, wiry Vietnamese pushed huge carts of luggage—mostly duffel bags—in the dim light. A gang of sweaty baggage handlers, all about five feet tall with lit cigarettes dangling out of their lips, wearing shorts and stained undershirts, muscled the bags off the carts onto wooden pallets. Using a bullhorn, an army MP directed the passenger traffic, telling the new arrivals to pick up their baggage and follow lines to officer, NCO, and enlisted arrival rooms.

Across the other side of the terminal was a line of servicemen—mostly army and a few air force and navy—all in clean, crisp uniforms waiting to board a flight home or to some R&R spot.

The terminal started to shake, followed by a low, rumbling sound. The line of servicemen waiting for their flight broke into a loud cheer, and several of the baggage handlers smiled and giggled.

Coburn glanced at Vernon, who had a puzzled look on his face.

"Jeez, Clark. These guys cheer for earthquakes?" Vernon said incredulously.

Before Coburn could comment, another MP who was within earshot smiled and said, "That, sir, was no earthquake. That, sir, is a B-52 Arc Light strike."

Coburn's eyebrows went up. "You mean they bomb that close to Saigon?"

The MP chuckled. "If you call fifty miles close, sir. They're carpet bombing the Ho Chi Minh trail."

Coburn, Vernon, and Lieutenant Commander Theodore's bags were close together, and the three grabbed adjacent seats in the officers' arrival room. The MP who had been directing traffic with his bullhorn walked to the front of the room and welcomed them to Saigon. He received several Bronx cheers and some nervous laughter. He told them to remove anything white or reflective because they would be driving through Saigon to their billet, the Military Assistance Command Vietnam's Koeppler Compound. They were led out of the terminal into the black stink of the Saigon night and aboard a dark-painted school bus. Each man shared his seat with his duffel bag.

As the bus pulled away from the terminal, Theodore pointed to the open bus windows. They were covered with chain-link fencing. "Must be to stop grenades, but it will make it tough to abandon ship."

They were in a combat zone.

The bus followed an MP jeep through the dark and deserted streets. Coburn could make out corrugated iron shacks and some hovels that seemed to be walled with thin sheets of metal stamped with Coca Cola and 7-Up logos—probably soft-drink can aluminum. The streets were wet and puddled. He could smell rot and sewage. As they drove into the center of Saigon, the buildings were more substantial, but the fetid air was just as bad. He did not see one person on the street during the half-hour drive. Just a few stray dogs. Or maybe they were big rats.

Sentries waved them through the gate and concertina wire, and the bus stopped at the low, white MACV indoctrination building in downtown Saigon.

The officers filed off the bus into a room with ceiling fans slowly stirring the wet, hot air. An army captain welcomed them, but this time everyone was too tired to make derisive noises. They were assigned beds and given a schedule of the next week's indoctrination. Coburn groaned to himself. This was going to be a rehash of the first few weeks of the counterinsurgency training he had gone through in Coronado.

Following Theodore and Vernon, he trudged into the sleeping quarters. Theodore's rank was the equivalent of an army major, and since MACV was an army command, a major was a field rank, so he was entitled to the privileges of that rank. Theodore said he'd see them in the morning at breakfast and went into his sparse but air-conditioned two-man room. Coburn and Vernon continued down the dim corridor to the junior officer bunk room. They stood at the doorless entrance. It was dark, hot, and humid, and it smelled of body odor and mildew and was silent except for loud snoring and insect chirps.

Vernon looked at Coburn and shrugged, then went into the darkness in search of his bed. Coburn stood in the hallway and thought about what had he gotten himself into. The room had about fifteen steel bunk beds with lockers lining the walls. If this was for officers, what were the enlisted sleeping in? Foxholes dug into the cement floor? Fucking army. In Coronado Coburn had had his own room with air conditioning, alarm clock, television, radio, desk, phone, and bathroom. Here he was sharing a dormitory with a bunch of army cannon fodder. Where was the fucking bathroom and showers? Where was his fucking bed?

He found his fucking bed, the top bunk in an airless corner of the room, above a body obviously responsible for the deep rumbling snoring he had heard in the hallway. Three hundred and sixty-five days of this? No way, thought Coburn. He fumbled open his assigned locker, stripped to his skivvies, and followed the sound of dripping water to the bathroom and showers, where

Vernon was brushing his teeth. Without a word they exchanged looks that spoke volumes. Coburn urinated, didn't bother to wash his hands, and padded barefoot back to his corner and climbed into the top rack, careful not to step on the body that was grinding walnut shells as it slept.

Coburn lay on his back on the lumpy mattress, wallowing in misery as he nodded off into short bursts of sweaty, uncomfortable sleep. At 0600 the lights came on, followed shortly by the dawn filtering through dirty windows covered with chain link fencing.

With his mouth tasting like somebody shit in it, Coburn grumpily rolled out of his rack, leaving a wet stain of sweat on the gray sheets. The snoring monster that had inhabited the rack below was gone, an early riser. Surveying the itchy red welts on his chest, arms, and legs, Coburn concluded that he had fed several hundred mosquitoes during the night.

After a cold-water shower and shave and a stored-up shit, Coburn put on fresh khakis and found Vernon, Theodore, and several other counterinsurgency school classmates in the officers' dining room. Although he hadn't eaten since the last snack on the airplane, Coburn wasn't hungry; the heat and smells killed any appetite that might have survived. He grabbed a cup of coffee, a glass of orange juice, and some flaccid toast served up by the little Vietnamese woman behind the steam tables. Coburn sat down with the others and drank his coffee and juice but just pushed his toast around the plate, uncharacteristically quiet. He promised himself that he'd get out of this fucking shit hole as soon as possible.

"Another fucking welcome from another fucking army asshole," muttered Coburn under his breath as he slumped at his classroom desk during the first indoctrination lecture. It was all stuff he had heard time and time again in Coronado. At least the classroom was air conditioned. Maybe he could sleep there? Coburn burped up a sour mixture of bitter coffee and orange juice. It couldn't get any worse, could it?

Just before the next class started, a young man wearing jungle greens and a US Navy first-class petty officer insignia on his collars walked into the classroom. A sailor. He looked at a clipboard and read off Lieutenant Commander Theodore, Lieutenant Vernon, and Lieutenant (Junior Grade) Coburn's names and ranks. The three stood up and walked over to him.

"Sirs, let's get out of this shithole. You need to meet the boss."

Coburn had no idea who the boss was, but he could have kissed the sailor. They walked out into the smoky morning and climbed into a jeep, Vernon and Coburn in the back. Outside the compound, Saigon was alive, noisy, and crowded, but it smelled no better than last night. The jeep-generated breeze felt wonderful. Coburn could feel the sweat drying on his face. Vernon's head was on a swivel, trying to take in his surroundings. Coburn had given up; his senses were already overwhelmed.

The jeep was waved through by sentries—two Americans wearing jungle greens, helmets, and flak vests and carrying M-16s, and two Vietnamese with the letters QC on their helmets and armbands that Coburn assumed meant MP or shore patrol. They were in a tree-shaded neighborhood, surprisingly clean and better smelling. The jeep pulled into a parking spot next to a sign that read "Commander, Naval Forces Vietnam, Senior Naval Advisor Vietnam." A three-star flag was flying from the flagpole in front of the entrance steps.

They followed the petty officer up the stairs and into a cool but not air-conditioned building, ceiling fans turning. Down a corridor and into a corner office. A short, wiry, bantam rooster of a US Navy captain stood up as the petty officer introduced them. This was the admiral's chief of staff, Captain Arthur Powell.

"Good to see you; we need you guys," said Captain Powell. "How was your first night at the beautiful Koeppler Compound?"

"Sucked," blurted out Coburn. "Uh...I mean, it sucked, sir."

Powell laughed. "Sucked? Well that's an improvement. The boss wants to meet you." They followed him across the hall to an open door leading into an outer office. Behind the desk sat the petty officer who had picked them up at Koeppler Compound. He looked up from his typewriter.

"Admiral Benjamin says to go in, sir. Anyone want coffee?"

Captain Powell answered for all of them. "Sure, bring in some coffee, please."

They walked into Vice Admiral Daniel Benjamin's office. Coburn was surprised by the three stars' youthful appearance. Benjamin was famous in the navy as a hot runner, being deep selected for early promotion at each rank from lieutenant commander through vice admiral, promoted ahead of his peers. He was in his early forties, husky and muscular.

He shook hands with each of them, introducing himself as "Dan Benjamin," not using his rank. Coburn, who was by no means slight or delicate, found that shaking hands with Admiral Benjamin was like shaking hands with a catcher's mitt. The petty officer walked in carrying a tray with a pitcher of coffee and four cups and saucers.

"Put the coffee down there, Culpepper," the admiral said, pointing at the conference table. "You guys take a seat. Serve yourselves. I gotta take a leak. Be right back. Culpepper, close the door and hold calls and visitors, please." They sat at the table as the petty officer shut the office door behind him, and the admiral stood at the commode in the bathroom off his office, peeing with the door wide open.

Coburn looked at Powell. He was wearing the gold dolphins that signified a submariner. Subs, thought Coburn. Either a World War II diesel boat guy or a nuke. The former were all daredevils with hard-drinking and risk-taking reputations. The latter were disciplined, humorless eggheads selected by the infamous Admiral Rickover for his tribe of Brahmins. Which one was Powell? Judging from his deliberate movements and obvious physical fitness, he was probably one of the nuclear submariners who seemed to be taking over the top navy echelons. As the chief of staff for Commander Naval Forces Vietnam, Powell would probably be reviewing or maybe even writing Coburn's fitness report. This Powell guy was worth sucking up to. But if he was a nuke, better be careful. They all had very sensitive bullshit detectors.

The toilet flushed, the faucets ran, and then Admiral Benjamin came to the table.

"Pour me a cup, please, Art."

Admiral Benjamin looked at a typed page in front of him. He went through Theodore's assignment first, calling him "Mr. Theodore." Theodore's job was a new position and an important one. With the acceleration of the Vietnamization of the war and the turnover of equipment and operation areas to the South Vietnamese military, the naval advisory effort was becoming critically important. Successful transfer of responsibility, administration, logistics, and equipment was the advisor's objective. Theodore would be working out of NAVFORV headquarters as liaison to the riverine assault group advisors, in the southern III and IV Corps. He would be reporting directly to Powell.

"Well, Mr. Vernon, I've heard about you before. A front-runner, and I'm glad you're here," said the admiral, smiling at Vernon.

Stifling a frown, Coburn maintained an interested poker face as the admiral told Vernon that his predecessor had been sent home early, via the hospital, so there would be no turnover. He had been wounded during an ambush on the river. Things had been pretty hot but seemed to have calmed down. Vernon just nodded, listening.

Benjamin read the last paragraph on his paper and turned to Powell.

"Jesus fucking Christ, Art. Those BUPERS guys have their heads up their asses and are fucking deaf. Mr. Coburn's counterpart is a lieutenant commander and this country's president's fucking nephew, and Mr. Coburn's a jaygee!" The admiral rubbed his hand over his mouth in frustration. "Don't they listen? Don't they read?"

"Admiral, as soon as I saw Mr. Coburn's orders, I called BUPERS and asked them what was happening. They told me that he had volunteered for the job, had good qualifications and a solid record, and should make lieutenant while in-country. They said the lieutenants they had available we wouldn't want."

Coburn saw this as his opportunity. "Admiral, Captain, I can do the job." Benjamin looked at him, sizing him up.

"Mr. Coburn, your ability is not the problem. And you can't help it if you were born too late. The problem's a political one, a cultural one. The South Vietnamese Navy seems to have accepted advisors of the same rank or maybe one rank less than their officer—your counterpart. But two ranks less is an insult, and any advice you give will be ignored."

"I think I can still do this, sir. I'd like to try, anyway."

Although Coburn was looking at Benjamin, from the corner of his eye he could see Powell staring at him, sizing him up. Powell definitely was a nuke, trying to decide if this confidence was genuine or just bullshit.

Powell spoke up. "Think we can frock him, sir?" Frocking was the advancement in rank of someone selected for the rank but not yet authorized to wear the rank. It provided all the privileges of the new rank but without the increase in pay.

"When's the lieutenant selection board meet?" asked the admiral.

"I don't know, sir." Captain Powell stood up, opened the door to the outer office, and ordered the petty officer. "Culpepper, please run down to personnel and find out when the lieutenant selection board meets. I think it's sometime late fall. When you find out, interrupt us and tell me." He turned back to the table, then quickly turned around and yelled after Culpepper, "And get me the regulation on frocking."

Benjamin leaned back in his chair, thought for a few seconds, and then slapped both hands on the table in front of him. "Here's what we have. Three choices. Number one, I switch you, Mr. Coburn, with some lieutenant or lieutenant commander whose counterpart is a lieutenant. Two, if Culpepper comes back with the right information, I will have the authority to frock you as a lieutenant, and you proceed as ordered. Three, if Culpepper does not come back with the right information, I'll just break the law and call you a lieutenant and hope you don't get passed over."

"Admiral, I hope it's number two," said Coburn.

It was obvious to Coburn that his orders had him going to a plum job with high visibility—especially since his counterpart was the fucking nephew of the fucking president of South fucking Nam. He didn't want this job going to someone like Vernon or whoever else might be in competition to be number one when the fitness reports were written.

"Me, too, Mr. Coburn." The admiral looked down at his briefing paper. "You just left the DeKalb, Mr. Coburn?"

"Yes, sir."

"The flag officer selection list came out this morning. Your old skipper just made rear admiral."

Coburn sat erect and smiled. "Really? That's great, Admiral."

This couldn't hurt. Coburn hadn't seen his last fitness report that his CO had written upon his detachment from the DeKalb, but it had to be a good one, with a recommendation for early promotion—a water walker who didn't get his shoes wet kind of report—signed by a guy who just made flag rank. This was all sounding very promising.

The door opened, and in walked Culpepper, followed by a chief petty officer carrying a thin document. Culpepper explained that he thought he'd better bring the personnel chief to explain the situation.

After a brief introduction by Culpepper to the three new advisors, the chief said that the lieutenant selection board would not meet until right before Thanksgiving, and the results would probably not be published until just before Christmas. Time in the previous rank to be considered for selection was two years. In order to be frocked, the officer had to be on a published selection list for that rank.

After some further discussion, they figured out that Coburn would not have the necessary time in his present rank to even be considered by the next selection board. Coburn's elation disappeared.

Then the chief said, "Admiral, I think if you give me a little time, I can put together a letter authorizing the wearing of the rank and the use of the title of lieutenant without the privileges of frocking or actual selection."

"Do so, Chief. And see if you can find some railroad tracks around here. We'll be meeting for another half hour or so. Can you get it done by then?"

"Fifteen minutes, aye, sir." Culpepper and the personnel chief hurried out of the office. In a few seconds, the sounds of the typewriter came through the closed door. Coburn felt much better again.

Benjamin took a sip of cold coffee, made a face, swallowed, and then looked at the three new arrivals. He leaned forward on his elbows and started talking evenly and quietly.

"Gentlemen. The navy's advisory effort has been running for six years now, and it has grown considerably. Including enlisted, we have over three hundred advising South Vietnamese Navy riverine and coastal units. And about half the number advising supply and headquarters. With the turnover of actual USN units to the Vietnamese, that number will probably double in the next year and a half.

"Our advisory effort has garnered a lot of glory and several unit commendations. Lots of medals for the advisors. And we've lost some killed and injured. The results have been, frankly, questionable. When the advisor abandons his advisory role and for all practical purposes assumes command or takes charge of a unit that is commanded by his counterpart, the units do well. And that is no good for anyone except the VC. Taking away the reins from the Vietnamese CO is a short cut to enabling and dysfunction."

The admiral saw a puzzled look on Coburn's face. "Follow me on this, Mr. Coburn. Vietnamization of this war—from us back to them—is going to be accelerated no matter whether LBJ or Nixon wins the election. There's a rumor around DC that the president may not even run again. Our orders are simple—prepare the South Vietnamese to be able to fight this war and win it on their own because we are not going to be here forever. In fact, front-line US troops and units will start leaving shortly, turning over equipment, boats, supply centers, and areas of operations to the South Vietnamese. And after a while, the advisors will be leaving, too."

The personnel chief walked in and dropped a typed sheet of paper with carbon copies and a small package in front of Powell.

The admiral continued. "I expect you advisors to do just that. Advise. I know that can be counter to the way you've been brought up in the navy—lead or get out of the way. I want you to work yourself out of a job. I want your unit to no longer need you so we can delete your billet." The admiral paused.

Powell spoke up. "You'll find it will be frustrating to watch your counterpart dither or take the wrong step, and you'll want to step in and take the radio away from him and start giving commands. But remember they're his men, not yours. The only time I want you acting like John Wayne is if your life or the lives of your own enlisted men are *in extremis*. You understand?" They all answered in the affirmative.

"I know you want to do well," said the admiral. "But this is not the army, where if you don't have a chest full of ribbons you don't get promoted. There will be no glory for you if you do your job right. But I will know it, and Captain Powell will know it, and your fitness report will reflect that." Not said but understood by all was that the reverse was also true. "Stand up, please, Mr. Coburn."

The admiral nodded at Powell, who stood and read the letter from the admiral to Coburn authorizing him to wear the rank and use the title of lieutenant. Benjamin signed the letter and gave it to Coburn along with the packet, which contained the double-silver-bar railroad-track insignia of the rank of a navy lieutenant.

"There you go, Mr. Coburn. I don't want you leaving the building with your jaygee bars on. Throw them away and put on your new rank." He shook Coburn's hand, and Coburn thanked him.

"Uh...Admiral?" It was Vernon, who had sat silent through most of the meeting. "I know Lieutenant Coburn has limited privileges, but do those privileges he does have include the requirement that he hold a wetting-down party?" Navy tradition for recently promoted officers was to host a party to celebrate the wetting down of their new stripes.

Both Powell and Benjamin laughed. "Good question, Mr. Vernon," said Benjamin. "Let's see, he's not getting paid for being a lieutenant, so he probably can't afford a wetting-down party. But I'd say that's his tough luck, wouldn't you Art?"

"Yes, Admiral, it is," answered Powell. "War's hell."

They shook hands with Benjamin and followed Powell down the hallway to a briefing room, its walls lined with maps and blown-up aerial photos.

Coburn was happy with his first morning in-country. From a miserable night in the hellhole of Koeppler Compound to a high-profile job and the three-star boss bending the rules and giving him a promotion, albeit a promotion in name only. Still, he had to go back to his damp upper bunk, dripping cold-water showers, and a serenade of snoring at the end of the day.

A full commander looked up from a chart table in the briefing room. Powell introduced him as the NAVFORV intelligence officer for III and IV corps, which included the Mekong Delta, the major southern rivers, and the southernmost coast. The commander gave them a concise and informative briefing, focusing on the riverine areas that Coburn and Vernon would be operating in.

From the edge of Saigon to the Cambodian border with the exception of the areas occupied by large army bases and a few provincial capitals, the civilian population seemed to support the Viet Cong, often providing shelter and food. The commander described an area that was not secure. "Indian territory."

Since Tet, VC ambushes and firefights had dropped appreciably. But infiltration of men and supplies into the area continued.

Coburn raised his hand. "Commander, does that lower level of activity since Tet mean the VC are hurting? You know, light at the end of the tunnel?"

"The VC and the NVA units took a beating during Tet. They lost a lot of men and used up a lot of resources. But so did we. Not as much as they did, though. My assessment is that they're regrouping and building up their numbers and supplies, especially via the Ho Chi Minh trail and through Saigon into your areas. So yes, they are hurting, but they've put a big hurt into us. In my opinion," the intelligence officer looked at Powell, who gave a slight nod of his head, "the VC and North Vietnamese scored a major strategic victory. Not here but in the United States. The American public's support for this effort is now a big question mark. Same for Congress."

Powell joined in. "I agree with that. This is a war of attrition for them, while for us it's a war of maneuvers and technology. If you have the patience, you will always win a war of attrition."

He looked at Coburn. "Mr. Coburn, do you know who said the VC and North are 'seeking victory by eroding and exhausting the enemy instead of engaging him'?"

"I don't know, sir."

Vernon spoke up. "Wasn't that President Kennedy, sir?"

"Yes it was, Mr. Vernon. You know your history. That's a valuable tool in this war."

"So, sir, do we have any idea when things will pick up again?" asked Coburn, trying to retrieve the attention.

Powell shook his head as the intelligence officer answered. "No, we don't. A lot will depend on the activity of friendly forces in your area—interdicting, seeking out, and destroying. But until the civilian population forsake the VC and the South Vietnamese get their act together, victory will not be ours." He paused and took a deep breath. "It may never be ours."

The intelligence officer wished them luck, and Powell, using the commander's first name, thanked him for the excellent briefing. They followed the captain back to his office. Coburn added another personal goal to his pile; get Powell's confidence in him to the point where he'd become Clark instead of Mr. Coburn.

Back in his office, Powell told them that Lieutenant Commander Theodore—whom he called Jim—would stay with him for the rest of the day and that Mr. Coburn and Mr. Vernon were to be issued their gear and weapons and then go to their reporting senior, the advisor to the Vietnamese Commander of III and IV Corps River Assault Groups.

Powell looked at Coburn and Vernon. "Lieutenant Commander Pete Mondello is your boss. Good man. Consider yourselves lucky. You'll be working in army areas of operations. It's their AO but you're not working for the army, you're working for Pete. Got that?"

Both lieutenants answered in unison. "Aye, aye, sir."

"Good luck to you two." The captain shook hands first with Vernon and then Coburn. He held onto Coburn's hand a little longer and looked him in the eye. "Mr. Coburn, keep in mind that you have only some of the privileges, but you have all of the responsibilities of your new rank."

"Got it, Captain. I couldn't forget that, even if I wanted to."

"Okay, you two. See Culpepper for transportation. Get to work."

A tall, husky black chief petty officer wearing jungle fatigues was talking to Culpepper when they walked into the office.

"Culpepper, Captain Powell said to see you for transportation for Mr. Coburn and me," said Vernon.

"All set, sir. This is Chief Gunner's Mate Robinson. He'll take you to get your gear and meet with Mr. Mondello." They shook hands and followed Chief Robinson out to a jeep. Sitting shotgun was a thin and suntanned lieutenant in jungle fatigues and a black beret. Embroidered in block capital letters above his right pocket was his name: "Gordon."

Coburn put out his hand. "You must be Arnie Gordon. I'm Clark Coburn, your relief. This is Doug Vernon."

In a Chicago Mayor Daley accent, Gordon replied. "Guilty as charged. I am indeed Arnold Gordon the short timer. You guys met Chief Robinson, I see."

The chief put on his beret and folded his bulk into the driver's seat as Coburn and Vernon climbed into the back seat. Robinson turned his big bulk so he could look at the two of them. "How'd you like to get out of Koeppler Compound before lunch?"

"Chief, are you shitting me? If you can get us out of there before the sun comes up tomorrow, Mr. Coburn here will suck your dick."

They all laughed, but Coburn did not. "Nah, Chief, Mr. Vernon's better at that. Take my word for it."

Again they laughed. Coburn continued. "But don't we have to be there for those indoctrination lessons and whatever else we're supposed to do?"

Gordon turned to look at Coburn and Vernon. "Indoctrination at Koeppler is really for the guys who haven't gone through the training you went through. Mr. Mondello says to pull anyone coming to the RAGs out of there as fast as we can. So far the army doesn't seem to notice—or care. We'll get your gear out of there, grab some *pho*, get your new gear issued, and then we'll visit the boss. You'll stay in the HQ hootch overnight, and then off to the RAG. Avanti, chief, avanti."

"What's *pho*?" asked Vernon.

"Noodle soup, sir," answered Robinson. "One of Vietnam's gifts to the world."

They drove to Koeppler Compound, and within thirty seconds, Coburn and Vernon were back in the jeep with all their gear. Robinson took them on a kamikaze ride through Saigon, entering a large traffic circle crowded with taxis, motorbikes, buses, motor scooters, trucks, and military vehicles. Honking the jeep's horn and yelling in Vietnamese, he bullied the jeep through the circle and off onto a slightly less crowded street, pulling across four lanes of traffic and alongside a sidewalk food stall. Child-sized tables with miniature stools were in the shade of an umbrella. In a cloud of steam, a tiny woman labored away. The smell was delicious.

They unfolded themselves from the jeep and walked up to the stall. Gordon looked at Robinson, who held up four fingers and without asking Vernon or Coburn what they wanted to eat, ordered four bowls of noodle soup in beef broth. The big man then walked down the block and turned into a store. Gordon led Coburn and Vernon to one of the tables, and they hunkered down on the stools, their bent knees a good six inches higher than the tabletop.

A small boy Coburn guessed to be about six or seven but who was probably twelve years old appeared out of nowhere and laid down four chipped ceramic spoons and four sets of chopsticks wrapped in paper, which Coburn was convinced was a square of slick, single-ply toilet paper. Small bowls of bean sprouts, sliced hot peppers, cilantro, and tiny lemons or limes—Coburn wasn't sure which—followed. On his third visit the boy delivered a plate with three jars of unrecognizable gunk colored red, brown, and nearly black.

"Be careful with those. The mildest will burn your asshole for two days unless you puke it up before it makes it that far," said Gordon. "Somehow the Vietnamese have been able to cross hot peppers with lava. If you want to try it, go slow."

Robinson appeared carrying four cold beers and four small glasses. The beer had a big "33" on the label.

"Welcome to in-country, Lieutenants," said Robinson. "Cheers."

They all filled their glasses, clinked them against one another, and took big swallows. The cold beer was a delicious elixir in the heat, soot, and humidity. Coburn thought that maybe this year wasn't going to be so hard after all. Plum job, frocked without being selected, first full day in-country, and drinking cold beer.

Robinson looked comical sitting on a tiny stool designed for someone a foot and a half shorter and half his weight. Coburn noticed that Robinson was carrying a .38 pistol in a holster and

Gordon had a .45. Both he and Vernon were unarmed. He had noticed flak jackets in the jeep.

Pointing at Gordon's .45, Coburn asked, "Should we be armed?"

Gordon shrugged. "Should you? I don't know. Will you? For sure. We'll get you a sidearm and M-16 at the hootch."

"You ever had to use that .45?"

"Let me count." Gordon looked up, apparently remembering the number of times. "I'd say approximately zero. No, make that exactly zero. I have fired it at some cans and junk for practice, but that's it."

Coburn looked at Robinson, who said, "Me, too, sir. Frankly, if someone was close enough to me that I could use my pistol and he was the bad guy, I'd first shit in my pants, then I'd throw the damn .38 at him. I'd have a better chance at hitting him that way then shooting the damned thing. Then I'd run like hell."

Gordon added, more seriously, "The M-16's another story. That gets used."

The boy appeared with two bowls of steaming noodle soup, put them in front of Robinson and Gordon, disappeared, and then came back with two more for Coburn and Vernon. Robinson gave a quick lesson on preparing the soup: squeeze the lime into the soup, throw in a handful of bean sprouts, pull some cilantro leaves off the stem, throw them in, and then judiciously take a hot pepper slice or a drop from the hot pepper sauces, mix with chopsticks, slurp broth with spoon, and slurp the solids with the chopsticks.

The *pho* was delicious, savory, filling, and satisfying. The beer made a pleasant tranquilizer. Coburn was quite happy in-country.

Vernon asked Gordon what their share of lunch was, and Gordon laughed it off, saying that they should do the same with whomever their reliefs were in a year. Besides, the entire meal cost about three dollars for the four of them, including the tip to the little boy.

After lunch they walked down to the Rex, a hotel taken over as a BOQ, and Coburn and Vernon exchanged their US dollars for Military Payments Certificates—MPCs—and South Vietnamese piasters. MPCs were scrip to be spent in US facilities in-country. They were an attempt to slow down the rampant black market in US goods and dollars. The piaster-to-dollar exchange rate was officially 138 p to a dollar. But an MPC could get you 250 p in any Saigon bar or market. A genuine greenback could get 500 or more. An American serviceman caught dealing in the black market or exchanging MPC at any unauthorized location could get a court martial. Or so the rumors went. Gordon and Robinson had never heard of anyone being arrested by the MPs for buying pussy at black market rates.

They drove to the billeting office to get space in a Saigon BOQ for their trips back from the rivers. Both Coburn and Vernon got rooms at the Le Qui Don, a small hotel in a quiet, tree-shaded part of town. They checked out their rooms and to their delight discovered old, noisy but working window air-conditioning units and bathrooms with dripping showers. A visit to the gigantic PX in Cholon came next. They picked up necessities like bug spray and soap. The PX was crowded with Korean and Thai soldiers grabbing TV sets and kitchen appliances as soon as they were put on the shelves.

Back in the jeep, they drove along the Saigon River past the South Vietnamese Navy headquarters, across a small bridge, through a river craft repair yard onto the South Vietnamese Navy's RAG Command compound. They pulled up to the combined quarters and offices—the hootch—of their boss, Lieutenant Commander Pete Mondello.

The hootch was empty. Mondello was probably meeting with his counterpart, Commander Minh—Commander of the River Assault Group Command. So Gordon and Robinson walked Coburn and Vernon over to the supply building, where a US Navy gunner's mate issued them weapons, magazine clips, ammunition, web gear, helmets, flack vests, duffel bag, backpack, ponchos, quilted poncho liners, two more sets of jungle boots, reef booties, olive-drab underwear and socks, sheath knife, pocket knife, emergency medical kit, survival kit, floppy hat, canteen, mess kit, mosquito netting, hammock, air mattress, flashlights with red and clear lenses, camouflage grease paint in olive-drab lipstick containers, rubber shower shoes, ballpoint pens, green pocket notebook, toothbrush, toothpaste, soap, shaving cream, and a pack of Gillette Blue Blades and razor holder.

"Holy shit," marveled Vernon as he stuffed the equipment into a duffel bag. "This is like Christmas morning when I was a kid."

Robinson chuckled. "Mr. Vernon, that's some valuable shit there. That poncho liner is worth a blow job in the finest of skivvy houses. Or so they tell me. Same for the hammock and air mattress. Don't pack away your fatigue blouses. We'll take them over to Ba Be and get them embroidered with US NAVY, your name, and rank insignia. She'll also get your berets."

"Who's Ba Be?" asked Coburn.

"She's sort of the mother of the hootch," said Gordon. "Cleans, cooks if you want her to, does laundry, tailoring, any domestic chores. The boss pays her a couple of bucks a day and all that she can lug away without our catching her. I guess there's a market for empty cans and bottles. She does all right. Owns a couple of houses in Saigon. Don't piss her off, though. She is the boss of the hootch."

"Shit, I found that out the hard way," laughed Robinson. "I had just come down from an operation, had mud on my boots, and walked across the deck she had just swabbed. She started yelling at me and then gave me the stink eye and the silent treatment for another month. At first I thought she didn't like colored folks. But no, she just didn't like me—or anyone else—fucking up her decks."

They walked back into the hootch and found Ba Be sweeping the office space. Gordon introduced her to the new arrivals. A pleasant-looking woman, probably in her early forties, maybe a bit older, thought Coburn. She had her black hair tied back in a ponytail and wore a loose-fitting white shirt, baggy dark-blue pants, and shower shoes. Coburn and Vernon gave her their jungle fatigue blouses. She noted their names from their black plastic name tags and their ranks from their insignia.

"Dai Uys," she said approvingly.

Dai Uy was Vietnamese for a navy lieutenant or army or marine captain. She had heard that Gordon was being replaced by a Trung Uy—a jaygee—and she didn't like it and had told Mondello so in no uncertain terms. It was an insult to Gordon and to his counterpart, she said. Now she was glad to see that the US Navy had listened to her.

She demanded that the two new arrivals bow down so she could reach their heads, and she measured the circumference of their skulls with a string and knot. Then she bustled out of the hootch, the jungle fatigues cradled in her arms.

As she left, a tall, officer in khakis walked in. Gordon jumped up and introduced Lieutenant Commander Pete Mondello to Coburn and Vernon. Coburn, as he usually did when meeting people who could influence his life for better or worse, sized up Mondello.

Mondello was handsome and physically fit, and he wore a command-at-sea badge on his chest, which meant he had early command of a ship. He looked like something out of a recruiting poster, like someone Hollywood would cast as a heroic naval officer with a girl like Doris Day back home. He moved with confidence. This guy's going to make admiral, and he's going to take me with him, thought Coburn.

"Welcome aboard, Clark. Welcome aboard, Doug. Or do you go by Douglas?" asked Mondello as he shook hands. Coburn liked that he was Clark, not Mr. Coburn, to his new boss.

Vernon said, "Doug's what I go by, but everyone else calls me 'hey you,' sir." Coburn noted that Vernon was at ease and confident enough to make Mondello laugh.

"Grab a seat, everyone." Mondello moved to the chair behind his desk. He looked at Coburn. "Did you get promoted since your orders were cut? I was expecting a jaygee."

"No, sir, no promotion. Still out of the zone for selection. Admiral Benjamin frocked me."

Robinson put a copy of the frocking letter that Culpepper had given him in front of Mondello.

"Well, congratulations, Clark. I'm sure Captain Powell wouldn't have let that happen if it wasn't deserved. I was worried about a jaygee in the job."

Gordon slouched in his chair. "You were worried, boss? How about me? I was afraid you wouldn't let me go home until Clark got promoted. I had to bribe Admiral Benjamin with that bushel of MPC I found when I was rifling through your closet." They all laughed, although again Coburn felt he was falling behind the other two lieutenants in the room.

"Arnie, I was wondering what happened to all that money. I want it back before you get on the freedom bird, understand? It was several hundred thousand dollars."

"No problem, sir. A check okay?"

The easy banter and the comfortable air of the hootch reminded Coburn of the DeKalb's wardroom when the XO wasn't on the rag. Mondello asked the two new advisors about their previous duty stations, hometowns, and families. Then he leaned forward on his elbows.

"Okay, Clark, you're relieving that criminal over there." He nodded his head at Gordon. "And despite his antics, he's done a wonderful job, and you have some big shoes to fill. He and Chief Robinson are going to show you around here the rest of today and tomorrow morning, and then I want you on Arnie like stink on shit for the next week in Phu Cuong and on the river. He gets on that plane in exactly eight days.

"Doug, unfortunately, the guy you were supposed to relieve is in Oaknoll Naval Hospital. Lost his left foot and got pretty badly burned. I want you with Arnie, Chief Robinson, and Clark today and tomorrow morning. Then I'll drive you down to Nha Be, your base."

Ba Be walked into the hootch, smiled hello to everyone, and held out the embroidered jungle fatigues. The letters were bold and black. US NAVY over the left pocket, COBURN and VER-NON over the right, black lieutenant bars embroidered on the collar, and the three black pips of a Dai Uy on the front button flap. She had a plastic bag slung over her shoulder.

"Good job, huh, Dai Uys? Only two hundred piasters. Nice work." Then she took two berets out of the bag and handed them to Coburn and Vernon. "Beret for RAG advisors. Number-one quality. Three hundred piasters."

Coburn and Vernon agreed that the work was nice, put on their berets, thanked her, and each forked over 500 p for the 50-p embroidering and 150-p beret.

Mondello looked at both of them. "You'll be more comfortable in those than in khakis. Unless you hear otherwise, that's the uniform of the day here and at NAVFORV. When you're off this base, wear a sidearm. Civvies okay in the hootch or if you're eating at the officers mess and off duty. I don't give a shit what you wear on the river, just don't embarrass the navy or your counterpart.

"Okay, get out of those khakis. Ba Be will get some bunks ready for you, and she's making dinner tonight if you want to eat here. Plan on starting at 0700 with me tomorrow morning. I'll give you my idea of how things are going and what I expect from you two. Then we'll pay a call on my counterpart, Commander Minh. Then, Clark, you go to Phu Cuong with Arnie and the chief, and I'll take Doug to Nha Be."

* * *

Mondello was at his desk drinking coffee out of a paper cup and reading the morning message traffic when Coburn and Vernon walked into the hootch. Both were in jungle fatigues. "Good morning, Doug. Morning, Clark. You sleep okay?"

"Boss, I don't know. I was asleep and didn't notice," quipped Vernon. Mondello smiled, and Coburn found Vernon's easy manner with Mondello and adopting Gordon's calling Mondello ''boss'' vaguely irritating.

"I don't remember hitting the pillow, sir," added Coburn, just to have something to say.

The rest of Mondello's staff of sailors were bustling around the open office, the chiefs in khakis, the lower ranks in dungarees. A sailor put two paper cups of black coffee on Mondello's desk by the two chairs facing it.

Mondello pointed at the chairs. "Sit down. I assume you had breakfast?"

"Yes, sir. At the mess. Not bad," answered Coburn.

"Good. I asked Arnie and Chief Robinson to debrief Commander Minh, so it's just the three of us." Mondello stood up and lifted a shade that was covering a bulletin board behind his desk. Maps of their areas of operations were thumb tacked to the board. He walked to the door, stuck his head out, and yelled for someone named Bill.

A few seconds later, Bill walked into the office, a stubby jay-gee in khakis. Mondello introduced them to Lieutenant (Junior Grade) William Wilson, the advisory unit's intelligence officer and counterpart to Commander Minh's intelligence officer.

For the next hour Wilson went through an intelligence analysis of activity in their AOs. He went into greater detail and specifics than the presentation of the day before in the briefing room at NAVFORV. And the conclusion was the same.

The VC and NVA were licking their wounds and rebuilding their forces and supplies. They were keeping their profile low. Following doctrine, they avoided large unit confrontations. Instead, they used guerrilla tactics, attacking in small groups and then vanishing.

"And, finally, the civilians in your two areas are for the most part apathetic or support the VC. Very few support the South Vietnamese government. As far as they're concerned, the government's a bunch of crooks." Wilson paused and took a sip of the coffee that Ba Be had handed him during his presentation.

"These peasants don't care who's running their government. They want their fish, their rice, their land, their security. They seem to prefer paying the VC tax collector rather than handing out bribes to the White Mice and province chief."

"White Mice?" asked Vernon.

"South Vietnamese National Police. They wore uniforms with white shirts. Their boss was that thug in the newspaper photo summarily executing a guy on a Saigon street during Tet. Not a very nice bunch." Wilson smiled with tight lips as he shook his head.

With Ba Be in the background sweeping and making sure the coffee cups didn't leave a ring on Mondello's desk, the three junior officers got into a detailed discussion about types of weapons and tactics being used by the VC, hot spots, safe spots, NVA unit locations, and the likelihood of VC or NVA escalation. Mondello sat mute, listening.

"Okay, guys," summed up Wilson. "That's my story, and I'm sticking to it. I'll see you when you drop in here, and occasionally the boss lets me out, so I might be in your neck of the rivers and ride along on an operation, especially if my counterpart decides to get out of his hammock and visit. Good luck."

Wilson shook hands with Coburn and Vernon, nodded to Mondello, and waved at Ba Be as he left the hootch. The fact that Wilson hadn't used "sir" when talking to Coburn stuck in Coburn's mind. He wore a rank on his collar that was one level senior to Wilson's. Where was the deference that rank demanded? Or is this place just casual and sloppy?

"Bill's done a good job here. Problem is that he's thinking about leaving the navy when this tour is up," said Mondello. "BUPERS wants to send him to grad school, and the Intel community is hot for him to change his designator to intelligence, but he just got acceptance letters from Harvard and Stanford MBA programs. How do I persuade him to pass that up?"

"Boss, you can't. At least not with a straight face. Maybe you can get BUPERS to pick up the MBA cost if he promises to stay in?" ventured Vernon.

"I already tried that. Bill did say he might stay in the reserves, but that's as good as being out," said Mondello.

Let him go, Coburn thought. The less competition for the good jobs the better. "Sir, how about Doug and I just break his kneecaps or something?"

Mondello laughed heartily at Coburn's suggestion and said he had some relatives on his wife's side who would be glad to take a contract for the work. Coburn felt he had gained the spotlight.

Mondello's face then turned serious as he hunched over his desktop and leaned on his elbows, his desk chair tipping forward a bit.

"You two need to know what I expect from you. I'm sure Captain Powell told you much of what you will hear from me.

"First, this will be your first time in a joint command. MACV is led by an army four star. You will be operating in army AOs with your support coming from the army. But you do not work for the army. You work for me, and that's navy. I expect you to be deferential and cooperative with the army people, but I expect you to keep me informed. If in doubt about what to do, you come to me before you do something stupid. I don't want to be blindsided by Captain Powell calling me up saying Admiral Benjamin is pissed because one of my people got out of the box. I want you to show and take initiative, but don't lose track of our objective." He let that sink in.

"Secondly, you're advisors. You do not have authority over your counterpart or his people or his equipment. You are going to advise an officer—who has never lived in a time of peace or a place of safety his entire life—on how to fight a war that you have no experience in fighting. He's been fighting a war for years. You have not. He's familiar with his equipment and men. You are not. But you bring something that he may have lost. Objectivity. And a bigger global picture, and fresh eyes. The fact that you got to steer a ten-thousand-ton ship loaded with technology through the Atlantic doesn't mean much here. But your brains and character do.

"The enemy is not to be underestimated. They are good fighters and tacticians, and they are brave. More importantly, they are patient. Their objective is unification under the government in Hanoi. Maybe I'm too jaded, but I don't know what the goal of the South is. Status quo? Unification under a coalition?

Democratization of North and South? I don't want to hear any counterinsurgency school bullshit out of either of you two about domino theories or saving the world for democracy.

"The RAGs you're going to are not bad, not good. Some good South Vietnamese naval officers are trying to do their jobs. Some of the officers are lazy and incompetent because of patronage or nepotism and waiting for a promotion to some cushy job in HQ. The noncoms are on the whole pretty good. Not the best technicians, but most of the gear is pretty simple. Good boat handlers. Fair mechanics. When fired upon, I've seen them fight like crazy—hard to get them to cease fire. The rest of the sailors are just trying to stay alive. Most have families living in huts near the bases. Pay is shit. If you capture any goods, rice, whatever, the command can sell it on the market, and supposedly the sailors get a cut. I think most of it goes to whoever arranges the sale and the connected officers."

He stopped for a moment, collecting his thoughts. Then he said, "Assume that you have VC in the crew. Be careful what you say.

"Now for the important part for you. How you do this will affect your fitness report."

Coburn had quit listening and was just staring off in the distance, thinking that he was getting hungry. What did they do for lunch around here? Eat at the mess hall? Maybe drive into the city for more of that soup? He noticed a gecko sunning itself on the windowsill.

"Clark, you listening?" barked Mondello sharply. Coburn snapped out of it. Mondello had a bite.

"Yes, sir, I'm listening intently."

Mondello looked at him for a few seconds and then resumed his instructions. Coburn was embarrassed.

"Vietnamization of this war is ramping up. More and more turnover of US equipment, bases, and AOs to the Vietnamese. This is their war to win or lose. It's your job to make sure your counterparts and their commands can function without American supply, administration, support, air cover, artillery, and lastly and most importantly, without you. I don't think there's a RAG that's ready."

He looked at Coburn. "Clark, Arnie has your RAG nearly there, but it's easy to slide backward in this place, especially since his—and soon to be your—counterpart is not the strongest. Well connected, well meaning, but weak. Maybe even stupid.

"Doug, your RAG is the one in the hottest area, even with this post-Tet lull. They've taken a lot of hits, and I think your counterpart has a real morale problem on his hands. But he's a good man."

More to show he was listening than anything else, Coburn asked a question. "Sir, sounds as if I've got a problem counterpart. Do we have any say in replacing him?"

"In your case it means going all the way up to the admiral and having him suggest to his counterpart, Commodore Chon, to make a change. Remember, your counterpart's the kid of the president's sister."

"That sounds hard to do sir," said Coburn with a thin smile on his lips.

"Damn right, Clark. But we may see a lot of personnel movement on the South Vietnamese Navy's side. For every unit we turn over, they'll commission the unit and will have to staff it with their own personnel. Experienced officers, noncoms, and sailors will probably be taken from existing South Vietnamese Navy units—like your RAG—and be assigned to the new units. That means someone has to fill in the spots they left. The other personnel moves will be those of the privileged like Clark's counterpart, who will be given a promotion and put into a do-nothing job with a prestigious title."

"Gee, boss, he could wind up being your counterpart," joked Vernon. Mondello stared at him for a second, then broke into a wide smile. "Y'know, Doug, you have a devious mind. That should take you far around here. I heard General Giap is looking for a new navy liaison in Hanoi. I'll put your name in."

The three men laughed, although Coburn didn't want to. Mondello's smile eased into a serious expression again.

"So my final instructions to you are to resist the temptation to call in American support or use our logistics channels for your counterpart's unit. Let him use the Vietnamese support. Let him call in Vietnamese air and artillery. They've got both, and they're not bad. Let him call in his own medevacs. Let him go to his own boss or staff to set up and plan an operation. You help in every way you can, but when you get on the freedom bird in a year, I want your unit running on its own. I want to be able to tell the admiral that your unit doesn't need an advisor anymore."

"Aye, aye, sir," said Coburn.

"Doug, Clark, let's not fool ourselves. What I want may not happen through no fault of your efforts. We're dealing with a culture that is different than ours, and we may be pushing on a rope. But we have to try."

"Got it, boss."

"Me too, sir."

"I'm sure you do. Let your counterparts take command, don't do it for them. They may resist, but step back as long as you and your sailors are not in danger. This is not how you were brought up in our navy. Because of that, being an advisor is a tough job. But from now on, it's better to let your counterpart and his staff do an adequate job then for you to do his job perfectly."

Mondello looked at both officers for a few moments in silence. "And whatever you do, don't get killed. Too much fucking paperwork for me. Let's grab some lunch and then visit Commander Minh."

They joined Gordon and Robinson in the mess for lunch. Gordon announced, "Gentlemen, 181 hours to go in-country, but who's counting?" After lunch they walked over to the headquarters of the commander of the RAGs, where a woman wearing an ao dai at a desk told them to take a seat and asked if they wanted tea.

Coburn checked her out. She was slender with beautiful, long, black hair parted in the middle that reached her shoulders. She appeared to have a full bosom, but whether that was her or a padded bra would need further investigation. And she was pretty, very pretty.

Commander Minh came out of his office and greeted Mondello, calling him by his first name. He shook hands with Gordon and Robinson, obviously familiar and friendly with both. Mondello introduced Minh to Coburn and Vernon. Minh was a foot shorter than Coburn and probably fifty pounds lighter. He spoke accented English effortlessly. His black hair was flecked with gray. Coburn guessed him to be in his fifties, maybe a bit younger. They followed Minh into his office and took seats on two very low couches, their asses five inches from the floor, their knees at the level of their ears.

After a few words of welcome and some questions about Coburn and Vernon's background, Minh told Coburn, "Dai Uy Coburn, you are replacing an officer who is brave, smart, and well liked by all of us. Dai Uy Gordon will be missed very much. He is truly our friend. As you Americans say, you have big shoes to fill."

"Yes, sir, I appreciate that. Maybe you can persuade him to stay another year and help me?" joked Coburn.

Gordon shook his head as the others laughed. "No way, Dai Uy, no way. Numbah ten." Gordon pronounced "number ten," the Vietnamese slang for terrible, in his best bar girl accent.

Minh looked at Mondello. "Pete, that's a good idea. Can you do something about that?"

"Commander, I don't want to. Let's get rid of him. Good riddance."

Again they all laughed. Minh turned to Vernon. "Dai Uy Vernon, you are going to a dangerous place. We need you there very badly. I wish you luck, sincerely. Please be safe, yes?"

"Aye, aye, Commander I will." Vernon was uncharacteristically solemn.

Minh stood up. "Gentlemen, I wish you all the best of luck. I am sure I will see Dai Uy Vernon and Dai Uy Coburn frequently in the next twelve months, and I am looking forward to our meetings." He turned to Gordon and took his hand.

"Dai Uy Gordon, I will see you in six days. At that time we will formally say goodbye to you, and also I am pleased to announce that you will receive several decorations from a grateful nation. One will be the Cross of Gallantry, first class."

Gordon smiled and shook hands with Minh. They all said good-bye and walked out of his office. Coburn stopped briefly at the secretary's desk and said in Vietnamese that he hoped to see her again. She smiled but did not reply. Maybe she hadn't understood him, thought Coburn. He looked up and saw Mondello looking at him, tight lipped and shaking his head in a silent rebuke.

So the boss didn't want him messing with the office help. Nevertheless, Coburn felt excited. If Gordon was leaving in a shower of medals, so would he. He wasn't going to blow this opportunity.

Mondello changed into jungle fatigues, flak vest, and helmet, with a .45 on his hip. He put an M-16 next to the driver's seat of his jeep. Vernon, identically attired, put his duffel in the back and climbed in the front seat, his M-16 upright between his knees. Gordon, Robinson, and Coburn, also in flak vest and helmet and sidearmed, got in their jeep, Robinson driving, Gordon in the back, and Coburn riding shotgun.

The two jeeps were side by side. Mondello started his engine, shut it off, and then got out of the jeep and walked between the two vehicles. He was standing beside Coburn, Vernon a few feet away.

"Clark, Doug, there's something I should have said to you yesterday, so let me say it now. You two are going off to war. And independent duty. There are rules to be followed, ethics to be preserved, and behavior standards to be met. But you are the only ones who can ensure that happens. There's no senior officer standing in the back of the bridge watching you handle the ship and your men. It will be very easy to bend the rules, to violate them, and a good chance no one will find out. But you'll know, and you have to live with that. Got it?"

"Aye, aye, sir," said Coburn and Vernon in unison.

He looked at both officers for several seconds. Then he smiled and patted Coburn's shoulder. "Okay, let's get you two to work."

Robinson followed Mondello's jeep out of the compound and across the bridge and turned northwest as Mondello turned southeast. They waved good-bye.

* * *

With liberal use of the jeep's horn, Chief Robinson wheeled through midday Saigon traffic. As he explained to Coburn, there was a hierarchy of right-of-way in Saigon. The bigger the vehicle, the greater the right. Jeeps had the right-of-way over everything except for buses and trucks and could usually outmaneuver and accelerate around those. The other big secret to Saigon driving was to never make eye contact with another driver. Doing so would immediately relinquish your right-of-way to the other guy. And the horn was your basic driving tool. Then your accelerator. Next your steering wheel. And finally, as a last resort, your brakes.

It was hot, but the movement of the vehicle created enough breeze to keep Coburn comfortable despite the flak vest and helmet. As they threaded their way north through the city, he saw that Saigon must have been the Pearl of the Orient. But now, for the most part, it was dirty, ramshackle, and stinky.

They passed the Ben Nghe channel, a small tributary of the Saigon River. It was a dark brown, almost black, scum-filled waterway choked with sampans and small barges; a pungent floating market. Two little kids were jumping off a waterside shack's porch into the water, playing some sort of game.

They skirted Tan Son Nhut and then crossed the Saigon River on the Binh Loi bridge onto the wide concrete pavement of Highway 1. Women were selling what looked like giant grapefruit or prickly looking fruit of similar size from little stands along the road. Only some military trucks and a few ancient Citroen taxis were on the road.

Robinson turned the jeep north onto Highway 13 near the village of Heip Binh. Gordon yelled into Coburn's ear that this stretch was called Thunder Road by the US Army, which sent convoys up and down it daily, servicing the big base at Cu Chi. The road threaded through the area of operations of "The Big Red 1" First Division, the Eleventh Armored Calvary Regiment, and the "Tropic Lightning" Twenty-fifth Infantry Division.

"Lots of US firepower in this neighborhood," yelled Gordon. "And the ARVN are all over the place, too. Our AO is the river over there," he swept his hand from his left to straight ahead, "all the way up to Cambodia." They were just east of the river, but Coburn couldn't see it.

Robinson accelerated the jeep as they rode up Highway 13. Vestiges of the city and its stink were gone. They were now hurtling though small villages, rice paddies, fields, and sparse woods. "We're in the rocket belt, sir. About the max range for the VC rockets to hit Saigon ends just a few klicks from us," said Robinson to Coburn.

"What's a 'klick,' Chief?" asked Coburn.

"A kilometer, sir. Speedometer on this jeep is in klicks. It's our jeep, but since we're advisors, it's configured for the Vietnamese. Better start thinking metric, sir."

"Roger that, Chief." Coburn thought for a minute then asked over his shoulder to Gordon, "Do we call in artillery in meters or yards here?"

Robinson grinned as Gordon answered. "Artillery, air strikes, medevacs, directions to the skivvy house, and the length of my dick are all in meters and kilometers, Clark. US and Vietnamese."

"Mr. Gordon's given to exaggeration, sir," said Robinson. "When you're dealing with his dick, better use millimeters and a magnifying glass. Now me, on the other hand..." Robinson quit talking and just smiled. Coburn relaxed in his seat. This was comfortable. He liked it. This was going to be a real good year.

They caught up with a rumbling convoy of trucks doing about thirty klicks, roughly twenty miles per hour. Two helicopter gunships circled overhead. The driver of the last truck waved his arm out the window to tell Robinson he could pass. Robinson blinked his lights, got into the narrow left lane, and accelerated, passing about twenty trucks and an MP jeep at the lead. He blinked his lights and tooted his horn as he passed each vehicle.

"You don't want to get too close to a convoy, especially one like that loaded with goodies. Charlie likes to ambush those. We don't need that, sir," said Robinson. "But it's been pretty peaceful on old Thunder Road lately."

Gordon shouted from the back seat, "Yeah, let's keep it that way until Arnie Gordon's ass is on that big bird back to Travis."

"What's your next duty station, Arnie?" asked Coburn.

"XO school at Newport and then XO on a guided missile destroyer out of Pearl, Clark. Pretty nice set of orders for a fuckup like me."

"Sounds good to me, Arnie."

"Yeah, me too. My wife is going nuts. She's already dieting and exercising so she can look good in a bikini on the beach while I'm floating around the Pacific. And she's telling her parents and her sister-the-bitch-beast's family to visit us for the winter. Since they're all from Buffalo, I think I'll be having house guests from October through March."

The jeep continued on through the villages of Lai Thieu, Buing, and Chinh Nghia, where Robinson pulled off and took a side road to a well-guarded motor pool where they stretched their legs and fueled the jeep.

"We're almost there, sir," Robinson said as they pulled back onto Highway 13 and headed north.

They turned off of Highway 13 and threaded through the quiet town of Phu Cuong. After a short drive to the waterfront, they turned left down a dirt frontage road, past a floating pier. Tied to the pier were several converted landing craft and smaller French-era vessels, all painted a dark gray, all bristling guns, all with the yellow-and-red flag of South Vietnam waving from their masts. The jeep turned into a riverside clearing and stopped at a steel gate and rows of concertina wire. A South Vietnamese sailor smiled and saluted the jeep. He pulled the concertina wire's wood frame back enough to open the gate and waved the jeep in. They stopped in front of a hootch with several antennas on its roof.

"Lieutenant Coburn, welcome to US Navy Advisory Group, RAG Bravo, the home of the pitiful motherfuckers," said Gordon.

"Yes, sir, home sweet home," said Robinson as he hefted his gear and Coburn's duffel out of the jeep.

Coburn, carrying his M-16, followed Robinson to the hootch. The solid, low structure was built by the navy's Seabees two years ago. Sandbags surrounded a cement wall, twenty centimeters thick and a meter high, that was the border of the fifteen-by-fifteen-meter cement slab on which sat the hootch. Leading from the back of the hootch to an open shower and toilet shack was a five-meter-long paved path. A cement wall and sandbags protected the shower and toilet. There were no breaks in the wall. Coburn had to climb up a three-step wooden stairway to get over the wall and then three steps down the inside.

The cement slab between the wall and hootch had been turned into a makeshift patio with some low-slung chairs, a small table, a fifty-five-gallon oil drum converted into a barbeque grill, and a Pawley's Island hammock strung between the corner of the hootch and a thick steel pole that supported an antenna platform.

The hootch had three rooms. The largest was the kitchen/office/lounge, which featured a plumbed sink and cold-water faucet, a refrigerator with freezer on top, a propane-fueled four-burner stove and oven, cushion-topped storage bins that also served as sofas, a table/desk with six chairs on casters, a landline phone, communications radios, television, reel-to-reel tape deck, and a radio. The next biggest room was the enlisted bunk room. Although there were only two occupants, the room contained two bunk beds, four lockers, and two writing tables. The smallest room was the officer's room, half the size of the enlisted bunk room and half the furniture. Electric lights hung from the rafters and outlets ran along the plywood walls. A box of candles, a hurricane lamp, a first-aid box, and a fire extinguisher were in every room.

Sitting against the wall of the big room was a locked weapons cabinet below a bulletin board that featured Elizabeth Jordan, the May 1968 Playmate of the Month with staple holes in her leopard-skin miniskirt. Next to the weapons cabinet stood an old treadle-powered Singer sewing machine and a box of red, yellow, and blue cloth.

Halfway between the hootch and the shower and toilet, surrounded by more sandbags, was a diesel generator and fuel tank. The generator was on automatic standby and would start if the hootch lost electrical power.

The shower, a small sink, and toilet were gravity fed and plumbed, as was the kitchen sink, to a septic tank. The water source was a large water tank that once had wheels and a trailer hitch. It had been hoisted onto a sturdy platform above the shower and painted flat black.

Robinson pointed to the tank. "That's our hot water." He then pointed to the sun. "And that's our hot water heater."

Gordon added, "If you don't want to freeze and have your balls and dick shrivel up, take your shower in the late afternoon. It won't be hot, but you won't die of chill shock either. And don't drink this water. The army has contractors who will fill up our tanks twice a week and claim it's been purified, but I wouldn't trust it. We have a container in the refrigerator with treated water."

"Tastes like shit, but won't give you the drizzlies, sir," added Robinson. "Okay to drink the water out of the taps if you boil it. We do a lot of iced tea and coffee and drink a hell of a lot of soda and canned juice."

"Think booze will kill the water germs, Chief?" asked Coburn.

"Probably. Cruz uses vodka as an antiseptic, mouthwash, and water purifier as well as an aftershave."

"Where is Cruz?" asked Coburn.

"Your future and very able assistant advisor Engineman First Class Orlando Cruz is probably on a resupply run with Ba Mei. I see the skimmer is gone," answered Gordon. "They're probably trading VC flags for coffee, chocolate milk, and whatever else they can scrounge from the army quartermasters upriver."

Gordon could see from Coburn's expression that he might as well be talking in Greek. "Don't worry about it. I'll explain it all to you later."

"Okay, I guess. But who's Ba Mei?"

"Our hootch mother, maid, domestic servant, laundress, cook, and if you miss your wife, nag."

"You mean like Ba Be in the boss's hootch?"

"Precisely, Clark. You can't expect us to clean up our own shit, can you? After all, we're busy being warriors. We don't have time to dump trash or wash our skivvies."

Coburn looked around and smiled, shaking his head in wonderment. This was sweet. Even a maid. This year could be a very good one, indeed. He looked around the big room in the hootch.

"Seabees built all this?" he asked.

"Yes, sir," said Robinson. "It's amazing the home improvements a phony VC flag, captured AK-47, or a bottle of Jack Daniels will get you."

The sound of footsteps on the wooden steps caused Coburn to turn around. A small woman wearing a conical straw hat, loose white blouse, baggy black pants, and rubber sandals came down the steps followed by a short and husky man wearing a sleeveless jungle fatigue blouse with CRUZ embroidered above his right pocket, cut-off fatigue trousers, floppy hat, and shower shoes. He carried a large cardboard carton on his left shoulder and a bulging duffel bag in his right hand.

Gordon introduced Coburn to Cruz and Ba Mei. Cruz offered a welcome-aboard cigar to Coburn. Ba Mei sized Coburn up from beneath the cone of her hat.

Cruz put the duffel bag and carton on the floor in front of the refrigerator. Ba Mei started unloading the bag, rapidly putting sodas, juices, and produce into the refrigerator; the contents of a cardboard box into the freezer; cans into the locker next to the stove; and cardboard boxes of cereal and bags of potato chips, pretzels, rice, and flour into a stainless steel container that Coburn had originally thought was a safe. Cruz hoisted the big cardboard box onto a refrigerator shelf and pulled out a white plastic umbilical tube with a clip in the middle. It was a carton of chocolate milk. Five gallons' worth. The bottom of the refrigerator was filled with rows of Australian beer. Ba Mei scurried out and up and over the steps and then reappeared with a large fish.

She looked at Coburn. "Fish, Dai Uy. Eat. Number one."

"That's dinner tonight, Mr. Coburn. In your honor. She insisted on it."

"That's nice, Cruz." Coburn bowed to Ba Mei and thanked her in Vietnamese. She took off her hat and smiled. Ba Mei was probably in her mid thirties. Tiny, delicate to the point of being skinny by even Vietnamese standards, but pretty.

But when she smiled, "pretty" was the last adjective Coburn would have used to describe her. Ba Mei had been chewing betel nut, and her teeth and gums were now a dark, nearly black, red. Coburn found the sight disgusting and hoped he hadn't grimaced.

He looked away. "Cruz, that's a lot of food you brought in. How do we pay for that? We all pitch in or does the army charge some account or what?" Cruz, Robinson, and Gordon all laughed.

Cruz walked over to the doorjamb between the big room and the enlisted bunkroom, reached around the corner, and took a key off a hook. He unlocked the weapons cabinet.

"We pay for it from our bank account, Dai Uy," said Cruz as he opened the cabinet. "And this is our bank."

The cabinet had a few empty slots for the M-16s that he, Gordon and Robinson were carrying. In the remaining slots were an M-16, which was Cruz's, a holstered .45, which was also Cruz's, an M-60 machine gun, and an M-79 grenade launcher. That inventory was what Coburn had expected.

But there were also six AK-47 assault rifles, three SKS rifles, four Chicom pistols, several boxes of various kinds of US, Russian, and Chicom ammunition, a machete, a Chicom mess kit, and a pile of neatly folded red, blue, and yellow Viet Cong flags.

Coburn let out a low whistle. Gordon explained that the pile of food Ba Mei and Cruz had just brought in—excluding the fish, which she probably bartered from a local fisherman for some no-longer-used piece of US Navy issued equipment—cost about half a genuine VC flag, which they had produced with the sewing machine.

"Ba Mei's a great seamstress, and Cruz is a crackerjack sales-man," said Gordon.

"You mean someone gave us all that for half a flag?"

Cruz explained. "Not really. They gave us that, and then we get another load later in the week for a whole flag, sir. Although sometimes we actually do have to buy something with MPCs or piasters. Then we pass the hat, but that's pretty rare."

Robinson added, "I figure we could get another jeep if we wanted one for one of those pistols or an SKS."

"Shit, Chief. I think we could probably get a tank or maybe even a destroyer for the whole fucking cabinet," remarked Coburn.

Gordon put his hand on Coburn's shoulder. "You are a man with vision, Dai Uy. You will go far. Probably wind up in the brig, though."

* * *

After moving his gear in, Coburn toured the RAG base with Gordon, Robinson, and Cruz while Ba Mei prepared the fish for dinner. Besides the hootch, the base contained several red-tile-roofed buildings that looked to be made of plaster-covered plywood. One was the RAG command center, which served as office, communication center, and the living space for the RAG commanding officer and his family.

The CO, Lieutenant Commander Nguyen Van Toh, was rarely at the base and never on operations, spending his time in Saigon and Nha Be supposedly working with headquarters. His executive officer, Lieutenant Le Binh Chang, occupied the quarters and for all practical purposes commanded the RAG. Coburn would meet the officers and senior enlisted the next morning.

The other buildings on the base were a combination repair shop and armory, a supply building, a mess hall that also served as a conference room and classroom, a small sick bay, and a toilet and shower. Outside the base across the frontage road were a barracks and a row of small wood buildings that served as officer quarters and housing for some of the married sailors' families.

Sandbags were stacked behind chain-link fencing, barbed wire, and concertina coils that marked the landside perimeter of the base. Coburn could see deadly Claymore mines planted every ten meters behind the concertina wire.

They walked onto the floating pier and looked at the RAG boats. The biggest were converted US Navy World War II medium landing craft, or LCMs, given to the French in the late 1940s. One had a large superstructure and antennae as well as machine guns and Honeywell grenade launchers—hand-cranked machine guns that spat out forty-millimeter grenades. This was the command boat. Topping the superstructure was a canopy that covered the flat deck, on which sat several beach chairs.

The next big boat was the monitor, festooned with more machine guns. A pit amidships housed an 80 mm mortar. On the bow enclosed in a steel turret was a 40 mm cannon, a converted antiaircraft gun.

The three remaining big boats were troop carriers, armed with machine guns. Big canopies covered the troop area to protect the passengers and their equipment from sun and rain. The large bow ramp of these troop carriers, hinged at the bottom, could be dropped flat, allowing the troops and any equipment a rapid exit—but also inviting enemy fire into the troop space.

Two smaller landing craft had been converted into river minesweepers, and they dragged grapples and chains. The hulls of the little minesweepers were as likely as the sweeping gear they towed to detonate a mine. Two lightly armed small French river craft, unchanged since the French Navy left them to the Vietnamese, made up the rest of the assault group vessels.

To Coburn the group was essentially floating armor, the waterborne equivalent of tanks and armored personnel carriers.

He had no doubt that they were slow, maybe six or eight knots at best. If they went in harm's way, they'd better be prepared to fight their way out because they couldn't run away.

The last vessel did not belong to the RAG. It was the advisor's skimmer—an open fiberglass hull with a Johnson outboard motor. This was the utility vehicle of the advisors, their waterborne jeep, the little boat that could go into tight places and travel at high speed. Robinson had tried to fix a mount for an M-60 machine gun in the bow but gave up when he realized the fiberglass hull could not withstand the recoil. A makeshift crab pot and two fishing poles were stowed in the skimmer.

"No water skis?" asked Coburn.

"Mr. Coburn, colored people do not water ski, Mexicans do not water ski. And we sure as hell aren't going to chauffeur a white guy around the Saigon River on water skis. So, no, no water skis," explained Robinson as Cruz nodded in agreement and Gordon chuckled.

"I tried to tell these two knuckleheads that I'd let them use the skis, but they accused me of trolling for gators or sweeping mines with them," said Gordon. "So, no skis."

After a delicious meal of fish, rice, and various vegetables that he did not recognize, Coburn sat with Gordon on the hootch patio, smoking Cruz's cigars and drinking cold Australian lager. A breeze and the cigar smoke kept the insects at bay.

They started the turnover of Senior Naval Advisor to RAG Bravo from Gordon to Coburn.

"Clark, consider yourself a very fortunate Dai Uy. In my opinion you're getting the cream of the crop of enlisted. The best I've ever worked with. Period."

"I'm getting that feeling," said Coburn.

"Chief Robinson is smart, real smart. And he's got a whole lot of common sense. He sizes up the situation instantly and then acts. The army pukes you're going to be working with really respect him, and these Vietnamese get scared when he's not around."

"What's his background?"

"I think he's been in the navy eighteen years. Mostly destroyers and a cruiser. Made rank in the minimum time. Wife and two kids in San Diego. The boss and I have been trying to persuade him to try for warrant officer or limited duty officer since he got here."

"When was that?"

"He got in-country about two months before you got here. That means you'll be with him for ten months. That's good."

"When did Cruz get in-country?"

"Cruz has been here nearly nine months, but he has asked to extend a year so you'll be leaving before he does. That's very good."

"How's Cruz?"

"The best. Funny as shit and a real cumshaw artist. I think he could trade river water for a case of steaks with the army guys. A lot like Robinson. Very cool when the green tracers go buzzing around. He knows engines and equipment. Good teacher, has those sailors actually doing preventive maintenance on the boats. We never have to tow a boat back because the engine crapped out. Irreverent as hell. Up for chief in a few months, and I'll be shocked if he doesn't make it. And I think Ba Mei and he have a thing going, but what the hell, huh?"

Gordon took the cigar out of his mouth, sipped his beer, and then looked at the cigar tip.

"Let's talk about the bosses."

"Bosses?" asked Coburn.

"Yeah, Captain Powell and Mr. Mondello."

"We get much interface with Powell?"

"More so than we used to. The admiral really relies on Powell for the entire advisory effort. Vietnamization is accelerating, so Powell pops up all over the place. Sometimes with Mondello, sometimes without. Powell's really a good guy, I like him. But he's one tough and demanding character. A real nuke."

Another sip of beer and a puff on the cigar.

"But not an asshole about it. Whatever you do, Clark, don't bullshit him. He's impervious to brown nosing. And if you think he's off track, especially in something that you are certain—and I mean certain without a doubt—tell him so. Politely, but tell him so."

"I'm all for that."

"I guess it's his nuke upbringing, but he'll talk about problems and shortcomings with you, and not hand out praise or attaboys. It doesn't mean that he's unaware of good work, it's just that he's focusing on the areas that need improvement. Don't get depressed when after he visits, you get a shopping list of things to correct. That's just his manner. Overall, he's a really good guy. Not the kind you smoke cigars and drink beer with. But a good boss for our boss. He'll probably leave here with two stars on his collar."

"And our boss?" asked Coburn.

"Mondello is as good as any guy I have ever worked for since I've been in the navy. He's my new role model. He's one of those guys who can sit you down and talk to you, and when you leave, you feel good even though you later figure out he just gave you an ass chewing."

"He looks like something out of Hollywood."

"Oh, I should say so. The guy's an unbelievable pussy magnet. You go into anyplace with him where human females are present, and the floor gets wet. The guy's charming with the ladies, but if he's dicking around, he's doing it when no one is watching."

Coburn chuckled and shook his head. "Yeah, I got the same problem. And my dick's too big. And I'm too rich."

Gordon smiled and looked at Coburn. "Clark, you are a handsome motherfucker. I'll take your word on the big dick." He puffed the cigar and looked at the smoke rising above his head in the dusk.

"Mondello is smart, every bit as smart as Powell. And he's like a mother lion with her cubs when it comes to his people, of which you are now one. He's got a temper, which I've seen directed at the guy Doug Vernon is replacing at Alpha group, the guy in the hospital in Oakland. Mondello found out that he was telling the army one thing, his counterpart another, and Mondello something else, trying to pad his KIA count and get the army and South Vietnamese to put him in for some medals or some shit.

"Mondello reamed him out in private, but I could hear him all the way in the mess hall. Told the guy he should can his ass but needed him on the river. Next operation he gets hit. Rumor is that Mondello fired the B-40 himself. You don't ever want to be on his bad side. Fortunately, it takes a lot to get there."

"How much longer will the boss be around?"

"Let's see, he's pretty new. I think he's got at least another nine months. I get the feeling that if Admiral Benjamin and Captain Powell need him, they'll keep him longer."

"So, I've got two great enlisted and John Paul Jones and Horatio Nelson for bosses. Not bad, not bad at all, Arnie."

"Now for the rest of the story, Clark. Your counterpart, Thieu Ta Nguyven Van Toh, is a zero. Nice guy but dumber than shit and lazy. Wears custom-made uniforms and hangs around Saigon instead of commanding his RAG. Before I got here he went out on one operation, they got in a big firefight, he got scratched or something. Wound up with a bunch of medals for hiding behind the splinter shields and never went out on an operation again. He supposedly will be up here tomorrow to meet you. Don't bet on it."

"This is the guy whose uncle is the president."

"Bingo. I wonder if LBJ was my uncle if I'd act the same way? Probably."

Coburn asked, "So what do I do for a counterpart? Every briefing I got said to let the Vietnamese command. How do I do that without a counterpart?" asked Coburn.

"You do what I did for a year. As bad as the CO is, the XO is good. He's a Dai Uy. Le Binh Chang. For all practical purposes, he's your counterpart. Mondello is well aware of the situation, as well as Commander Minh. Chang is a good man all the way around. Skuzzy-looking, always needs a shave, and smokes in his sleep. Excellent English, so if you don't trust your Vietnamese when the shit hits the fan, stick with English. He's your counter-part."

"Got it. But I can see some problems, probably more for the boss and Chang than for me."

"Probably, Clark."

Gordon put down the empty beer can and stretched.

"You'll be working closely with the army guys since this is their AO. We'll visit them maybe tomorrow. Two guys are important—Major Teller, who is the operations advisor to the Fifth ARVN Division, and Captain Neal, the intel advisor. You should visit Bob Neal often. His secretary is gorgeous and has California-size tits."

"I will heed your advice. Intelligence is very important to me."

Before Coburn went to bed, he wrote three letters. The first was to his parents, giving them a mailing address, telling them he had been promoted, and assuring them that he was safe and that they shouldn't worry.

The next was to Kelly, the nurse in San Diego. It was much like the letter to his parents, but with an added paragraph about being recognized by the admiral for his potential and given a promotion, witnessing air strikes and running the gauntlet from Saigon to Phu Cuong at high speed in full battle dress. He added some double entendres about missing her and wanting her and hoping she'd join him for R&R in a few months. He also asked if she had heard from Jean, Doug Vernon's girlfriend.

The last letter was to Betsy.

Dear Bets:

Sorry I haven't been able to write to you sooner, but we've been busy since I got off the plane.

I must be doing something right because the admiral gave me a promotion, so now I'm Lieutenant Coburn. No more Lieutenant (Junior Grade).

Please drop me a line when you have time. My address on the envelope is the one to use. Unless I'm in the jungle on an operation, I should get mail in less than a week from the States. I'd like to hear how you're doing.

I hope the job is going well, and I'm sorry my duties wouldn't let me make it home before I left for this place. But that's war, Bets. I've got to run.

Clark.

* * *

Gordon and Coburn met Lieutenant Commander Toh, RAG Bravo's CO, and Lieutenant Chang, his XO, in the mess hall.

Toh was immaculately outfitted in a tailored uniform and followed by an entourage of South Vietnamese Navy Saigon-warrior junior officers. He was pleasant and seemed genuinely happy to meet Coburn, asking all the proper questions about where he was from, what he thought of Vietnam so far, and telling him how much he was looking forward to working with him. Over cafe sua, Toh emphasized the importance of the transfer of in-country and coastal US Navy assets to the South Vietnamese Navy and the overwhelming importance of the advisor-counterpart relationship.

Coburn caught Gordon's eye and lifted an eyebrow in question. Toh was saying all the right things. Maybe he wasn't so dumb after all. Then again, maybe he was just well briefed. Who knew?

During the polite chitchat, Chang sat quietly, sipping his coffee and lighting a cigarette from the one he had in his mouth. Gordon was right. Despite obviously having spruced up for Toh's visit and meeting Coburn, Chang did look skuzzy, disheveled. He was more broad shouldered and lanky than most Vietnamese. Sinewy in a miniature Johnny Cash sort of way. His uniform shirt was tight across his shoulders but baggy down his chest and waist. The officer's hat sitting in his lap had seen better days, and the gold-braid lieutenant insignias on his shoulder boards were tarnished green.

Chang looked at Coburn as Toh and Gordon discussed the latter's departure. The XO had deep-set but very large, round eyes. Bony cheeks and chin. Big-boned hands without a lot of meat. Chang was staring into Coburn's eyes, then he gave a slight shrug and his lips formed a thin smile. They both knew who ran the RAG, and it wasn't the pretty boy in the tailored uniform.

After their coffee, Toh introduced Coburn to the other RAG Bravo officers. Two lieutenants (junior grade) and an ensign. Then they walked out where forty sailors were standing in rank. A chief petty officer saluted Toh, announced that the men were ready for inspection, and led Toh, Coburn, and Gordon through the ranks.

Toh barely looked at the men, but Coburn took his time and looked at each person, saying something in Vietnamese to each sailor. If these men had gone through the effort to prepare for an inspection, they deserved more than just a cursory glance from some spoiled brat from the big city. Toh waited impatiently for Coburn to finish. Robinson and Cruz were standing at attention to the side.

Toh shook hands with the RAG officers and then Coburn and finally Gordon. He told Gordon he was looking forward to the awards ceremony back in Saigon. Toh put on a flak jacket and helmet offered by one of the Saigon lackeys, climbed into the first of two jeeps, and was driven out of the compound.

Robinson and Cruz walked up to Coburn and Gordon. "Well done, Mr. Coburn. You made that asshole wait for you to finish the inspection," said Robinson.

"Yes sir, Mr. Coburn. I could see the XO smiling at that. He couldn't help himself. Couldn't wipe the grin off his face," added Cruz.

Gordon spoke up. "That will probably get to Toh's uncle, who will talk to the ambassador or some other big shit, and the next thing you know the boss is going to get a call from Captain Powell wanting to know who's fucking with American and South Vietnamese relations in Phu Cuong."

Coburn asked worriedly, "Really? Toh would complain to the president because I inspect the sailors the way they're supposed to be inspected?"

"I dunno. He might squeal to uncle, but I think uncle thinks he's a pain in the ass anyway. Besides, if Powell or the boss got wind of it, they'd laugh their asses off."

The next few days were busy with visits to the army advisors at the Fifth ARVN Division. More time was spent in the intelligence office than needed, mainly due to the attributes of the secretary. They traveled to Cu Chi, the big base of the Twenty-fifth Infantry Division, to meet the operations officers.

A surprising amount of time was spent conducting inventories and transferring custody of weapons, radios, equipment, classified documents, furniture, TV, tape deck, generator, accounts, the skimmer, and the jeep. Coburn was surprised that the AK-47s, SKS rifles, Chicom pistols, and the ammunition for these weapons were not in any inventory. For all practical purposes, they didn't exist. The RAG advisors held onto them to use for barter with the rear-echelon army types.

CHAPTER 17
BINH TRANH, SOUTH VIETNAM

After sunset the guide led Vo and Ky out of the farmer's hut. They walked single file through the rubber trees for nearly four hours, skirting houses and hamlets. Outside of the village of Binh Tranh, the guide motioned them to stop. The three sat down on the hard ground and waited. Silent.

Vo leaned back against a tree trunk and shut his eyes, but knew he would not fall asleep. Ky took a drink from his water bottle and offered it to the guide, who shook his head.

Vo felt the presence of the men before he saw them. Ky startled as shadows moved and then turned into two men armed with AK-47s. Vo and Ky got to their feet, and the guide motioned for them to follow one of the men. The other walked a few meters behind them.

They walked to a darkened hut and were met by another armed man. The guide stopped at the hut entrance, looked into Vo and Ky's eyes, and shook hands without saying a word. He turned around and disappeared into the night. Two of the armed men stood guard while the third led Vo and Ky into the hut. In the filtered moonlight, they could see a bare table, two stools, and a ring of stones surrounding a pile of ashes on the floor. Their guard bent over the cooking fireplace, grabbed the ring of stones, and lifted the entire fireplace, uncovering the entrance to a tunnel. They smelled candle wax and dank earth.

Vo and Ky climbed down into the tunnel and followed it for a few meters until it opened up into a small cavern lit by a lantern. At a table made of a slab of the steel matting the Americans used for their airstrips sat two men, both middle aged. Their seats were simple stools. Two empty stools sat across from them. Another armed guard stood in the corner. A pot of tea and metal cups were on the table.

One of the men stood up and held out his hand to Vo.

"Gentlemen, welcome. We have been expecting you." He shook hands with Vo and then Ky.

He continued, "I am Tran Van Tra. Do you know who I am?"

Ky nodded and Vo answered, "Yes, sir. You are the Commander of the National Liberation Front."

"Yes, I am. And this is Lo Anh Hoang, the Commander of the National Liberation Front forces in the district you will be operating in." Hoang did not stand up or offer his hand. He just studied the two young men.

Vo introduced Ky and himself.

Hoang asked abruptly, "Where's your third man?"

"He contracted malaria and could not travel. We left him before we crossed into Vietnam," answered Vo.

"When will he get here?" asked Hoang.

"I do not know. He may have died by now. We are proceeding on our mission without him."

"You abandoned your comrade to die on the trail?" asked Hoang aggressively.

Ky looked nervously at Vo, expecting him to lose his temper.

"We made a decision to carry on with our mission as best we could. Taking him with us would have jeopardized our mission. He was left under the care of a doctor. To die, probably," Vo said in an even manner. He stared into Hoang's eyes, challenging the older man.

The NLF Commander sat down and waved at the seats.

"Lieutenant Vo, Lieutenant Ky, sit down please. You put your mission first, which is what you must always do."

Hoang relaxed and put his elbows on the makeshift table as his senior officer continued.

"General Nguyen Sy Ong—the Transportation Group Commander, your mentor and reporting senior—has briefed me on your mission. Your task is strategic, but much of what we do here is also tactical. You are not in the university in Hanoi, you are here in the South. Both General Ong and I expect you to think both strategically and tactically. To win the war, to unify our country, we need to fight battles. Do you understand that?"

Vo and Ky said they agreed as the NLF Commander poured tea into the metal cups.

"Good. You will work with force Commander Hoang, who will provide whatever support and services he can—which may be less than what you need and certainly less than what you want. Your communications to and from General Ong's people will be handled by his liaison staff."

The NLF Commander took a sip of his tea and then said in a slow and deliberate manner, "Your decisions are yours to make; you do not need any approval from me or Comrade Hoang. But only a fool would make important decisions without seeking our thoughts, recommendations, and counsel."

"Yes, sir," agreed both Vo and Ky.

"Good. We have enough to do fighting the Americans and their puppet Southerners without fighting one another. I must go now."

The NLF Commander stood up, as did the other three men. He shook hands and disappeared down the tunnel and up the ladder, the silent guard following him.

Hoang smiled a relaxed smile at Vo and Ky. "I hope you two university scholars can help me. Resupply of my forces is a mess, complete chaos."

For the next hour Hoang described the post-Tet status of his forces. Offensive operations had to be reduced not because of a lack of fighters, but because he did not have enough ammunition and weapons. He suggested that the two young officers travel through the district and meet with his subordinates for as long as it would take for them to grasp the problems he was facing.

"I know General Ong is wondering how he can supply tanks and battalions of troops in the future as we enter the third and final phase of our war for reunification. But I am looking at how I can keep our forces fighting tomorrow and the next day. We'll never drive tanks into Saigon without first winning the battles for hamlets and villages."

Hoang told Vo and Ky that he had arranged for them to stay in Binh Tranh, the nearby hamlet. He would be working out of the underground complex they were sitting in. One of the armed guards appeared at the cavern entrance. Hoang stood up, shook hands with Vo and Ky, and instructed the guard to show them the subterranean headquarters before taking them to Binh Tranh and their quarters.

Vo and Ky had to stoop as they followed the guard on the tour of the rabbit warren of tunnels. In some places they crawled on hands and knees. They were shown a communications center of captured American radios; an armory; a store room containing wooden boxes of Chinese ammunition, medicine, rice, and a thriving family of rats; an empty, four-bed hospital and dispensary; a claustrophobic sleeping dormitory; a kitchen; and a latrine that made Ky gag. Both men were glad to be above ground as they followed the taciturn guard to the hamlet.

In a small, nondescript hut on the southern edge of Binh Tranh, a tiny, gray-haired woman greeted them. A candle lit the single room. In one corner was the raised wood platform that was to be Vo and Ky's bed. Her sleeping platform was across the room. A small table with a single low stool stood in the middle of the room. A cupboard and a metal box that protected the food from rats and the village dogs made up the rest of furniture. The cooking area was a stone and ash circle just inside the entrance. The floor was dirt, swept clean by a short-handled broom of twigs. The hamlet's well and toilet area were fifty meters from the hut in opposite directions.

"Thank you for inviting us into your home, Grandmother," said Ky as they dropped their packs. She smiled, bowed her head, and silently watched them unpack their gear.

"Grandmother," asked Vo, "where can we put these?" He was holding his pistol, ammunition, money belt, maps, and mess kit.

She moved the metal food box and swept the dirt where it had stood with the twig broom, revealing a piece of wood. Under the board was a hole big enough to hide all their gear or a person.

Later, as they lay side by side on the sleeping platform, Ky asked, "Vo, what's your take on Hoang? He seemed hostile when Commander Tran introduced us. The way he was acting when you told him about Ninh."

"He acted the same way I would have, Ky. If I had been fighting for twenty years and two overeducated, privileged children walked in to tell me how to fight my war, I'd not be very friendly, either. But then Tranh said our decisions are ours to make, not being fools, and that we didn't need to be fighting among ourselves."

"I was glad to hear him say that, Vo. I was looking at Hoang then, and he visibly relaxed."

"Despite his aggressive questioning at the beginning, Hoang must know that our decision to not take Ninh with us was the right one. By the time we left, he was even solicitous, asking us for our help. He's no fool. And we have to be sure we don't act like fools."

"Yes. That's right." Ky glanced out the open hut door. The sky was lightening. He could see the sleeping shape of their hostess across the room.

"It's almost dawn, Vo. Let's get some sleep. Good night."

"Good night, Ky."

* * *

For six weeks, Vo and Ky roamed the area along the Saigon River from northwest of Saigon to the Cambodian border. They moved at night, sometimes with the help of a local NLF guide or cell commander. Moving inland up to thirty kilometers from the river, they observed Southern and American camps, fire bases, headquarters, depots, helicopter pads, and the lone naval facility at Phu Cuong.

Whenever they were near Binh Tranh, they debriefed NLF division commander Hoang on their activities. Hoang usually listened attentively in silence, took no notes, and always asked them to continue to keep him informed.

It was obvious that Hoang had instructed his subordinates to provide assistance and cooperation as they traveled, observed, and questioned. But it was also obvious that while these NLF fighters were following Hoang's orders, many were skeptical about the two Northerners. Some were hostile and begrudging, looking at the visitors as unnecessary burdens on their time and scarce rations.

CHAPTER 18
PHU CUONG

As the Senior Naval Advisor to RAG Bravo, Coburn inherited Gordon's call sign. He was now Crazy Razor.

With two days left before Gordon departed to Saigon, the RAG went on an operation. This would be Coburn's introduction to riverine combat. A platoon of Regional Forces/Provincial Forces soldiers and their advisor, an army special forces captain, were to be inserted upriver.

They would be landed near a village, sweep through the village looking for an elusive VC command post, and then be extracted a few kilometers downriver. The operation, if all went well, would take about ten hours. While the troops conducted their sweep, the RAG boats would act as a blocking force, stopping and searching any waterborne traffic and looking for VC trying to escape across the river.

At 0500, Coburn, Gordon, and Cruz left Robinson in the hootch to monitor the radios and walked down to the floating pier. Each wore helmet, flak vest, and jungle combat boots. Each carried an M-16, a .45 in a holster, two full canteens, and a backpack containing a poncho, food, bug repellent, and suntan lotion. Cruz carried the PRC 25 radio, better known as the prick 25.

Coburn had slept little that previous night, happily nervous and excited about the day on the river.

The two little river minesweepers were already underway, making lazy doughnuts in the river while waiting for the rest of the boats. The command boat, the monitor, and one of the big troop-carrying boats sat with their engines idling, still tied to the pier. The advisors boarded the command boat and greeted Chang, who was on this third cigarette of the morning. Chang signaled to the command boat coxswain, who yelled to the other two boats. Engines revved up, lines were tossed to sailors on the pier, and the three big boats followed the two minesweepers single file up the Saigon River.

At the first bend, the XO flashed a spotlight at a large concrete bridge. A tank sat across the traffic lanes on the center of the bridge, its muzzle pointed upriver. In a sandbagged bunker beneath the bridge's roadway sat ARVN sentries who played their spotlights upriver and randomly dropped anti-swimmer percussion grenades into the water.

A year before, the bridge had been dropped into the river by a floating explosive charge, cutting the supply route to Cu Chi. The VC responsible for destroying the bridge surprised everyone by becoming a *Chieu Hoi*, a defector.

The VC who had bombed the bridge told an interesting story to his interrogators. He had sat on the riverbank for a few nights, just watching the bridge, and determined when the bridge sentries changed. On a moonless night, using a rudimentary snorkel made of bamboo and rubber bands from a truck tire inner tube, he floated downstream to the bridge with a load of captured C-4 explosives and two time detonators wrapped in a black plastic garbage bag he had salvaged from a garbage can near an ARVN compound. He wedged the bag under a piling, swam to the riverbank, climbed out, walked a kilometer upstream, and sat under a tree waiting for the explosion.

The US Army intelligence report estimated that the VC spent less than a dollar for the materials to blow up a concrete bridge and disrupt a vital supply line. Because that estimate was based on the assumption that the VC actually bought an inner tube to cut up into rubber bands, it was considered by many to be sixty cents too high. The cost to repair the bridge was over ten million dollars.

As the lead minesweeper approached the bridge, a small skiff with an outboard motor pulled open the log barrier to let the line of boats through. The sentries in the sandbagged bunker waved at the sailors and yelled a heavily accented "Cruz Numbah One" as they passed under the bridge. Cruz waved back and tossed a package of Swisher Sweets rum-soaked cigars into the bunker. He turned to Coburn and winked.

Gordon looked down at his feet, shook his head and said more to himself than anyone in particular, "You know, I may be nuts, but I'm going to miss this place."

After passing under the bridge, the troop carrier ran its bow onto the riverbank at a clearing. The sun was coming up, and Coburn could make out some military-looking buildings, a jeep, and two trucks. About thirty Vietnamese soldiers with packs and weapons were sitting in a group. One was standing next to a tall figure, the American advisor. The prick 25 squawked, and Cruz listened to the handset.

"Thirty-one Ruff-Puffs and one co van My coming aboard," relayed Cruz. He turned to Coburn and explained, "Co van My is Vietnamese for American military advisor. Ruff-Puff is the RF/PF, the Regional Forces/Provincial Forces, Dai Uy."

Barely stifling a growing irritation with Cruz, Coburn said, "I know, Cruz. I just finished thirteen weeks learning that stuff in Coronado."

Cruz nodded and shrugged his shoulders.

The two river minesweepers put their sweeping gear in the water and moved upriver, one near each bank. The monitor followed them in the center of river. The command boat loitered by the pickup point, waiting for the troop carrier to lift its bow ramp and back away. A few minutes later, the troop carrier pulled alongside the command boat, and an RF/PF officer and the American advisor jumped aboard. The troop carrier moved ahead and got in line between the monitor and the command boat.

The Ruff-Puff officer and his advisor obviously knew the XO, Gordon, and Cruz from previous operations. Gordon introduced them to Coburn. Coburn was surprised that the Vietnamese, although only a second lieutenant, looked to be in his forties. That seemed much too old for such a junior rank. The American, however, fit Coburn's image of a Green Beret. Fit, self-confident. His hand was bandaged.

"Punji stick," said the special forces captain. "I tripped and fell right on it. Dumbest move I made all that day. Charlie nearly put me out of action without having to waste a single bullet." Coburn knew from his class work about the punji stick, a sharpened bamboo strip dipped in feces and then hidden, usually in a pit. The trauma of the wound wasn't as bad as the infections that could follow.

"You get that cleaned out, Al?" asked Gordon.

"Sure as hell did. Medic was with me. Alcohol, sulfa powder, who knows what else he did. Got back to the hootch, and he really flushed it out, put some junk on it, bandaged me up, and gave me a shot in the ass. It's healing okay, so whatever he did must have worked. Another star for the Purple Heart. Each star shows how dumb I can be."

They were all under the canopy on the top deck of the command boat. Chang spread a map on the steel deck, and they pulled up the low beach chairs. The RF/PF officer pointed out the insertion area and the village to be swept, talking in Vietnamese. Coburn was able to follow the conversation and translated for the Americans. He could tell from the looks the Green Beret and Cruz gave him that he was making points.

They talked about the best placement of the blocking force and the location of the extraction. Chang asked if they expected any resistance at the landing area. Did they want the RAG to soften up the area with gunfire? The Ruff-Puff officer and his advisor discussed this in Vietnamese, and then the Vietnamese shook his head.

The American advisor said, "Charlie's been pretty elusive these days. I expect he'll keep out of the way. This will probably be a walk in, a walk around, and a walk out with no contact. Showing presence, waving the flag."

He pointed at the troop carrier. "We've got a medical team with us that will hand out soap and aspirin, so this will probably be more a psyops operation than anything else. Still, Charlie's out there, so we do want you guys at your radios and guns, but we don't need to shoot up the beach."

Coburn didn't show it, but he was disappointed. He wanted some action.

The sun was up, and the day was turning into a hot one. Gordon and Cruz took off their flak vests and jungle fatigue blouses and sat bare chested on the beach chairs with helmets on their heads. Coburn followed suit. This was not what he had thought an operation would be like.

As they approached the insertion point on the east bank, the minesweepers pulled in their gear, and the command boat moved alongside the troop carrier and transferred the Ruff-Puff officer and his advisor back to their troops. With all guns manned, the monitor and troop carrier nosed onto the riverbank as the minesweepers and command boat loitered in midstream. The bow ramp dropped at 0700, and the troops and their advisor walked into the sparse tree line surrounding the clearing.

Coburn grabbed the squawking radio, listened, and acknowledged. The Ruff-Puffs were ashore, there was no contact, neither hostile nor friendly, and they were moving toward the village. The boats backed off the bank, formed a rough single file, and headed downstream with the current, the monitor closest to the bank, its turret slowly sweeping fore and aft, waving the cannon barrel like a baton.

The next eight hours were a monotony of idling downstream with the current, then turning upstream and powering back to the insertion point, then repeating the cycle again and again. A few sampans were on the river, and the minesweepers stopped them to check papers and look at whatever was in the shallow craft, usually fishing nets and crab pots. Farmers toiled in their fields, not bothering to look at the big gray boats. A bunch of little kids stood on the banks in shorts, dripping wet from bathing in the river. A few waved, most just stared. Two helicopter gunships flew down the river, circled over the RAG boats like giant dragonflies, and moved on.

At one point, Cruz reached into his backpack and took out a box of C-rations. Gordon followed suit and told Coburn to do the same. Cruz collected the C-rations and went below. Half an hour later, a crewman came up with a plate of stir fried vegetables and what had been the contents of the C-rations main course cans, a thick soup, and a large bowl of rice. He placed that all down on the metal deck, went below, and then came back with a kettle of tea, a bunch of chipped bowls and cups, aluminum spoons, lacquered chopsticks, and two little bowls of fish sauce and hot peppers.

Lunch was served.

Chang, Coburn, Gordon, Cruz, and the coxswain who had just been relieved sat on the beach chairs or their haunches and ate the communal meal. Coburn wondered if they gave medals and commendations for enduring boredom and eating with chopsticks.

"Is this what's it like?" he asked Gordon.

"Lately, it has been. Last year at this time, we were hugging the deck calling in air strikes."

Chang asked Coburn, "Dai Uy, you want a firefight?"

"No, no, Dai Uy," said Coburn, hoping he sounded convincing. "But this is more like a vacation for me than what I thought it would be like."

"Enjoy it, Dai Uy," said Chang. "They're out there. I am sure we will be in combat again. More than we want to be. But we are doing our mission even now. It may not be heroic, but we are fighting the war even so."

Coburn wasn't sure if this was a rebuke or just well-intentioned conversation and indoctrination. He went on eating.

"Well, Dai Uy Chang, you are right," said Coburn through a mouthful of rice and vegetables. "If they're out there, they are seeing us in force, and they have to deal with that fact."

Cruz said, "Mr. Coburn, it's a day at a time in Nam. A day at a time."

"Yeah, just like serving time in prison," joked Gordon, lightening the conversation.

At 1530, Chang's radio squawked a few seconds before the advisors' radios squealed. The troops were about fifteen minutes from the pickup point. The monitor nosed into the bare riverbank, then the troop carrier lowered its bow ramp. Led by their CO and the Green Beret, the troops filed out of the tree line and onto the troop carrier.

All were present. They were tired, their clothes sweat stained, their boots covered with dust and dried mud. Most of the troops had their helmets cocked back on their heads to catch more of the nearly nonexistent breeze. The command boat pulled up to the stern of the troop carrier, and the Green Beret jumped aboard. His counterpart stayed with his troops.

The boats backed off the bank and formed up in single file— the monitor leading, then the troop carrier, the command boat, and the two small minesweepers. They headed downriver. The tall army advisor dropped his radio and backpack, took off his flak vest and then his jungle fatigue blouse and green T-shirt, both almost black with sweat. Cruz handed him a can of pineapple juice, which he drained.

"Thanks, Cruz. Man, that was a long, hot walk."

They had found no sign of VC activity in or around the village, which was no surprise. And the villagers were not friendly. In fact, pretty hostile if glares and body language counted for anything. Even the medical team's offers to provide examinations and treatment were not well received, although a few mothers did let them look at their babies, all of which were healthy.

Coburn was curious. "Your counterpart looks pretty old to be a Thieu Uy."

"Yes, he is old for a butter bar. He was a senior noncom in the French army, mustered out but then decided to get back into the military. The RF/PFs needed officers, so he took a commission from them instead of going back to enlisted in the ARVN."

"What's the difference?" asked Coburn.

"It's like the difference between the regular army and the national guard or reserves in the States. The Ruff-Puffs have been a long-running joke in this war. Then some genius decided that we have to 'win the hearts and minds of the people,' and that included beefing up the prestige and capabilities of the local guys, the RF/PFs. Lot of US Army and US Marine Corps advisory effort going into that."

"Your counterpart any good?"

"He's one tough fighter. And hard on his troopers. But he doesn't give a shit about politics and kissing the province chief's ass. He should be a Dai Uy, but that's never going to happen. His boss is a Dai Uy and worthless."

A flicker of light caught Coburn's eye on the west bank. An instant later he heard the barking of a gun. More flicker and more barking. He was seeing the flash of two black muzzles sticking out of a bush on the bank.

"Shit, gunfire 060!" Coburn grabbed his M-16, sighted on the bush, and squeezed the trigger. Nothing. He flicked the safety to full automatic and sprayed the bush, his tracers on target.

His magazine was empty, and as he reached for another in his duffel, he saw Chang grab the radio and rapidly give orders to the boats. Gordon, Cruz, and the gunners on the command boat were firing at the bend in the river that Coburn had lit up. The sound was deafening; the smell of cordite filled his nostrils. The Green Beret was on his radio, speaking in Vietnamese.

Coburn felt as if he were outside his body, watching himself in slow motion.

He turned his selector switch to single fire and kept shooting at the bush. The monitor fired its 40 mm cannon and 20 mm machine guns turned into the riverbank. A puff of smoke rose amidships as the mortar fired. The command boat and troop carrier turned into the same point, firing as they closed in.

Coburn was exhilarated, giddy. He had never felt so alive, his senses so sharp.

As soon as its bow touched the bank, the troop carrier dropped its ramp. The Ruff-Puffs fanned out, firing indiscriminately. Chang was trying furiously to get the boats to cease firing to avoid hitting the soldiers. Next to Coburn the Green Beret was on the radio, talking to a helicopter light fire team.

Coburn looked happily around. Shit, this was life! This was exciting!

Then he noticed Gordon.

Gordon was a chalky white, almost a blue tint. His eyes were wide, he was dripping sweat.

"You okay, Arnie?" asked Coburn almost cheerfully.

"Yeah, sure," answered Gordon in a wavering, clipped voice. "Sure, I'm good. Anyone hit?"

"I don't know." Coburn realized that for the first time, he was recognizing fear, real fear, in a human being. Arnie Gordon, the big hero who was going to get some medals the next day, was scared shitless. Coburn was not afraid; he was on an adrenaline high. He loved this.

Chang finally got the boats to cease fire, and then the sounds of the soldiers' M-16s and M-79 stopped. The two helicopters circled the boats as the Green Beret talked to them on his radio. The only sounds now were his voice and the wop wop wop of the helicopters. Chang picked up his radio and demanded a casualty report from all the boats.

Ten minutes had passed since Coburn opened fire. The boat crews had suffered no casualties, and it looked as if none of the boats had been hit. All the Ruff-Puffs were accounted for, and other than one fellow who had been hit in the eye by a bush limb, no casualties. The helicopters could see nothing other than the soldiers and the trees. The old Vietnamese second lieutenant said the only signs of the VC were spent cartridge casings. No blood, no bodies, not even footprints.

Coburn floated happily on his adrenalin-induced high. Gordon was back to his normal color but still wide eyed and shaky. Cruz puffed a cigar as he reloaded his magazines with ammunition.

"Shit, you mean we shot off all that ammunition and they got away?" asked Coburn incredulously but with a grin. "How the fuck did they do that?"

The Green Beret looked at Coburn with a serious face. "Better get used to it, Dai Uy. That's how this war is. Maybe if the war ends, they'll tell you how they do it." There was a touch of disdain in the man's voice, which Coburn missed completely.

Chang agreed. "Yes, Dai Uy. While they had us occupied, they probably moved a platoon across the river behind us."

Two hours later, the soldiers and their advisor disembarked. As the sun set, the boats passed under the concrete bridge and tied up at the floating pier. Back at the hootch, Cruz told Robinson how the day had gone, and Ba Mei put out a dinner of chicken, vegetables, and instant mashed potatoes.

Gordon and Coburn put together an after-action report, which was sent to the local Tactical Operations Center, or TOC, for distribution to a long list of commands, including NAVFORV and Mondello. Under the paragraphs for enemy KIA, WIA and captured, they entered "none."

Coburn remarked that they must have hit someone. They had fired all that ammunition; they had to have hit someone.

* * *

Over dinner the four advisors did an informal debrief of the mission. They all agreed that Chang was doing a good job, and more importantly, they didn't take his job away from him. The same for the Ruff-Puffs, except the advisor, not the Ruff-Puffs, had called in the support helicopters.

As Coburn ate his meal and drank his beer, he felt himself coming off the high. Probably the beer, he thought. By the end of the meal, he was nearly depressed. He had felt so good just a few hours before. He wanted that high back.

* * *

Gordon was departing from Phu Cuong.

The night before started with Chang coming to the hootch with a bottle of the potent Vietnamese rice-based white lightning that burned a path down the throat and induced double vision and a thick tongue, followed the next morning by a migraine.

Within a few minutes, most of the Vietnamese officers and senior enlisted were on the hootch patio, trying to get Gordon to chin-chin with them. Each filled a glass for Gordon and one for himself and tried to down the harsh liquor while everyone chanted "chin-chin." After exactly 363 days and twelve hours, seventeen minutes in-country, Gordon was well acquainted with the art of chin-chin and had decided that he'd limit the ritual to just Chang and the senior noncom. The rest of the Vietnamese decided that rather than let the evening go to waste, they would welcome Coburn aboard with a round of chin-chin.

By midnight, Gordon had burned his jungle fatigues in a small fire on the riverbank, shook the hand of every Vietnamese in the RAG, sang "Anchors Aweigh" and "Roll Me Over in the Clover," and packed his duffel bag. During that same time, Coburn got drunk as a skunk, and to the delight of the Vietnamese, demonstrated his college days' prowess at producing blue flames by using a borrowed Zippo lighter to ignite his farts. Then he vomited until he had nothing left to vomit and started dry heaving and was put to bed by Robinson and Cruz.

Hung over, wearing sunglasses and a gray complexion, Coburn helped Gordon load his duffel bag in the jeep. Chang and a row of sailors stood as honorary side boys by the base gate. Ba Mei stood next to Coburn and Robinson, crying. Cruz got into the driver's seat and started the jeep's engine. Gordon, dressed in starched and pressed khakis, turned to Ba Mei and gave her a hug. She buried her face into this chest, sobbed once, then pushed herself back and smiled through her tears.

Gordon turned to Robinson, who saluted him smartly. Gordon saluted back, took Robinson's hand, and shook it. "Chief, I'm going to ask BUPERS to send you to my ship when you leave here."

"I'd be honored to serve with you again, sir," said Robinson. "Good luck, have a safe flight, and enjoy your family."

"Thanks, Chief. I will. Say hello to your wife and kids for me."

Gordon turned to Coburn, who reached out his hand. Gordon took it and held it.

"Arnie, thanks for showing me the ropes. You're a tough act to follow," said Coburn, mustering up more enthusiasm and steadier hands than he felt. "Good luck with the XO job."

Gordon looked at Coburn seriously. "Clark, you've got the best possible job in the navy here. Chang's great, Chief and Cruz are the best. But don't forget, Clark, this isn't a game. This is dangerous, people die. There's nothing to celebrate in that."

"Roger that, Arnie," answered Coburn and wondered why in the hell Gordon was giving him a lecture.

Gordon put on his flak vest and helmet, then climbed into the seat next to Cruz. As they approached the gate, Chang called the side boys to attention and saluted smartly as a sailor trilled a bosun's pipe. Gordon returned the salute, and the jeep drove out of the base.

The shrill of the bosun's pipe and exhaust of the jeep did not help Coburn's hangover as he followed Robinson into the hootch to drink a cup of strong coffee. *It's my time now*, thought Coburn with a smile on his grey face.

* * *

Life as Senior Advisor to RAG Bravo turned into a dull and boring routine. Coburn's day consisted of meeting with

Chang, walking around the base, occasionally looking at the boats, visiting the local army advisory group—especially the intelligence office to sharpen his focus on the big-bosomed secretary—reading the *Stars and Stripes* newspaper, going through the message traffic, and collecting the mail. He often spent evenings at the army advisory group's BOQ, which had a decent enough mess and on the top floor a bar, and a movie every evening.

He soon became known by the army officers as Dai Uy Nuoc. Nuoc was Vietnamese for water. And since the navy operated on water instead of ground, he became Dai Uy Nuoc.

The RAG went on an upriver operation about once a week, downriver from Phu Cuong less frequently. Most of the operations involved picking up a load of troops—usually ARVN and RF/PF but occasionally US Army—inserting the troops, idling along the river as a blocking force, extracting the troops, and motoring back to Phu Cuong.

Rarely did the troops get into a firefight, even rarer did the RAG get shot at. Coburn's operations uniform deteriorated to shorts or jungle fatigue trousers rolled up to his knees, shower shoes, and his helmet nearby. He sat on his flak jacket but rarely used it for anything more than a cushion.

The three advisors had been rotating through the river operations two at a time, the odd man staying at the base and monitoring the radios. Coburn soon realized that his chances of getting into action needed to be improved.

One morning he announced to Robinson and Cruz that as senior advisor, he wanted to have more time with Chang during operations. Coburn would go on every operation, and Robinson and Cruz would rotate through every other operation. Both men said nothing more than "Aye, aye, Dai Uy" but seemed skeptical of the wisdom and the rationale of the change. Coburn didn't care what they thought.

At the end of Coburn's third week in Phu Cuong, Cruz brought in the mail and handed him four letters and a *Sports Illustrated*. The letters were from Betsy, Kelly, his parents, and his sister. Coburn poured himself a cup of coffee and sat in the sun on the sandbagged wall around the hootch to read the letters.

The first was in his mother's handwriting, relating family happenings, concern for his safety, and how proud they all were. His sister's was a brief note of how excited she was to be starting student teaching and that she was still dating whatshisface, whom Coburn had supposedly met but did not remember.

He opened Betsy's letter.

Dear Clark:

I just received your letter and want to respond while I have time. It was really nice to hear from you. Congratulations on the promotion. You must have been pretty proud when that happened.

And yes, I love my job and really enjoy living in New York City. It's all very exciting and maybe a little too exhausting. But I like it a lot.

Clark, I want to be frank with you. And clear the air. Ever since the last time I saw you in Newport, I have had a feeling that we were drifting apart. At first I thought it was the separation and our jobs. But it's more than that. Your letter before you got on the plane confirms that. And I share your feelings.

But I never understood why you could not write or call me more frequently when you were in California. One of my office mates is engaged to a navy lieutenant whom I think is going to something called a Swift(?) boat and was in school part of the time you were there. He was able to write and call frequently. Couldn't you have? Or were we already finished? Perhaps we were, and you should have written that letter from Travis three months earlier.

Have we run our course and now it's come to an end? Do we just move on with our separate lives? I don't think we can just be "friends," do you, Clark?

Please be safe. I don't like war, especially this one. It doesn't make any sense to me. I'm obviously not alone. Ever since Walter Cronkite made his comments about the futility of it all, a lot of people have very serious doubts. Clark, I don't want you getting hurt fighting a stupid war.

I want to get this into the mail, so I'd better close off.

Take care, Clark.

Betsy

Coburn reread her letter two more times. When he sent the letter from Travis, he had only wanted to put Betsy on hold. Not this.

He looked out at the river. Who the hell was the Swift boat driver? Which one of those guys had a girlfriend who worked with Betsy? Son of a bitch. And now she's becoming a war protestor. Probably wants to date some draft-dodging Madison Avenue guy who drives a Corvette.

Coburn decided he'd not reply to her letter right away. She didn't even say she loved him. She had written him a "Dear John" letter. He stuffed the letter into his pocket. He needed time to think up a response.

He opened Kelly's letter.

Dearest Clark:

First, I want to tell you—again—how much I love you. And now how much I miss you. I think of you all the time.

I'm so glad you were able to write and give me an address. I have much to tell you.

After I dropped you off, I think I cried all the way from Travis to San Diego. I was more emotional than normal the whole wonderful trip up the coast. The emotions were more than just being with you. Hormones were at work. The day after I got back home I went to my doctor. Clark, I'm pregnant.

I suspected I was pregnant when we started the drive north but wasn't sure. So it wasn't as much a surprise to me as I'm sure it is to you. I have been giving much thought as to what to do, but this is a decision that we need to make together.

As much as I'd like to have a baby by you, now may not be a good time for either of us. On the other hand, it may be the perfect time. I just don't know. But our options are clear, dear Clark. Either I have the baby, or I do not. If we decide now is not the right time, I need to know quickly.

Please let me know what you want us to do as soon as possible, Clark. Remember, I love you no matter what we decide to do. I'll understand whatever you say.

I hope you haven't fainted from shock. On another happy note, Jean and I have exchanged letters several times since you and Doug left. I really like her. When you come back, let's make it a point to see them.

That's wonderful that the admiral gave you a promotion just like that! He's no fool, and I'm very proud of you. But I'm not real happy with your running around in a dangerous place. You be safe, please.

Do you see Doug over there? If so, say hi for me.

Remember, I love you and miss you. Please write back soon so I know what to do.

With all my heart,

Kelly

Coburn's scalp prickled, and his stomach churned. He couldn't believe it. She had gotten herself pregnant. Why did he even open her and Betsy's letters? Why was the world picking on Clark Coburn this morning? He sighed, shook his head, and stuffed Kelly's letter in the same pocket with Betsy's.

"You okay, Dai Uy?" Cruz was standing behind him. "Bad news from home? You look sort of shocked or something."

Coburn shook his head and smiled. "Nah, I'm okay, Cruz. Women letters."

"That's not good. Dear Dai Uy letters? 'I love you no mo'?"

"I wish that was the problem. No, this is more in the commitment arena."

Robinson walked out of the hootch, a weapons manual in his hand. "Somebody getting committed? Does that get you out of here sooner? Sign me up."

Cruz replied, "No, you're crazy enough to get committed, but you're here forever. Dai Uy has a woman demanding a commitment from him."

Robinson smiled and looked at Coburn. "That true, some woman wants you to do the right thing, Dai Uy?"

"Well, Chief, it's a little more complicated than that. It's women, not woman."

Both Cruz and Robinson broke into laughter. "I respectfully suggest, sir, that you stay in Nam until both of them marry someone else," said Cruz.

"I may have to take that advice. Or get some mafioso goombah to do some marriage counseling for me."

The next night, while sitting on the command boat waiting for the dawn extraction of a company of ARVN, Coburn wrote Kelly.

Hi Kelly,

That was indeed some shocker of a letter you sent. It was waiting for me when I came off a real rough operation. But I'm okay. I should wait a bit for my nerves to settle down, but I wanted to write you as soon as possible.

There are just too many factors in play for me to make a decision for you, Kelly. You're right, this is not the right time for me to be a father. I don't know what the future will bring. The probability of my making it through this year is not as good as someone selling insurance or doing face-lifts in California. I also got the feeling that you were not ready for the domestic lifestyle either, but you're the one who has to answer that question—I can't.

I don't want to sound harsh and cruel, but I cannot make a commitment to you, much less to your baby. I can't make a decision about a baby that is for sure yours and may be mine. I'm sorry for how this sounds, Kelly, but it's the only way I know how to say it.

Let me know what you decide, Kelly. You've a good head on your shoulders. You'll do the right thing.

I'll drop this in the mail as soon as we get back to base. I'm writing it by candlelight on the river.

Clark

PS: I haven't seen Doug in a few weeks, but when I do I'll say hello to him for you.

CHAPTER 19
NHA THO

The messenger walked into the small base camp hut. In silence he warily eyed the candlelit strangers before being assured by the NLF village squad leader that it was safe to talk.

He said an ARVN platoon was going to conduct a sweep near the river ferryboat crossing at Bin Suc. They were searching for a supply depot, an ammunition cache. The sweep would start at 0700 from Route 15 and head north to the river. The ARVN intelligence officers were sure there was a cache in the area.

Smiling, the NLF squad leader told the messenger that they would meet the Southerners and surprise them. The runner disappeared back into the darkness.

"We have been using our sources to plant false reports of a supply of arms in that area," said the village leader to Vo and Ky. He took a US Corps of Engineers map out of his waistband and pointed to the location.

"We will ambush them here. Our plans are set. We have four hours to get in place. Would you like to come along?"

Four hours later Vo and Ky were seated next to the squad leader behind the heavy foliage of an overgrown rubber plantation's foot trail. Concealed in a half circle were ten other NLF soldiers—five equipped with rifles, the rest with grenades. The squad leader held the detonator of a captured Claymore mine, camouflaged in the grass a few meters in front of them. The killing zone was the center of the half circle.

Trip wires were placed along the expected escape routes of the ARVN soldiers. The wires led to booby traps of grenades or captured mortar rounds. Sharpened bamboo sticks, dipped in human feces, were planted in concealed holes along the escape routes as well as the footpath leading to the fictitious arms cache.

A dense tree canopy filtered the sunlight. Vo looked around, trying to spot the other NLF soldiers and the trip wires. Even though he knew where they were, he couldn't make them out. Grenades made of soft drink cans and a bamboo throwing handle were given to Vo and Ky. They had no other weapons.

0700 came and went without any ARVN troops sweeping the area. The NLF ambushers just sat in their positions, sweating, hungry, rationing their water. They let the insects feast on them rather than give away their position with a swat. Both Vo and Ky had to fight to stay awake.

It was noon. Vo was irritable and bored and sleepy. But he knew there was nothing to be done about that. Ky had shut his eyes and dozed off. Vo debated on waking him but decided to let him sleep. If they were still here in an hour, he'd wake Ky, and then he'd try to sleep.

About an hour later, Vo reached over and shook Ky's shoulder. He was about to tell Ky that he wanted to nap when the NLF leader tensed. They could hear something moving toward them.

An ARVN soldier with his M-16 across his body came out of the tall grass, walking quietly in a crouch. Two meters behind him followed another with an M-60 machine gun, then another with just a sidearm, and a fourth with an American PRC 25 radio on his back. Next to the radio operator was a very tall soldier, an American advisor. They walked toward the invisible semicircle's center. A platoon of soldiers followed them out of the tall grass.

The Claymore fired, startling and deafening Vo and Ky. The center of the semicircle turned into a ball of smoke and dirt.

Vo could see the muzzle flashes of the NLF rifles but couldn't hear them because of the ringing in his ears. He saw Ky punch through the wax plug on his grenade handle, pull the wire, and then throw the grenade into the smoke. Vo did the same.

Leaves started to fall above their heads, the return fire of the Southerners pruning the foliage. Shooting at invisible targets, the ARVN fired wildly, rapidly replacing their spent ammunition clips with full ones.

With a wave of his hand to follow him, the NLF leader and his men retreated along their preplanned extraction route, leaving behind the ARVN, who kept firing at ghosts.

High on adrenalin, the NLF fighters regrouped two kilometers from the killing zone. One of the grenadiers was missing. They decided to stay where they were for another six hours and then move out under the cover of night. Perhaps the missing fighter would catch up with them before they left the rendezvous spot.

Three sentries were put out at each corner of a triangle with fifty-meter sides. The rest of the squad lay on the ground in the shade of the tree canopy. Most immediately fell asleep. But Vo and Ky were too pumped up, too excited to sleep. The leader sat next to them, eating a small ball of rice he had taken from his pants pocket. They could hear the shuttling medical evacuation helicopters and the patrolling helicopter gunships circling above the ambush site.

"That was the first time we have ever been on the attacking side in a battle," Ky told the leader. "Every other time, we were part of the target. We never were able to fire back."

"How does this feel? Better than being a target, I hope."

Vo answered, "Yes, anything's better than that. We have some questions for you. Can we ask them now?"

The man nodded.

"Why did we withdraw after just a few minutes?" asked Vo. "It appeared we had complete surprise, and they were in our killing field. We could have wiped them out."

"You are correct that we did have complete surprise. But we could not wipe them out. We have no ammunition left. They

313

could have just one person able to fire, and he would have more firepower than all of us put together. And if he ran low on ammunition, these helicopters," he pointed skywards, "would resupply him and bring in reinforcements. That's why I ordered the retreat when I did. We had no ammunition. Just empty rifles."

Vo nodded his head in understanding. Ky asked the next question.

"The man who is missing. If he is captured, won't he be able to provide valuable information to the Southerners?"

"It's the fortunes of war, Comrade Ky. I hope he walks into our spot here in a few minutes. If he doesn't, he is probably dead or captured. I hope the first. Otherwise he will be tortured and imprisoned. And if he is tortured for his information, what valuable information does he have? He knows just the comrades in his cell and me. I'm sure the Southerners already know my name."

"What damage did we inflict?" asked Vo.

"I don't know yet, Comrade. But we will know in a day or two. Our sources will find out." The man smiled. "Since it's the ARVN, I imagine that they will accurately describe their losses but claim that they killed twenty or thirty of us but that the dirty communists dragged their dead away."

* * *

Vo and Ky went out on many more operations with local NLF units. None had the success of the first one, which accounted for the deaths of one American advisor and twelve ARVN soldiers including an officer, and the wounding of eleven ARVN troops at the cost of one dead NLF fighter. Most of the operations were long walks in the jungle and rice paddies, sitting in ambush waiting for an enemy who never appeared, and then the long walk back.

During several operations it was the NLF that was ambushed or ran into Southern or US forces. The NLF fought back until their magazines were empty, losing men and fleeing, scattering as the enemy pursued them. And sometimes they hunted the enemy, ambushed him, and then suffered unsustainable losses to artillery and air strikes. Except for the times when nothing happened, they always came back with no ammunition.

Once they sat in spider holes along the banks of the Saigon River with three NLF armed with two AK-47s and a single B-40, waiting for the Southerners' big river craft to come back downriver. They shot the rocket and missed, sprayed the thick-hulled steel boats with all their rifle bullets, then ducked out of sight as the boats opened fire on a nearby tree line and called in two helicopter gunships that accomplished nothing more than killing several trees.

CHAPTER 20
SAIGON

At the end of his first six weeks, Coburn drove down to Saigon with Cruz for a meeting with Mondello. Cruz dropped him off at Mondello's hootch and then went shopping for more cloth for Ba Mei to sew into VC flags. Since Mondello was in a meeting with his counterpart, Coburn slumped down into a chair by his boss's desk and reread a letter from Kelly.

Clark:

You are an unbelievable son of a bitch. How dare you imply that you are not the father? That's a terrible insult to me. And it says a whole lot about you.

I feel like a fool for falling for you and your line of bullshit. That's my fault. But your behavior is not my fault. Enjoy being alone because the rest of the women in this world are not as gullible as I have been.

At least you had the decency to send your asinine response in a timely manner so I can make my decisions and get on with my life.

Do not write me. If I receive a letter from you, it will go in the garbage unopened.

Kelly

317

"Bad news, Clark?" Mondello startled Coburn, who folded the letter in half and stood up.

"Not really, sir. Letter from an ex-girlfriend."

"A 'Dear John' letter?"

"Not really, sir. Sort of a 'you won't commit to me so go fuck yourself ' letter."

"I assume you won't be writing her anymore this tour."

"That's a pretty safe assumption, sir. She's jealous of the navy and my commitment to it."

Mondello didn't respond to that, and Coburn wondered if he had said one sentence too many. He sat back down after Mondello seated himself behind his desk. Banging on the partition behind his desk, Mondello yelled out for Wilson, his intelligence officer.

Wilson popped his head around the partition, saw Coburn, smiled, walked over, and shook hands.

"How's life in the boonies, Clark?" Coburn bridled inside that Wilson did not address him as "sir" or at least "Dai Uy."

"Not too bad, Bill. Still learning how to load a latrine and flush an M-16. Or is it the other way around?"

Mondello and Wilson both laughed, as well as the yeoman at his typewriter across the office. Coburn relaxed.

"I asked Bill to sit in. He needs your take on what's happening on the Saigon River, and you need an intel update from our perspective," said Mondello. Coburn liked the sound of that. Mondello was acknowledging that Coburn was the expert in his own area of operations.

Mondello started the discussion by saying that he often monitored the radio traffic and read all the after-action and operations reports. It appeared to him that Coburn's part of the Saigon River was relatively quiet. Charlie was not on the offensive.

Coburn agreed but added that the VC seemed to be able to take potshots at the RAG every operation, especially when coming back downriver. More harassment fire than anything else, but if they got lucky with a B-40 or could put together more than a couple of guys with AK-47s, things could get pretty serious.

Riveting Coburn with his eyes—which Coburn knew meant an important question was coming—Mondello asked, "Your RAG ready for a bigger show of force?"

Coburn didn't hesitate.

"Yes, sir, it is now. After the first week or so, I noticed that they were getting a little sloppy, complacent. Nothing big. Not wearing helmets, gunners sitting on the gun tubs instead of in them, squinting through the gun sights. Basically not at general quarters when they should be."

"What did you do?"

"I got Chang, the XO." He added the XO part for Wilson's edification. "Got him over to the side and had a quiet discussion with him. He responded well and quickly. It didn't take much, but he smartened the whole RAG up."

Coburn put on a serious face, knowing that it was Chang who had politely told him that it would be better to wear his flak vest and helmet on the river. Mondello didn't drop his stare, making Coburn wonder if Commander Minh had told him about that. Shit, better drop the bullshitting.

"Any take on the activity from your army buddies up there?" asked Mondello.

Coburn knew that Wilson regularly communicated with Bob Neal, the army intel advisor to the ARVN division. Neal's office was also the workplace for the beautiful secretary Coburn had his sights on. Better be careful here.

"They think Charlie's still around but avoiding anything head on until they build up their strength. Every time the army or ARVN go out in the field, they run into little contact but often find a cache of food, medicine, or ammo. No weapons. Locals are pretty hostile but nothing overt. Phu Cuong seems friendly enough, but that's because of the money they can make from us and the ARVN."

"What's your take?" Mondello was giving him the stink eye again.

"Sir, I don't know what it was like a few months ago, but it's very quiet now. If there's a force of any size, I don't know where it is. I haven't seen anything."

"Quiet, huh?"

"Yes, sir, it is. But that's good for our business."

"What business?"

Coburn deadpanned. "Manufacturing and selling VC flags. One flag for a case of steaks or a couple of those big cartons of chocolate milk. Lack of firefights has reduced the supply of the real thing." He looked at Mondello. "Boss, I can get you a new jeep if you want. Four genuine VC flags."

Mondello's handsome stern face twitched, then cracked into a laugh. Wilson was already laughing.

"Where do you buy those things in Phu Cuong?" asked Wilson.

"I'm shocked that you'd ask that, Trung Uy," replied Coburn. "You know it's against the law for the Vietnamese to make those things, much less sell them. We make them. Well, really Ba Mei makes them, but we supply the sewing machine and cloth. We... uh...do the marketing. In fact, Cruz is shopping for red, blue, and yellow material right now."

"Tell me more," said Mondello.

"Well, sir, we usually set up production if Ba Mei's making chicken or duck. When she butchers them, she collects the blood in a bowl. Then Cruz lights up one of his stogies. We dip the flags in the blood, and Cruz puts in some bullet holes with the cigar. Genuine real thing. Guaranteed. No refunds, however." Coburn looked around the room. "Hey, we need the money. Do you know how much it costs for pedicures and custom tailored skivvies in Phu Cuong?"

"I heard enough," said Mondello. "Bill, when we get done, call NAVFORV and ask the JAG to send over some shore patrol and arrest Clark and his buddy Cruz."

"Aye, aye, boss," said Wilson with a salute.

"While we wait for the police to come, Bill, give Betsy Ross here an intel brief." Mondello walked over to the coffee pot, smiling and shaking his head as he poured himself a cup.

Wilson spent the next half hour detailing the suspected VC and NVA units in the III Corps riverine area. Out of the four

RAG areas of operations, Vernon's RAG, Alpha, had the most activity. Coburn's area was spotty with a large concentration of VC in the area farther upriver than where the RAG usually operated.

Wilson said he suspected this was a safe staging area for the VC, near the Cambodian border and out of the normal reach of the US and ARVN divisions headquartered near RAG Bravo. Electronic surveillance, air reconnaissance, and human intelligence sources on the ground could not identify any single large unit, but the numbers of small units, cells, and individuals were gradually increasing—but still well below pre-Tet levels.

Coburn walked over to the large wall map that Wilson was using and traced the Saigon River from Phu Cuong to the northwest. He looked at Wilson.

"If we start operating up here now, do you think they'll take us on, or will they just sit and watch us steam by?"

"Clark, I don't know. I think if you get near a big cache or base camp or staging area, they'll probably try to unload on you. But then they risk losing it all to an air strike or artillery."

Mondello said, "That's the $64,000 question, Clark. My guess is that they won't open up unless they absolutely have to. If we had some hard intelligence and targeted an insertion at a vulnerable spot and caught Charlie in the latrine or hammock, they'd have to fight. But given their intelligence, they'd probably know we're on the way, so they'd either *di-di* the hell out of there and relocate or set up a hell of an ambush."

Wilson continued his briefing and opined that the local population in the III Corps riverine area outside of Saigon and a few provincial towns were neutral at best. In Coburn's area, he thought they were not neutral but instead passively against the South Vietnamese government.

"Roger, that," said Coburn, acting as if his experience matched Wilson's assessment. In fact, Coburn had no idea what the local population was like, having rarely ventured out of the confines of the RAG base, US and ARVN establishments, or the local noodle soup shop.

"Think you can get some psyops going, Clark?" asked Mondello. "Win the hearts and minds of the people stuff?"

"I'll try, sir. When I get back, I'll sit down with Chang and Bob Neal and Major Teller, the G3 advisor. Maybe get some medical pecker checkers to go out with us."

"Good. That's probably better than us dropping napalm and H&I fire. Certainly worth a try. Talk to Chief Corpsman McGruder before you go back."

Wilson finished his intel brief and went back to whatever he did behind the partition. Coburn was envious of the easy camaraderie between Wilson and Mondello, especially with the difference in rank. He consoled himself that Wilson and Mondello had been working together for four months, and he had just a bit over a month in-country. He just needed more time.

Mondello suggested they stretch their legs and continue their discussion while walking around the base. He went over to the refrigerator and took out two cold cans of Coca-Cola and gave one to Coburn.

"Thanks, boss." Coburn was consciously calling Mondello what everyone around there called him. They walked in the direction of the boat repair yard on the riverbank.

The monitor from Vernon's RAG Alpha was in the graving dock, high and dry on wooden blocks. The bow was bent up thirty degrees. Through a ragged hole on the port bow below the waterline, Coburn could see the boat's innards. Small dents peppered the side, the armored turret and the splinter shields. A hole big enough to put a fist through punctured the after part of the hull. Bubbled and blackened paint covered the stern.

"That's Alpha's monitor," said Mondello. "Mine, automatic weapons, and a B-40. They grounded her on the bank, and once the firing stopped, towed her off, but she started to sink, so they pushed her back onto the mud. Repair yard sent a salvage team up there, and we just towed her back and got her on the blocks two days ago."

"Jeez, boss. You mean this just happened?"

Mondello nodded, looking at the damage. Several Vietnamese yard workers were rigging scaffolding around the hull.

"Doug okay, sir?" asked Coburn.

"He was on the command boat. They caught some fire, but everyone's okay. This one got the brunt of it. We lost Chief Howell in there." Mondello pointed at the rocket hole. "Killed him and the Vietnamese engineman he was working with. Detonated in the engine room and ignited the diesel fuel. Inferno. Couldn't get the bodies out until it cooled down. If you could call what we got 'bodies'."

He pointed at the gun turret and the bent bow. "Both gunners have broken legs and some cracked vertebrae."

"What happened, sir?"

"Ambush. A well-planned one. They were inserting an ARVN company. Once the shooting started, Doug's counterpart was too busy screaming at the helmsman and on the radio to the other boats, so Doug called in an airstrike. Lots of body parts when they finished."

Shit, thought Coburn. I'm on a vacation cruise interrupted by two kids with BB guns, and Vernon's calling in air strikes.

Mondello kept staring at the damaged boat. "How's your counterpart doing?"

"Boss, I've seen my counterpart once for about an hour. If I hadn't met him then, I'd think he was fiction, some mythical guy. He doesn't exist."

Coburn continued. "But the XO, Chang, is top notch. For all practical purposes, he's the CO. And he has a good ops officer who's smart and aggressive."

"Could they operate if we took you three guys out of there? And we didn't replace you, Chief Robinson and Cruz?" Mondello gave him that stare that said, "don't bullshit me."

"If you're asking can they run the RAG on an operation, yes. At least at this tempo. If you're asking are the officers and sailors capable of administrating, maintaining, repairing, and supplying the RAG, yes. Do they know how to call in artillery and an airstrike, I think so, but they haven't had to," Coburn paused. "But…"

"But what, Clark?"

"I don't think the South Vietnamese Navy can provide them the repair parts, logistical support, and training of new sailors. At least not from what little I've seen. Until that happens, they'll be dependent on us. I think the ARVN can handle artillery, and my RAG can use it without me. But I don't know about South Vietnamese medevacs, air support, command and control."

Coburn paused, thinking.

"Maybe that's okay, but I haven't seen any evidence one way or the other. Chang's real capable, boss, and his men are good. If we can get him the tools, he'll know how to use them. But I just don't see the tools coming from anyone but us. And I don't mean guns and fuel and ammo, I mean support. If my real asshole counterpart is typical of the leadership in the rear…"

Coburn let his sentence drop. He realized he was on a rant. Crapping on the president's nephew may not be the right thing to do.

"Clark, before you go back to Phu Cuong, write down just what you told me in a report from you to Captain Powell, via me. Copy to Jim Theodore."

"Lieutenant Commander Theodore? He was the senior student in our counterinsurgency training."

"One and the same. Give the draft to the yeoman, and he'll type it up."

Mondello, who was taller than Coburn, put his arm around the junior officer.

"You've got a tough job ahead of you, Clark. How are you going to get the rest of the Vietnamese military up to the standards of RAG Bravo?"

"Sir, beats the shit out of me. And that's no bullshit."

"I believe it. What say we go to the Rex and try to eat steak tonight. I'll see if we can get Commander Minh to join us."

Coburn had captured Mondello's confidence and attention. He felt as if he were walking on clouds.

* * *

Chief Hospital Corpsman McGruder was a lanky Kentuckian. Before coming in-country, he had spent his twenty-three years in the navy working mostly with the marines, with a few assignments at sea on destroyers and two short shore-duty assignments at the big navy hospitals in San Diego and Portsmouth, Virginia. He was now the advisor to the South Vietnamese Navy's medical personnel assigned to Commander Minh—a physician and two corpsman in Saigon and the three corpsman assigned to each of the four RAGs. When Coburn and Cruz walked in, Chief McGruder was sitting at his desk in the small sick bay.

Taking the unlit pipe out of his mouth, McGruder stood up and said, "Cruz, Thieu Ta Mondello warned me that you were in town, so I locked up everything that could fit in your duffel bag. The only thing you can steal are the geckos. You still dribbling from the clap?"

Cruz laughed, then shook hands with McGruder and introduced him to Coburn.

"Welcome aboard, Dai Uy. The boss and Commander Minh said that last night you three were talking about doing a psyops upriver with a medical team. About fucking time someone thought of that. I understand it was your idea."

"If it works, Chief, it's my idea. If it doesn't, it's Cruz's idea," Coburn replied.

Cruz put on a mock frown. "Shit, I get blamed for everything around here. *Stars and Stripes* and the Armed Forces Network said I was responsible for Tet. Bunch of anti-Latino assholes running this place."

"Nothing wrong with hating beaners, Cruz. Now if those assholes were complaining about rabid puppy dogs or cute little rats, that'd be another story," retorted the chief corpsman.

The three advisors sat around the chief's desk and planned a psyops mission upriver, beyond the Michelin rubber plantation. Indian country.

McGruder would arrange the medical personnel, Cruz and Robinson would work with the RAG, and Coburn would act as overall coordinator and direct liaison with the advisors to the ARVN division.

Coburn left Cruz with McGruder and walked over to Mondello's office. He borrowed a paper pad and one of the ubiquitous black ballpoint pens produced by the millions by Skillcraft for the US Government. He roughed out the report that Mondello wanted him to send, proofed it, and handed the handwritten draft to the yeoman for typing.

Grabbing a cold Coca-Cola from the refrigerator, Coburn walked over to Commander Minh's office. The pretty secretary was typing a letter in the outer office. After a few minutes of unsuccessful flirting in Vietnamese, he drained the Coke, tossed the can in her wastebasket, and walked back to the hootch. With nothing to do and a rejection-bruised ego, he decided to practice his Vietnamese with Ba Be.

She said she had two children, both girls, ages ten and eight. If he understood her correctly, she had tossed her husband out of the house for drinking and whoring, and as much as he wanted back in, she was steadfast. She thought Mondello was wonderful—"numbah one"—and very handsome. She called Wilson her good friend. And she warned Coburn that if he didn't meet her standards of behavior, he was number ten.

When she asked if he had a wife or girlfriend and he said he did not, Ba Be looked at him fixedly and asked if he liked men. Coburn burst out laughing and told her he was just too young for marriage, and all his girlfriends had dumped him—which was pretty close to the facts.

She said in a low, conspiratorial voice that maybe she'd find him a nice Vietnamese girl to marry and take back to the United States. Again Coburn laughed and said no thanks, he didn't think he'd be up to the standards of Ba Be's matchmaking.

The yeoman handed him the typed report. Coburn reread it, signed the original, and handed it back to the yeoman for distribution. The yeoman gave him one of the carbons and put the original on Mondello's desk.

"The boss doesn't let paper sit on his desk too long. He'll probably stick an endorsement on it and get it to Captain Powell tomorrow," said the yeoman.

Cruz and Coburn were scheduled to drive back to Phu Cuong in the morning. Until then, Coburn's time was pretty much his own. Cruz was going to hang around with McGruder, leaving Coburn the jeep. At about 1700, Coburn drove to the Rex BOQ, parked the jeep, and locked the steering wheel and gas cap with a chain and padlock. The roof of the Rex was starting to fill up with Saigon warriors. Coburn found an empty table by the roof edge, sat down, and ordered a beer from a white-jacketed Vietnamese waiter.

Taking out Kelly's and Betsy's letters from his pocket, he unfolded them and reread each slowly, looking for some nuance that he had missed, some chink in the women's armor he could use. How would he respond? If at all. Kelly was damaged goods, and he had little doubt she would shit can his letters before opening.

The hell with Kelly and good riddance. She got knocked up, and it was not as if he were really going to get serious with some girl he picked up from the Mexican Village. Kelly was now officially history.

The waiter brought his beer as Coburn tore Kelly's letter into little pieces and put them in the ashtray.

Betsy was another matter. She was beautiful and had adored him. What to do about that? Had he been too hasty with the letter he sent from Travis? After a week in-country, he fantasized meeting her for R&R in Hawaii and spending an entire week in some air-conditioned hotel room on Waikiki, then see what opportunities his next set of orders would bring.

"You must be one of those cocksuckers from the DeKalb."

Coburn looked up from Betsy's letter. Mathew Geralds was standing by his table. Jumping to his feet, Coburn grabbed his old shipmate's hand.

"Matt, what are you doing here? They don't let homos in South Vietnam."

"Ever since they let you in, Clark, they do." Geralds looked at the lieutenant bars embroidered on Coburn's jungle fatigue blouse. "Congratulations. It looks as if they're promoting homos, too."

"Sit down you asshole. Buy me another beer and tell me what you're doing here."

Betsy's letter got stuffed into his shirt pocket. The reunion of the DeKalb shipmates went from a couple of beers to dinner.

Geralds had left the ship as soon as the DeKalb reached the Mediterranean and reported directly to an abbreviated language course in San Diego. After a week of weapons training and then another of SERE, he arrived in-country three weeks after Coburn. His job was the director of petroleum—fuels—management for the Naval Supply Centers in Saigon and Danang. Geralds was not an advisor to the South Vietnamese Navy; his clients were the US Navy and US Marine Corps units in-country.

As the waiter cleared their plates, Geralds leaned back in his chair and lit up a cigarette. He blew a smoke ring that hung intact in the still, humid air.

Pointing at the lieutenant bars, Geralds said, "I didn't even know you were in the zone."

"I wasn't. COMNAVFORV gave me a spot promotion when I called on him."

"No shit? It's good to see that the navy sees value in promoting guys with little, teeny dicks." Geralds launched another smoke ring. "Have you heard from Betsy?"

"Yeah, Matt, got a letter from her," Coburn replied flatly.

"She finally got your address, huh? She wrote me on the ship when you were in Coronado, wondering if you were all right since she hadn't heard from you for a while."

"What'd you say?"

"That you had probably found a nice flock of sheep and had started fucking furry animals."

"Don't knock it, Matt. Sheep aren't half baaa-a-a-ad." Coburn made bleating sounds. "Seriously, did you write her back?"

"Yeah, sent her a quick note saying I hadn't heard from you either, training was probably keeping you busy, needs of the navy, that kind of bullshit."

"She's pissed that I missed her graduation, and some bitch she works with is engaged to some Swifty I guess was in Coronado about the same time as I was. The fucker wrote and called all the time," said Coburn.

"She dumping your ass? 'Dear Clark it's not you, it's me' letter?"

"Nah, no one dumps Clark Coburn. Clark is the dumpster, not the dumpee." Coburn looked at his hands. His smile was gone. "Well, I sort of put an end to it all back in Coronado. Gently, I thought, y'know, maybe start things up again later if the embers were still hot when I get back. Keep in touch so she won't forget me—that sort of bullshit. I think she just decided to put the nail in the coffin of our relationship." He looked up. "Want another drink or something?"

Geralds pushed his chair back. "Let's go out in town for a bit. Been to the Red Door?"

"Nope, but I'm going there now with you," said Coburn.

The Red Door was a bar with bedrooms upstairs. It was noisy, garish, smoked filled, and crowded with American military officers, a few Australian army officers, and American civilians. Coburn could pick out the Saigon warriors from the company and platoon leaders who were in Saigon from the field for a little R&R. The guys from the field all had that gaunt look, tan skin, and old eyes.

Several of the patrons wore holsters with loaded pistols. Coburn thought that was stupid—booze and loaded guns in the same crowded room. This was a bizarre Saigon version of a saloon in the Wild West.

A sound system blared the Stones and the Beatles. Young Vietnamese women, wearing tight miniskirts or ao dais sat on bar stools next to the men, cruised around the room, or leaned against the wall, arms folded across their chests as they sized up the newcomers. Several had obviously been to Hong Kong for breast enhancement, and a few more had dyed their hair blonde or red. Two walked up to Coburn and Geralds as they waited for the Vietnamese woman behind the bar to pour their beers.

One stabbed Coburn in the right arm with her Hong Kong breast, pressing her thigh against his leg. "You new here, huh? Where you from?" she asked in thickly accented English. "You navy."

She was surprised by Coburn's fluent response in Vietnamese. "Yes, miss, I'm an American navy lieutenant. Where are you from?"

Not switching to Vietnamese, she replied in English, "I from Vung Tau. You know Vung Tau? You buy me Saigon tea?"

Geralds was getting the same script from the other girl. He ignored her and told Coburn, "You buy them Saigon tea and they sit, and talk to you for fifteen or twenty minutes. You buy enough and they fuck you. Or you just buy them out for the night, and they fuck you."

"What's Saigon tea?"

"Orange soda pop in a martini glass. 250 p."

"Two fucking dollars for an ounce of orange pop?"

"Yep, that's the price of pussy. Or you can just buy her out for the night, I think that's about twenty dollars. And they take MPC."

"You're shitting me. Isn't that illegal?"

"Of course it is. And every so often the White Mice or the MPs raid this place or somewhere else down the block. But this is about as good as it gets in Nam."

"What're my options?"

"Leave, pay for some Saigon tea, buy the girl out, make the girl drink real booze and then watch her puke, or just sit by yourself and suck a beer and watch this fucking zoo. Or any combination of the above." Geralds took a swallow of his beer.

"Dai Uy Coburn's never paid for pussy in his young life. He ain't gonna start tonight."

"Not a bad move, Clark. No one ever caught the clap by drinking alone. I'll follow your example and become an innocent bystander and observer of life in Nam."

After two beers and five approaches by various bar girls, Coburn and Geralds walked back to Coburn's jeep. A young girl, about ten or twelve, was asleep in the back. Coburn rousted her out, unlocked the steering wheel, and drove Geralds to his BOQ room. They exchanged contact information and agreed to get together when Coburn was in Saigon next. He drove back to the boss's hootch.

Coburn walked in to find Mondello was sitting in the headquarters hootch with a pile of papers on his lap, half listening to the television that Wilson, Cruz, and McGruder were watching. The blonde weather woman had just finished the weather reports for the R&R destinations and then, as she did every night, gave her body measurements. Standing behind Mondello, Coburn tried to read the top page of what Mondello was going through but figured it was just some routine paperwork and turned his attention to the television set.

A Star Trek rerun was about to begin. Coburn watched for a while, then said good night and climbed into his rack. He thought about Betsy, Kelly, Doug's girlfriend Jean, and the bar girl with the big knockers and masturbated before brushing his teeth and going to sleep.

Cruz drove them back to Phu Cuong early the next morning.

* * *

After briefing Cruz and Robinson on Wilson's intelligence report and the report he wrote to Captain Powell, Coburn explained his plans for the psyops medical team visit.

The location would be farther upriver than their normal area of operation—unfriendly Indian country. He'd sit down with Chang and the army advisors to pick an appropriate village—big enough to have more than a few occupants and remote from convenient access to medical services. Chief McGruder would set up the medical team. Robinson remarked that it would be good to get McGruder out of Saigon and on the river with them.

They discussed security for the operation. This was to be a "winning the hearts and minds of the people" operation, not an assault. But they were going into an unsecure area. While the entire AO had been quiet and the VC were maintaining a low profile the last few months, it would be foolish to park the boats on the riverbank and then simply walk into the village.

Should they use the sailors to set up a perimeter and keep the monitor and the command boat's guns manned? Bring with some ARVN or US troops for security? Ask for helicopter gunships and artillery to be at the ready?

Coburn wanted as low a profile as possible. Cruz and Robinson, who had experienced a lot of combat on the river, wanted troops along. They decided that they needed Chang to make these decisions.

Coburn found Chang on the command boat, discussing a diesel engine problem with one of his senior petty officers. After exchanging pleasantries, Chang leaned against a grenade launcher and said, "Commander Minh tells me that you had a good meeting with Lieutenant Commander Mondello."

"News travels fast, Dai Uy," said Coburn, genuinely surprised how fast the grapevine really worked. "It was a good meeting."

"And you want to do a medical assistance operation."

Again surprised, Coburn smiled and nodded. "I want to, yes. But this is your RAG, not mine, Dai Uy Chang. I think it would be good to do that."

"I do, too. But we may be poking a sleeping tiger."

"No doubt about that, Dai Uy Chang."

"Better to wake up the tiger before he is fully rested than to wait for him to wake up on his own." Chang was smiling at Coburn. "I think you look forward to tiger wrestling."

The two discussed the operation in detail. Chang suggested the village of Bau Sinh just west of the rubber plantation. He also did not want to use ARVN or US troops.

"Dai Uy, if we bring troops, we will need to take at least one troop carrier. I'd rather put together a security force of my sailors and just use the monitor and the command boat, maybe you take the skimmer?"

"Sure." Coburn liked the way this was going.

"I'm taking risks, Dai Uy," said Chang as he exhaled cigarette smoke out his nostrils. "But if we go to the ARVN, even if they decide we should use our sailors for security instead of their troops, the VC will know when and where we are going. We will be ambushed, probably as we go into the village. I do not trust ARVN security of classified information. And I am not allowed to go to the US forces unless we go to the ARVN first. I think our plan has the least risks."

"It's your show, Dai Uy Chang. For what it's worth, I agree with you. But I do not mind risks."

Chang looked hard at Coburn without saying anything. Then he told the petty officer working on the engine that he'd be in his office and invited Coburn to join him for lunch. While relations between Coburn and Chang were good, this was the first time Coburn had been invited to join Chang in anything other than business. Coburn wondered if Gordon had ever been extended the honor.

In the small dining room of Chang's quarters, the counterpart and his advisor ate a meal of stir-fried vegetables and fish, rice, a pungent dipping sauce, and tea. The meal was served silently by Chang's wife, a pretty woman wearing a loose-fitting, white blouse, black trousers, and rubber shower shoes. Coburn could hear small children playing in the next room.

Chang lit another of his French cigarettes and leaned back in his chair, squinting at Coburn through the acrid smoke. He offered a cigarette to Coburn, who refused, saying he wondered how Chang could smoke those things. They smelled like burning dog shit. For the first time ever in Coburn's presence, Chang burst into laughter.

"Dai Uy Coburn, they smell better than the river at low tide, and they keep mosquitoes away."

"I'd rather breathe through my mouth and live with the mosquitoes."

Chang stubbed out the last of the cigarette on the sole of his shoe. "You and I are much alike, Dai Uy."

"Really? How so?" Coburn was genuinely surprised at the comment.

"We both like war. We both like the excitement, the clarity, the life of combat. I saw that the first operation with you."

"I don't know if I like war."

"Oh, but you do, Dai Uy Coburn. You like the fighting, you like the power. And you like the glory. And you don't think of the horror. Or when you do, you like that, too."

Chang paused and lit another cigarette. "And so do I. But I have much more opportunity. You will be here for what, another ten months? I have been here all my life and will be here for the rest of my life, however long or short that may be."

"I don't know, Dai Uy Chang. I haven't had much combat exposure since I got here. You know, a few guys shooting at us when we came downriver, and that's it. Yeah, I get excited and it feels good to me, but I don't think I've really been in war or combat yet."

"We can make our war and combat. We can meet the VC and kill them. I have no problem with killing."

Coburn was still off balance with the conversation. "How was Dai Uy Gordon? With this?"

"Dai Uy Gordon is a very brave man. He hated combat and the killing. But he never ran, he never avoided what he had to do. He won many medals from us and I think from your navy, too. He was afraid until the day he left here. Doing what must be done when you are afraid is courage, true courage."

"You don't think I will get frightened, Dai Uy Chang?"

"Not of the dangers of war. Of other things, yes. Maybe of losing power or control, not being recognized. But not of war."

Coburn was still trying to comprehend the breadth of Chang's statements. "And you? What drives you?"

Chang smiled and stubbed out his cigarette. "I thought it was hatred of the communist, the VC, Uncle Ho. I still do carry that hate. But now I'm driven by something else, an...I don't know the word...what do you say for a strong need for something that you cannot do without? Not like food or air but like heroin?"

"An addiction?"

"Ah, thank you, Dai Uy. I am addicted to war, to the fighting, to the killing. When I am not fighting, I want to be fighting, and I look to find reasons to fight."

"How will you be when the war ends?" asked Coburn.

Chang smiled and looked at Coburn and then at the doorway to the room from where children's voices could be heard.

"I don't know if this war will ever end. If it does, another will start. That's the history of Vietnam. And before it does end, I may very likely be dead, either of wounds or of old age."

After a pause that Coburn did not want to interrupt, Chang said, "But if I am still alive after the war ends I will be happy for my wife and children. They have never tasted peace. I want that for them."

"But how will you feel, Dai Uy Chang, without the taste of combat to satisfy your obsession, your addiction?"

"I will feel like a major part of my life is missing. I will probably turn into an old man doting on memories. Or maybe even remembering days like this talking to you. I will miss my opiate of the battle."

* * *

Dear Bets:

I wanted to drop you a quick note before I have to shove off. I don't know what exactly to write. It's a war here, and we live it a day at a time. And it takes tremendous focus and attention. Distraction is dangerous. But please keep me in your thoughts until I am done with all this. This letter sounds so awkward, Betsy.

As for your friend's fiancée, the Swift boat officer, what he goes through and what I go through are as different as apples and oranges.

*That includes our time in Coronado. So please don't compare me to him.
That's not fair to me.*

*I saw Matt Geralds when I was in Saigon last. He's in some air-conditioned office job and seems pretty happy. He asked about you and
mentioned that you wrote him.*

Clark

After he reread the letter, Coburn put it in an envelope,
addressed and sealed it, and dropped it on the floor. He scuffed
his boot on the envelope, turned it over, and then scuffed the
other side. He put it in the outbox with the other letters and
messages.

Satisfied that the envelope's appearance would stand out
from the sterile mail received in a Manhattan office, Coburn
hoped that the combined effect would be a guilt trip for Betsy.
She would have to feel bad about giving a self-sacrificing hero
fighting for his country cause to worry. He wasn't sure how long,
if at all, Betsy would tolerate waiting. It was probably already over.
But this couldn't do any harm.

It was the day of the medical team psyops. Win the hearts and
mind of the peasants, and win the attention of the brass.

Despite Chang and Coburn's efforts to keep the operation
focused and free of security leaks, the mission almost became a
public relations event. The first and biggest problem was Toh,
the RAG's titular CO and the nephew of the President of South
Vietnam. Toh realized this mission could generate a lot of good
publicity—for him. He wanted to lead the mission and have his
photo taken handing out medicines to adoring peasants and
their children.

When he heard that the village chosen was in unsecured territory upriver, he tried to change the village to one about seven
kilometers upriver from Saigon. Commander Minh and Mondello tactfully suggested to the South Vietnamese Navy's Chief of
Naval Operations that a secure village that was walking distance
to a government hospital was not a place that needed a visiting
medical team.

Realizing that the location was not going to be changed to his liking, Toh then decided that a battalion of ARVN or US Army was needed to adequately protect the peasants from the Viet Cong. And he should be brought in by helicopter along with the journalists. This time Chang and Coburn were on the landline telephone to Toh, respectfully pointing out that a psyops should not look like an invasion or search-and-destroy mission.

Chang said he was confident that the RAG sailors could provide more than adequate perimeter security and that Coburn would have artillery and a light fire team of two helicopters on call. Toh called back the next day saying that due to requirements from a higher authority, he would not be able to be there leading the operations from the command boat but would be monitoring the radios and be in command of the operation from his office in Saigon.

Both the US Army and the nearby ARVN division wanted a piece of the spotlight, but the army advisors quickly squelched that, pointing out that a US Army nurse would be with the team and both ARVN and US Army artillery and helicopters would be on standby. Besides, they had other things to do.

Coburn tried to get Theodore to get some press coverage. Despite Coburn's urgings that good press would be good for Vietnamization, Theodore was concerned about the risk of a media circus to the mission's security. He quietly let the request die on his desk.

Finally, after four weeks of planning and negotiations, the operation was about to begin. Chang had given up on any idea of keeping the mission secret. By now, even Hanoi must be aware that the village of Bau Sinh was about to be visited by a medical team that afternoon.

They would take the command boat, the monitor, and the advisors' skimmer. Coburn and Robinson would be there as well as Chief McGruder. McGruder arrived early in the morning with a US Army nurse from Saigon, Captain Peggy Griffith. He also brought the South Vietnamese Navy doctor assigned to RAG headquarters. The rest of the medical team would be made up of two RAG Bravo corpsmen. Three big cartons of medical supplies and propaganda material were in the back of the jeep.

Captain Peggy Griffith worked on the wards of the army hospital in Saigon. Coburn studied her as they loaded gear on the command boat. She was a big-boned woman, but not fat. As typical of most of the nurses, her hair was short cropped for practicality in the humid heat of South Vietnam. She was dressed in jungle fatigues, jungle boots, helmet, and flak jacket. Instead of a weapon, she carried a large canvas bag and backpack, both marked with a red cross. In her left breast pocket were a bandage scissor and a thermometer. On her wrist was a large-dial, stainless-steel-cased wristwatch—all function, no fashion. And on her left hand was a gold wedding band.

Coburn made a show of being on top of it all, checking radio frequencies, confirming that artillery and light fire team helicopters were on standby. He made it a point to check maps and stare off into the distance through his dark sunglasses when he knew she was watching. Unlike his usual floppy hat, shorts, and shower shoes, Coburn wore freshly ironed jungle fatigues with his trousers bloused above his jungle boots, flak vest, and helmet with mosquito repellant held in place with a large elastic band around the helmet's camouflage cloth covering.

Chang looked at his counterpart, smiled to himself, and got the boats underway and moving upriver and under the bridge. Robinson and McGruder followed them in the skimmer and once through the bridge, tied the small boat to the command boat and climbed aboard.

A crewman brought a bunch of ceramic cups, most of them chipped, and a kettle of tea to the top deck and poured tea for all. Chang hung back by the coxswain, but the Americans and the Vietnamese doctor sat under the canopy on the low deck chairs. Coburn kept the PRC 25 radio near him and the large-scale maps of the river open on his lap.

He was sitting next to the nurse. She was chatting with the Vietnamese doctor, Robinson, and McGruder, asking about the area they were passing through. Coburn took that as his opportunity to show his knowledge of the area. He moved his chair around and pointed out where they were on the map. Robinson chuckled quietly to himself.

Chang joined the group and added a narrative to the steady passage of the boats upriver. At certain points he and Robinson pointed at a bend in the river or a place where the bank jutted out from the shore and identified them as ambush and firefight sites. Both men avoided saying when the actions occurred, purposely leaving the impression that Coburn had been involved in some fierce battles on the river. The nurse zipped up her flak vest and listened intently.

The day was hot but dry, the sun brilliant. Occasionally they'd pass farmers—older men, women, children—working in their fields and paddies, sometimes with a water buffalo and stray dogs in attendance. The adults never looked up, toiling bent over under their conical straw hats. Some of the children would wave. At one shallow spot along the north bank, two boys were washing their water buffalo, then standing on its broad back and doing cannonballs into the river.

"This is almost idyllic," said the nurse in her thick, West Texas drawl. "It's hard to believe we're in a war."

The Vietnamese doctor said that what she saw was what Vietnam could become, but there were many problems to be solved before that could happen. He hoped for his children's sake that would happen soon. Chang nodded and flicked his cigarette over the side. The smell of sautéing garlic and fish sauce drifted up from the small galley below, the odors mixing with the diesel exhaust.

They had been underway for three hours when the crewman came up, collected the teacups, and then reappeared with several bowls, more teacups, and chopsticks. He went below again and this time came up with the relief coxswain, both men carrying bowls of steaming food and rice. Chang invited everyone to eat lunch. They would be at the village in about half an hour.

The meal was a mixture of fresh vegetables from the local market in Phu Cuong and canned entrees from half a dozen

C-rations that Robinson had brought aboard. The nurse was amazed.

"I have never had C-rations taste like this before. This is delicious," she said.

McGruder laughed. "It shows you what can be done with ham loaf and wienies and beans, huh, Captain?"

"Y'know, Chief, I'm going to be a civilian soon, and I'm tired of the titles and saluting. Please call me Peggy."

"You're on, Peggy. But only if you drop the 'Chief' and call me Don and that asshole over there," he pointed at Robinson, "Chuck."

"And me Clark," added Coburn. "You going home soon and leaving the army, Peggy? Where's home?"

"Yes, I'm out of here in four weeks on my way back to being Missus George Griffith, civilian, and living a normal life in El Paso. That's home."

"Husband in the army?"

"Was. We were both stationed at Fort San Houston. He's an orthopedic surgeon. We got married six months before I got my orders here. His time was up. He didn't mind the army, but the travel, relocation, and separation was a burden. So we decided that he'd buy into a practice in El Paso and I'd finish my obligation."

"You've been separated a whole year?" asked Coburn.

"Almost. I met him in Hawaii for a week's R&R two months ago, and that was nice. I'm taking thirty days leave when I leave here, and he's meeting me in Australia. Then back to CONUS, separate from the army, and buy a house in El Paso."

"Going to work as a nurse there?"

"For a while. Then babies."

"Sounds, nice," said Robinson.

"You have kids, Chuck?" she asked.

"Indeed I do. Two daughters." Robinson took off his helmet and pulled a photograph out of his helmet liner's webbing. He gave the picture of his wife and daughters to the nurse.

"Hey, I want to see that. I never saw your kids, Chief," said Coburn.

McGruder chimed in. "Yeah, let me see that, too. I want to see if it's true that they look just like me."

Chang interrupted the laughter by saying the village was just around the next bend. He would send the monitor in first and land the sailors, who would set up the security perimeter. Then the command boat. He wanted the medical team and Dai Uy Coburn to get into the skimmer and stay near the far bank until he was certain the area was secure. It was a little before noon.

Once the team and he were in the skimmer, Coburn started the outboard and let loose the towline. He motored away from the command boat and stayed in mid-river, idling while the two big boats maneuvered into the bank. Coburn was not happy that Chang had unilaterally decided that he'd go into the skimmer. If the landing turned hot, he'd be out in the river taking care of a bunch of non-combatant pecker checkers instead of shooting back and directing fire.

On the other hand, he was with the nurse, who was the only round-eyed woman for miles around. She wasn't bad looking, had a beautiful smile, but for a big-boned woman had little tits. Still, she was a worthy target. She, the Vietnamese doctor, and Chief McGruder would not be returning to Saigon until tomorrow morning, which meant she had to sleep over at the hootch.

An older man, the village chief, met the sailors. After the sailors were in place around the perimeter, Robinson, Chang, his operations officer, and leading petty officer walked into the center of the small village, which was not much more than two dozen huts at the junction of two dirt paths.

Chickens, ducks, and a couple of pigs strolled through the center. The only villagers in sight were the village chief and several children watching Robinson and the RAG officers with poker faces. Chang walked around, then satisfied that the village was safe, directed the petty officer to notify Coburn to bring in the team and the command boat to bring in the supplies and equipment.

Within half an hour, two tables were set up in the village center next to an empty hut. A generator-powered loudspeaker and tape player blasted the nasal twangs of a Vietnamese folk song interspersed by announcements from one of the sailors inviting all villagers to receive free medical aid. Seated at the table were the two RAG corpsman, McGruder, the nurse, and the Vietnamese doctor. Chang, Coburn, and Robinson hung around in the background, Coburn carrying the PRC 25 radio on his back.

Nothing happened for another half hour, and then a woman walked up carrying her baby. She talked to one of the RAG corpsman, who escorted her to the empty hut where the doctor and nurse examined her, treated a skin infection, and examined the baby. Within ten minutes, a line of women and children was waiting at the table.

One RAG corpsman worked with McGruder and Peggy, and the other worked with the Vietnamese doctor. Occasionally all five conferred on a patient. A few old men watched, not getting in line. Only the children smiled, especially at McGruder, who handed out candy, toothbrushes and toothpaste, South Vietnamese flags, and bars of soap that contained a series of cartoons and patriotic phrases that appeared as the soap was used.

Out of boredom, Coburn walked around the small village. This area, he thought, is VC controlled. And here he was walking around as if he were back in Newport on a weekend afternoon. Except he was carrying a radio and had a loaded pistol in a holster. The few villagers who looked at him did so without emotion. Neither friendly nor angry. They just stared at him. He smiled at one older woman, but she just stared at him. Coming around one hut, he found Robinson standing in the middle of a gaggle of children. One little boy was holding Robinson's hand while a girl whom Coburn guessed to be about eight years old rubbed the back of his forearm.

"She's trying to rub my color off, Dai Uy. They've never seen a colored man before."

"Chief, you are the life of the party. This village definitely does not like me."

"You're just not dark enough, Dai Uy. Too bad we didn't use some shoe polish on you before we left."

Together they walked back to the village center, Robinson trailing a wake of children. Peggy and the doctor were taking a break, stretching their legs and backs. Chang walked up, smoking a cigarette.

"How's this going?" asked Coburn.

"Pretty good, I think," said Peggy. "This is the first one of these things I've been on, and I'm sorry I haven't done more of them. I think we've seen more people than live in this village."

"You have," said Chang. "According to him," Chang pointed at the village chief, who was talking to one of the RAG corpsmen, "the village population is about fifty, and we've counted over seventy, and there's still a line waiting. The word must be spreading."

"That's good. And gratifying," said Coburn. He turned to the doctor. "What have you been treating? Anything real serious?"

The doctor looked at Peggy for confirmation and said, "These villagers are overall healthy. The most common problems are stomach and bowel disorders and skin infections. Several of the women were here for their husbands, describing what sounds like arthritis. We've told them to get their husbands, but it's been a couple of hours and none have shown up."

Peggy nodded and added, "The babies are all chubby, although everyone else is skinny. They give them a lot of sweetened condensed milk when they're weaning them. I'm also surprised at the condition of the children's teeth. No cavities, no plaque."

"I probably put a stop to that, Peggy. Don and I've been passing out candy to all the kids," said Robinson. "But I've been also passing out toothbrushes, too."

"If I could prescribe anything to these villagers, it would be the frequent use of soap and water. Infections and stomach problems would drop precipitously," said the doctor as he and Peggy returned to the table.

At 1700 Chang told Coburn that they had better pack up and head downriver. He wanted to get some kilometers behind them while they still had daylight. An ambush timed as the sun set could hamper the support of a light fire team or artillery.

The line at the table was gone, and the few villagers who showed up were examined without having to wait. Chang talked to the RAG corpsmen, who started packing up the medical team's gear while Coburn stood back and watched. The nurse got up, looked around, and saw Coburn. She walked up to him.

"Clark, see that woman over there with her baby?" She was looking at a woman standing by herself, holding a baby covered in a scarf.

"She's been hanging around all day but would not get in line. Your corpsmen asked her if she needed help, and she refused but kept on standing there." Peggy put her hand on Clark's forearm, a move he had always interpreted as a woman's desire to get intimate. She lowered her voice and stood closer.

"Your corpsman asked one of the other women what's the matter with her. From what we figured out, the baby's face is disfigured. I want to take a look, but I don't want to upset her. I'm going to try."

Peggy walked over to the woman and smiled at her. Then without further ado, Peggy took the baby from the woman's arms. The woman surrendered the child without protest. Peggy looked at the child's face and handed the baby back to its mother. The nurse walked back to Coburn, who by this time had been joined by Chang, Robinson, McGruder, and the doctor.

In a low voice, Peggy said, "The baby has a bilateral cleft palate. Seems fine and healthy otherwise. It's very disfiguring, but that can be repaired. We have an excellent oral surgeon in Saigon who has done this surgery on Vietnamese children several times."

"What's it entail?" asked McGruder.

"Two surgeries. We bring the baby and mother to the hospital. One day for surgery to fix one of the clefts, two days recovery in the hospital, then we send the baby and mother home to recuperate for three weeks or a month, then we do the other side. Results are good, risks are minimal," answered Peggy. "Can we take them with us?"

"Yes, if she wants to go," said Chang. "She would ride in the monitor in case we get ambushed. It's the safest boat."

Coburn thought of the monitor from Vernon's RAG Alpha, lying in the dry-dock with its innards exposed. "Maybe we could call in a dust-off and fly them out?"

"Let me talk to her," said Chang. Coburn followed him, although there was little he could do to help Chang. After nearly a quarter hour of explaining and cajoling, most of which Coburn was able to follow, they walked back without the woman and her baby.

"No joy," said Coburn purposely putting gravity and sadness in his voice. "She won't go with us. I think she's afraid of retribution or something. Even if her kid gets stuck as the village freak. We told her that if she changes her mind to let the village chief know, and we'll come and get her."

Again per Chang's instructions, the medical team and Coburn left first, taking the skimmer and idling in midstream. Then the command boat backed out, and finally the monitor after loading the perimeter security sailors.

Coburn toyed with the idea of taking the skimmer all the way back to Phu Cuong since it could go three times as fast as the other two boats. But he wasn't sure if he had enough fuel, and their only defense would be speed. He kept the idea to himself, knowing it was a stupid one. Instead he motored over to the command boat, transferred the team, secured the towline, and climbed aboard.

They had another hour of daylight left, and the passage would take at least three. Chang had all his guns manned and had both boats at full throttle. With the current, the boats were making nearly eight knots. Not fast enough to water ski but faster than they normally ran. The medical team and Robinson took seats under the canopy. Coburn hung around the coxswain with Chang, acting very alert and in charge. He keyed his radio and checked in with the Tactical Operations Center using military jargon and slang he had picked up from listening to the army units and helicopters on the radio.

Robinson looked at McGruder and rolled his eyes. McGruder smiled back and shook his head.

Chang walked forward and explained to Peggy that it was common for the VC to shoot at them as they came down the river. He said he was surprised at how quiet the day had been; maybe they'd be lucky and not get shot at this trip. Coburn nodded his head knowingly but wished to himself that they would get into a firefight. He wanted the rush. He wanted to look like John Wayne before this woman from West Texas.

The doctor asked Chang why they had not been opposed. Did he think they surprised the VC, and they had not expected them this far upriver? Chang said he doubted that the VC were surprised. Maybe they just wanted to get some quality medical aid. Who knew?

Coburn understood the Vietnamese conversation but kept quiet. He didn't want to give Peggy the impression that they were upriver because the VC let them go upriver. Rather, he wanted her to think that they were upriver because he had taken an operation into harm's way.

It was dark when they passed under the bridge. The trip downriver had been quiet and uneventful, and the doctor, Peggy, and McGruder napped in their low deck chairs, and Coburn wrote his after-action report draft with help of a flashlight.

Cruz was waiting for them on the floating pier and invited Chang, his operations officer, and the doctor to join the Americans for dinner in the hootch. Chang made sure the boats were securely tied up, and Robinson moved the skimmer to its normal berth. After washing up, they all gathered in the advisors' hootch.

Ba Mei and Cruz had been busy. Grilled chicken, rice, stir fried vegetables, and, of all things, cheesecake that Cruz had made from a boxed mix. Cold Australian beer—about half a VC flag's worth—was the beverage, along with grape soda. Not having eaten in nearly seven hours, the guests attacked the food with gusto. As second portions of the cheesecake were being served, Chang went back to his hootch and returned with a bottle of cognac.

The beer, cognac, and Cruz's cigars, combined with the exhaustion of the day, made for a very relaxed crowd. Since he had to call in the after-action report and wanted to keep his mind clear, Coburn avoided the beer and liquor. He also wanted to be sharp for whatever transpired with Peggy—hopefully an alcohol-lubricated seduction. Leaving everyone at the table, he used the landline to call in his report, reading from the form he had filled out on the river.

Sleeping arrangements were next. The South Vietnamese Navy doctor would bunk with Chang. McGruder would bunk in one of the spare bunks in the room shared by Cruz and Robinson. Coburn announced that he'd sleep in the other spare bunk in Cruz and Robinson's room and that Peggy could have his room, which had two bunks. She protested that as silly. Why should Coburn have to leave his bunk? She'd just sleep on the padded bench in the main room or in the upper bunk in Coburn's room. Coburn's optimism increased. A little more cognac and beer and she'd be ripe.

"If you insist, Peggy. I think the upper bunk in my room will be more comfortable than sleeping out here," said Coburn, straight faced.

Cruz raised an eyebrow and shot a quick glance at Robinson, who winked back. The table was cleared of dishes, which were stacked in the sink for Ba Mei in the morning.

Peggy sat outside on the sandbags surrounding the hootch as McGruder, Robinson, and Cruz washed up, said goodnight, and went to sleep. Coburn joined her, offering her a beer, which she refused.

"It's nice out here, Clark. Certainly beats Saigon."

"It is nice, Peggy. But it's Indian country and still plenty dangerous. Today was a rare exception."

"The anticipation of trouble is sometimes worse than the trouble itself, isn't it? I'm convinced that's the cause of a lot of stress disorder cases we're seeing in the psych wards."

"Shell shock?"

"Something like that. You seeing a lot of action up here?"

"Too much. It gets pretty tough, but it's my job," said Coburn.

She changed the topic. "Got a wife or girlfriend back home?"

"Neither. Had a girlfriend, but she had a breakdown. Her doctor said she sort of collapsed mentally when she heard I was hurt. Got a 'Dear John' letter a few weeks later saying she just couldn't take it."

"That's tough. How'd you get hurt?"

"B-40 went off. Blew me over the side, but my flak vest caught all the shrapnel. Knocked me out and gave me a concussion and a few burns, but no scars to speak of," lied Coburn.

She looked at him quizzically. "Concussions can be pretty serious and nothing to mess with."

"Hey, Doctor said I was okay and said I was fit for duty," said Coburn. He realized he was bullshitting in an area where she was the expert, not him. He changed the topic. "Miss your husband? You know, must be hard being away, and…well, you know."

She looked at him with that beautiful smile of hers. "I miss George terribly. And it is hard not being near him, especially since R&R. But I don't miss anyone or anything enough to sleep with you, Clark. Even when I'm full of beer and cheesecake."

Coburn's spirits plummeted, but he laughed deeply and falsely, pretending that she had made a joke and seduction was the last thing on his mind. She got up, grabbed her backpack, and went to the head and the sink to wash up for bed. Wearing an olive-drab T-shirt and cut-off tropical fatigue trousers, she said goodnight to him on her way to his room and the upper bunk. He walked in a few minutes later after peeing and brushing his teeth. She was sound asleep, breathing deeply.

What a bitch, thought Coburn to himself. Prick tease leads him on for the entire day and then kicks him the nuts after she gets him all excited. Bitch.

* * *

The rocket hit while Coburn was sitting on the toilet reading the *Stars and Stripes* newspaper. It sounded like a freight train followed by a deafening explosive clap. Dirt and sand pelted the side of the latrine and the black water tank. He heard Robinson shout "Incoming!" before the echo died.

His heart racing, Coburn stood up and nearly toppled over; his feet had fallen asleep. Rapidly wiping himself and pulling up his pants, he could feel his heart pounding in his chest. He was about to wash his hands and thought what a stupid idea that was and ran back to the hootch and the shelter of the sandbags.

As he ran, he heard whistling sounds followed by a series of explosions as black blossoms sprouted in the area between the hootch and the floating pier. Huddled behind the sandbags were Peggy, Cruz, Robinson, and McGruder, all wearing their helmets and flak vests. Cruz tossed a helmet and vest to Coburn. Robinson was on the PRC 25 reporting to the TOC and giving the coordinates of the small hamlet across the river.

"TOC Crazy Razor Alpha. Affirmative. I saw the flash of the mortar tubes. Have eyes on the spot now. Nothing moving. No weapons visible. Over."

The radio buzzed. "Crazy Racer TOC. Wasp in the air. Has coordinates. Should be overhead your location in five. Will be on this frequency. Out."

Coburn looked up over the sandbags. It was quiet. He stood up, and Cruz said, "I wouldn't do that yet, sir."

Cruz's admonition was immediately followed by a series of six mortar rounds walking closer to the floating pier and the RAG boats tied up there. Gravel and dirt landed on the corrugated iron roof of the hootch. Shrapnel pierced the green plastic sand-bag covers. McGruder was crouched with just his helmet show-ing above the protecting sand bags, peering through a pair of binoculars resting on the top layer.

"Fuck, they must have moved the mortars. No flashes that I could see. They must be behind that hut or in the tree line." Robinson relayed McGruder's report to the TOC and helicopter light fire team that was on its way.

Chang was running toward the RAG boats, yelling orders. Coburn looked up above the sandbags and then stood up, ready to follow Chang.

"Hold on Dai Uy," said Robinson. "They're waiting for us to get moving into the open, and they'll start lobbing in more rounds."

"I got to be with Dai Uy Chang. He's my counterpart," said Coburn, sounding like a comic book superhero.

He vaulted over the sandbags and ran after Chang. Within seconds, a pop was followed by more pops and whistling, and then another half dozen mortar rounds exploded at the edge of the floating pier.

When he reached Chang, Coburn was gasping for air, his heart pounding, exhilarated. The sailors were starting the boat engines, getting ready to move them away from the pier. Chang had ordered the monitor's mortar crew to fire on the tree line across the river. His operations officer was observing the fire, giving adjusting orders to the monitor's mortar crew. Two helicopters swooped overhead and across the river, circling the hamlet.

Chang yelled at Coburn, "Dai Uy, have them fire at the tree line. They're in there!" Coburn didn't have the radio; Robinson did.

"Where's your radio, Dai Uy?" asked Chang incredulously.

"I'll go back and get it." Coburn turned to run back when Chang tackled him and knocked him onto the hard-packed dirt. Four mortar rounds hit, showering them with dirt and rocks. Chang dragged his advisor up by his flak vest collar, and the two ran to the monitor.

The helicopters started their runs on the tree line, shooting rockets and minigun fire. At the end of each run, the monitor's mortar crew would fire continuously until the helicopters were in position for their next run. The deadly ballet of mortar fire and helicopters was being choreographed by Robinson and the RAG operations officer, although neither could talk to the other. The incoming fire ceased.

Chang ordered a squad of sailors and his leading chief to cross the river and assess the damage. Coburn was on an adrenalin high tempered by a bruised ego and embarrassment. Without telling Chang, he jumped on the RAG boat as it left the pier with the squad for the short trip across the Saigon River.

The Vietnamese chief looked at Coburn in surprise and asked in Vietnamese, "Lieutenant Coburn, where's your weapon?" Coburn's M-16 and his .45 were in the small arms cabinet back at the hootch. He felt pissed and embarrassed.

The Vietnamese sailor's radio crackled. It was obvious to Coburn that Chang was asking this sailor why Coburn was aboard. Coburn looked back at the RAG base and saw Chang holding the radio handset. Robinson and Cruz were standing next to him. Fuck those assholes, thought a humiliated Coburn.

The damage assessment squad walked around the hamlet across the river from the RAG base. It was deserted, although cooking fires still smoldered. They walked through the tree line and the damage caused by the monitor's mortar and the helicopters.

At the far side of the tree line, they found what looked to Coburn like chicken fat and pale meat scraps, a blood trail, and the tread marks of Ho Chi Minh sandals that disappeared after twenty meters. They searched for an hour but found nothing more.

Coburn was coming off his adrenalin rush and feeling depressed, unappreciated, foolish, and, worse, not admired. His sailors and the Vietnamese had made him look like a fool. With that nurse and McGruder and probably that doctor watching the whole thing.

They boarded the boat, and the Vietnamese chief radioed his damage assessment to Chang. No bodies, no weapons, a blood trail, and entrails to nowhere. Hamlet empty, no men, women, children, ducks, or dogs.

Chang, Robinson, and Cruz were not on the pier when Coburn disembarked. He trudged back to the hootch and found McGruder, Peggy, and the doctor standing by their jeep, packed and ready to go.

McGruder said, "We wanted to wait until you got back before getting on the road, Dai Uy. Thanks for the hospitality. I think yesterday's mission was as good as it gets."

McGruder put out his hand, and Coburn shook it. "Thanks Chief. I'll try to put a report together for the boss. Drive safe."

Coburn knew it was a dumb idea for McGruder to salute him in a combat zone but thought the offer of a handshake was crossing the line between superior officer and underling.

Then Peggy smiled her brilliant smile, said thanks, and shook hands. They climbed into the jeep, and McGruder drove out the gate, waving at the sentry. Coburn was in the dumps. That nurse's smile wasn't a smile. She was laughing at him. He's out there putting his ass in danger, and she laughs at him.

Back in the hootch, Robinson was sitting at the table drafting out the after-action report. Cruz was about to go down to the pier to look for any damage and then instruct some of the sailors on how to change a diesel engine ejector. Both were very businesslike. Robinson poured himself a cup of coffee and one for Coburn, then handed him the draft report.

"Here's my take on the after-action report, Dai Uy. Dai Uy Chang says no boats damaged but the floating pier took a hit on the southwest corner. Put a hole in the deck plating, but nothing structural. That's in the draft. I don't have the damage assessment from across the river, so I left that part blank for you."

Coburn took the coffee and the draft. He hoped Robinson hadn't noticed the uncontrollable shaking of his hands. The shaking was from excitement and leftover adrenalin, not fear.

"Thanks, Chief. The place was deserted, found some blood and guts in the tree line but nothing else. Zip. Nada." He read through the draft, penciled in his information, and then called in the after-action report.

"Care to talk about it, Dai Uy?" asked Robinson.

"Not much to talk about, Chief. I thought yesterday went as good as could be expected. Maybe better than expected. This morning? Shit, we take incoming from a friendly hamlet in our backyard. Not much damage on our side. Somebody or maybe somebody's French poodle got hit on the other side."

"Want to sit down with Cruz and me and do our own assessment and 'lessons learned'?"

Coburn visibly stiffened at the suggestion. Yes, these two had been in-country longer than he had, and yes, the two probably had more time sitting on the shitter than he had in the navy, but he was in charge, not these two. Coburn also knew that the senior enlisted were the backbone of the navy and only a fool would ignore their skills, expertise, and most importantly, their advice.

"Chief, I think that's a good idea. I was going to suggest that myself. Maybe get Chang at the table, too?" Coburn hoped that Chang, Cruz, and Robinson would catch a mortar round and get wiped out before that would happen.

"Sounds good to me, Dai Uy. I'll corral Cruz and Dai Uy Chang. Maybe after the noon siesta?"

* * *

The three advisors met with Chang in his cigarette-smoke-filled office. Coburn took the initiative and brought up the medical team operation. The consensus was that it had been an overwhelming success although Chang was curious as to why the VC had let them do it. No opposition, it had been a holiday river cruise in the sunshine.

Coburn lost the initiative when Chang turned to the morning's events. Chang went through the action in a methodical manner. They all thought that the response of the RAG and the support from the helicopter gunships went well and the coordination was excellent. Chang praised Robinson, who modestly said it was just a team effort. Coburn silently stewed.

After lighting another cigarette from the stub in his mouth, Chang turned to Robinson and Cruz. "But you two need to take care of your Dai Uy. You have the experience, which you must share with Dai Uy Coburn. You should not have left him unarmed and without communications. My sailors take care of me; you must do the same."

Cruz spoke up first. "You're right, Dai Uy Chang."

"I'll take responsibility for that fuckup, Dai Uy Chang," added Robinson.

Coburn saw that Chang was letting him save face, the all-important rule of the Asian cultures. These three were treating him like a baby that couldn't wipe its own ass. He took advantage of the pause in the conversation with his second attempt to take back the initiative with a question.

"Why did the VC attack us this morning? A secure hamlet, right across the river. They knew we'd knock the snot out of them. I just don't understand it, especially since yesterday was so quiet."

"I've asked the army intelligence people to investigate the hamlet residents," said Chang. "Perhaps the Viet Cong just want to show us that they can strike whenever and wherever they like. And maybe to show the hamlet the damage the American helicopters and we caused."

"Sort of like why a dog licks his balls," said Cruz.

Chang looked at Cruz, questioning. "Why?"

"Because he can," answered Cruz with a deadpan expression.

Chang stared at Cruz for a second, looked at Robinson, who was smiling, and then burst into a robust laugh. "That's very good, Trung Si, very good. Yes, the Cong shoot at us because they can."

CHAPTER 21
BINH TRAMH

Vo and Ky sat across from Hoang in the subterranean head-quarters, going over their impressions of the last several weeks. As always, Hoang listened but said nothing. Vo and Ky exchanged quick glances, and Ky nodded his head in answer to Vo's unasked question.

Vo leaned forward on his stool. "We want to put together our plan and move forward. But much of what we want to do is insep-arable from the NLF. We will keep you apprised of everything. Both Comrade Ky and I are worried about getting into areas that are outside our field of expertise."

"Like what, Comrade Vo? Tactics?"

"Yes, like tactics. Like coordination of missions and focusing on the long-term objective of reunification. We see glaring prob-lems that have nothing to do with logistics."

Hoang nodded and looked down at his teacup, then back at the two young officers sitting across from him.

"Your primary mission is the one assigned to you by General Ong. Strategic logistical planning, right?"

"Yes, that's right," answered Vo.

"But you are here, now. And you are seeing things that General Ong cannot see. And if you are seeing problems that need to be corrected, I can assure you that I, General Ong, Commander Tran, and even Ho Chi Minh insist that you address these problems. Give me your recommendations. And don't let your egos get in the way if some of them I shit on. Do you understand me?"

"Yes," answered Vo and Ky in unison.

"I want you integrated into the NLF, reporting to both me and General Ong. Let me use your education and brains as well. Who knows, I may become a supply depot specialist, and you might become heroes of the battlefield."

As they stood up to leave, Hoang handed over a paper package wrapped in string. "These came for you from Hanoi. I recommend you open the package and read its contents here."

They opened the package as Hoang watched. A typed letter from Sergeant Nguyet informed them that Ninh had died, his cremated remains returned to his parents, and that a replacement would not be sent. Vo passed the letter to Ky, who read it and gave it to Hoang to read.

Another note from Sergeant Nguyet acknowledged receipt of all the reports Vo had sent from the trail, extended General Ong's appreciation for the astute comments and recommendations, and directed that all future correspondence be sent via the NLF leader in their operation area—District Commander Hoang. Again they shared the letter with Hoang.

The rest of the package was a pile of personal letters to Vo and Ky.

The two men silently went through their letters. Vo read the ones from his mother and father first, saving Ngoc's for last. Ngoc had written him eighteen letters, one a week since he had left Hanoi.

She wrote how much she missed him, worried about him, and loved him. She wrote that her medical studies were going well, and she would be finished in another year. She wrote about visiting his parents and how well they looked and told him his brothers were in good health, too. One letter included a formal photo of Ngoc in an ao dai. And in one letter she asked him to say hello to Ky and Ninh for her.

"Ky, Ngoc says hello to you."

Ky looked at Vo and smiled. "That's nice. Send her my love when you write back, huh?"

Hoang watched the two men read and reread their letters while he went through some reports on his desk. Finally, he closed the last file and said, "Do not take any correspondence out of here. Destroy them all. I'm sorry, but that's a precaution you must take."

"Should I keep this photo, sir?" asked Vo.

Hoang looked at the picture of Ngoc. "Very pretty girl, Vo. Sure, you can keep that picture. But we'll burn everything else. If you want to write back, please do so now and keep it short. What you write will be read by others before it leaves here."

For the next half hour, Vo and Ky wrote letters. Vo sent one to his parents saying he was in good health, appreciated their letters, and to say hello to his brothers and Ngoc when she visits.

And then he wrote a letter to Ngoc.

Dear Ngoc:

I want to write you this short letter to tell you that I received eighteen letters from you today! They mean so much to me. Do not worry about me; I am fine and healthy. Ky sends his regards and was flattered that you sent greetings to him. I'm glad and proud that your studies are doing well.

I miss you so much and love you even more. I think of you all the time.

I love you,
Vo

* * *

The memory of Ninh kept both men awake in their hammocks in the dark and dank underground dormitory. Vo with a start realized that Ky was standing next to him, holding two cups of a fragrant tea.

"Drink this, my friend, it will help us sleep," said Ky.

The tea smelled familiar, but Vo couldn't place it. "What is this, Ky?"

"The flower tea. The same as when we left Ninh."

Vo and Ky drank their tea, a mildly narcotic and hallucinogenic brew from a flower that grew along the banks of rivers and streams. They fell into a deep sleep with vivid, colorful dreams of home, orange napalm blossoms, and Ninh.

* * *

Vo and Ky spent a week sequestered in a corner of the subterranean headquarters complex, organizing their thoughts and recommendations in a report to General Ong and NLF Commander Tan. Once they finished the first draft, they would present it to Hoang, incorporate his thoughts and edits, and then implement what they could while it went to Hanoi for review.

They gave the draft to Hoang.

Hoang hefted the thick draft, thumbed through it briefly, and told the two young men that he wanted to have time to read the report thoroughly before they discussed it. He told them to be back in his headquarters in five days.

Vo and Ky continued to travel around their area of operations, observing, questioning, learning. As always, they traveled at night, sleeping during the day in a safe location, often within a short distance of American or Southern troop concentrations.

The night before they were to return to meet with Hoang, they were outside Phu Cuong meeting with Canh Chien Pham, the local NLF communications and liaison agent. During the day the NLF agent ran a small factory that made luminescent lacquer ware out of eggshells and local woods. The finished trays and bowls were popular objects for sale in the US military post exchanges throughout the south. During the night, he ran the communications network for Hoang.

An attractive woman dressed in ao dai walked into his small factory office in the early evening.

She was introduced to Vo and Ky as Nguyen Hao Yung, Mrs. Nguyen. Vo and Ky exchanged quick glances. Mrs. Nguyen was very good looking. The factory owner and NLF agent explained that while he was a strong proponent in limiting knowledge for the sake of security, he wanted Vo and Ky to meet Mrs. Nguyen because she was vital to their work.

Mrs. Nguyen's husband was Major Nguyen, an ARVN Ranger in I Corps, operating south of the Demilitarized Zone. Their marriage had been arranged by his influential Saigon parents and her parents, a wealthy commodities trader father and socialite mother. Her parents hoped the marriage would force their bohemian-minded daughter to forsake the crazy ideas she had picked up during her university years in Paris. While the young officer and his bride made a handsome couple, there was little love between them. The marriage was a marriage in name only, for convenience, and the financial and social gain of both families.

Two years ago, Major Nguyen's father had used his influence to get MACV to hire his daughter-in-law to be a translator at MACV headquarters in Saigon. She spoke fluent English and French. As she had pointed out to her father-in-law, she had too much time on her hands while her husband was away, the money was good, and the senior level translator jobs were prestigious and much sought after.

The South Vietnamese security and background checks, lubricated by favors and money, were quickly finished and showed no problems. The Americans, in need of people with her capabilities, pushed their own investigations through quickly and found her background impeccable. After a few months working as a translator, Mrs. Nguyen was encouraged by her US Army supervisor to take a promotion to become an intelligence analyst in the joint MACV and ARVN intelligence center in Saigon.

As an intelligence analyst, she worked with American military personnel and civilians, one of which was US Army Captain

Robert Neal. Neal had spent two months in the joint center and was being reassigned to be the intelligence advisor to the ARVN division's intelligence officer located northwest of Saigon. Part of Neal's orders was to develop a division-level joint intelligence center for both the ARVN division and the US forces in the area.

He convinced his superiors that he needed Mrs. Nguyen to come with him. She was offered another promotion and relocated to Phu Cuong to work with Captain Neal in the G2 office. Mrs. Nguyen was the only Vietnamese civilian in the office. She was hardworking, pleasant, and intelligent. Neal and the others in the G2 office trusted and relied on her.

A month after Mrs. Nguyen moved to Phu Cuong, she received a phone call from her father-in-law. Her husband, Major Nguyen, had been killed in Hue during the Tet offensive. Mrs. Nguyen took leave for two weeks in Saigon for her husband's funeral and to comfort her in-laws. She returned to her job in Phu Cuong and resumed her work in the G2 office.

Within a short time, she had become the office go-to person. Her recall of names and dates and where the files were located was nearly as valuable as her analytical skills. Mrs. Nguyen could piece together apparently unrelated and obscure facts and anecdotes from raw intelligence and come to logical and accurate conclusions. Neal often said that if she left, he'd have to shut down the office.

While a student in Paris, she had a lover—a sardonic, alcoholic French man twenty years her senior. As a young man, he had fought in the resistance against the Nazis and then became a freelance journalist. He introduced her to his circle of acquaintances, which included exiled communists from Saigon and Hanoi. Within a short time, she had joined a group of Parisians sympathetic to the NLF.

She was undecided between staying in Paris after graduation or going to Hanoi and offering her services to Uncle Ho. But her parents changed her plans when they brought her back to Saigon and married her off to the handsome Captain Nguyen.

The two newlyweds had problems from the beginning. As much as she tried, she could not stifle her disgust of what she saw as the corrupt regime of the Southerners and her husband's patriotic blindness to the corruption. And her beauty could not overcome his preference for sex with other men. When he received a promotion and was sent to the DMZ, she felt relieved and reprieved.

At that time she was approached by an NLF recruiter. Without hesitation she asked how she could help the reunification of the country for the good of the people. And so she became a translator and an intelligence analyst with bona fide, top-secret clearance granted by the governments of South Vietnam and the United States of America.

She sat in the G2 office six days a week, absorbing valuable intelligence and passing it on to the NLF communications and liaison agent at the lacquer factory outside Phu Cuong. Her analyses for Captain Neal often contained false information she planted in coordination with her NLF comrades.

Paradoxically, she liked Captain Neal, her mentor, and in fact had sent his wife and two small daughters silk ao dais. She thought some of the ARVN officers she worked with were arrogant and lazy, happy to be in intelligence instead of in combat with the infantry.

She intensely disliked the lone American naval officer who always found a reason to visit Captain Neal. She became adept at ignoring his obvious advances as he hovered around her desk, trying to brush against her.

Vo and Ky listened as she told them her history. This was a brave woman.

"Mrs. Nguyen, on behalf of General Ong, I express sincere gratitude for your bravery and sacrifices," said Vo.

"Comrade Vo, Comrade Ky, I will do everything I can to ensure the success of your mission."

* * *

To their surprise, the NLF Commander was waiting with Hoang. With no preamble or pleasantries, Hoang asked Vo to summarize the findings and recommendations contained in the draft report to General Ong.

For the next two hours Vo and Ky went through their draft. They were so familiar with what they had written that they never looked at the document on the table before them.

"Comrade Commander, Comrade Leader, reunification for the good of the people cannot be obtained militarily without first gaining the will of the people," stated Vo.

The issue of Vo and Ky's jurisdiction was brought up next. While they had been sent as logistical experts working for Hanoi and the NVA, there was much they could offer to the NLF in the Saigon River corridor between Saigon and the Cambodian border. If nothing else, they would be another set of eyes, ears, and hands.

The recommendation that they should be integrated into the NLF structure and vice versa was a bold one for two young men to make, risking stepping on the polished boots of the generals in Hanoi and the rubber sandals of the NLF in the south. Hoang and Tran sat in silence, watching and listening.

Vo shot a quick glance at Ky, who gave a nearly imperceptible shrug, and Vo continued. If their audience of two wanted to interrupt them or ask questions, they certainly would.

It was apparent to Vo and Ky that the shortage of ammunition was the most critical factor in limiting operations, both strategically and tactically. NLF units could engage the Americans and the Southerners at will, but usually had to disengage prematurely because they ran out of ammunition. Having no bullets to shoot, they were extremely vulnerable to counterattack or future engagements until they could replenish their armories. Exacerbating the ammunition shortage was the failure of a weapon to fire, often due to poor construction, lack of maintenance, and shoddy repair. Medical supplies, rations, footwear, clothing, and personnel were important, but none so critical as ammunition and weapons.

Ky presented their recommendations. First, fire discipline and ammunition controls must be instituted throughout all NLF units. A certain number of rounds of bullets, rockets, and grenades should be allocated each unit member before an engagement. No unit should ever use all its ammunition in an engagement but should disengage when 30 to 25 percent of the unit's ammunition was left. Secondly, well-guarded armories should be established in secure areas where new weapons and parts could be received from the North or Cambodia, and broken weapons could be repaired or cannibalized for parts. These armories would be under the command of the NLF area leader. Ky looked at Hoang for a response but saw none.

Thirdly, many of the locally produced grenades and reloaded bullets failed to fire or fired prematurely. Standardization and quality control could only be enforced if ammunition and reloading facilities were standardized and supervised by dedicated workers and managers. As with the armories, factories needed to be established in secure areas under the supervision of the NLF area leader.

The supplies the NLF brought into an engagement were all they could rely upon. Unlike the Americans and the Southerners, there were no armored supply vehicles or helicopters to deliver hot meals and bullets to a unit engaged in a battle. Engagements had to be planned with this fact foremost. Depots primarily for munitions but also for other supplies within a day's travel of the farthest unit should be established for rapid resupply.

Ky's final point before turning the floor back to Vo was that any armory or factory or depot must not only be small, compartmented, and portable, but also expendable.

"We cannot afford to have large quantities of supplies in one location, no matter how well protected."

Again seeing no reaction on the part of Hoang or Tran, Vo took over from Ky. The Tet offensive had exhausted supplies—especially ammunition, weapons, and medical supplies. While these supplies were being slowly replenished, poorly thought-out ambushes and attacks by NLF units were exhausting material and personnel for little or no benefit.

Often, the overwhelming response by the enemy to an NLF-initiated action decimated the unit. Vo recommended that all NLF-initiated operations be approved by a senior command structure with a greater strategic understanding.

Vo had expected that this recommendation would certainly raise a question, but again the two men remained impassive.

Trying to answer what he thought was the unasked question, Vo said, "I am not recommending a ponderous bureaucracy, but rather an agile committee or group that has the authority to approve or disapprove a military operation."

Vo went on, explaining a paradox. Their demands far exceeded the supply chain's capacity to deliver. And the supply chain's capacity, as meager as it was, exceeded the ability of the units to utilize what was delivered before foodstuffs spoiled, caches were captured by the enemy, or bribery and pilfering put the supplies on the black market. In addition, the supply chain, which was mainly by boat or on land from Saigon or by land from Cambodia, could not deliver the amount of supplies needed to sustain any operation bigger than a battalion sweep, much less an armored invasion of the South.

To develop the logistics needed to conduct military operations in the corridor for the reunification of Vietnam would take possibly a decade or more. Vo paused, thinking that he was being presumptuous lecturing two very senior officials. But he continued.

"We cannot rely on the small factories, armories, and depots to sustain any major military operation. Our Soviet and Chinese allies must provide the military hardware and expendables. A factory hidden in a rubber plantation cannot be expected to produce a missile that will shoot down a helicopter or jet air plane," he added with more force than he intended.

"We will need more advanced weapons in the future." Now he felt he was overstating the obvious.

"But we must take the steps that we can take, now. Without delay." Vo paused again. "It is our opinion that the Saigon River is the key. Goods moving up the Saigon River are stopped at the bridge at Phu Cuong for inspection. Bribes can get some through, but not at a sustainable rate. The option is to move the supplies to land transportation below Phu Cuong and truck them to an upriver spot beyond Phu Cuong. But that is cumbersome and requires driving our supplies through ARVN- and US-controlled areas of operations. The other alternative to bring in the supplies via the Cambodian ports and up the trail, or from the north down the trail. Then transfer the supplies to the river and bring the goods downriver.

"We recommend that option because the river is unpatrolled. A single river assault group of slow but dangerous vessels is in Phu Cuong and occasionally operates on the river, but that's all. The Americans fly observation helicopters and reconnaissance aircraft up and down the river but would not be able to detect hidden cargo on a river fishing sampan."

Ky stood up and took over the narrative. "A motorized sampan can carry five hundred to a thousand kilograms of cargo. It can tow even more. A nomotorized sampan can move with the downstream current and carry an equivalent amount. Ammunitions and weapons can be waterproofed by sealing them in grease and wrapping them in plastic and rubber. These packages can be made neutral or slightly negatively buoyant and towed down the river. At certain points, or if approached by a patrol or one of the Southerners' river boats, the sampan merely cuts the package loose, and it settles on the river bottom but is marked by fishing buoy or a reed or similar natural object. The next sampan picks up the tow and moves it to the next drop-off spot, and so on until it reaches a depot."

Vo said, "We have also recommended the implementation of a strategy that may be considered a harsh one. The Americans and the Southerners have overwhelming firepower at their disposal. The Americans in particular do not hesitate to use it. Their soldiers do not seem to worry about costs. We have recommended using their strength against them.

"If we can get them to use their destructive prowess on the civilians they are trying to win over to their side, they will lose their battle for the hearts and minds of the populace. The Americans' massacre of the village of My Lai was a tragic loss of life but a tremendous strategic victory for us. Our strategy should be to cause the enemy to attack the people, even though it means the loss of lives. Neither Comrade Ky nor I will apologize for making such a recommendation."

Vo took a deep breath. "Commander Tran and Leader Hoang, Comrade Ky and I have presented our observations and recommendations to General Ong in the draft you have here. We respectfully request your comments and recommendations. We will incorporate them in the next draft for your review."

Tran spoke quietly and slowly. "Sit down, please, Lieutenant Vo. There will be no next draft."

Vo felt a wave of disappointment and anger sweep over him. They were going to kill the report. He looked at Ky, whose face was red, his lips pressed together in a thin line. Ky leaned forward on his stool about to say something when Tran smiled.

"There will be no next draft," Tran said, "because Comrade Hoang and I agree with what you presented. We concur with your recommendations, and it was very well written. We had it encrypted and sent to Hanoi yesterday along with some additions of our own."

Ky sat back on his stool and let his breath out in a long sigh followed by a smile. "Thank you, sir."

Hoang spoke for the first time in two hours. "General Ong was told that effective immediately, we have established a Military Affairs Committee that will oversee the developments you recommended—the factories, depots, armories, and river transportation. And also the establishment of a review and approval process for operations and supply requests. This committee is made up of three people and will be kept secret. The three are you, Comrade Vo, or in your absence Comrade Ky; my communications and liaison agent or his designee if he cannot participate; and me."

"Thank you for the honor, Comrade. We will do our best," pledged Vo.

"I have no doubt about that. I also want you two to relocate near Phu Cuong. Perhaps become lacquer workers in our agent's factory. I am going to relocate these headquarters shortly. I will also move closer to Phu Cuong. There is a danger in that, but I believe the proximity will lead to increased communications and efficiency. This is your last visit here."

CHAPTER 22
SAIGON

It was the first time the two friends had been together since Koeppler Compound over four months ago.

Both had arrived that morning in Mondello's office for a debrief and a few days in Saigon. Coburn almost didn't recognize Vernon. His friend had lost weight, although he was still husky and muscled. Deeply tanned, his skin was taut over his cheekbones, his eyes sunken. His right forearm was wrapped in an olive-drab dressing of gauze and tape. But he acted and sounded the same—smiling, energetic, optimistic.

They sat around Mondello's desk, drinking coffee and waiting for Wilson and the NAVFORV liaison, Theodore, to join them. Mondello asked Vernon how his arm was coming along. The young officer replied that all the shrapnel had been picked out and the infection seemed gone. The wound was healing nicely.

Coburn didn't want to ask what had happened. Not because he wasn't curious but because he didn't want Vernon talking about combat and heroics and whatever else would grab the boss's attention. Especially since Coburn's RAG seemed to be doing nothing but pleasant river cruises in the sunshine.

He was upset that Vernon had probably been awarded a Purple Heart for cowering in some bunker somewhere. Probably got scratched trying to open a can of C-rations when some gook lit off a firecracker.

Theodore and Wilson walked in together and shook hands with Coburn and Vernon. Theodore asked Vernon how his arm was healing. Coburn rolled his eyes and then realized that Mondello had caught his expression of exasperation.

After an intelligence briefing from Wilson, Theodore talked about the directions coming out of NAVFORV, specifically to wean the South Vietnamese Navy from the US tit. America would continue to provide money and equipment but not people.

Mondello added that he didn't know if the objective would ever be met. Some parts of the South Vietnamese Navy were doing fine and could probably stand on their own. But most could not. And the country's overall military and government leadership, infrastructure, and economy were even further from the goal. Theodore agreed.

The other major directive from NAVFORV—and also MACV—was gaining the support of the population. Theodore asked Coburn to describe how the medical psyop went.

Aware that everyone in the room with the exception of Vernon had read the after-action reports, that McGruder had probably given Mondello a colorful and entertaining but accurate verbal report, and that Chang's and the Vietnamese navy doctor's impressions had been shared with Minh and therefore Mondello, Coburn knew he'd have to control the bullshit and stick to the facts.

He methodically went through the operation from planning to execution, stopping at the point they returned to the Phu Cuong RAG base. Vernon seemed interested and impressed, which heartened Coburn.

"Clark, do you think it worked? I mean, are the people more… what's the word…predisposed to your guys?" asked Vernon.

Coburn put on a face of gravity, pretended to be thinking deeply. He already knew what he thought was the answer since he had asked himself that question many times in the weeks since the operation. It was going to take a lot more than a visit and a bottle of aspirin to "win the hearts and minds."

"Doug, if that village was made up of just the kids ten and under and the puppies that hadn't made it into the stew pot, yeah, we did okay. But judging from the stares I got from every adult, they don't trust us at best, hate us at worst. Don't get me wrong. We didn't do any harm, and in the long run we probably did a little good, but it's going to take a whole lot more than a single visit with a medical team."

Wilson asked, "I read that you went all the way upriver and then back down with no engagement. That's pretty unusual, isn't it?"

"Yeah, Bill, unusual it is. As far as I'm concerned, the VC just let us. There was no way we sneaked up there and back without their knowing about us."

"Would you recommend to your counterpart to do more of those?" asked Mondello.

"Yes, sir, I would. In fact, I did."

"What about the other RAGs? Think Doug's group should try it?" asked Theodore.

"I don't know the situations on the other rivers, sir. If it's anything like what I'm dealing with, sure, they should try it. Might keep some dink kid from putting on the black pajamas and picking up a B-40."

"Any bits of advice you'd tell the other RAG advisors like Doug over here?" asked Mondello, pointing at Vernon.

"Lots, sir. I'll tell you what we did that worked well. First, don't make it look like a sweep or a search-and-destroy mission. We used our own sailors for security, not a platoon of ARVN, US, or Ruff-Puffs. We just took two boats and the skimmer so it didn't look like Iwo Jima.

"Secondly, line up artillery and air support and put them on standby during the operation. We did, and didn't use it, but if we had run into a problem, it would have been very handy.

"Third, keep the team small and predominately Vietnamese. Chief McGruder and a US Army nurse were the only round eyes at the table.

"Finally, let your counterpart and Chief McGruder take the lead in the planning."

Mondello nodded his head and said, "Good, Clark. Very good. What would you have done different?"

"Brought a reporter or military journalist to get some press out of it. Probably would have been good to have a Vietnamese media person or two along. Bring lots more stuff for the kids. Especially that soap with the slogans that appear when you use it. And candy. Chief Robinson was like Santa Claus—we ran out of stuff. I'd also ask Chief McGruder and the *Bac Si* what kind of medicine, or whatever, they need. I don't think we ran out of anything, but I don't know."

Coburn was feeling good. They were listening to him. He was being recognized, his advice and opinions sought. He decided to take it a step further, show the human side of Dai Uy Coburn the advisor. "Uh, one last thing, if I may, boss," said Coburn, looking at Mondello.

"Sure, go ahead."

Coburn told the story about the woman with the baby with the bilateral cleft palate. He described how they tried to get her to go with them, but she refused. For whatever reason, she was condemning her child to a life of ridicule and scorn. "Short of actually kidnapping her and the kid, I don't know what we could have done."

Theodore was listening intently with his chin on his fists, elbows on his knees. "I want to think that one over a bit, Clark." He looked around the rest of them. "If any of you get any ideas, let me know."

"Ideas like what, sir?" asked Vernon.

"I don't really know, Doug. That's a heartbreaking story, and I just think we can do something about it. But I don't know what we can do."

Coburn felt as if he had just hit a grand slam home run and won the World Series.

Mondello asked the next question. "Clark, you were rocketed and mortared the next morning. That's the first time that happened to that base, ever. Think it's related to the psyop?"

Not even wanting to think about that morning, Clark forced himself to maintain his confident air and answered. "That's the big question, boss. Chang has asked the ARVN intel guys to look into it, and I asked the G2 advisor to do the same. It's been a couple of weeks, but so far no response. I doubt if we'll get anything much more than what we have now. I just don't know, sir."

"Want me to look into this, boss?" asked Wilson. Mondello gave him a thumbs-up and a nod.

Theodore asked Vernon for a report on the enemy tactics his RAG was encountering. Coburn hoped that NAVFORV's push for Vietnamization would take some of the glory out of the action that Vernon was dealing with.

RAG Alpha's area was a hot one. Ambushes and firefights were commonplace. While less than the pre-Tet levels, the VC and NVA were still active and aggressive.

Vernon told them of a new and dangerous twist to the enemy's tactics. It had been almost routine that after extracting troops and returning from a mission that the boat column would be ambushed with rocket and automatic weapons fire. The tried-and-proven response was to turn into the incoming fire, open up with every weapon on the boats, and land the troops in the center of the ambush area while the boats suppressed the enemy's fire. If the enemy fire was intense, artillery or air support would be called in before landing the troops. Up until recently, the troops wound up chasing the enemy and counting bodies.

During the last two encounters, the enemy fire subsided as usual after the boats opened up. The troops were landed. But instead of counting bodies or chasing VC, they walked into a booby-trapped killing zone. As soon as the booby traps detonated, the enemy opened up with a murderous cross fire.

"Charlie seems to have changed his target from the boats to the troops," said Vernon grimly. "They had it well planned. We couldn't suppress fire without hitting the ARVN. The troops were pinned down, and all we could do was watch and take potshots where we could. I think the only reason Charlie quit firing was because they ran out of ammunition."

With a sour face, Vernon added, "I wouldn't be surprised if they add some B-40s to the mix and shoot at the boats, or put a couple of mines right off the beach."

"What would you two suggest to counter this?" asked Mondello. Coburn was surprised that he was included in the question.

"Call a truce or surrender, and let's all go home," joked Vernon. The atmosphere lightened a bit.

Coburn said, "Return fire but don't get near the beach. Then call in artillery or air and bomb the shit out of the place. Then land the troops."

"I'm with Clark on that one, boss. It could be like using a sledge hammer to kill a gnat, but it could save lives," added Vernon. "Another move would be to return fire and maneuver to put the troops in flanking position. Both times it happened on points of land. Figure out the killing field and then flank it."

"Or combine that with the artillery and air," said Coburn.

Theodore and Wilson were taking detailed notes, Mondello just sat and listened.

Then Theodore looked up from his notes. "You think your counterparts are working this problem?"

"I don't know if 'working' is the right word, Thieu Ta Theodore. I know my counterpart's scared shitless about it," said Vernon.

Coburn said, "If you mean Thieu Ta Toh as my counterpart, unless it's posted on the bulletin board at some high class Saigon whorehouse, I doubt he even knows about it. This is the first I've heard about it, so I doubt if Chang is looking at the problem. Toh won't do anything. Chang certainly would be concerned."

"Pete, does Minh know about this?" asked Theodore.

"I don't know, Jim. I share the after-action reports with him, and Bill does the same with his staff. But I haven't talked to him directly about it. Let's you and I go see him after we throw these two river rats out of here."

"Want us to go with you, boss?" asked Vernon. Brown nose, thought Coburn.

"Not yet. Let's finish up. What's your take on your RAG's progress on Vietnamization? How's your counterpart doing?"

Vernon led off by saying that RAG Alpha was in bad material shape and should probably be decommissioned as soon as some of the US Navy's River Assault and Interdiction Detachments boats could be turned over. His counterpart, while a good tactician and leader, would probably run away to Hong Kong if he had to rely on South Vietnamese combat and logistics support. Vernon glumly made the assessment that he could never envision RAG Alpha operating on its own without American advisors and support.

"Sorry, boss, but that's the picture I'm seeing," Vernon added.

It was Coburn's turn. He painted a very different picture for RAG Bravo. Toh, his counterpart, was useless, but Chang was ready and capable now to take command and operate without advisors if the South Vietnamese logistical and combat support was ready. The boats were in good material condition, the sailors well trained. If Chang left, the operations officer could probably handle it, but then they'd have to find a new ops boss.

Theodore laughed. "You sure you two are in the same country?"

As he did with all his RAG advisors when they visited, Mondello asked them to write a report to Powell. Coburn and Vernon spent the rest of the working day drafting their reports, handing their handwritten drafts to the yeoman around 1800.

* * *

They could see flares over the Rung Sat zone from the roof of the Rex. A red ribbon snaked from above the flares to the ground and shattered into red sparks.

"Snoopy's shooting. Someone's getting killed down there," said Vernon as he took a gulp of cold beer. Coburn didn't know what the red ribbon was until Vernon identified it as the tracer trail from the US Air Force's heavily armed DC-3 known as Snoopy.

"You think the Vietnamese will ever get equipment like that, Clark?"

"Dunno, Doug. I shudder to think of something like that in the hands of my counterpart. Toh would probably use it for a palace coup or maybe sell it to the Cambodians or some other gooks." He looked into his beer. "You hear anything from Jean?"

"Sure do. I try to write her every day. Don't always succeed. But she's been dropping me a line or two daily, it seems. Sure is nice to get a letter with her handwriting and that scent of perfume on it."

"Shit, stop it, Doug. You're giving me a hard-on."

"Here's a scary thought. What if by coincidence my mom used that same perfume and I get a letter from her and the smell gave me a boner? Talk about a dilemma." Vernon took another drink of beer.

"That's one for the chaplain; I can't help you there. But then, if your mom's good looking, why not?"

"Jeez, man. My mom looks like a mom. Now your mom is another story. Got any more nude pictures of her?"

"I wish you had told me earlier. I left them in the hootch," said Coburn.

"How's Kelly doing?" asked Vernon.

"Kelly's history. Wanted a whole lot of commitment out of Dai Uy Clark and his magnificent appendage. So over the side with her."

"No shit? I'm surprised. She seemed pretty cool with the status quo. You still got that girl on the East Coast?"

"Betsy? Don't know. Sort of the opposite's happening with her. As hard as it may be to believe it, Clark Coburn may be getting dumped." Coburn looked up. Matt Geralds was walking toward them. "Oh oh, here's trouble. Homo 025, ten yards and closing."

After introducing Vernon to his old shipmate, Coburn waved down the waiter and ordered a round of beer. In the small world of the navy, Geralds learned that a friend of his from the supply corps school in Athens, Georgia, was a pork chop on Vernon's last ship. The three young officers fell into an easy banter, relaxing, enjoying the evening air and looking forward to a steak dinner.

"This looks a whole lot better than fish heads, rice, and C-rats, my friends. I'm digging in; cover me," said Vernon as he picked up his knife and fork to attack the steak sizzling in front of him.

Geralds asked what food was like at Vernon's RAG base, and Vernon made a face. Coburn told the two that he was eating pretty well, thanks to the really good hootch mama Ba Mei, Cruz's culinary skills, and a steady supply of good food bought with locally produced counterfeit VC flags.

After they finished, they wandered down Tu Do Street past the string of raucous bars and into the Red Door, Geralds's sanctuary. Coburn and Vernon chatted with a girl and bought her a couple of Saigon teas but called it quits about 2200, leaving Geralds at the bar with a buxom woman who claimed to be his girlfriend.

* * *

The next morning, Coburn walked into the kitchen of the headquarters hootch to find Ba Be sweeping an already spotless floor. She looked up as he greeted her and told him that Mondello wanted to see him. But he should eat his breakfast first. Coburn drank two cups of coffee and ate a big piece of French bread with a big glob of Cheez Whiz squirted on it. He smiled to himself. This wasn't too far off from his typical morning meals in college.

He found Mondello at his desk.

"Wanted to see me, sir?"

"Yeah, Clark. I got a call from Captain Powell this morning. Do you know Lieutenant Mathew Geralds?"

"Sure do. He was my roommate on the DeKalb. Doug and I had dinner and drinks with him last night. Something up?"

"Captain Powell thought you might know him from the DeKalb. He died last night, or early this morning."

The words didn't register at first. He didn't feel anything. Rather, he felt as if he was watching himself and Mondello from a corner of the room.

"He's dead? Matt's dead? What happened, sir?"

"I don't know, Clark. Wasn't enemy action. You're supposed to go over to the MP office at MACV and see this guy." Mondello handed him a piece of paper with a name, building number, and telephone number on it.

"Then call Captain Powell's office. He'll probably want you to drop by. That's all I know. See me when you come back and fill me in." In a quiet voice Mondello added, "My sympathies, Clark."

The MACV Military Police office was right next to the sprawling compound's main gate. An army first lieutenant was the MP Coburn was sent to see.

"What happened?" asked Coburn.

"As best we can piece it together, this fellow..." he searched for the papers. "Captain Mathew Geralds..."

"Lieutenant Mathew Geralds. Navy officer," corrected Coburn.

"Right. Yeah. Navy. Anyway, he was sitting in the Red Door after curfew, and the White Rats decided to raid the place for serving booze after hours, that kind of bullshit. Bar owner probably was late with her bribes. They come pouring in the front door, and Geralds and a bunch of others go running out the back. The bar boy jumps on his Honda and offers him a ride. So Lieutenant Geralds climbs on the back, the bike's loaded too heavy in the rear, does a wheelie, and Geralds falls off and hits his head. Bought the farm. Lousy way to die, even in a war."

"Roger that. What do I need to do?"

"We ID'd him from his dog tags, but we'd like somebody who knows what he looks like to ID the body. Then you're supposed to call Colonel, shit, I mean navy Captain Powell at this number." The MP handed him a sheet of paper.

"Okay, where do I go to, uh, ID him?"

"I'll take you to Graves Registration. He's over there."

They rode through the MACV compound to Graves and walked into an air-conditioned room. Without preamble, the MP officer said to the enlisted soldier at the desk, "Geralds ID."

The soldier took them through a double door into a chilled room with what looked like a wall of giant file drawers. In the middle of the room were six stainless steel tables above a concrete floor with several drains. A lone body covered with a white sheet was on the nearest table. The soldier lifted the sheet, and Coburn saw Geralds lying there, his left eye open wide, his right eye squinting, his skin waxy and pale blue-white, a deep scrape on his right shoulder.

"Sir, do you recognize this man?" asked the soldier.

"Yeah, that's Matt Geralds. I mean Mathew Geralds. Lieutenant, US Navy." Coburn felt no emotion. He wasn't shocked, sad—not even curious. His emotions were flat, just flat. Almost uninterested. He might have been looking at a park bench.

"Sign here, please, sir," requested the soldier.

Coburn wrote his signature and added his rank and service and the date. The soldier tore a carbon copy from the form and handed it to Coburn.

They drove back to the MP office in silence. He still felt nothing, absolutely nothing. For no particular reason, he asked what would happen to the body. The MP officer said Geralds would be cleaned and sealed in a body bag and coffin, then shipped home on a C-141, probably for a military funeral at his wife's or parents' town.

"He wasn't married," said Coburn, just to have something to say. He looked at the copy of the form in his hands. Under cause of death a block labeled "Non-Combat Related" had been checked, and under that the block "Vehicular Accident" was checked. Typed near the bottom of the form was "cerebral hemorrhage."

"What do I do with this form?"

"That's for his command. NAVFORV."

Coburn called Captain Powell's office and talked to the ever-efficient Yeoman First Class Culpepper, who told him that Powell wanted him to come to the office as soon as he finished at MACV.

Half an hour later, Coburn was shown into Powell's office. Another navy captain was already there. Powell introduced the other captain to Coburn as the head of the Naval Supply Center in Nah Be and Geralds's boss. He asked Coburn about his relationship with Geralds and what had happened last night and this morning.

After handing Powell the copy of the form he had signed, Coburn kept standing and methodically repeated what he had been told by the MP officer and told them about his witnessing and identifying the body and signing the form. The supply captain thanked him for doing that, especially the identification of the body.

Powell said, "Mr. Coburn, you probably knew Mr. Geralds better than anyone else here. In addition to the letter from the deceased's CO, we always send out a letter of condolence under the admiral's signature to the next of kin. Normally, that's drafted by the deceased's CO. It's important that the letter be personal, not just a sympathy card."

"I understand that, sir," said Coburn, uncertain whether to sit down or not.

As if reading his mind, Powell said, "Sit down, Mr. Coburn." Coburn sat next to the supply captain on the couch.

Geralds's CO looked at him and said, "Matt only worked for me for a few months, and I got to know him well, but you knew him better. And the circumstances of his death are not such that a parent can find pride or solace. I'd like your help. You don't have to do so if you don't want to. This may be a tough time for you."

"I'm okay, Captain. What do you need?" asked Coburn.

"I'd like you to draft the letter to his parents from the admiral. I'll chop on it and will probably plagiarize portions for my letter to them. Then Captain Powell will take a crack at it, and then the admiral will do a final review, edit, and sign it. We can't tell them he fell off a motorbike drunk while running from the police. Just write the body of the letter. We'll take care of the salutation and closing."

"Aye, aye, sir. Somewhere I can write?"

"Get some paper from Culpepper and grab a seat in the conference room," said Powell. "Get yourself some coffee."

After several false starts, Coburn finished his draft in half an hour.

Dear Mr. and Mrs. Geralds:

On behalf of all the men and women of the United States Naval Forces, Vietnam, I extend to you my deepest condolences upon the loss of your son, Mathew W. Geralds, Lieutenant, Supply Corps, United States Navy. While I know this is a painful and trying time for you, I hope you can take solace that your son died in a combat zone in the service of his country, upholding the finest traditions of a commissioned officer in the United States Navy. His sacrifice, and yours, are sincerely appreciated by all of us who knew Matt.

Matt 's career, which ended so tragically prematurely, was marked by intelligence, fortitude, and good humor. His shipmates will always remember Matt as the one to be relied on, the one to confide in, the best and most loyal of friends. Matt's expertise in logistical management were unmatched and will be missed. His image of a handsome young man in uniform is indelible in our minds, a wonderful young man and an outstanding officer. We share your grief and your loss.

While Matt did not die in combat but instead in a tragic vehicle accident, he is entitled to all the military honors his country can provide.

Please do not hesitate to contact me if I, or the Navy, can be of any assistance to you during these trying times. I am so sorry for your loss.

Sincerely, etc. etc.

Coburn handed the draft to Culpepper, who read it over. "This is pretty good, Mr. Coburn. I'll type up a double-spaced draft and get it in the hopper. Captain Powell would like you to stick around until he gets a chance to read it. He'd like you to come to his office at 1300. There's a geedunk on the second deck if you want to grab some lunch. Not bad, won't give you the shits."

The snack bar was air conditioned, and clean. A wiry Vietnamese man in a chef's hat and apron tended a griddle behind a Formica counter and stools. Coburn thought of the burger joint near his college dormitory when he inhaled the delicious perfume of sautéing onions. After a surprisingly good cheeseburger, fries, and Coke, Coburn waited outside Powell's office while the senior officer was on a muted landline telephone conversation punctuated with some loud and colorful expletives. The yeoman smiled and told Coburn that was pretty standard behavior.

Coburn chuckled and thought that all in all, things were going fairly well. Good meeting with Mondello and Theodore—his psyops may have trumped Vernon's firefights. And thanks to his former shipmate and now-dead good buddy, he was getting some very quality time with the brass. Sorry Matt was dead, but there was nothing he could do about that.

"Come in, Mr. Coburn. Grab a seat," said Powell, pointing at the chair next to the desk. "Nice letter draft. More importantly, in four paragraphs you said absolutely nothing and said nothing concisely enough that we can get it on one piece of flag letterhead."

Coburn deflated. Powell had just said his letter said nothing.

Powell must have read his thoughts for a second time that day. "The ability to say nothing and make it sound as if you're saying something, or at least the admiral's saying something, is invaluable and will hold you in good stead in this man's navy."

He smiled broadly at Coburn. "In fact, after reading this I thought, 'holy cow, I found my replacement. I can go home now.' How'd you like my job, Dai Uy?"

"Thanks for the offer, Captain, but I think I've my hands full with RAG Bravo. Now, if you want to give me O-6 pay and an office like this, well, maybe I'd consider it."

That got a laugh out of Powell. "So you'd sell your soul for a few shekels, some mahogany paneling, and an air conditioner?"

"Yes, sir," quipped Coburn. He wondered for the first time if Powell was really the nuke hard-ass he had sized him up to be three months ago. Powell reminded him now of his skipper on the DeKalb.

"How's it going on the Saigon River? I noticed that psyops mission. Good. I understand that was your idea."

Coburn almost blushed. He decided it was time for the "aw shucks" kind of modesty. "Yes, sir, it was. But it took a whole lot of work by a whole lot of people besides me to make it happen. At the end, I was just a spectator."

"So was Ike during D-Day. Saw you guys got attacked the next morning."

More cautiously this time, Coburn shuffled in his chair and said, "Yes, sir. Charlie lobbed in a rocket and then about thirty mortar rounds. Dinged up the pier and put some craters in the dirt, but that was about it."

"Think the VC are starting to get active again?"

"I don't know, Captain. Frankly, I wouldn't mind it if they did. Hard to fight a war when there's only one side."

"Your counterpart capable of fighting a war?"

Coburn dropped all pretenses. "No sir. The RAG CO stays in Saigon, letting his XO do all the work. I've seen the CO once in four months, and that was for an hour when Arnie Gordon left. XO's running the show, and if you ask me if he's capable of fighting a war, the answer is yes."

"What do you think would happen if the CO was forced to operate out of Phu Cuong, go on missions, do the stuff the XO's doing now? And the XO—what's his name?"

"Chang, sir. Dai Uy Chang."

"And they promoted Chang out of there and gave him another command? What do you think would happen?"

"We'd better have the supply system stock up on toilet paper because the CO would shit all over himself. Morale would plummet, and the RAG would never move the boats away from the pier. The guy's a zero. A well-connected, good-looking, zero. Uh…in my opinion, sir."

"What would you recommend the Vietnamese do?"

"Promote Chang into the CO's job. He's already doing it, might as well get paid for it. Promote the ops officer to XO. Find a new ops officer. Send the president's nephew to war college or Monterey for PG school or find him a job as military attaché in some embassy somewhere."

"Thanks for your opinions, Mr. Coburn. These are to be kept close. Keep them to yourself unless asked by me, the admiral, or our representatives. And of course Lieutenant Commanders Mondello and Theodore."

"Of course, Captain." Coburn didn't like being told the obvious. Was Powell looking at him as a possible loose cannon with a big mouth?

"How do you like being a RAG advisor?"

This was a loaded question, thought Coburn. He didn't like being a RAG advisor. But he liked what being a RAG advisor could get him—recognition, medals, an early command at sea, some cushy job somewhere. The problem was that his RAG might as well be on the Hudson River for all the action they saw. He'd finesse the answer.

"Captain, I like the job a lot. But if there's a job with bigger challenges, I'd want that."

Powell didn't respond to that but just stared at Coburn for a few seconds as if sizing him up. Coburn realized he was getting a lot of these kinds of stares this trip. Mondello, Theodore, now Powell. Probably because of the bullshit report they got about the morning mortar and rocket attack. Probably some crap from McGruder and maybe Chang and Minh, and probably Cruz and Robinson.

"Okay, Dai Uy. That's it, I've got to brief the admiral. Thanks for taking care of this condolence letter and dealing with the MPs. Keep up the good work in Phu Cuong. Be safe." Powell stood and put out his hand. Coburn stood and shook it.

Powell held onto Coburn's hand and added, "And sorry for the loss of your friend, Clark." For a few seconds Coburn was puzzled by what that meant, then realized that Powell was talking about Geralds.

With a sad face Coburn said, "Thank you, Captain Powell. I appreciate that."

Coburn walked out to his jeep. The old fart said he was doing good work, he called him by his first name, he asked his opinions. The old man loved his ass.

* * *

Cruz looked up from cleaning the skimmer's outboard motor's points and plugs as Coburn entered the hootch. "Chao, Dai Uy. How was the trip to Saigon? Anything new to worry about?"

Coburn took out a cold can of Australian beer before he tossed his bag and holstered sidearm on the table.

"Not bad, Cruz. They liked the medical team visit we did. Hell, what's not to like? Saw a buddy of mine who has RAG Alpha, and he mentioned some nasty new tactics the VC are doing down there. Got to spend some time with biggies at NAVFORV. Anything happen here?"

"Yes, sir. Something happened. We got a confirmed KIA and maybe hit another. Captain Neal called in that they had intel that some VC tax collector or recruiter was going to be at that little fishing village just the other side of the bridge at dawn yesterday. So we tell Chang, and he puts together a squad of sailors. We take the skimmer under the bridge at midnight, park it in the weeds, and sit in the mud on the bank all night."

Cruz held up a spark plug and inspected its tip, then continued.

"River mud stinks, and I kept falling asleep. Sun starts to come up and sure as shit, there's these two dinks poling a sampan up that inlet. Chang puts the binoculars on them and sees an SKS rifle in the boat, so he gives the order to open fire. Robinson pops two flares, I'm on the radio telling the TOC to stand by, and the sailors open up. Both guys go into the water, one gets hung up on a tree root. More holes in him then a sieve. Had some documents on him that Chang sent to ARVN G2. Couldn't find the other guy, but if he's not dead, he's hurting. Most likely he's breakfast in crab city. Chang got the rifle and a Chicom pistol."

"This happened yesterday morning? Did you send an after-action report to Mondello? I didn't know shit about this," said Coburn angrily.

"We were dragging the inlet trying to find the other guy and any other shit that might have gone overboard, then we waited for a Ruff-Puff patrol to scout the area for the other guy. We didn't get back here until maybe 1600, and Chief filed a report as soon as we got back. Copy's on the bulletin board, Dai Uy."

"Shit, I didn't know about this," repeated Coburn.

"I called Thieu Ta Mondello's office on the landline, hoping you'd be there. Mr. Wilson picked up the phone and said you went off to NAVFORV and took all your gear with you, so he assumed you were on the way here. He said he'd let everyone know and if he ran into you, would let you know and have you call us on the landline. I guess you didn't go back there, huh?"

"NAVFORV kept me all day. By the time I got back, everyone had hit the sack, and I got up early and got underway this morning before anyone was up," said Coburn.

Cruz didn't say anything but gave him a skeptical glance, punctuated by a raised eyebrow.

When Coburn left NAVFORV in the early afternoon, he decided he was due a celebratory drink and sat on the veranda of the old Continental Hotel. For decades the Continental had been the informal headquarters of the Saigon press corps.

After a few beers, he joined a table of reporters and photographers, one whose father was allegedly a movie star. After more beers they went up to one of the reporter's room and sheared a Buddha stick—a marijuana cigar wrapped in opiate-soaked cotton twine.

Coburn giggled at the thought of being stoned with a loaded .45 on his hip. At around 2200, he went to the Red Door, found the buxom blonde who called herself Geralds's girlfriend, bought her a few Saigon teas, and then bought her out of the bar for twenty dollars in scrip. She led him to the Hung Dao, a ramshackle hotel down the street, and into a second-floor room furnished only with a bed. He woke at dawn with a terrible hangover, downed an open warm beer sitting on the floor, and stumbled out onto the street. The whore never woke up.

After downing three stung Vietnamese coffees with condensed milk at a street stall, he puked. More by luck than by memory, he found the jeep and drove back to Phu Cuong.

"Okay, I'm going to hit the rack for a siesta unless there's something else I need to know about," said Coburn, resigned to that fact that he had been cheated out of a kill. And Cruz making faces calling him a liar. Fuck him and fuck Robinson and fuck Wilson for taking the call.

"A letter for you by the stove, Dai Uy," said Cruz as he returned to his work.

Betsy's handwriting addressed the envelope. He put his sidearm in the weapons locker, grabbed his bag from the table, picked up the envelope, and went back to his room. He threw the letter on his bunk, pulled off all his clothes, and padded naked to the toilet and then the sun-warmed shower.

He flopped onto his bed and opened the letter.

Dear Clark:

I want to be as clear and direct about this as I can. We have drifted apart, and too far apart to come back together. The separation, growing into the next phases of our lives, our work, our interests, our values. Who knows why? I don't really know.

Our relationship is over. I won't write trite things, Clark. It's simply over.

I wish you luck and happiness in whatever you do with your life, Clark. I mean that sincerely.

Goodbye,
Betsy

The cunt, he thought. The bitch. Different "interests"? Probably some Ivy League asshole whose parents had paid off the draft board so he could work on Wall Street. While Charlie is lobbying shells at Clark Coburn's unprotected ass. Hell, he's fighting for her right to shop at Saks Fifth Avenue. And now he probably won't be able to fall asleep. With images of Betsy dating some Ken doll look-alike, he drifted off to sleep.

* * *

For several days Coburn moped around Phu Cuong, thinking alternately of how to get even with Betsy or how to forget her. Keeping busy seemed the best salve, and he tried—running over to the ARVN advisors' offices, meeting with Chang, reading the message traffic and intelligence reports. But the afternoon siesta, bedtime, and early morning were the worst.

He toyed with writing a bullshit letter from a nonexistent hospital bed recovering from nonexistent wounds to make her feel like the selfish thoughtless cunt she was. But then he decided that silence would be better. She'd wake up in the middle of the night, wondering what he was doing—had she made a mistake, could she ever get him back? And there was no way he'd take her back.

One afternoon before taking a shower, Coburn noticed a pus discharge from his penis. It burned when he urinated. He had the clap. Too embarrassed to mention it to Robinson or Cruz and not trusting the RAG's corpsman, he went to the ARVN advisors' medical group and asked the army doctor what to do. Within a few minutes, he was examined and given a shot in his ass and a bottle of pills to take until finished even though the symptoms would rapidly subside.

"And, sir, use a rubber and wash your hands and dick after fucking. Don't eat pussy, either. At least not any gook pussy," added the enlisted army medic as he handed him the pills. Mortified and angry, Coburn shuffled back to his jeep thinking these army enlisted pukes needed some lessons on military decorum.

* * *

Robinson and Cruz were waiting for Coburn when he returned from the medics. Half an hour before, the mother and her baby girl with the double cleft palate had arrived at the floating pier. The two had traveled by themselves in a small sampan.

The mother wanted to have her baby's birth defects repaired. Robinson had just talked to McGruder on the landline. The mother and baby were sitting in sickbay with one of the RAG's corpsmen. The landline phone rang in the hootch. Cruz went in to answer it. A minute later he came out.

"That was Chief McGruder. He talked to the nurse you guys were with, and she said to bring them in. McGruder says to deliver them to him, and he'll get them over to the army hospital. I told them we'd be there within two hours."

Robinson and Cruz both looked at Coburn, expecting some response. Coburn was still preoccupied with his broken heart, damaged ego—and dripping dick.

Realizing they were expecting him to say something, Coburn said, "This is a pleasant surprise, huh? Sure, let's throw them in the jeep and get them to Saigon. Cruz, you drive and maybe take one of the corpsman with you. I'll let Chang know what we're doing."

"Aye, aye, sir," answered Cruz. "I'll stay overnight and be back in the morning."

"McGruder is letting Thieu Ta Mondello know what's happening, Dai Uy," said Robinson.

"Good, Chief. Maybe we need to send out a brief message to all concerned. I'll do that." Coburn wasn't going to lose an opportunity.

A few minutes later, Cruz rolled out the gate with the mother and baby in the seat next to him and the corpsman in the back seat of the jeep.

Later that afternoon, Robinson answered the landline. It was Major Teller, the operations advisor to the ARVN division. Coburn and Chang were to be at the TOC at 0800 the next morning for an important planning meeting.

* * *

The next morning Robinson and the RAG's operations officer joined Coburn and Chang in the crowded TOC. Coburn recognized most of the Americans in the room, mainly advisors to the ARVN and Ruff-Puffs in the area. The few Americans he didn't know were probably staff and company commanders from the US infantry division near Cu Chi. Half the people in the room were Vietnamese from ARVN and Ruff-Puff units.

An ARVN lieutenant colonel and Major Teller, the advisor to the ARVN G3, walked to the front of the room, followed by two senior noncoms armed with a flip chart and collapsible pointers. After a brief welcome in English and Vietnamese, the ARVN officer, with the help of the flip chart, a large map posted behind him, and the well-choreographed movement of pointers by the two sergeants, described a major operation that would start in thirty-six hours.

Recent intelligence indicated a large VC supply depot and a growing number of VC units were in the area northwest of the Michelin rubber plantation. There also were reports of NVA personnel permanently assigned to the area, although their missions were still unknown. The entire area was neutral at best, hostile at worst, to the South Vietnamese government. A large-scale coordinated sweep-and-blocking operation was planned.

The RAG would land three companies of ARVN a kilometer upriver from the rubber plantation. The noise of the diesels as well as the size and number of the river assault craft would destroy any hope of surprise, so opposition to the landing could be expected. The RAG was authorized to use whatever firepower it had at its disposal at the landing area, but not during transit for fear of hitting friendly troops.

Ruff-Puff and other ARVN forces would be approaching the landing zone parallel to the river by foot in a pincers movement while US forces would be airlifted into LZs farther inland and would sweep to the river. The RAG would stay in place as a blocking force. The primary goal was to squeeze and kill the

VC between the ARVN, Ruff-Puffs, US forces, and the river. The secondary objective was to find the supply depot and any base camps in the region.

All units were to be in place at 2315. Completion was scheduled for 1800 the next day or whenever the objectives were reached, no matter how long it might take. Nearly 900 South Vietnamese and US military personnel would be in a shrinking area of operation, making fire control discipline a priority. No one was to open fire without permission.

Radio frequencies were identified for command and control, artillery support, and air support. The ARVN lieutenant colonel and Teller answered some questions, and then Coburn raised his hand.

"Sir, the RAG can provide fire support if needed. We've eighty mike mike mortars, forty mike mike cannon, and a lot of heavy machine guns and Honeywells." Coburn tried to appear casual and at home with the jargon of the weaponry of Vietnam.

"Got that, Clark. It's in the operations orders everyone's getting. When we get done, we'd like to see you and Dai Uy Chang."

The TOC cleared out. As they waited for Teller to finish talking to a small group of US and ARVN infantry officers, Coburn said to Chang that it would have been nice if they had more than a day-and-a-half notice for an operation like this.

Chang surprised Coburn by saying, "I've been involved in the planning for over a week, Dai Uy. I knew the dates, so we refueled and resupplied the boats. For security everyone involved in the planning was told to tell no one else. I couldn't tell you, not even my own officers."

"No shit?" said Robinson. "Makes sense. I was wondering how we were going to get ready in time, but looks as if you took care of that, Dai Uy Chang." Coburn and the Vietnamese operations officer nodded in agreement.

But Coburn wasn't happy that he had been purposely kept out of the loop until just now. He thought Chang was cheeky in keeping this information to himself and wondered if Chang was trying to undermine him. On the other hand, he consoled himself, if the operation goes tits up, Chang can take the blame. If the operation goes well, Coburn would find a way to grab the glory.

Teller walked up to them, shook hands all around, and led them back to the operations office. He shut the door behind him. Sitting on the conference table was a large fiberglass case, much like what a cameraman might carry but three times larger. Teller unsnapped the lid locks and opened the case. Nestled inside shock-absorbing foam was what looked like a gigantic camera lens or a stubby telescope. With Robinson's help, Teller hoisted the black matte lens onto the table, then pulled a sturdy, black collapsible tripod and a bunch of olive-drab cylinders from the bowels of the case. They mounted the lens on the tripod.

"Gentlemen, this is for you. On loan. One of the first in-country. A starlight scope."

"What's a starlight scope, Thieu Ta?" asked Robinson. Coburn was glad Robinson asked the question. He didn't want to betray his own ignorance.

"Low-light scope. Magnifies the ambient light so you can see sharply in the dark. Not like those infrared scopes. We tried it out last night, and it really works well. Division got this one two days ago for operational evaluation. It's too big for the grunts to carry. Really designed for perimeter security or recon from a stationary position. It's too big to be portable. We figured that putting this on your command boat for this operation would be a good first test."

"How do we work this, Thieu Ta Teller?" asked Chang, who was obviously fascinated with the scope.

Teller opened a compartment at the eyepiece end of the scope and placed two of the olive-drab cylinders into the battery compartment. Then he closed the compartment and flicked a switch. A faint buzz could be heard for a few seconds. Then silence.

"That's it. Take off the lens covers, focus as you would a telescope with that knob by the eyepiece. Batteries will last about two nights, and we have two sets. Recharger's in the case." Teller smiled at them. They were silent.

Teller continued. "Don't fall in love with it. We're only lending it to you. This equipment is classified, so I can't have Dai Uy Chang take custody. You sign for it, Clark. You can't let Charlie get this. If you have to, throw a thermite grenade on it."

"Shee-it," said Robinson. "We'll have fun playing with this when the sun goes down."

The RAG base made its final preparations for the operation.

Cruz was back from delivering the mother and her disfigured baby girl to Saigon. McGruder and Peggy had been waiting for him when he arrived at Mondello's office. They took the mother and baby to the army hospital. Two hours later, the oral surgeon walked out of the operating room, and with the RAG corpsman translating, told the mother that her baby was fine and the left side of her face was repaired. Barring any complications, she could take the baby home in three days. In three weeks she was to return to have the other side repaired. Cruz hadn't seen the baby after the operation, but McGruder, who watched the surgery, told Cruz the repair was perfect.

Later that night the three advisors, the Vietnamese officers, and several of the Vietnamese senior enlisted practiced with the starlight scope. They were all excited to use it on the river. It would sit near the helm and radios on the command boat.

CHAPTER 23
PHU CUONG

Vo and Ky moved into the lacquer factory outside of Phu Cuong, sleeping in a converted supply room during the day. Their identification papers now included ARVN discharge documents for loss of mental faculties due to concussions from bomb blasts.

Ky said, "This is good, Vo. Now all we need to do if we are stopped is to act stupid. I'm already very good at that. Lots of practice."

Pham, the factory owner and communications and liaison agent, had told them that the Southerners had approached the chief of a village far upriver. They were planning a medical team visit, not an armed sweep or harassment and interdiction operation. Supposedly the entire operation would be run by the Southerners using the river assault group out of Phu Cuong.

The operation had become very popular in Saigon, due to the fact that the river assault group's commanding officer was the president's spoiled nephew. The American army and its puppets wanted to share the publicity but finally settled on just sending an American nurse. Except for the nurse, it was now strictly a naval operation.

The team would travel on the assault group craft, use the group's sailors to set up a secure perimeter, and then move the medical team into the village where they would run a clinic for six hours. Air, artillery, and support troops would be on call.

The senior Vietnamese corpsman, an assault craft coxswain, and an engineman were a covert NLF cell embedded in the puppets' river assault group.

Vo, Ky, and Pham discussed the operation and the opportunities it presented. The Southerners had little to gain militarily in the operation but certainly could enhance the Saigon government's image in a hostile village.

"It will take a lot more than handing out laxatives and bandages to change those villagers' minds," said Pham. "They've lost too many men, cattle, crops, houses, and even pet dogs to the government and American troops."

On the other hand, the villagers would get badly needed medical attention for the cheap price of letting the government sailors walk around their village. They discussed whether to take advantage by attacking the medical team and the sailors but dismissed that immediately as suicidal since they did not have the resources to sustain an attack, especially after air, artillery, and troop support arrived. And more importantly, what would be gained? The loss of a village friendly to the NLF?

Should they attack the vessels as they traveled upriver? Should they attack on their return? After a short debate, they agreed that either action would be a waste of resources for little gain, at the risk of terrible retribution in the form of an airstrike.

But they did agree to Vo's suggestion to wait until the assault group was back at its base in Phu Cuong. Then they would send a rocket and mortar team into the Southerner-friendly village across the river and shell the assault group's base and its boats. The navy would respond, firing on a hitherto friendly village.

"If your child is killed by a bullet, whether fired by someone you like or not, you will hate that person forever," said Vo.

A week later, Vo and Ky woke up in their lacquer factory quarters to the early morning sound of weapons being fired from both sides of the Saigon River.

* * *

For the next two months, Vo and Ky separately toured the area. They stayed with NLF units, sometimes observing missions. But they spent most of their time overseeing the implementation of their recommendations for small weapon and ammunition factories, ammunition reload facilities, and repair shops.

Within a month, several were completed and operating with a few workers and more than a few security troops. Others were a slow work in progress, treated by the local NLF as an intrusion into their private war by a bunch of overeducated dilettantes.

In some places they were treated with disdain and told to tell Hoang and Tran to come and tell them in person what to do. Until then, Vo and Ky could kiss their asses.

The movement of supplies downriver was increasing. Sampans with false bottoms and compartments hidden beneath fishing equipment were moving down the unpatrolled reaches of the Saigon River. Waterproof packages of weapons and munitions were being shuttled from point to point, towed beneath the surface and then allowed to settle on the river bottom to wait for the next tow.

None of the local commanders liked the idea of having their operations approved by the Military Affairs Committee and liked even less the restrictions on ammunition and resupply. Some, in fact, openly ignored the instructions and did whatever they had been doing before. Hoang, the overall NLF leader in the area, was meeting with each recalcitrant local leader and offering him the option to comply with his instructions or to be replaced and "dealt with appropriately as insubordinate and subversive, preventing the pursuit of the people's struggle." Progress was being made, but slowly.

Stores of supplies slowly increased, which caused a problem. There was not enough depot capacity, and the distance to some of the outlying NLF cells was much more than a day's travel. The capture or destruction of a full depot had to be avoided. Vo and Ky stepped up their efforts to establish more secure depots.

One rare evening when they were both at the lacquer factory, Ky asked Vo, "When do you think we'll have the depots established?"

"Five years, maybe six. If we can finish that by the end of 1974, Ky, I'll be happy."

* * *

During a meeting at Hoang's new headquarters outside of Cu Chi and the massive American infantry division base, Pham told them about a woman who had taken her disfigured baby to the River Assault Group's base in Phu Cuong. During the medical team visit, the American nurse and Vietnamese doctor had begged her to go with them to the American hospital in Saigon so her baby girl could have her face repaired. At first the mother had refused but then left with her baby several weeks later.

The American advisors took her to Saigon, and the surgeons fixed half her face. The mother and baby returned to the village and waited for the baby's surgery to heal. Then she was going to take her back to Phu Cuong and Saigon and have the final surgery performed.

"The surgery done so far is quite remarkable," said Pham. "The woman is very proud and shows off the Americans' work. There's an undercurrent running through the village that perhaps good can come from the Americans and their Southern friends."

"Do you think we have a problem, Pham?" asked Hoang.

"I didn't at first, but I think we will have a problem when she comes back from the final surgery. This isn't just a case of curing an infection or dysentery. The women in the village are treating this like a true miracle. That child will be a living monument to American goodwill."

"What about her husband?" asked Vo.

"He's a reluctant soldier in the regional-provincial forces. He's rarely around. As much as he may dislike wearing a government uniform, I can only imagine he would be indebted to anyone who could perform a miracle on his child."

"Can we offer her this surgery?" asked Vo.

"No," said Hoang flatly.

"What do we do?" asked Pham. No one said anything for half a minute.

"The child and the mother must quietly disappear," said Vo.

* * *

A week later, Vo walked into the woman's village. He had taken a sampan to the village. Vo told the village chief he was a fisherman on his way to Phu Cuong to get a new motor for his sampan and would be sleeping by his sampan on the riverbank that night and then leaving in the morning—if his balky engine would start. The chief seemed skeptical—Vo was aware that he looked much too healthy to be a man who made his living off the river. But the chief offered him a meal and bed at his home. Vo declined, saying he wanted to be near his sampan and his supplies He added that he'd like to stretch his legs and walk around the village.

From information provided to Mrs. Nguyen by the NLF cell embedded in the Southerners' river assault group, Vo knew where the woman lived. He strolled around the village and identified the hut. A woman holding a baby was walking toward it. Vo caught her eye and smiled. She smiled back and said hello. He walked up to her and looked at the baby. Half the baby's mouth looked normal, the other half disfigured by a deep cleft.

Vo asked what had happened to her baby's face, and she enthusiastically told him everything he already knew.

"That's a wonderful story, sister. When will the doctors come to fix this dear child's face?"

She laughed. "No, no, they do not come here. I have to take my baby to Phu Cuong, and they will drive me to Saigon. I want to go soon."

"Phu Cuong? I am going to Phu Cuong. My sampan motor is old, and I need a new one. I'm leaving tomorrow morning, sister. You are welcome to go with me." Vo touched the baby's fat cheeks.

The woman's face broke into a radiant smile. "Oh, yes, thank you! Thank you very much, brother. I will bring food for you. When do you leave? How long will it take us?"

"If my engine doesn't break again, maybe three or four hours. I want to leave early, as soon as the sun is up, so we can see where we're going. Please be at the riverbank at dawn."

She took his hand and squeezed it, then scurried into her hut. Vo walked down to the sampan and sat on the bank, watching the sun go down. He had food but no appetite.

Wrapping himself in an old, damp, and mildewed blanket, he tried to sleep but only dozed off for a few minutes at a time. Forcing all thoughts out of his mind, he sat like the mindless, stupid person his identification papers said he was. At last the eastern sky lightened.

Vo stretched his legs and folded the blanket. He made sure the heavy, cast-iron net weights and sisal rope were piled on the nets in the sampan. After checking the small motor, Vo made sure the three glass bottles of fuel were secure under the seat boards.

Just after dawn, the mother noisily walked down the path to the riverbank, baby in arms and a satchel of clothing and food over her shoulder. She was excited, chattering about how grateful she was that he would take her to Phu Cuong and how in a few days her baby would be as cute as any baby in the world.

Vo pushed the sampan into the water, loaded the woman's satchel in the bow of the small boat, and held the cooing baby as she climbed over the gunwale and into the middle seat, facing forward. He gave her the baby, untied the boat, climbed in behind her, and let the boat drift into the center of the river. The engine started easily, and he turned the sampan downriver. She nursed the baby.

Mercifully, the engine noise made conversation impossible. After an hour, the woman put her sleeping baby onto the piled fishnets and reached forward into her satchel. She took out an aluminum container of rice and vegetables and two sets of chopsticks and placed them next to her on the middle seat as she turned to face Vo. She signaled for him to eat.

Vo shouted over the engine noise, "Sister, let's stop for a minute to eat and relieve myself. Too much tea this morning."

The woman laughed, nodded her head, and turned to check on her baby. Vo looked for a landing spot on the riverbank with heavy foliage blocking the view from inland. There were no other boats in sight. He nosed the sampan into the bank, shut off the engine, and waded into the river and onto the bank, pulling the sampan up. He tied it to a tree trunk.

Checking to see that her baby was still asleep, she told Vo she needed to excuse herself and walked up the bank and squatted behind a bush. Vo slid the hidden bow compartment door open and took out his pistol. He worked the slide once, putting a round into the chamber.

She came around the bush smiling broadly, walked to the sampan, and bent over to pick up her baby. Vo put the pistol to the back of her head and pulled the trigger. The bark of the gun woke the baby, and she started to cry, her dead mother's hand on the little girl's forehead. Vo put the barrel of the gun on the side of the screaming baby's head and pulled the trigger a second time.

Numb and acting mechanically, Vo tied the heavy net weights to the woman's feet and around her waist. He tied another weight tightly around the dead infant's neck. Then he tied the mother to her dead child. Sweating in the hot sun, he rolled both mother and child in the fetid blanket and wrapped several turns of rope around the blanket, running a net weight through each turn.

Vo put the food and baby blanket into the woman's satchel with another weight and fastened that to the corpse-filled blanket. He lugged it all back into the sampan.

Dully staring at his hands and sleeves and then looking around, Vo slowly came to the realization of what he was seeing. There was blood, flesh, bits of bone, and brains splattered all over the boat, the riverbank, and him. He took off all his clothes and washed them and himself in the river. Using a bailing bucket, Vo washed down the sampan, feeling foolish for worrying about getting the blanket wet. River rats were already cleaning up the bank.

After pushing the sampan with its cargo of the dead mother and child back into the river, Vo started the engine and headed down stream. A helicopter flew overhead, not bothering to investigate the lone figure in the sampan. He passed another sampan, children playing in the river, and some women doing their wash, but they all ignored him and the terrible rolled and trussed blanket.

At a quiet bend in the river that Vo knew was over fifteen meters deep, he cut the engine and let the sampan drift. He could see no people on the river or the land. The only sound was the lap of the water on the sampan. The sky was clear of helicopters and airplanes.

Vo rolled the blanket with its weights and bodies into the river. With a few small bubbles, it sank out of sight in the muddy river water. He started the motor and steered the sampan downriver for another half hour and then ran it onto a shallow riverbank.

With the bailing bucket, Vo tried to wash the remaining blood, bone fragments, flesh, and brains from the sampan. He worked feverishly until he lost the sunlight. Exhausted and still not allowing his brain to think, Vo lay down in the sampan and fell into a dreamless sleep, not waking until dawn.

He woke up disoriented, then remembered in excruciating detail what he had done. Hungry and thirsty, Vo drained his water bottle and ate stale rice balls. The chemical odor of brains was on his hands and clothes.

Something caught his eye on the floorboards of the sampan, something that didn't belong there. Looking closer, Vo found a button, a small button from a baby's sweater. The little button was nearly lost in his big hand.

Standing up, he threw the button as far as he could into the river and saw a fish break the surface, trying to catch it.

Should he burn the sampan? Or take it back to the little fishing hamlet north of the bridge at Phu Cuong? Vo decided that sampans were too valuable to destroy, no matter how badly desecrated. He sat on the sampan for nearly an hour, staring numbly at the floorboards. Then he pushed the boat back into the river and finished his journey.

CHAPTER 24
PHU CUONG

At 1800 a line of trucks pulled up outside the RAG gate and unloaded nearly three hundred ARVN troops and their American advisors, and an amazing amount of rations, weapons, and ammunition. Chang and Coburn met the officers and said the boats were ready for boarding but they would not get underway until 1930. They suggested that the soldiers eat a meal before embarking. The RAG compound seemed to be a sea of olive drab, the helmets giving the impression of a field of mushrooms.

At 1930, the RAG got underway. This was the first time since Coburn had been in-country that every RAG vessel was moving upriver. Coburn and Robinson were on the command boat with Chang, the ARVN major in charge of the troops, and his US Army Ranger counterpart, also a major. Cruz was on the monitor along with the ARVN XO, a captain, and his US Army captain advisor. Because of the size and duration of the operation, Cruz and Robinson had recommended that they all go on the river and forsake monitoring the operation from the hootch.

The command boat was the first under the bridge, accompanied by the good-natured banter between the bridge sentries and the sailors. The monitor followed, and Cruz's whiskey baritone could be heard calling back to the sentries.

Once all the vessels were through the bridge, Chang ordered the minesweepers to deploy along the riverbanks, the two small patrol vessels to scout ahead, and the monitor to lead the main body. The command boat followed the monitor with the three troop carriers in single file behind.

They moved slowly and cautiously against the current, navigating in the moonlight with the help of the command boat's pathfinder radar and the new toy, the starlight scope. The Ranger major had heard about the scope but had never actually seen one. He was fascinated by the technology and wondered out loud if the scope could ever be miniaturized and mounted on a rifle.

Already bored, Coburn checked and rechecked his radio, made sure he had a clip in both his M-16 and his .45, and tried to doze off by closing his eyes and fantasizing about Betsy and how he could best throw a guilt trip on her and screw her up for the next guy. There were nearly three hours to go before they reached Xa Thanh Ahn and landed the troopers.

He couldn't even read the Michener paperback at the bottom of his duffel since there was no light. Maybe Charlie would do him a favor and waste some B-40s and get some excitement going. Anything was better than death by boredom. A Buddha stick would be nice just about now. A good two, maybe three hours of don't-give-a-shit mellowness.

The boats were about two kilometers from the landing area, running nearly due north. The ARVN major and his counterpart shook hands with the RAG advisors and their counterparts, thanked them for the ride, boarded one of the small patrol boats, and shuttled to the first troop carrier. Chang radioed his boat crews and told them to hold their fire. No one was to open fire without permission from the command boat.

Coburn walked aft to the coxswain and looked through the starlight scope and saw a river and land in shades of yellow and green. There was movement, men moving single file a few meters from the riverbank. Most had on packs and were carrying weapons. The file was moving under the cover of darkness but could be seen clearly through the scope. Coburn grabbed the handset of the PRC 25.

"Stallion, Crazy Razor, over."

There was no reply from Stallion, the operational command headquarters. Robinson had moved to Coburn's side; Chang had turned around and looked at him.

"Stallion, this is Crazy Razor. Have thirty-plus armed people at coordinates 518411. In the open. Request permission to open fire, over."

Robinson grabbed Coburn's arm.

"Crazy Razor, Stallion. Wait. Over." The radio went quiet.

Coburn looked at Robinson in disbelief. "Chief, we've got a whole platoon or more of Charlie strolling through the rice paddies, and these jagoffs have me waiting? Can you believe that..."

Robinson cut him off. "Sir, those are the Ruff-Puffs moving into position."

"Bullshit. You take a look through that scope and tell me what you see, Chief," said Coburn indignantly, pulling his arm away from Robinson's grasp.

"I have been watching them, Dai Uy. They're the Ruff-Puffs."

The radio crackled. "Crazy Razor, Stallion. Permission denied. You're looking at friendlies. Permission denied. Over."

Coburn wanted to open fire, call in a light fire team or some ground support aircraft, open up with the RAG's guns. He couldn't believe they'd denied his request. He swallowed and said into the handset, "This is Crazy Razor, Roger, over."

"Stallion out."

Chang was now standing by Robinson and Coburn. He had a cigarette dangling from his lips, unlit.

"Dai Uy, it has been three hours since my last cigarette. With luck we will have some flares so I can light this one. I'll never last until dawn."

The coxswain, Robinson, and Coburn all pointed at once. A rocket trail shot out from the east bank and traveled across the river, crossing the command boat's bow with a few meters to spare. Chang spun around in time to see the white trail bury itself in the west bank. Both Chang and Coburn picked up their radios.

In a high voice and staccato speech, Coburn reported the rocket shot and again asked permission to fire. The coxswain and one of the gunners had seen the launcher flash come out of the low hanging mangroves at the river's edge. The Ruff-Puffs were about fifty meters inland.

The response came quickly. "Crazy Razor, Stallion. Hold your fire, repeat, hold your fire. Friendlies too close. Continue as planned. Do you understand? Over."

"Stallion, Crazy Razor, Roger, understand. Continue as planned. Over."

"Crazy Razor. Be advised your counterpart has been ordered to consider LZ hot. Provide landing fire, including illumination. Provide supporting fire as requested by land forces. Over."

"Roger. Understand. Provide fire at LZ and supporting fire as requested. Over."

"Out."

The radio went quiet again. Coburn was angry and excited. His lethargy was long gone. They should have opened fire at the rocket-launching site. The dinks had shot at them. Coburn wanted to kill someone, and he didn't care who it was.

"We are to fire on the landing area, Dai Uy," said Chang. "We will use illumination, so I can light my cigarette." Coburn gave a nervous, jittery laugh. He picked up his M-16. His olive-drab wristwatch's illuminated face said 2327. The minesweepers and the patrol craft were nearly at the landing area. The RAG would be in position right on time.

At 2330 Chang gave a one-word order on the radio, which was followed immediately by a series of pops from the monitor as it fired illumination rounds. The gunners must have been waiting with the mortar shells in their hands above the tube mouth. Within a few seconds, the east bank was bathed in a brilliant light. Every RAG gun that could be brought to bear opened fire and raked the landing area.

The 40-millimeter cannon, the 20-millimeter, the .50- and .30-caliber machine guns, and the Honeywell grenade launchers barked and rattled. The mortar pop-whooshed round after round. The smell of cordite mixed with the hot smell of the oil that coated their gun barrels. Smoke and dirt tossed into the air obscured their view. Red tracers crisscrossed and ricocheted off the hard, dried mud and rocks. Some tracers hit each other, bouncing away like red-hot billiard balls at the speed of sound. Nothing could live through that, thought Coburn, holding his M-16 at his shoulder.

Firing blindly into the spider's web of tracer arcs and smoke, Coburn emptied two magazines. He was about to reload when Robinson yelled into his ear, "Cease fire, cease fire. Chang's bringing in the troop boats."

The three troop boats approached with their forward .30-caliber machineguns sweeping the riverbank. The ramps opened, and a sea of olive-drab mushrooms rushed off the boats and fanned out as the last illumination round went out. Everyone stayed in place, regaining their night vision, their ears ringing.

Coburn watched through the starlight scope. His heart was pounding. His hearing was muffled and ringing. But his thoughts and his vision were crystal clear. He felt so good. He loved this. The troops started moving inland toward a grove of trees.

A line of brilliant green dashes followed by the distinctive sounds of an AK-47 moved from right to left over the troops. At different angles, three more green lines snaked across the field. Another fanned toward the river and ricocheted upward after bouncing off the monitor's armored turret. Chang's and Coburn's radios came alive simultaneously.

"Crazy Razor, Stallion Alpha Alpha. Small arms incoming from tree line along southern edge of our location, fifty meters. Request illum ASAP. Am calling in light fire team. Over."

Stallion double Alpha was the Ranger major advisor to the ARVN commander of the troops they had just landed. Chang had already given orders to the monitor for illumination and was telling his gunners to concentrate fire on the tree lines once they could see it. The monitor's mortar popped.

Coburn said into his handset, trying to control his voice, "Stallion Alpha Alpha, Crazy Razor. Illum on the way. We will fire on tree line. Keep your heads down, over."

"Roger that. Light fire team on the way with darts. Arrival in two. Cease fire in one but keep illum going, over."

"Understand, cease fire in one minute, keep illum up, over."

"Stallion Alpha Alpha out."

Robinson was already standing next to Chang, telling him that helicopter gunships were coming in and to cease fire but keep the illumination going. The RAG's weapons stopped. Green tracers still crisscrossed over the field, mixing with the ARVN troops' return fire. Coburn plugged a small speaker into his radio so they could hear the chatter.

Stallion double Alpha was talking to the lead gunship pilot. The pilot's voice was calm and quiet but quivered with the vibration of his aircraft. A plume of purple smoke rose out of the field, and the pilot identified it as the location of the advisor. The helicopter came in from across the river, over the command boat and along the tree line. The Cobra unleashed volley after volley of rockets, and the minigun in the chin turret sprayed the trees. The helicopter turned to its right, and the second gunship came in. Each made three runs. A few green tracers arced futilely toward the Cobras. The pilot said they were out of ammo and on their way home to refuel and rearm. Stallion double Alpha thanked them and said he thought they could stay at their base but on standby. The pilot's last message was a request for the enemy body count. "My Charlie Oscar's big on numbers."

The ARVN troops advanced into the tree line. In the brilliant illumination, black-clothed figures could easily be seen running toward the river or to the south, trying to avoid the ARVN. Coburn and Robinson opened fire with their M-16s, as did the command boat's gunners. The black figures dove behind a paddy dike, and Robinson directed the Honeywell operator's fire to the dike. Chang was talking to the ARVN commander on his radio, giving him the location of pinned-down VC.

Chang finally lit his cigarette, inhaled deeply, and exchanged a smile with Coburn, who giggled and gave his counterpart's shoulder a squeeze. The only firing coming from the RAG was the constant pop-whoosh of illumination rounds from the monitor.

"Crazy Razor, Stallion Alpha Alpha. We have three WIA. We'll need a dust-off. Once tree line is cleared, I'll call it in. Our medic swamped. One WIA pretty serious. Can you provide medical support? Over."

Chang had eavesdropped on the speaker. He nodded to Coburn.

"Stallion Alpha Alpha, that's affirmative. Want us to make a house call, or do you want to drop him off at the office? Over."

"House call. I don't think we can move this guy. Over."

Chang gave the order to send ashore one of the corpsman from the troop carrier.

"Roger, corpsman on his way with medical bag, over."

"Thanks, Crazy Razor. Stallion Alpha Alpha, out."

As soon as the corpsman walked off the troop carrier ramp onto the riverbank, the tree line opened up again. Two lines of green tracers converged on him as he threw himself onto the ground. The RAG gunners fired with everything available, pounding the tree line. Coburn emptied another clip, spraying without aiming. Shooting for the sake of pulling the trigger, ejaculating bullets.

They could see the corpsman crawling on this stomach and elbows toward a group of ARVN. The fire from the tree line dribbled down to an occasional round or two and then stopped. The ARVN were moving forward again.

From behind the dike, men in black ran away from the advancing ARVN. Most went south toward the rubber plantation, but three were headed toward the river. They were carrying AK-47s and heading toward the command boat. The gunner at the .30-caliber machine gun next to the coxswain opened fire, and the three hit the dirt, burying for cover in the razor grass. The machine gunner stopped, waiting for them to move again. Chang, Robinson, and Coburn watched silently.

An arm raised out of the grass holding an AK-47 by the hand-grip and tossed the gun to the side. "Chieu hoi! Chieu hoi! Toi chieu hoi!"

"They're surrendering," said Robinson, looking down the barrel of his M-16. Coburn had his sights on the spot, finger on the trigger. Another AK-47 was tossed out of the grass.

"Chieu hoi! Chieu hoi!" One man stood up, his hands held high. A few meters to his right, another stood up, trying with his left hand to staunch the blood flow from a ragged wound in his right arm. The third stood up, with his weapon across his chest, blood running down from his scalp.

Coburn pulled the trigger of his M-16, and the third man's face exploded. Coburn was turning his rifle to point at the other two when Robinson grabbed it and pushed the muzzle vertical. Coburn sent a shot through the overhead canopy.

"What the fuck are you doing? That man was surrendering, you fucking idiot," yelled Robinson, his face an inch from Coburn's.

Coburn yelled back. "Watch your fucking language, Chief. That gook is VC, and now he's dead VC. Who the fuck do you think you're talking to?" Coburn wasn't going to take any crap from some nigger enlisted.

"You just shot a man who was wounded and surrendering. If I hadn't grabbed your rifle you'd have killed the other two. With all due respect, Lieutenant Coburn, I'd be yelling at the fucking Chief of Naval Operations if he had just done that." Robinson was nose to nose with Coburn, screaming in his face. "You want to put me on report, sir? Go ahead, do it. But you'd better be prepared to answer a lot of fucking questions."

Coburn felt like taking out his .45 and shooting Robinson, the mutinous son of a bitch. But some shred of self-preservation made him stop and collect his thoughts. Again, he felt as if he were outside of himself, watching this chief and this frocked jaygee yelling at each other. He unlocked his eyes from Robinson's and looked around. Chang was staring at them, stone faced. The command boat's crew who were on deck were either mimicking their XO or nervously giggling in embarrassment for the two Americans. Coburn let out a deep breath. Then another. He took off his helmet and ran his hand through his hair.

"Chief, the guy had his weapon in front of him. I thought he was going to shoot. I thought it was some trick, they were coming for the boat with some satchel charge or something." Coburn said in a hoarse voice. "And they opened fire on our corpsman," he added lamely.

"Mr. Coburn. This is your first real firefight. Shit happens, sir," said Robinson quietly, almost paternally. "That's why you got guys like me and Cruz watching your ass for you."

"Appreciate that fact, Chief. Thanks." Coburn walked up to Chang and bummed a French cigarette off of him. He was still hopped up, and there was a battle going on, but he knew he had to get himself settled down. Using Chang's lighter, Coburn lit the Gitanes, inhaled, and went into a coughing fit.

Robinson handed him a canteen. "Sir, those French cigarettes are worse than Cruz's cigars. I think that's why the French suck so much cock, get something soothing down their throats."

The last illum went out. They were in darkness, sitting in a blocking position while the ARVN troops moved inland. The RAG boats were nosed into the bank about 150 meters apart, each scanning a section of the river for anyone trying to cross in the night.

Dizzy from the cigarette smoke, Coburn lay down on his air mattress, not even bothering to smear himself with insect repellant. He was nauseated. He needed something in his belly; he'd eaten nothing since lunch sixteen hours earlier.

Coburn felt alive, his senses acute—the crackling of the radios, the sounds of ammunition being reloaded, the cigarette smell, the stink of cordite and diesel oil, the garlic and fish sauce odors from the galley a deck below him, the confrontation with

Robinson, the killing, the battle. Drunk on adrenalin and life, he was now omnipotent.

An hour later, Coburn woke up disoriented. He lay on his air mattress, looking up at a hole in the boat canopy. One of the sailors handed him a small cup of thick coffee and a piece of a baguette. He finished off both, then pissed over the side. He guessed it to be about 0400, maybe later. Chang was below in his rack. Robinson was asleep on the foredeck.

It was dark and quiet. He couldn't even see the boats on either side of the command boat. Coburn nodded at the sailor in the coxswain's seat and looked around through the starlight scope.

Nothing was moving on the land on either side of the river. All quiet. Downriver he could see some of the sailors on the troop carrier nosed into the bank. Upriver he could see the monitor and the distinctive, husky shape of Cruz walking aft. Cruz's cigar tip was bright yellow in the green of the scope. Coburn looked upriver, saw nothing, then swiveled to look at the far bank.

As the scope moved from the river to the bank, he thought he saw something. He brought the scope to the right, slowly, looking. Then he saw it, low in the water, moving across the river, on the far side of the monitor. He increased the magnification, losing the image for a second, then finding it.

It was running crosscurrent and crosswind; it couldn't be a log or collection of branches. Increasing the magnification to the maximum, he refocused and saw the figure of a man standing on the stern of a sampan, sculling across the river.

"Wake up, Lieutenant Chang," Coburn told the coxswain in Vietnamese. He didn't want to take his eye off the scope. In less than a minute, Chang was by his side and looking through the scope. He lit a cigarette and gave the coxswain and duty gunner orders.

The command boat had a telescoping ladder mounted on the upper deck with a .30-caliber machine gun, splinter shield, and seat at the top. It could be raised seven meters above the top deck. The coxswain and a gunner turned the wheel, which raised the machine gun to its full height. Chang climbed up the ladder and into the seat. Coburn could see the bottom of his shoes dangling above. The coxswain launched a handheld pop flare, a miniature version of the mortar's illumination shells. As soon as the flare ignited and began floating down beneath a small parachute, Chang opened fire on the sampan. He fired over two hundred rounds.

"Crazy Razor, Crazy Razor Bravo. What's happening? Over." It was Cruz.

"We got a guy trying to cross the river. He's near the far bank. X-ray Oscar has one of the small boats going over to investigate. If there's anything left. Over." Coburn had an eye to the scope the whole time and had watched the figure fall.

"Roger, that. If you need illum, be aware we're running low. Out."

Ten minutes later the patrol boat pulled up alongside the command boat. A body in the fetal position lay on the small boat's afterdeck. One of the corpsman, Robinson, and Chang had boarded the patrol boat. Coburn joined them.

Robinson held a red-lens flashlight while the corpsman cut off the man's wet black cotton top. He was missing the left side of his body from below the rib cage down to his hip. Coburn could see the man's guts. Surprisingly, there was little bleeding. The corpsman was wrapping a large dressing around the man, who was conscious and moaning. Chang was interrogating him, but the man would only say he was not VC and was a fisherman going to check his crab traps. Coburn understood every word. Robinson looked on dully.

The sampan, splintered and riddled with bullet holes, was tied up to the patrol boat. Sweeping his flashlight, Coburn saw fishing twine on a primitive spool, an aluminum thermos, a small hatchet, and several empty woven baskets. And he saw pieces of flesh and bone and a black puddle of blood. The boat smelled of fish and shit.

"Any weapons?" Coburn asked the patrol boat coxswain in Vietnamese. The sailor shook his head.

"Anything in his pockets? Identification?" The sailor pointed up at Chang, who was holding a plastic bag that he handed to Coburn. It contained an identification card, a few piasters, a clear plastic cigarette lighter, half a pack of Gitanes cigarettes, and a black-and-white photograph of a woman in an ao dai with two small children.

"He VC," said Chang with finality.

"What are you going to do with him, Dai Uy?" asked Robinson before Coburn could. Coburn was starting to get irritated at Robinson taking the lead.

"Wait for morning and see what the army wants us to do. If he lives that long," answered Chang. "He's not worth a medevac."

Coburn looked back at the man lying on the hard steel deck. The hell with him. If he was a fisherman, this was a free-fire zone, which meant if you're here you're VC, a fisherman VC.

Two hours later the man died, another enemy KIA. They put his body on the riverbank with his plastic bag pinned to his trousers, the sampan beached alongside the body. The cigarettes and the piasters were not in the bag.

* * *

Dawn found the area quiet. The RAG boats were all nosed into the riverbank, evenly spaced at 150-meter intervals. On each boat a sailor stood watch, looking up- and downriver for any movement. The day turned hot with no breeze. Despite the battle of the night before, the landing area looked untouched and tranquil.

By noon, flies were everywhere, attracted by the blood and the dead bodies that lay in the field and the sole corpse on the riverbank. The sickly sweet smell of decaying human flesh intensified as the day went on. Under the supervision of the RAG's operations officer, a squad of armed sailors, wearing cloths soaked in river water over their mouths and noses, searched the landing area for bodies and wounded. Any bodies found would be classified VC, even if a child or old woman.

416

"What are you going to do with the bodies, Dai Uy?" asked Coburn.

"Burn them. Usually we just leave them for the villagers or their comrades to identify and dispose of. But with this heat and the fact that we are going to be sitting here for the next day and a half, we're burning them. Maybe get rid of these flies, that stink, and that." He was pointing at two rats nibbling at the body next to the sampan.

The sailors collected fifteen bodies and two wounded who would probably be dead by evening if not given medical aid and water. On a bed of mangrove limbs by the far tree line, they stacked the dead like cordwood, dosed them with diesel oil, and threw a thermite grenade on top. Black smoke billowed. The smell of burning flesh reminded Coburn of a dentist's office or his grandmother singing feathers off a freshly slaughtered chicken destined for the Sunday dinner table.

Cruz had walked up the riverbank from the monitor and offered Coburn, Robinson, and Chang some of his cigars to cover up the smell. Chang refused, sticking with his acrid cigarettes, but both Coburn and Robinson lit up. Several sailors vomited. Robinson puffed his cigar, took it out of his mouth, and walked aft. He threw up over the side.

A RAG corpsmen worked on the two wounded prisoners, both suffering from concussion, flesh wounds, and dehydration. The corpsmen dressed their wounds, forced water and tea on them, and then moved them to one of the troop carriers, where they joined the two chieu hois under armed guard. Chang got on the radio to find out what the operational commander wanted him to do with these prisoners.

He put down the handset and said that one of the US Army platoons was moving toward them on foot. They'd take over custody of the prisoners. As soon as the platoon arrived, probably very late that day or early the next morning, they would embark, and the RAG could return to base.

Coburn liked the sound of that. Sitting here stuck to a riverbank in this heat and stink with nothing to do other than look up and down the river sucked. The platoon's arrival would get him out of here a day early. Back to the hootch to sit on a porcelain throne and shit, then wash his pits and shave.

Chang must have been thinking the same thoughts. Sort of. The RAG was nearly out of illumination rounds and was low on all the other ammunition. One of the minesweepers' engines was balky, and they'd probably have to tow it back. And the sailors would be back in time for their payday.

The US Army platoon arrived just after midnight. Chang and his three American advisors greeted the soldiers on the riverbank. A slump-shouldered, lanky first lieutenant was the platoon leader, and a baby-faced butter bar was his assistant. Two officers in an army platoon was luxury, Coburn thought. This kid must be in training to replace the hayseed, who must be going home soon.

The two dozen soldiers were ragged looking, their uniforms sweat stained. All needed shaves, and all smelled of sweat and dried rice paddy mud fertilized with shit. Coburn walked with the two army officers up the riverbank to the troop carrier they'd be riding in. The soldiers filed up the ramp. Most dropped their packs and weapons and lay down on the boat's canopied deck.

"This is pretty sweet," said the first lieutenant, shrugging off his pack and M-16. "Dry and clean, and we don't have to hump through the boonies to get where we're going."

"Everything's relative, Lieutenant," said Coburn. "We've already got the perimeter security covered, so I don't think you need to use any of your troopers for that. Get a good night's sleep. We'll probably get underway an hour or two after dawn. That's the plan."

"Sounds good to me, sir. Maybe we'll get a chance to wash some of this grime off us in the morning. No sharks or piranha in this river, huh?"

Cruz had walked up and was listening. "Well, sir, we don't really know. We were hoping somebody would jump in there so we could find out. Glad you volunteered," said Cruz through teeth clenched on a cigar stub. The army officers laughed and joined their men, most of them already in a deep sleep.

* * *

The dawn found Coburn sitting in the low deck chair with his poncho liner wrapped around him, sipping a cup of Vietnamese coffee. With luck they'd be back in the hootch in the early afternoon. He was surprised when the platoon leader came aboard the command boat.

"Sir, we just got word that we're supposed to find an LZ for a slick and put security around it, and you and I are supposed to be there," said the tall first lieutenant.

"What's up?" asked Coburn.

"Dunno, sir. Maybe they want to pick up those two prisoners."

"Okay, no problem. Where they going to land?"

"It's flat right here," said the army officer. "I'll give them the coordinates, put my men on the perimeter and pop smoke."

"Sounds good to me. What time?"

"They said 0630, but they'll radio when they're five minutes out. Seems pretty quiet around here. I don't think they'll get shot at. I'd better get back and shave; might be some chickenshit pogue from staff."

Coburn looked at his watch. Plenty of time to take a shit off the fantail, maybe jump in the river and then eat something. Probably better invite Chang.

It was turning into another hot day. Coburn and Chang were in their normal attire for a hot day on the river. Short, baggy trunks, shower shoes, flak vest, helmet, dog tags, sunglasses. No shirts, no insignias. At 0615 nine of the soldiers filed off the troop carrier, walked out to the center of the field, and fanned out, hunkering down on the perimeter of a fifty-meter circle. The two officers followed, standing at the center of the circle with their backs to the wind.

A lone Huey came in from the east and flew over the river. Green smoke appeared on the landing zone and drifted with the breeze to the south. The helicopter made a descending circle that ended in a hover a few meters above the ground as the baby-faced second lieutenant held his hands up, guiding the pilot in. The slick landed gently. Coburn and Chang walked from the command boat to the helicopter.

The paint on the Huey was a polished dark green, like the paint job of an expensive automobile. Aft of the doors was a large orange shield with a black slash and silhouette of a horse head on it. It was the command chopper for an armored cavalry regiment. A major in crisp jungle fatigues, shined boots, helmet, and flak vest jumped out of the nearest side door as Chang and Coburn approached. Walking around the front of the slick with meter-long strides was a ramrod-straight colonel.

The colonel nodded at the two platoon officers, looked at Coburn and Chang, then stopped.

"What the fuck are you two kids supposed to be? What the fuck kind of cocksucking uniform are you two shits wearing in my fucking area of operation?" he bellowed.

Coburn looked at the name embroidered over the colonel's pocket. It was the same as a famous general from World War II.

The colonel took a step closer, eyes riveted on Coburn. "Major," he shouted without looking at his aide, "take notes, I want a report on this shit."

He walked forward, now standing directly in front of Coburn. The colonel was a good two inches taller than Coburn. Instead of the army-issued holster and .45, he had a tooled leather holster and a nickel-plated .45 with white grips. The major had a small note pad in his hand, ballpoint pen at the ready.

"One of you two pieces of shit Crazy Razor?" asked the colonel.

Recognizing a bully and remembering that he didn't work for the army but for the Commander of Naval Forces, Vietnam, Coburn recklessly answered. "This piece of shit is Crazy Razor, Colonel. Lieutenant Clark Coburn, US Navy. This other piece of shit is my counterpart, Lieutenant Le Binh Chang, Navy of South Vietnam, sir."

The colonel's eyes flicked over to Chang and then back to Coburn. "Navy. Fucking navy give up on wearing uniforms? Fucking navy give up on wearing boots? At least you're wearing your goddamn dog tags so you can remember what your names are. Why in the fuck are you dressed that way, son?"

"Colonel, fits the environment we operate in. As advisors we're supposed to fit in with our counterpart's culture. And it saves on laundry. Sir."

"You insubordinate son of a bitch. I'm going to bust your ass down to private as soon as we finish talking here."

"No privates in the navy, sir. And may I suggest we go aboard the command boat, and you can finish yelling at me there."

The colonel stared at him, his face cold granite. "Lead the way, son. Major, stay here. You," he pointed at the platoon leader, "come with us."

Aboard the command boat, Coburn introduced the colonel to Robinson and then Cruz, who had come by to pick up some rations. Chang introduced the operations officer. Robinson, Cruz, and the Vietnamese RAG sailors were dressed much like Coburn and Chang except that a few had on shirts.

One of the sailors brought up cups of coffee and sweet crackers on a platter. They sat in the low deck chairs except for Cruz, who stood by the coxswain.

"Got another cigar, there?" the colonel asked Cruz.

"Sure, sir." Cruz pulled a fresh stogie out of his shorts pocket and gave it to the regimental commander. The colonel unwrapped the cigar, bit off the end, spit the tip over the side, and lit the cigar with an engraved Zippo.

The colonel took a puff, looked at the cigar between his thumb and forefinger, and bellowed, "This is the most fucked-up-looking outfit I have ever seen. Period. But you appear to know how to do your job, and you know how to kill the enemy."

He dropped down a few decibels.

"Out of the whole fucking operation, the landing on this beach and the movement of that unit inland was the only thing that went right. Lot of KIA, two prisoners, few friendly KIA and

WIA. That's fucking outstanding for the ARVN and you guys. Fucking outstanding."

"You," he looked at Coburn, "must have been the trigger-happy asshole who wanted to shoot our own forces before we even had the units in place. But this unit can fight and fight well, even though you look like the biggest pile of crap I've ever seen."

"Thank you, sir. I think." said Coburn.

"Son, that mouth of yours is your biggest liability and probably your one and only asset," said the colonel. He pulled a map out of his trouser pocket and unfolded it on the deck.

"We're here, right?" said the colonel, putting his forefinger on the exact location of the boats. "The VC have a supply depot here." His finger stabbed a point southeast of the first finger stab.

He described how he was maneuvering two battalions of his regiment to the north and east of the suspected supply depot and then having them move toward the river. He was going to capture the depot. The operation was all American except for the RAG. Chang leaned forward and looked at the map closely.

"I want you to take the platoon you have aboard and set up a blocking force like you have here, but I also want you to patrol the river from here to here." His fingers pointed at two locations about ten kilometers apart.

"At night we're expecting a lot of movement across the river as we squeeze in, gentlemen. I want your boats moving up and down the river. You see something, you pounce on it. The embarked platoon will take on any shit on land. This is a free-fire zone. You get your boats down there ASAP. My battalions are already moving into position."

Chang and Coburn exchanged glances. Then Coburn looked at Robinson and then at Cruz, whose eyebrow was the highest Coburn had ever seen it. He had to speak up.

"Colonel, our fastest boats can only do maybe five knots upstream. And we only have two of those. It would take them two hours to cover the area you want them to patrol. I could swim across the river before they could get to me."

"Five knots? What's this shit about patrol boats that go twenty-five knots?"

"Not us, Colonel. Those are the PBRs. We don't have anything like that."

"I can't turn off this operation now, son. What in the fuck would you have me do?"

"Crap, Colonel, we're just not high-speed mobility. What we can do is space our boats so we can see all the river, and if we see something, we shoot at it. Or call in the Cobras."

Cruz interrupted. "Colonel, Dai Uy, we're just about out of illumination and low on forty- and twenty-millimeter and .50- and .30-caliber."

Robinson jumped in. "Colonel, we're also towing a boat that lost its engine, and we're low on rations. Plenty of fuel, though."

The colonel exploded. "You're out of ammo and beans? How in the fuck did you let that happen? No one told me you needed replenishment."

Chang finally spoke up. "Dai Ta, we brought with enough supplies for the operation that was scheduled. We made a report of fuel, ammunition, and rations remaining last night to the ARVN division headquarters. We asked to be resupplied if we were going to stay on the operation past this morning."

The colonel stared at Chang for a few seconds. "Lieutenant Chang, what did ARVN say? When are you going to get your supplies?"

"They only acknowledged our report and request. No response, Dai Ta."

"Did you ask for anything?" the Colonel asked Coburn.

"No sir, my orders are to let the Vietnamese military support the Vietnamese military. Vietnamization, sir."

"Fuck. We're fighting a fucking war here. These people couldn't resupply their way out of a supermarket. Bunch of political ass wipes at the State Department and the fucking White House with this bullshit, and there's a war going on over here. We going to win this, or we going to walk away from it and lose it? Fuck!"

He kicked the steel gunwale and stood up. The colonel rubbed his hand over his mouth, then looked at the lanky platoon leader.

"Lieutenant, you find out from these people what they need to operate another three days. Then you go out to that fat-assed major getting a suntan by my helicopter and tell him I want a resupply by air of what these people need right here no later than noon. You got that?"

The platoon leader jumped up and looked at Chang, who pointed to his operations officer. Cruz joined them, and together they went below decks. Two minutes later, the platoon leader was running across the field to the helicopter with a list in his hand.

"Gentlemen, I'm getting out of here. Lieutenant Coburn, escort me to my helicopter."

The two walked in silence until they were halfway between the riverbank and the helicopter. They were out of earshot of everyone.

The colonel stopped and looked at the burned spot near the tree line. "What happened there?"

"We burned the KIAs, sir."

The colonel made a grim smile and shook his head, then turned to Coburn. "Son, you're a smart-assed son of a bitch. You going to make a career of the navy?"

"Yes, sir," said Coburn with new conviction.

"I'm going to tell you something about Vietnamization and this war and your career. The military of the United States is there to fight, to go to war, to create a big enough threat to keep the peace. The only way you can find people to lead in war is to pick them from those who do well in war. That make sense to you?"

"Yes, sir, it does. Seems evident to me."

"Vietnamization is all well and good and something that these people will never be able to accomplish. They're too fucked up, too corrupted, too busy feuding with one another to get together and beat the fucking communists. It's an end game.

If we don't win this war for them, then it's lost. And when we go home, they'll lose the war we just won for them."

"That's pretty pessimistic, sir. My counterpart's top notch."

"Son, I believe you. I could see that back at the boat. But he's just one damned naval officer. Half the ARVN officers are shit. I have a general for a counterpart who makes me sick. Looks good, custom uniform, and his wife is making monthly trips to Hong Kong and Paris to buy luxuries and put their bribes in the bank. Yeah, there are some good ones like that fellow Chang here, but there are a lot more crooks and a bunch who are, at best, mediocre."

Coburn looked at his feet and nodded.

"So here's some unsolicited advice from an old army fart who just got picked for one star. This is the only war we got. If you want to make rank and get ahead of your peers, you'd better get some glory. And in this war, that means body counts and medals. I don't care if it's the army, navy, marines, air force, or even the fucking coast guard. Your mission is to put ordnance on the enemy and kill him. Until they're all dead or surrender.

"It's a numbers game, son. The generals and admirals of the future will be those with the most medals and body counts. Get yourself some medals. Get some glory, son. Or else just keep your ass down, keep on hiding behind Vietnamization, sleep with your flak vest on, and hope you get to go home before Charlie comes down from the north and takes over the presidential palace."

"Aye, aye, Colonel."

"You kicked ass the night before last. Put a hurt into Charlie. Your bosses in Saigon are going to hear about that from me personally. They're also going to hear that you're the worst-looking outfit I've ever seen. Now go kick some more ass, and the next time you see me, shave, put on a uniform, and wear your fucking boots."

"Yes sir," said Coburn, smiling and saluting.

"You trying to get me killed you idiot? Drop that fucking salute."

The colonel turned around, strode to the helicopter, climbed through the door held open by the major, looked at Coburn, and tapped his helmet in salute. The major slid the door shut, went around to the other side, and got in. The Huey lifted off, circled to gain altitude, and flew north.

An hour later, just before noon, a big twin-engine helicopter landed on the field in front of the command boat. For the next half hour, the RAG sailors ferried supplies from the helicopter's ramp to the boats.

* * *

For three days, the RAG boats sat spread out along a ten-kilometer stretch of the Saigon River. They scanned the river, popping illumination at night and using the starlight scope. And they found nothing, absolutely nothing.

For three days the embarked platoon sent out reconnaissance squads and patrols. And they found nothing, absolutely nothing.

At least once a day the armored cavalry regiment's command slick flew down the river and then up the river. Radio communications consisted of radio checks and status reports of no contact, no supply depot, nothing at all.

Coburn managed to read the Michener novel between naps and a daily swim in the river. Cruz ran out of cigars. Robinson kept himself busy going from boat to boat and checking on supplies and equipment. Chang was sullen and restless.

Three days of doing nothing but sitting nosed into a riverbank.

The sailors threw grenades into the water and harvested the stunned fish that rose to the surface. Instead of C-rations and rice and maybe some vegetables, they were now eating C-rations mixed with fresh fish, rice, and vegetables. Coffee was all gone.

The boredom was driving Coburn nuts. He even asked the platoon leader if he could go along with a squad on patrol. But he did find himself thinking—and amusing himself—with what the armored cavalry regiment commander had said to him about medals and combat and killing the enemy. But how the hell was he going to win any medals sitting here sweating off his insect repellant?

Coburn was worried about Cruz and Robinson.

Gordon had fostered an informality in the advisory unit that blurred the traditional boundaries between officer and enlisted. That was probably inevitable with three men isolated from the traditional navy and working in a very foreign environment. And he realized that Robinson and Cruz had years of experience and technical skills he lacked. But Gordon had created a team—a partnership—of equals, and as far as Coburn was concerned, they were not equals. He had the rank, he had the privilege, and he had the responsibility. Robinson and Cruz's readiness to step in and seize the opportunity—and the attention—bothered him.

He almost felt as if they were undermining him. It was hard for him to miss the raised eyebrows, winks, smirks, and subtle head shakes. Robinson's grabbing his M-16 when he was shooting at the VC and then going nose to nose with him in front of the Vietnamese was inexcusably mutinous. Not to be forgotten or forgiven.

Robinson and Cruz were witnesses to his behavior. While everything Coburn did he could justify, the two knew stuff they could twist and use against him. Either one could do a real job on him if they wanted to plant some bullshit ideas in Mondello's or even Powell's minds. It was best to be super careful around Cruz and Robinson, he decided.

His musings were interrupted by the squelch on his radio speaker.

"Crazy Razor, Stallion, over."

He keyed the handset. "Stallion, this is Crazy Razor, over."

"At 1200 embark your passengers and return to your home base. Inform passengers Charlie Oscar ground transportation will be waiting at your base. This operation over effective immediately. Your counterpart being informed by separate comms. Over."

"Roger. Embark passengers and depart this area 1200. Over."

"Stallion out."

Chang was already passing the word to the RAG boats. The sounds and smells of diesel engines filled the air for ten kilometers. The platoon leader was standing at the bow of the command boat yelling that all his people were aboard and ready to move. Without waiting for noon, Chang started moving his boats from the upriver locations. By the time they picked up the boat at the last downriver location, it would be well past noon. They were headed back to the base.

With guns manned and the crew in flak jackets and helmets, the RAG sailed down the Saigon River. The one minesweeper capable of moving under its own power led the column of boats, sweeping close to the northeast bank, the side deemed most likely for an attack. The monitor followed next, then the troop carrier with its US Army platoon aboard, then the command boat, followed by the two empty troop carriers, one towing the disabled minesweeper, the other towing one of the small patrol boats that had steering problems. A lone patrol boat, like a sheep dog herding cattle, ran alongside the column.

They were several kilometers away from the area known as the mushroom and anvil due to the shapes the river formed on the charts. The mushroom and anvil were areas where they always caught some kind of incoming fire—usually nothing more than a few rounds of AK-47 fire but sometimes a full-blown ambush.

Since they still had at least an hour before they'd reach the mushroom and anvil, the crew was at their battle stations but relaxed. The column was coming up to a sharp bend where the river did a hairpin turn and reversed course around a narrow spit of land. The minesweeper in the lead had to slow down to shorten its sweeping gear to negotiate the turn, causing the entire column to telescope in on itself and slow down.

The minesweeper and the monitor were already on the other side of the flat point of land, the loaded troop carrier and the patrol boat were at the apex, and the command boat and the rest of the column still moving toward the turn.

Between the loaded troop carrier and the command boat, a column of water a meter wide shot forty meters into the air, mushroomed, and rained river water, mud, and dead fish on the boats. Simultaneously, a rocket hit the patrol boat's wheelhouse as the boat passed the troop carrier. The patrol boat veered left, bounced off the side of the troop carrier, and drifted drunkenly to a stop, dead in the water. Automatic weapons fire raked the command boat, the troop carrier, and the monitor, as well as the drifting patrol boat.

Grabbing his radio handset, Coburn tried to control his voice. "TOC Crazy Razor, taking incoming at coordinates 472534, south side of river. One boat badly damaged, casualties unknown. Engaging, over."

The response from the operations center was immediate. "Roger, Crazy Razor. Keeping this frequency clear. Over."

The three boats at the point of land—the monitor, the troop carrier, and the command boat—opened up with every gun they could point at the spit, sweeping the vegetation with bullets but seeing no people. Due to the tight turn in the river, they were also firing at each other across the low, flat land.

Chang was yelling into his handset for fire discipline. Rounds pinged against the boats' steel sides, some of the bigger rounds penetrating the shells of the hulls.

The boats turned into the incoming fire and moved toward the beach, firing as their bows grounded against the riverbank. Another rocket shot out and flew between the monitor and the troop carrier. Then another hit the monitor's armored forty-millimeter cannon turret. The cannon stopped barking out shells, its barrel drooped.

"Dai Uy, we need air strike!" yelled Chang, lying flat on the deck with his radio acting as a shield for his head.

"TOC, Crazy Razor. Request air strike ASAP. Coordinates the same, over."

"Roger Crazy Razor. FAC on this frequency. Call sign Vulture. Over."

A new voice came out of the speaker. "Crazy Razor, Vulture. I'm above you at your niner, I have visual your boats. Bringing in two birds with HE. I'm marking target with rocket and smoke. Get your boats away from there. At least half a klick. Over."

"Vulture, glad you're here. Can't move boats due to damage. We'll batten down. Over."

"Making my run. Spot my Willie Peter. Over."

A small, gray, high-wing plane with an engine at the front and one at the rear of a small fuselage between two booms, buzzed over the command boat, attracting ground fire. The O-2 turned and made a second run, launching rockets. Through his binoculars Coburn watched where they impacted. He had no idea where the VC were, but he guessed a spot in the middle of the spit in heavy vegetation.

"Come right fifty meters. Over."

The small plane did a third run and launched another pair of rockets. They hit exactly where Coburn was looking.

"On target, Vulture. We're hunkered down, over."

"Keep behind some armor, Crazy Razor, I'm bringing them in now, over."

From the north a Super Saber came in a steep dive, silently. A few seconds later, the thunderous sound followed. The jet pulled up over their heads and lofted a bomb with drag fins extended onto the area that Vulture had rocketed. The ground erupted, and the sound followed a split second later. It was a sound that went beyond hearing, pushing in on Coburn's stomach and lungs and deafening him. Dirt and pulverized rock rained on the boats.

For the next five minutes, the planes made run after run, lofting their bombs onto the spit of land. Finally the jets' thunder stopped, the eruptions stopped, and the rain of dirt and rocks stopped.

"Crazy Razor, Vulture. Birds flying home. You need more? Over."

"Vulture, Crazy Razor. Great job. Nothing could live through that. We got it now. Over."

"Leaving frequency. You get a KIA count, let TOC know, please. Out."

The exhilaration that Coburn craved was back. How could they get a KIA count here? Everything must be pulverized and vaporized. He stood up and could see craters in what used to be thick growth.

The minesweeper had picked up Robinson and the corpsmen immediately after the air strike and tied up to the patrol boat. Robinson and sailors were climbing aboard the crippled vessel. Across the spit, Cruz and some of the monitor sailors were trying to pry open the jammed turret hatch. The incoming fire had stopped.

The platoon leader was standing by the coxswain's station on the troop carrier, a few meters away from the command boat. He wanted to drop the ramp and send his platoon onto the spit to conduct a patrol and damage assessment. Coburn told Chang to drop the ramp.

"Dai Uy, I don't think we should. Let's stay in place, take care of our own wounded and dead, and then move at nightfall. The VC are setting a trap for us here."

This was uncharacteristic of Chang. Coburn didn't like his idea. Why leave before they had a body count? He needed that. Besides, these were US troops, and the platoon leader even wanted to go ashore.

Coburn argued that because they were US troops, he had the final say and again asked Chang to drop the ramp. Chang shrugged his shoulders and ordered the ramp dropped.

With the platoon leader in the lead of a dozen men and the assistant platoon leader at the head of another dozen, the troopers fanned out in front of the troop carrier and moved down the spit. Chang ordered his men to stay alert. Coburn sat in the deck chair, thinking about how to write the after-action report.

A muffled explosion brought Coburn back to reality. He could see the soldiers lying on the ground, smoke rising in a column. The distinctive sound of AK-47s opened up in a murderous cross fire, pinning down the soldiers. He couldn't see where the fire was coming from; they weren't using tracers. Then another explosion went off about twenty meters from the first. His radio came alive with the sound of the platoon leader's voice. They had walked into a minefield and ambush. He had troopers down, needed suppression fire and a medevac. Two more explosions went off.

Without waiting for Coburn to relay the platoon leader's message, Chang ordered his boats to pour suppressing fire on the perimeters of the VC's killing zone. Robinson had just returned from the minesweeper with the corpsman, covered with other people's blood. He grabbed Coburn's handset.

"TOC Crazy Razor Alpha. Taking automatic weapons fire from coordinates 472534. Platoon pinned down in minefield, same coordinates. We're suppressing fire. Request medevac for unknown number of WIA. LZ will be hot. Will pop smoke when safe to come in. Over."

"Roger Crazy Razor Alpha. Dust-off launching now. Will hold off until you pop smoke. Stay on this frequency. Over."

"Crazy Razor Alpha, out." Robinson turned to Coburn. "Boss, I'm going to need this."

He took the radio, strapped it on his back, and ran forward, jumping off the bow of the command boat onto the riverbank. Chang ordered a corpsman to follow Robinson.

The incoming fire stopped. Chang ordered the suppressing fire to cease. Robinson and the corpsman walked in a low crouch to the entrapped soldiers, stepping in their footprints to avoid any mines. Coburn watched through his binoculars, incensed that Robinson had taken the initiative. He scanned the area and saw Cruz standing on the monitor's bow, watching Robinson. Cruz had an M-60 machinegun in his hands and a sailor next to him holding the ammunition belt. Smoke from gun oil rose off the hot barrel. John Wayne wannabes, thought Coburn bitterly.

Robinson and the corpsman reached the platoon leader. Cautiously they stood erect. The corpsman looked around and immediately started administering first aid to the wounded soldiers. The soldiers who could move slowly started to retrace their steps back to the troop carrier.

An AK-47 opened up to the left of the monitor, firing from a hole in the riverbank vegetation at the soldiers. Cruz immediately suppressed the fire with his M-60, shooting in bursts and sweeping the weapon like a fire hose. A lone helicopter circled above. It was the shiny green command slick of the armored cavalry regiment.

Chang was listening intently to his handset. He looked at Coburn,

"Dai Uy, Chief Robinson says the best place for the medevac is right here." He pointed to the flat area in front of the command and troop carrier boats. "No mines."

Robinson and the platoon leader organized the movement of the wounded and dead back to the medevac LZ. Chang ordered his wounded to the same spot. A helicopter with large red crosses on its nose and sides circled the boats as the command slick moved out of the way. Two Cobras circled low over the boats and the land spit, looking for targets.

"Sir, this one is an officer, probably NVA. Dog tags and officer-issued pistol and some documents," yelled Robinson up to Coburn, who nodded and gave him a thumbs-up. Robinson was pointing at a Vietnamese wearing black pajamas but with boots instead of rubber-tire-soled sandals. The man was laying on his back on the ground, his forearm over his eyes, a large bandage across his chest and another around his thigh. A brass bracelet was on his wrist. He was pale, motionless.

Purple smoke plumed in front of the platoon leader, and the medevac helicopter came in, its rotors causing a cyclone of dirt and foliage, whipping the flags on the boats. Robinson, the corpsman, and several of the soldiers started loading stretchers into the helicopter.

The priority was obvious to Coburn. The US soldiers who had a chance of living first, then the RAG sailors who had a chance of surviving next. Then the US soldiers who were still alive but probably wouldn't make it. Then the US dead. Then the RAG sailors who were still alive and wouldn't make it. Then the VC who would live long enough to be interrogated. The helicopter lifted off with a full load of US soldiers and two RAG sailors.

Coburn jumped off the command boat's bow and walked over to the other wounded and dead. He felt no emotion as he looked at them. They might as well be butterflies in a collection, he thought. He stood next to Robinson, who pointed out another wounded VC and two VC dead. It would probably take another two more dust-offs to get the wounded and US KIAs out.

The suspected NVA officer moved his arm from his face, the brass bracelet flashing in the sun. He squinted in the strong sunshine. Coburn thought he looked childlike, baby-faced. He walked over to him and looked down, his body casting a shadow across the wounded man's face. Their eyes met.

"Hello American," said the man in accented English.

"*Chao ong*," answered Coburn, greeting the man in Vietnamese.

The wounded man smiled. "You speak Vietnamese. Very good."

Coburn had a four-pack of US cigarettes and a small book of matches from his morning C-rations. He didn't smoke but carried them to give to Chang or the RAG sailors. He pulled out the pack and took out a cigarette.

"Smoke?" he asked the Vietnamese in English. The man smiled and nodded his head.

Coburn kneeled down and put the cigarette in the man's lips. He tried to strike a match, but the wind was too strong. Still kneeling, he twisted his body to shelter the match from the wind, turning his back on the prisoner.

Someone shoved Coburn to the ground, and he heard what sounded like a thud against a heavy punching bag. Coburn spun around and saw a soldier standing over the prisoner, who was writhing on the ground, gasping for breath.

"Sorry to push you like that, sir. This gook was reaching for your .45."

"Thanks, soldier, I owe you." Coburn felt nothing, nothing at all.

He pulled out his .45, rolled the Vietnamese onto his back, and grabbed his hair, pulling his head up.

"You want my gun?" he asked coldly.

Coburn shoved the pistol barrel into the man's mouth, knocking out his front teeth. He pulled the trigger, blowing the top and back of the man's head off.

The only sound was the wop wop of the Cobras, the slick and the returning medevac. Without looking at anybody, Coburn holstered his pistol, climbed aboard the command boat, and sat on his low deck chair under the canopy. He felt cool, almost chilly despite the day's wet heat. He felt calm, relaxed, and more content than he had ever felt in his life.

CHAPTER 25
CU CHI

The radios were silent. Vo sat in the underground tunnel headquarters. Waiting.

* * *

A month earlier, Vo and Ky had been in their shack at the lacquer factory. Ky was looking at a report. A shipment of medical supplies from France had passed through customs in Nha Be, the port outside of Saigon. Taking custody of the shipment was an international aid group that was a cover organization for a local NLF supply cell—set up by Ky and Vo. The problem now was how to get the medical supplies from Saigon to the new supply depot at the junction of the Saigon River and the Rach Cau creek.

Breaking a large shipment of medical supplies into smaller, easier to conceal and transport packages meant, in Ky's experience, losing much of the original amount. Some would be siphoned off by local area cells for their own use, some sold and used for bribes, and some intercepted by the national police. But moving a shipment this large intact invited a search of the trucks by the American and puppet Southerner armies.

Looking across the lacquer factory's supply shed to Vo, who was trying to write a report to General Ong, Ky said, "What do you think about this idea, Vo?" Vo looked up, eyebrows raised in question.

"We've got that big medical supply shipment sitting in Nha Be. We can get it out of the city without breaking it down. The local cell is very good at that. But getting it up to the new supply depot is a problem. I don't want to break it down—too many losses. So here's my idea. It's a bit of a gamble, but let me know what you think."

"What I think about what, Ky?"

Ky nervously twisted his brass bracelet that Sergeant Nguyet had given them a lifetime ago. Seeing Vo's eyes on his wrist he said, "My good luck charm."

Ky leaned forward. "We use our sources to plant false intelligence that makes the Southerners and Americans mount an operation away from the depot. A big operation so that everyone's concentrating someplace else while we deliver the supplies."

"That might work, but how do we do that?"

"We let the ARVN intelligence office find out that a large headquarters and supply complex is operating outside the village of Bin Tranh, Hoang's old headquarters tunnel. Maybe we even salt it with some supplies and false documents. We know what their operations are going to be about five minutes after they know. So while they're all off running around Bin Tranh, we're driving a truck or two to our depot."

The idea was presented to Hoang and Pham, the two other members of the Military Affairs Committee, and approved on the spot. Hoang immediately put his operational planners to work while Pham initiated the planting of false intelligence.

Within a week they received intelligence from Mrs. Nguyen that a major operation was being planned for a joint force of Southern and American forces to conduct a search-and-destroy mission with the objective to capture a provincial headquarters complex. Hoang looked at this as an opportunity to not only confront the enemy on the NLF's own terms but also to observe the enemy in action, to learn how the enemy fought and thought.

It was also a time to test his NLF units, some of which he had doubts about. This would test their stomach for battle and their dedication to the people of Vietnam. Ky's original objective to transport the medical supplies while the enemy was busy elsewhere had become the genesis of a major NLF operation.

By the end of another week, the NLF knew the order of battle and the schedule of the enemy's plan to capture the abandoned tunnel complex and nonexistent supply caches.

From the growing supply depots, the NLF units took weapons and munitions in quantities to sustain them for a day of fighting. Medical supplies were shipped to the hidden hospitals and aid stations. Enemy radio frequencies were passed to the NLF communication officers for monitoring. And an ambush of the enemy's river assault group as it came downriver was added to the planning.

Two days before the US and Southerners' operation was to start, the NLF units moved into position. False planning documents and troop displacement maps were placed in the abandoned headquarters, as were obsolete munitions and weapons in the subterranean armory, and spoiled food in the supply room. Random personal gear and counterfeit letters from home were left in the dormitory. Two old French Army radios sat in the communications room. And the NLF men urinated and moved their bowels in the latrine area.

Twenty kilometers to the southeast, Ky would be supervising the transfer of the medical supplies to the new depot.

A part of the plan was to keep the Southerners' heavily armed riverboats occupied so that NLF troops and supplies could cross the Saigon River above and below the assault area. Then, when the boats headed downriver with their load of troops, an ambush would take place at a hairpin bend in the river.

The planners copied a tactic from their NLF comrades in the delta. They knew that the enemy navy assault groups when carrying troops always turned into the fire and landed troops. They booby-trapped and mined the killing zone, including a large mine in the river. The hairpin bend would also cause the river assault craft to have to shoot at each other if they returned fire.

Hoang asked Vo or Ky to observe the attack on the assault craft and troops. Since Ky would be closest at the new supply depot, he would join the NLF forces at the hairpin river bend and take part in the ambush. Besides, Ky added, by then he would be bored counting pills and bandages.

* * *

Vo sat in the communications room in Hoang's headquarters tunnels, half listening to the banks of PRC-25 radios. An NLF radioman sat next to him, keeping a log. American and Vietnamese voices interrupted the buzz and static as they marched, flew, and floated to the battle. A lone dedicated radio was silent. It was set to the NLF command frequency and broke silence only for short coded reports. Vo busied himself reading letters from Ngoc, his parents, and his brothers. A half-finished letter to Ngoc was on the table in front of him.

Hoang walked in and sat down. "Comrade Vo, I've found sitting while my men fight to be the hardest thing a commander is ever asked to do."

"Blue flower," emitted from the NLF command radio. "Blue flower. Blue flower." Then silence. That meant that the force around the helicopter landing zone was engaging the enemy. Hoang looked at his wristwatch and nodded. When the Americans were involved, things happened on schedule.

Vo finished his letter to Ngoc. Then one to his parents and one to each of his brothers. He stretched, he napped. He wasn't hungry but forced himself to eat a little bit of steamed tapioca root and peanuts. He toured the complex, running into Hoang doing the same thing. Waiting out the hours, waiting for the code words. They knew they wouldn't get accurate reports for at least a day or more.

"White dog. White dog. White dog." The NLF force was disengaging from the battle with the River Assault Group boats and its troops.

Looking over the radioman's shoulder, Vo read down the log. While he was walking around the complex, a report had come in—"Wood bridge." Vo felt his spirits pick up for the first time since the woman and her baby.

"Wood bridge" was from Ky. The entire medical supply shipment was safely delivered to the new supply depot. Ky was now on his way to the ambush spot at the hairpin bend.

"Does Comrade Hoang know about this one?" asked Vo, his finger on the "wood bridge" entry.

"Yes, sir. Comrade Hoang was sitting here when it came in."

Vo sat down to listen and wait out the hours, watching a centipede cross the table and listening to a family of rats in the corner. He debated on whether or not to throw something at them but decided otherwise. They were the NLF headquarters' pets. Ugly, dirty, impossible to get rid of. Just like the NLF, thought Vo with a rare smile.

Slowly, messengers arrived with reports, filling in the spaces and details of the coded radio reports. Like most combat, little went according to plan. Helicopters had been downed or damaged. Regional and provincial forces fought halfheartedly and retreated, many killed or wounded in the process. ARVN and American forces suffered heavy losses in the landing zones but inflicted serious damage by advancing, outmaneuvering the defenders, and calling in artillery and gunships.

Some NLF groups fought well, causing heavy damage and capturing valuable weapons, rations, medical supplies, radios, and ammunition. No prisoners were captured. The enemy was either killed or left to die on the field. The NLF could barely care for their own wounded, much less the enemy's.

Some NLF fought poorly. Their gunfire was undisciplined. They wasted their ammunition. Leaders panicked or fled. There were many reports of surrender.

And there had been one odd report of an American shooting an NLF squad member as he tried to surrender to the Southerners' navy boats with his comrades.

The ARVN captured the abandoned tunnel complex and gathered all the documentation and letters, collected the ammunition and weapons, then burned the food. The documents and letters were being sent to the joint intelligence office where Mrs. Nguyen—who had forged those documents and letters—would analyze them.

For the next two days, Vo hung around the headquarters complex, going over the reports, trying to determine the strategic impact of the operation and what to do next. He felt cautious pride in the ability of the logistical system to support such an operation without depleting its supplies. If need be, the system could support another operation like this one tomorrow.

When he returned to Phu Cuong, Ky would tell him the details of moving the medical supplies and the hairpin-bend ambush.

Four hours ago, the code word was received indicating the ambush of the Southerner's navy assault craft and its troops had started. The disengaging code word came in an hour later. The NLF operation was finished. Having been awake except for brief naps for nearly a week, Vo went to the dormitory cave and climbed into a hammock.

"Sir, Comrade Vo. Wake up, sir." It was the duty radioman. Vo was groggy; he had been deeply asleep. "Comrade Hoang asked for you, please."

Vo climbed out of the hammock, knocked a spider off his sandals, and followed the radioman through the dark tunnel to the communications room. Hoang was sitting on a stool. He looked tired, defeated, resigned.

"Sit down," ordered Hoang. Vo sat on the radioman's stool.

Hoang let out a low deep breath, looked at Vo, and said, "Ky is dead. He was killed at the ambush on the river."

Vo's scalp prickled. He felt his head growing cold, his ears plugged, the blood rushing out of his head. Putting his head between his knees, he stopped himself from fainting. A wave of nausea came over him, and he started gulping air in through his mouth, hyperventilating. The radioman pushed a cup of cold tea into his hand.

"Drink this, sir. It has sugar in it."

Sitting up straight to drink the tea, Vo felt dizzy and chilled. He dropped the teacup on the dirt floor and put his head between his knees again. After a few minutes, his breathing returned to normal, and he cautiously sat up.

"What happened?" Vo croaked quietly.

"The ambush went off as planned. Successful. An air strike was called in. High explosives, not napalm. Ky was injured, and the American soldiers captured him. He was conscious but could not walk. The American navy advisor executed him," said Hoang.

"Better that than capture." Vo was surprised at his own words and his lack of feeling.

"Yes, Comrade Vo, better than capture. This American doesn't seem to realize the value of a prisoner."

"I had better report this to General Ong, Comrade Hoang."

"Yes, I'm writing a report of the operation. Please add your thoughts, and I'll send them with mine."

* * *

The bottle of the harsh, clear rice liquor was half empty. On the small table in the lacquer ware factory supply shed was a little pile of letters, clothing, mosquito netting, hammock, and photographs. Vo collected the pile in his arms. In the late afternoon shadows, he walked to the back of the factory's yard, where a small fire was burning.

Vo tossed Ky's belongings on the fire and watched as they charred, flamed, and then turned to white ash. He stirred the ashes with a broom made of twigs, nodded at the factory worker, who threw some scraps of wood onto the fire, and walked back into the supply shed. The sun was setting.

Vo opened the liquor bottle and tipped it over his glass but then put it back down without pouring. Drink wasn't going to make him feel any more human. He sat down at the table, lonely. Sad. Numb. Why didn't he hurt? Why didn't he cry?

Vo reached for the bottle again, poured a bit into the glass, and swallowed it. The raw liquor burned and made him cough. He poured another. It was getting dark, and he hadn't lit his lamp.

There was a soft knock on the shed door. Vo wasn't sure he had really heard it. Maybe it was the spirit of the dead? Then he heard the knock again, followed by a soft woman's voice. "Vo? Are you there?"

"Come in," he said in a voice hoarse from lack of sleep and too much liquor and no tears.

The door opened, and in walked Mrs. Nguyen, looking around the darkness. He stood up, fumbled for his matches, and lit a candle. She looked at him with a questioning, sad expression of compassion. In her left hand was a cloth-wrapped package.

"Uh...please, Mrs. Nguyen, come in. Sit down. Please."

"Vo, please call me Yung. Comrade Pham said you were back. He told me about Ky..." her voiced stopped, choked with tears.

Standing there, Vo didn't know what to do. He finally led her to his chair and took the package from her. She sat down heavily, leaned her elbows on the table, and wept silently into her hands. He poured a little of the liquor into his glass and offered it to her.

"Drink this, Yung."

She looked up at him and smiled through her tears. Then she swallowed the liquor and started coughing.

"I'm sorry, it's very strong and..." he apologized, but she interrupted him.

"No, no. Don't say you're sorry. It is strong. I'm just not used to it." She smiled and then giggled a bit. There was an awkward long silence.

"Have you eaten anything, Vo? You look so tired, so sad." She stood up and took the cloth off the package, revealing several aluminum canisters stacked together. "I brought pho."

"I don't know when I ate last. I don't know when I slept last. I don't even know if I can eat now."

She opened the canisters. Then she took two bowls off of the makeshift shelf above the table and assembled the bowls of pho.

"Sit down and eat, please, Vo. With me, please. I want to eat with you tonight, Vo. I don't want to be alone."

He sat down next to her, and she slid a bowl in front of him and handed him a spoon and chopsticks. To the sound of slurping noodles and broth, the officer and the beautiful woman ate pho in the supply shed. He drained his bowl, and she refilled it.

"I know this is a war, a struggle for the people. Many die in war. I know that, Vo. And more will die. I thought I was hardened to that. But I've worked so closely with you and Ky, we became friends. I must not be as strong as I need to be, Vo. I hurt so much. Especially for you. You two were brothers..." She couldn't finish her sentence and buried her face in her hands, her shoulders shaking with silent sobs.

Standing, Vo reached down to Yung and cradled her elbow in his hand, lifting her from the chair. He turned her to him and wrapped his arms around her. She buried her face in his chest. Her body shook as she cried. Pushing back from him, she looked up into his face.

"Vo, you're crying," she said as she wiped a rivulet of tears from his cheek with a gentle thumb. She held him in a tight crush. Vo could feel her full breasts on his chest and her thighs against his. And then he started to sob. Deep, deep sobs.

Together they stood in the little supply shed, holding each other, crying. The floodgates of Vo's tears were open. He cried as he had never cried before. She held him tightly against her. Vo cried for Ninh, for the woman he shot, for the disfigured baby he killed, for Ky, for this woman he held who hurt so bad. He couldn't stop crying.

She lifted her head from his chest and looked at him through her tears. Her hands reached up to his face and gently brought it down to her lips, and she kissed his wet cheeks. Then she kissed his lips. Gently. He held her tighter. The kiss turned into a lover's kiss as her tongue ran over his teeth and then into his mouth.

Holding onto her shoulder, Vo guided her to the raised sleeping platform in the corner. He moved the mosquito netting aside as she unfastened the small hooks and eyes on her ao dai top and put the garment on the back of the chair. She slipped off her black silk pants. Vo extinguished the candle, turning the supply shed into a pitch-black space with no dimensions. His shirt was off, thrown onto the dirt floor. He felt her hand reaching out to his chest, finding him.

She moved into his arms, her heavy, full breasts warm and firm against his chest, her hands around his waist, his hands on the small of her back. She leaned back and untied the drawstrings on his trousers, and he stepped out of them.

They lay in each other's arms beneath the mosquito netting, their tears dried. She kissed his cheek and then his lips, her breast brushing his chest as she leaned over him. He was excited, hard.

"Yung, I have...Ngoc..."

She put a finger on his lips, silencing him. "I know you have Ngoc. You have told me much about her. I understand, Vo. I understand." She lay her head on his chest. "But now, right now, Vo, we have each other, here. This is what it is, and I don't know what to call it. This war is terrible. And it will be long. And this, what we are doing, is right. It can never be explained to anyone, but it is right. Isn't it, Vo?"

He nodded his head, stroking her hair.

"While you and I are here, in this place, in this war, we need each other, Vo. I want you to make love to me. To hold me. To cry with me. And only we can know this. If we survive this war, and Ngoc survives this war, you must never tell her of this. That's another ironic tragedy of this war." She lifted her head and kissed him long and hard.

Turning her gently onto her back, Vo kissed her neck and shoulders and breasts. Following the line of her rib cage with his lips and tongue he kissed her hips and thighs and then her labia and clitoris. She brought his head back to her lips, arched her hips, and guided him into her. For the rest of the night they made love, cried, and dozed, never letting go of each other.

WAR

CHAPTER 26
SAIGON

"What's a matter you? You no wanna fuck me?"
The big-breasted whore with long hair dyed blonde was shaking Coburn awake. He rolled over, a shaft of sunlight tortured his half-opened eyes.

"What's a matter you? You no love me no more?"

Her whining, singsong voice cut through his hangover like a dull, red-hot knife. Lying on his back with his arm over his face, Coburn tried to collect his thoughts and figure out what had happened. She kept on shaking him.

"Leave me alone, bitch," he snarled at the working girl.

"Bitch? You call me bitch? You bitch. You no fuck, you bitch."

She punched his shoulder and rolled out of bed, put on a thin bathrobe, slipped into rubber shower shoes, and flip-flopped out of the little room.

Two days ago Mondello called Coburn, telling him to come to Saigon for an important meeting. Coburn drove the jeep down a day early. Rather than go to the RAG headquarters or his BOQ room, he spent the rest of the afternoon and the evening on the terrace of the Continental Hotel, drinking with the correspondents and photographers and then smoking dope in one of their rooms.

He vaguely remembered eating a meal with two of the photographers and smoking a Buddha stick but had no recollection how he wound up in a whore's bed upstairs of the Red Door. His mouth felt as if it were caked with mud, and his eyes were dry and ached. A headache threatened to blow his head apart.

Sour burps were followed by tidal waves of nausea, and then he vomited on the floor next to the bed, scoring a direct hit on his fatigues and boots. He only hoped that the whore was right and he hadn't fucked her because he didn't want to repeat the embarrassment of having the clap.

Naked except for his dog tags and wristwatch, Coburn got out of the bed and stepped into his own warm vomit, which made him gag and then throw up again. He looked at his watch. He had two hours to get to his meeting with Mondello if he didn't die first.

Padding naked down the hallway to the whores' washroom with his soggy fatigues in hand, Coburn caught a disdainful stare and grimace from one of the girls. In the bathroom he washed out his mouth with tap water, a surefire invitation to loose bowels, but he didn't care. Besides, whatever was still in his system would surely kill all living things. He tried to rinse out his fatigues and then dipped his head into a full sink of cold water. He put on his wet clothes, walked back to the bedroom, and found his wallet and keys in his boots.

After another trip to the bathroom to rinse the vomit out of his boots, he looked into his wallet. There were a few piasters and ten dollars in scrip. He had spent about thirty dollars on Saigon tea and with any luck unconsummated sex. After he put on his boots, he went downstairs and passed the big-breasted blonde Vietnamese hooker sitting in the quiet bar. She held up her middle finger, scowled, and called him a faggot.

Breathing an alcohol- and vomit-flavored sigh of relief that his jeep had not been stolen, Coburn unlocked the chained steering wheel and then unlocked the compartment under the driver's seat. His .45, change of clothes, toothbrush, and shaving gear were still there in the small duffel as well as the pile of reports, letters, and messages for Mondello.

He drove through the Saigon traffic. The smell of diesel exhaust, rotting vegetables, and sewage in the hot, sticky air did little to settle his stomach or ease his headache. With an hour to spare, he parked the jeep in the compound.

Coburn was relieved to find only Ba Be in the hootch. She looked up from her cooking and stared at him.

"Chao, Dai Uy. You sick?"

"Chao Ba," answered Coburn. "No, I just need a shower and shave. Where's Thieu Ta Mondello, Ba?"

"He with Dai Ta Powell. Back soon. You hungry?"

At the thought of food, Coburn's stomach fluttered, but he didn't vomit. "No, maybe I'll drink a Coke." He pulled his wet and dirty clothes away from his chest. "Ba, can you wash for me?"

"You give me after you wash. When you go Phu Cuong?"

"Thieu Ta said I should stay here until tomorrow. So can you get them clean and dry by tomorrow morning?"

She looked at him more closely, her nose twitched. "Yes, Dai Uy. But you sick? You look sick."

Smiling but getting irritated at her questioning, Coburn shook his head, a movement that initiated another wave of nausea, "No, I'm fine. I just need to wash and shave." He took a cold Coke from the refrigerator, and holding it against his forehead, went to bathe and change.

Half an hour later, a freshly bathed and shaved Coburn, with teeth brushed and mouth cleansed by a pint of Lavoris, handed Ba Be his filthy clothes. He sat at the table, reading the *Stars and Stripes*.

A section of the paper included a listing of medals awarded that week to US servicemen. A lone Navy Cross, a few Silver Stars, a few more Bronze Stars and Distinguished Flying Crosses, some Purple Hearts, and a lot of Air, Commendation, and Achievement medals. He didn't recognize the names of any of the awardees. Most were Army and Marines, a few Navy and Air Force.

The time for the meeting came and went. This was unusual; Mondello was always punctual. Coburn was feeling better and nosed around the refrigerator, looking for something to put into his tender and empty stomach. The ever-perceptive Ba Be told him to sit down and she'd make him a package of the Japanese dried noodles and powdered broth flavoring—the hootch's most popular hangover medicine.

"Chao Dai Uy," said McGruder in his booming and ever-cheerful voice. "What you doing down here?"

"Hi, Chief. A meeting with the boss. You seen him?"

"Not since he left to go to NAVFORV this morning. He was supposed to be back by now. I have some papers for him to sign. Ba, you seen Thieu Ta?"

Ba Be said she hadn't seen Mondello and ordered McGruder to sit down since she was making him noodles, too. Knowing better than to defy or ignore Ba Be, he took a can of orange juice out of the refrigerator and sat across the table from Coburn. Coburn put down the newspaper, grabbed another Coke, and returned to his seat.

McGruder looked at him. "You feeling okay, Dai Uy? You look like shit, sir."

"I'm okay now, Chief. Something I ate last night gave me a real bad case of Ho Chi Minh's revenge."

"Looks more like something you drank, sir."

Coburn didn't like that comment. He felt that McGruder didn't believe him and was calling him a liar.

"How's the sore dick doing, sir?" asked McGruder.

"Sore dick? What sore dick, Chief?"

"Your sore dick, Dai Uy. You still draining?"

Coburn felt himself blush. He was embarrassed and angry. Somehow Robinson and Cruz had found out that he had the clap and must have told McGruder. These enlisted assholes were tight with one another and loved to fuck over the officers.

"Shit, Chief, how do you know about that?"

"Medical reports, sir. That medic has to file a medical report, info all the medical types in III Corps, MACV, and NAVFORV.

That's how we know if there's an epidemic, as well as who gets a Purple Heart. I'm the medical officer for this advisory group, so I get a copy. So does the boss."

Crap, thought Coburn. Mondello knows. Fuck. That's not going to help.

"Sir, I wouldn't sweat it," added McGruder, as if reading his mind. "If the navy kicked out everyone who had the clap, syphilis, or beat off, we'd have a bunch of empty ships and no crews. Besides, you know the old navy corpsman motto: the sailors have the clap, the chiefs have gonorrhea, and the officers have a cold. They all got the same thing. Just don't go dipping your wick after your PCOD."

"What's PCOD, Chief?"

"Pussy Cut-Off Date. Take your rotation date, then back off six weeks. That's the last time you get laid in this country. We figure it takes six weeks to diagnose and cure a venereal disease. So, no pussy after your PCOD so you don't give mama the clap when you get back home."

Coburn laughed and started in on his noodles. A few minutes after he finished, a grim-faced Mondello walked into the hootch.

"Clark, Chief, sorry I'm late," he said as he looked around the room then focused on Coburn. "You feel okay, Clark?"

McGruder answered before Coburn could think of what to say. "I think too much *nuoc mam* and Ba Muoi Ba beer, Thieu Ta."

Coburn, upset at the chief for interrupting and telling Mondello that he was hung over instead of letting him come up with a more presentable excuse, just smiled and nodded his head.

"Looks far worse than that," said Mondello, his face still grim. He looked at the two bowls on the table and turned to Ba Be. "Ba Be, will you please make me a bowl of noodles, too?"

She smiled broadly and turned to the stove. Mondello took a Coke out of the refrigerator and sat down heavily next to Coburn. Mondello opened the soda can and took a long drink, put the can down on the table, and stared at it. Then he let out a long breath, leaned back in his chair, and looked at the slowly turning ceiling fan.

"Lieutenant Doug Vernon is dead. Died late last night," said Mondello.

McGruder quietly asked, "Fuck. What happened, sir?"

Ba Be started to sob, loudly.

Coburn didn't say anything. His first thoughts were that he'd now be the number one lieutenant when fitness reports were written and Jean Miller no longer had a boyfriend and was fair game. But he knew he had better put on a somber and sad face.

"Shit, sir, shit," Coburn said, putting a hoarseness into his voice. "What happened, boss?"

Mondello looked at Coburn. "I know you and Doug were good friends, Clark. Sorry."

Ba Be was wailing into a dishtowel, leaning against the kitchen counter. McGruder walked over to her and put his arms around her. She buried her face into the tall man's stomach. Her cries quieted to a whimper.

"Dai Uy Vernon my favorite. He gone. He gone. He dead." She pushed herself away from McGruder, turned off the burner, and poured Mondello's noodles into a bowl. She put the bowl down in front of him. Standing, her head was the same height as Mondello's sitting. He wrapped his arm around her and put his cheek against hers. She started to cry again, then pushed back, sniffed, and wiped her cheeks with the dishtowel.

"I okay, Thieu Ta," she said.

"Ba Be, why don't you go home for today? Take all the time you need," said Mondello.

She looked at him, then around the room. "Okay, I go to temple."

She turned to wash the dishes, but McGruder took her by the arm and led her away from the sink and helped her collect her bag. Coburn worried that she wouldn't be able to do his laundry.

As he ushered her out of the hootch, McGruder turned and said, "Thieu Ta, I'll give her a ride home. I'll catch up with you later, sir. Nothing urgent, those papers can wait."

"What happened, sir?" Coburn asked again.

"Ambushed his jeep. He was driving from the hootch to the boats for a night op, and Charlie was waiting for him. Had his flak vest on, but rounds made it through the side webbing. Wounded Chief Willits. Willits grabbed the wheel and got the jeep out of the ambush and called in a medevac. But Doug bled out while Willits was holding him. Willits was sitting the other side of Doug, so Doug caught most of it, but Willits is pretty shot up. Hip and chest. He'll be okay. Doug's at Graves Registration, and Willits is in the hospital in Saigon."

"What do you need me to do, sir?" asked Coburn.

Mondello stared at him for a long time. "You okay? You just lost a good friend."

"Yeah, I'm okay," said Coburn. "What do you want me to do, sir?"

Mondello looked hard at Coburn, his lips pressed into a thin line. For a few long seconds Coburn held his gaze, then looked at the floor.

"Okay, Clark. I asked you down here for an important meeting and a change in your assignment. And we will address that. But I also want you to help with Doug's affairs. I'll write the letter to his parents, but I want you to take a look at it before I send it up to the admiral. I also want you to inventory his personal effects. They should be down here tomorrow. Better plan on staying here another two days or more. Robinson and Cruz can handle anything that comes up in Phu Cuong."

Change in assignment? Important meeting? Coburn was puzzled and excited. Were they going to give him a big job? Assign him to something that would lay the foundation for a plum stepping-stone when he rotated out? Maybe the detailer needed him to fill some high-profile, do-nothing job back in San Diego or Pearl Harbor or DC. The curiosity was killing him, but he knew he'd better play it cool.

"Keep yourself busy for a couple of hours, Clark. I want to collect my thoughts. We're driving over to NAVFORV at 1600 and then tomorrow morning to the MACV Compound. In between, we'll be dealing with Doug."

"Aye, aye, sir." Coburn got up and went back to his sleeping quarters. He was finally feeling human. The noodles had settled his stomach, and the Cokes had rehydrated him. It looked as if he had another opportunity to shine, and he intended to take full advantage of it. After trying to nap, he found the yeoman and borrowed a couple of sheets of blank paper and a clipboard.

Dear Jean:

I want to tell you how sorry I am about the loss of Doug. We were good friends, and I still can't accept the fact that he's gone. I'd have written sooner, but it's been too hard emotionally for me. I kept on crying.

I know the Navy has notified Doug's family and helped them through this terrible ordeal. I asked if I could escort his body home and be at the services, but the doctors said my wounds had not healed enough for me to travel.

I was with Doug when we were ambushed and tried to keep him talking to me, but unfortunately he died in my arms before the medical evacuation helicopter arrived. It was a very bad time, Jean.

If there's anything I can do, please let me know.

With sympathy and deep feelings,

Clark

Coburn reread the draft and laughed out loud. He thought his audacious behavior hilarious, entertaining. Out loud he said, "Clark, my man, you are a rascal. A true cad." Then he started laughing again.

After rereading the draft letter a few more times and making some small edits, Coburn put the letter away. He'd find her address in Vernon's personal effects and then wait a few weeks before sending—after she had quit crying.

CHAPTER 27
PHU CUONG

The dispatch box contained letters from his parents, Ngoc, and Ky's father. They were all dated a month earlier and had been opened and read at Transportation Group headquarters before being sent south. Vo suspected that General Ong's formidable assistant, Sergeant Nguyet, was the government censor.

Waiting until he was back at the supply shed in the lacquer factory, Vo read the letters as the sun came up before he went to sleep. His parents wrote that his eldest brother had been wounded and had been transferred from the south to a hospital not far from their home. His war was over. He was now blind but otherwise healthy and in good spirits. They also wrote that Ngoc visited them frequently, and they felt as if she were their daughter.

Ngoc wrote of her love for Vo, how happy she was when she received a letter from him. Her medical studies were interesting, and she was at the top of her class, impatient to move on. During her last trips to his parents, they visited his brother in the hospital. His parents were acting very brave, but they were hurting over what the war was doing to their family.

The letter from Ky's father was short. He thanked Vo for his letter and said he would save it forever. He wrote that the letter from Vo let a father know how his son lived, fought, and died and made him proud and patriotic. As much as he wanted to reunify his country, as much as he wanted to defeat the Southerners and throw out the Americans, Ky's father wanted peace even more. He asked how many fathers would shed tears for their sons before peace came.

After Vo reread each letter, he tossed it onto the small fire he had started behind the shed. He watched the pages curl and blacken then turn into white ash and the flames die. With his sandal he crushed the ashes into the brown dirt. Having watched the Americans and Southerners search bodies for information, Vo knew better than to save letters from home.

Back in the dark shed, he lay beneath the mosquito netting. This was the worst part of the day for him—chasing sleep while trying to make his mind stop racing. He tried to stop the guilt, the loneliness, and the hopelessness. With eyes closed, he hoped for exhaustion to put him into a deep sleep, but instead he would nap for a few minutes and then toss and turn before sleeping for a bit more.

Vo had tried liquor to stop his insomnia, drinking until his mind slogged to a halt and his emotions were deadened. But a stupor during war endangered not only his life but more importantly threatened his mission. So he had sworn off alcohol.

The dream-inducing tea sometimes put him to sleep, but the dreams were as vivid as life and left him agitated.

The only time he slept well was when he was with Yung. Since Ky's death they would make love to each other as often as they could. Once or twice a week, she would come to the lacquer factory in the evening after leaving Captain Neal's intelligence office. Often she brought food that would sit untouched until they finished their tender, slow, and passionate acts of sex.

Sometimes, to push the raging emotions out of his mind, Vo would try to relive erotic memories of Yung or fantasize about the next encounter with her. He would masturbate to the thought of how she looked in the dim light of the shed, her long, thick hair, silken skin, and full, round breast and prominent nipples. Thoughts of her warm, smooth moistness as she guided him into her and then the pressure of her breasts on his chest as she held him tight brought him to a climax that sometimes let him sleep a bit.

Later, the guilt would creep back in. He loved Ngoc. But he also loved whatever one called what he had with Yung. As she frequently told him, "It is what it is."

And the images would return. Yung naked and the baby with the cleft palate. Ninh and Ky laughing as their adrenaline burned off following a B-52 strike. His school mate Le sitting in his wheelchair in the northern sun. A man's face exploding as an AK-47 bullet hit beneath his nose. The green tracers crossing the red tracers, some colliding and veering off at odd angles. A rocket trail in the night missing its target. The orange napalm blossoms. Stunned fish floating on the river after a mine detonated.

Sometimes smells crept into his brain as he tried to sleep. Acrid cordite. That odd chemical odor of brain tissue. The slaughterhouse smell of blood and intestines. Fish sauce. Garlic. Yung's female spoor. Rotting river vegetation. Sulfur. Infection and gangrene. And the sickly sweet smell of a dead man.

Vo pushed back the mosquito netting and stood up. Cracking open the door to the shed, he squinted in the bright sunlight. No one was in sight. He stepped out and sat on the dirt with his back against the shed and his head back, letting the warm sunshine bathe his pale face.

A wave of disappointment came over him. How could he let himself act and feel this way? How could he be so selfish?

The sun was hot on his face, making him sweat, which felt good. He had an important obligation to the people of Vietnam that surpassed everything else. Resolved to that mission, Vo opened his eyes, blinked, and then squinted in the sunlight. He stood up a different man than when he had sat down.

Vo knew he had the fortitude and self-discipline to always do what needed to be done. He could steel his mind and act no matter if others or even his own self-preserving instincts were telling him to do otherwise. The only way he could be stopped was either by a bullet or with the completion of the people's mission. The mission was all that counted.

As for his feelings, they were secondary. He would protect the innocents in his life if that did not conflict with the mission. And he would sacrifice them if they did. As for Ngoc and Yung, he thought, it is what it is.

CHAPTER 28
SAIGON

Grim faced, Theodore and Mondello were sitting across from Coburn in the conference room at NAVFORV. Mondello had not said a word during the short jeep ride, his handsome face frozen in a jaw-clenched frown. Coburn knew his boss was upset over the loss of Vernon and decided that trying to make small talk was not a good idea. He kept silent, trying to display an equally sad face.

"Clark, I'm sorry you lost a good friend. I know you two were close buddies," said Theodore, shaking Coburn's hand.

"I appreciate that, sir," said Coburn deciding that saying too much might screw things up. He wanted to portray himself to these two as tough, someone who could handle the worst and keep on functioning.

"Okay, let's get on with business," said Theodore. He opened a red striped folder marked "Top Secret—NOFORN," and skimmed the top sheet inside.

"First off, this meeting is classified Top Secret, No Foreign Dissemination. Don't take notes, don't talk about his to anyone except me, Mr. Mondello, Captain Powell, or the admiral. Sign this, Clark."

Theodore pushed the top sheet from the folder in front of Coburn. It was a statement of commitment and agreement to the security requirements Theodore had just summarized, and it said that he understood the failure to act in accordance with the security rules was a serious crime. Coburn signed it and gave it back to Theodore, who passed it to Mondello, who signed as witness.

Theodore continued, "You're being given a change in assignment, but we're not moving you, Clark. You'll stay with RAG Bravo and in Phu Cuong. Your title will still be Senior Naval Advisor RAG Bravo—but in title only."

"Title only, sir?" asked Coburn.

"We'll get to that, Clark," answered Theodore, who looked at Mondello to take over the meeting.

Mondello leaned forward and started talking. "Thieu Ta Toh, the president's nephew and your official counterpart, is going to receive orders tomorrow to attend the Naval War College in Newport for a year. Chang is going to relieve him as RAG Bravo CO, and the ops officer is fleeting up to XO."

"About time they got rid of that no-load," grumbled Coburn.

Theodore said, "Agreed, Clark. But sending someone to the war college is not exactly what I would call getting rid of someone. The admiral and ambassador got personally involved in that move."

"I guess, sir, but it's good to see Chang get the reins. He's been doing the job; he might as well get paid for it. He going to get promoted?" asked Coburn.

"Yes, he puts on the Thieu Ta stripes at the change-of-command ceremony, which is going to occur next Monday in Phu Cuong. Better break out your dress whites, Clark," said Mondello.

"We had identified a relief for you as Chang's senior advisor. He's starting SERE training and should be in-country in three weeks," said Theodore. "Our original plan was to bring you down to NAVFORV once he got in. But with Doug's getting killed, he's going to go to RAG Alpha instead. That's why you're staying in

Phu Cuong. At least until we find somebody in the next class in Coronado."

What the fuck is going on? thought Coburn. They were going to move me to Saigon and give me a new job, but now they're keeping me in Phu Cuong, but I still get the new job? This wasn't making sense, but Coburn figured he'd better keep listening until these two were done.

"Tomorrow, Clark, we're going to MACV, and you'll get briefed on your new assignment," said Mondello.

He couldn't stand it any longer. He had to speak up. "Sirs, I'm not sure what you're telling me. I was supposed to work here in Saigon? And Chang is CO, but I'm no longer his counterpart, but I still am his counterpart? With all due respect, I'm pretty confused," said Coburn.

Mondello looked at Theodore, who nodded for him to answer. "There's a new development that can better utilize your strong points, Clark. We were moving you to a new billet, a liaison billet with special operations. That's why I called you down here in the first place. We were pulling you out of Phu Cuong and bringing you into NAVFORV. But now that we have to use your relief to fill the vacancy caused by Doug's death, that would have left a vacancy in Phu Cuong, and we still need to have the senior advisor billet to RAG Bravo filled."

"Couldn't it be gapped?" asked Coburn, hoping to get the chance to move to Saigon and civilization. He was also feeling pissed off that he lost a chance for a cushy Saigon job because Vernon had gotten himself killed.

"No, RAG Bravo is part of the Saigon special defense zone order of battle and by treaty has to have a full advisory team unless the South Vietnamese say otherwise. We asked, they said no. At least, not yet," answered Mondello.

"So I'm sort of filling the seat at the RAG but not really doing anything at the RAG, I'm working doing something else?" asked Coburn.

Mondello's use of the phrase "utilize your strong points" had just sunk in. Coburn knew that could be fitness report verbiage for "minimize your weak points," but he had no weak points. At least none that anyone had complained about. Was somebody bad-mouthing him to the brass?

"Sir, why can't I stay as the de facto senior advisor? I mean, why not just let me do my current job and whatever the new stuff is?" he asked, looking at Mondello. Coburn knew he might not like the answer.

"Several reasons, Clark. First, we expect your new assignment to be a full-time job. Let Robinson and Cruz handle the RAG and Chang." Mondello noticed that Coburn momentarily grimaced at the mention of his two enlisted men. He stared hard at Coburn, who held his gaze for a second, then looked at the tabletop.

"What's the problem, Clark?" asked Mondello.

This was all moving too fast for Coburn. He needed time to think, to say the right thing. But Mondello and Theodore were looking at him.

"I just don't know if those two can handle the top job, sir. I mean, they're good sailors and have a good rapport with the RAG but...uh...are they senior enough? Chang's going to be a lieutenant commander, y'know. And...um...I don't think they're aggressive enough, sir."

"What do you mean by that, Clark?" asked Mondello.

Shit, thought Coburn. How much have Robinson and Cruz told him about me? They've been wanting to fuck me. Mondello and Theodore were waiting for a reply.

"I mean, sir, this is combat. Not a fleet exercise in the middle of the Atlantic. You can't just sit there and open a manual and figure out if you return fire or call in an air strike or something. You have to react and react aggressively, or you and your men can die."

Coburn stopped, looking at the two senior officers for any signs of how they were taking his response.

"Clark, Chang is aggressive enough. Robinson and Cruz won't be the CO. Chang's in charge. And both Robinson and Cruz have been recommended for awards recognizing their bravery under fire by your predecessor. I favorably endorsed both recommendations. They're aggressive when they need to be. As for the seniority, Chang couldn't give a shit, Clark. He'll be okay with Robinson and Cruz." Mondello stopped and took a sip of the cold soda the yeoman brought in. "The only one who cares about seniority is some guy in the South Vietnamese Navy headquarters—and maybe some military liaison in the ambassador's office. That's why you have to keep your title as Senior Advisor to RAG Bravo."

"But there's a lot of work left to do," said Coburn lamely.

"Clark, you did a very convincing job on me, Mr. Theodore, and Captain Powell that Chang was ready to be the skipper and take care of the RAG on his own. If it weren't for the liaison with the US support, we probably wouldn't even need Robinson and Cruz."

Coburn was disheartened. "So why even keep me in Phu Cuong, sir? What am I supposed to be doing there that I can't do here?"

Theodore answered, "The operations you will be involved in will be in the Saigon River corridor. You have also established good rapport with the army advisors in the area. And you will probably be working with Chang and the RAG on some of the operations, but as a passenger and liaison, not as the senior advisor."

"That's right, Clark," added Mondello. "We thought of bringing you back to Saigon, but when Doug died, we reexamined that. Even if we had your relief here, I think we'd still keep you up there. If nothing else, it will save you a lot of travel time. And your digs up there are pretty comfortable."

"Just what the fuck is my job, sir?" asked Coburn, swearing out of frustration and anger. He checked himself. "Sorry, sir."

"No need to say 'sorry,' Clark," smiled Mondello. "We need to brief you on that part in preparation for tomorrow morning anyway."

Theodore spoke up. "There's been an increase in NVA and VC activity in the movement of supplies on the Saigon River.

There's also been an apparent change in when and how the VC pick their fights. Fewer engagements, but much more effective. And the general feeling is that the population in the river corridor from Saigon to Cambodia is shifting from neutral to anti-Saigon government. I've heard intelligence estimates that supplies and forces are almost to where they were before Tet. And the level of sympathy for the VC is even higher. US politics are going to accelerate Vietnamization. We've got to reverse these trends before we leave, or we can expect a collapse as we walk out the door."

"Do you know what the Phoenix program is or a Provincial Reconnaissance Unit?" asked Theodore.

"No, sir"

"You'll get a more in-depth briefing tomorrow. But here's the Cliff Notes version. The CIA ran a program called ICEX, intelligence collection and exploitation. Sneaky Pete cowboys trying to undermine the VC, use their own tactics against them. MACV got control of it—although the CIA is still very much involved—and turned it into the Phoenix Program. Same thing, different name. The objective of the Phoenix Program is the neutralization of the Viet Cong Infrastructure through the collection of data on them that could lead to their identification and subsequent neutralization."

Mondello joined in, "Clark, that can also include a lot of shit that can be embarrassing to the United States and the South Vietnamese governments."

"Ends justifying the means stuff, sir?" asked Coburn, genuinely interested.

"Yeah, ends and means stuff," answered Mondello.

Theodore continued his explanation. "Provincial Reconnaissance Units are outside the regular forces of the US and the South Vietnamese. Special forces, mercenaries, hired guns. They're supposed to neutralize the Viet Cong cadres and infrastructure. And the rule is there are no rules. The PRU enforce Phoenix."

Coburn let out a low whistle. This was not what he expected. Was he going to have to work with these guys? He sat there wide-eyed.

"You okay, Clark?" asked Theodore.

"Uh...sure, sir. This is just sort of...I don't know."

"Eloquently put, Dai Uy," quipped Mondello. "The decision has been made at the highest levels to reverse the trends along the Saigon River. That means, among other things, gearing up special ops, bringing in silent equipment and low-light vision devices, PRUs, and a detachment of PBRs for quick transportation and support. You will be the liaison between the army, special operations, PRUs, and the floating assets—the RAG, the PBRs, and even the skimmer assigned to the RAG. There's going to be a lot going on, and it will all be covert."

"PBRs? We could have used those when that colonel was ripping my ass about having the RAG boats zoom up and down the river," said Coburn.

"That's where we got the idea, Clark. You wrote we need something fast and heavily armed on the river in your report about that armored cavalry martinet," said Mondello with a chuckle.

Theodore looked at his watch. They had been at it for three hours. "Let's call it quits and start over tomorrow at 0800 at MACV. Unless you guys want to continue?"

"Not me," said Mondello. "Let's go up to the Rex and have a drink to Doug Vernon. I got the first round."

"I'll stick with 7-Up, sir," said Coburn sheepishly.

* * *

The secure conference room at MACV headquarters was large and air-conditioned, with a long, polished table and padded leather chairs down the middle. Captain Powell walked up to them, shook hands, and greeted Mondello by his first name but used the formal "Mister Coburn" as he greeted Coburn. They were early, and besides Theodore and a few civilians in short sleeve shirts and khaki trousers, the room was empty. Powell waved them out of the room and into the corridor.

"My sympathy to you for the loss of your friend Lieutenant Vernon," said Powell to Coburn. "Jim Theodore tells me you two were close friends. That's two you've lost."

"Thank you, Captain. I appreciate your concern." It took a while before he realized that Powell was referring to Matt Geralds as well as Doug Vernon. He had forgotten both, his mind occupied with his new assignment and what it all meant.

"We've got a few minutes. I want to talk to you, Mister Coburn." Powell looked at Mondello. "Pete, you stay with us, please."

Powell waited for two soldiers to pass down the corridor, then turned to Coburn. "Tell me your side of shooting prisoners," he ordered.

Feeling like the kid who was found cheating on an exam, Coburn put on his most sincere face. But his stomach was churning and the hairs on the back of his neck were standing up. "Sir, if you're talking about the operation on the upper part of the river and then the ambush on the way down, I didn't have a choice."

"I'm talking about precisely those two incidents. Why didn't you have a choice?"

"How do you treat a man in a firefight who is yelling 'chieu hoi' at you but sticking an AK-47 in your face, Captain? I shot him. I had to react instantly, and that was the right thing to do at the time. Otherwise I probably wouldn't be standing here answering your question. You'd have already written my parents a sympathy letter, sir."

Coburn was purposely displaying a muted anger and an air of indignation. This nuke captain wasn't there and who the hell is he to be to be judging me?

Powell was obviously ignoring or immune to Coburn's theatrics and calmly asked, "And the second one?"

"The gook grabbed my .45, Captain. I shouldn't have let him get close enough to do that, but it happened. I shot him in the struggle to get my sidearm back. I don't think I could have waited for someone to come help me, sir. Again, I reacted to the situation in front of me." Coburn had added defiance to his tone.

Powell looked at Coburn without saying a thing. Coburn looked at Mondello, but he was wearing a poker face. Coburn looked back at Powell. "Anything more, Captain?"

"Yes, one more question. You were briefed by both Lieutenant Vernon and Lieutenant Wilson of a VC tactic of ambushing RAGs and sowing a minefield and booby traps for the debarking soldiers. A counter maneuver was recommended to not follow the previous practices of turning into the fire and debarking the troops but instead flanking the fire and debarking the troops on the flanks. Or calling in air or artillery and not landing at all."

"Yes, sir. In fact, I made those recommendations," confirmed Coburn.

"Then why, given that information, did your RAG ignore those recommendations and debark troops into a minefield?"

"I tried to stop that, Captain," said Coburn, "but the army platoon leader insisted on the maneuver we executed. He ran his men right into the killing zone."

Powell looked at Mondello and then at his wristwatch. Without another word he turned and walked back up the corridor to the conference room, followed by Mondello and Coburn.

Coburn was seething inside, furious at Robinson and Cruz for crying to Daddy that their boss was showing initiative and trying to win a war while they farted around waiting to go home. He calmed himself down, confident that not only had he answered Powell's dumb-shit questions but also came out ahead. He had Powell's number, and he could manipulate the old fart like a marionette.

The conference room was now crowded. He found a place card with his name on it and sat down. Mondello and Theodore grabbed chairs along the wall; they obviously did not have a place at the table. Coburn felt good about that. Again, he thought, he was one of the select few.

Captain Neal and Major Teller walked in and found seats across from Coburn. That was reassuring. At least he'd be working with friendly and familiar faces.

Two navy lieutenants found their names at the tables and sat down. One was wearing gold jump wings, the sign of a SEAL. A couple of civilians sat down. An army colonel who obviously knew Captain Powell sat at the end of the table.

A two-star army major general walked in followed by his aide, who stood at the back of the room, then an older, beefy civilian with a .38 pistol in a hip holster, and an armed MP who shut the door and stood at parade rest in front of the doorknob. Before the door shut, Coburn could see another MP guarding the doorway in the corridor. The room came to attention as the general walked in. He quickly told them to take their seats and relax. The general and the civilian shook hands with Powell and the colonel and took their seats.

The two-star introduced himself. He was the head of MACV's special operations. After warning everyone that the meeting was classified as top secret, NOFORN, he introduced the civilian as the CIA manager of the Phoenix Program. Then self-introductions were made around the table.

The navy officer with the gold jump wings was indeed a SEAL, and the other lieutenant was the CO of a PBR squadron. One civilian was from the embassy, another the CIA, and a third was an intelligence analyst. The rest of the strangers were Rangers, a Green Beret, and an Air America pilot.

Speaking without notes, the general repeated much of what Mondello and Theodore had discussed with Coburn the day before. Some of the officers and civilian seated along the wall gave brief presentations to educate those at the table. Important to Coburn was that all operations would come through Teller and all intelligence through Neal. That was good, that was familiar, that was comfortable.

After an hour, the general summarized the meeting, and again warned that the meeting was Top Secret. As he stood up and the room again came to attention, he made a final statement.

"Gentlemen, all communications from this point on will be limited to just those in this room. Operational leaders will be the only ones submitting reports. As far as the world is concerned, we do not exist. Keep it that way."

* * *

Two cardboard boxes on the table in front of Mondello's desk contained Doug Vernon's personal effects. McGruder and Coburn were inventorying the clothing, books, photographs, letters, camera, wallet, dog tags, and money. An unofficial but always-followed rule of such inventories was to look for items that could unnecessarily hurt the recipients, usually the widow or the parents of the dead. Those doing the inventory would find and throw away drug paraphernalia, nude photos, Playboy magazines, or love letters from women other than the wife. Coburn picked up a rubber band bound stack of letters, the envelopes all addressed by the same hand, the return address of a Miss Jean Miller.

"Chief, what do you think we should do with these? They're from his girlfriend," asked Coburn, handing the pile to McGruder.

"That's a big pile of writing there, Dai Uy. They must have been pretty serious."

"Yeah, I think so, Chief. Think we should send them back to her?"

"No, I don't think so. I'm sure his parents will let her know they have them. Let's just send them to his mom and dad."

"Think I should read them, Chief? You know, take out the 'I can't wait to get your big cock in my mouth' stuff?" asked Coburn, half joking, half not. He was curious to read what Jean had written. McGruder laughed, shook his head, and put the letters on the inventory sheet and tossed the pile into the box to be sent to Vernon's parents. Before that, Coburn had ripped off the corner of one of the letters, stuffing Jean's address into his pocket.

Mondello walked into the hootch, a piece of paper in his hand. He gave it to Coburn. "Read this for me, Clark. No pride of authorship involved, so you make any edits you think are needed."

The letter was sad, sympathetic and genuine. Coburn was upset by Mondello's using the phrase that Vernon was "the best of the best" and a paragraph praising his bravery under fire. But he consoled himself that with Vernon dead and not able to brown nose the boss, he was now the number one Dai Uy.

"Looks fine to me, boss. I wouldn't change anything," said Coburn and handed the draft back to Mondello.

"Thanks, Clark. I just got word that there's a memorial service at NAVFORV for Doug tomorrow afternoon. You got any khakis with you?"

"Uh...no sir. Just jungle fatigues. I was planning on going back tomorrow morning. Brief Robinson and Cruz on the new assignment and then get going on the new job," answered Coburn.

"Robinson and Cruz are already briefed. Bill Wilson went up there this morning and will be back this evening." Mondello had sent his intelligence officer to talk to Coburn's subordinates about Coburn's assignment without telling him.

"You should be at the service, Clark." He looked at Coburn. "We're about the same size. I'll lend you a set of khakis, and Wilson must have a spare pair of lieutenant bars around. You wash your ass and put on clean skivvies before you wear my uniform."

"Got it, boss," said Coburn glumly. Too much was happening without his control. He really didn't like Wilson's talking to Robinson and Cruz.

"And I told Ba Be you'd drive her to and from the service. Keep an eye on her. Bring a clean handkerchief."

"Aye, aye, sir."

The next afternoon, wearing Mondello's khakis and Wilson's rank insignia, Coburn sat next to a weeping Ba Be dressed in mourning ao dai. A navy chaplain conducted the memorial service. Two thirds of the attendees were Coburn's classmates from training in Coronado. They all seemed to have the same taut-skin, tanned look with deep shadows under the eyes.

After the service the entire group, including the chaplain, Captain Powell, and Ba Be, went to the rooftop bar at the Rex for a somber class reunion and a drink in memory of a fallen comrade. As he passed his handkerchief to Ba Be, Coburn looked around the collection of officers.

He tried to figure out which ones were his competition for the best job out of here and then rank them. When he finished, there was no doubt in his mind that he was the number-one lieutenant, especially now that Vernon was dead. Upset that he had to drive Ba Be home, Coburn refused another round with the group and led her to his jeep.

The next morning he left for Phu Cuong.

CHAPTER 29
CU CHI

The three members of the Military Affairs Committee were meeting in the tunnel complex near Cu Chi. Vo had requested the meeting to discuss an odd proposal he had received.

"Comrade Leader Hoang, Comrade Pham, I have been approached by one of our men who move the weapons and ammunition shipments down the Saigon River. I trust this man. A group of Cambodians has asked him to have shipments of contraband sent into Vietnam via the river."

"What do you mean by 'contraband,' Comrade Vo?" asked the NLF leader.

"Narcotics, sir. Morphine and heroin."

Both of the older men looked at each other in surprise.

"Do these Cambodians know the workings of our river logistics, Comrade Vo?" asked Pham.

"According to our man, no. All they know is that our shipments have a low probability of being intercepted," said Vo. "What these Cambodians know exactly and how they learned that information is unknown to our man and me."

"Do we know if these men can be trusted? Could they be enemy agents, playing both sides?" asked the lacquer factory owner.

"We do not know if they can be trusted, Comrade Pham. I certainly don't."

Hoang quietly asked, "How do you think they know of our success in moving supplies?"

Pham, the communications and liaison agent, answered for Vo. "Comrade Hoang, success is harder to keep secret than failure. Too many claim to be the father. Too much talk on the trail or at the border. Drunken bragging, maybe. A spy in our organization? Somebody's favorite nephew boasting to impress someone. Who knows in such matters?"

Hoang took a sip of cold tea, made a face and asked, "Why do these men think we would ship their opiates?"

Vo leaned forward in his chair. "They claim that heroin and morphine use among the Americans has reached epidemic proportions in III Corps. Some of the soldiers are even shipping drugs in caskets and the fuel tanks of vehicles. An addicted enemy is a weak enemy, Comrades." Both of the older men listened impassively.

"Second, these Cambodians claim that there is much money to be made as the demand rises. They will pay us in hard US currency, gold, or goods such as weapons and ammunition."

Hoang posed a question. "And what if we refuse these people?"

"I think they will find someone else. Recruit their own river men and use the Saigon River as we do. This may bring unwanted and dangerous attention to river traffic from the Americans and the Southerners. They also may intimidate or bribe our own people into carrying their drugs."

"And if we decide these men can be trusted or at least dealt with?" asked Pham.

"Then, Comrade Pham, we may be partners with ruthless forces that have little interest in the success of our mission."

After another hour of discussion, Hoang read a list of options from his notes.

"First, we kill these Cambodians. Get rid of them. Second, we use our resources to determine whether these men can be trusted or not. Then we can tell them 'no' and kill them, or enter into agreement. Third, we simply refuse but monitor their operations as best we can. Fourth, we plant the information about these men and their drugs with the Americans and let them handle it. Anything else, Comrades?"

"Comrade Leader, I think your summary is complete," said Vo. "I respectfully recommend we pursue the second option immediately and then meet again to review our investigation findings, and plan our next step."

Everyone agreed that Pham would lead the investigation and they would meet within two weeks. No action would be taken without the approval of NLF Commander Tran.

Three weeks later, four Cambodian military officers disappeared near the Vietnamese border. Mrs. Nguyen reported that the US Army intelligence office was concerned, and special forces had been sent to look for them.

CHAPTER 30
PHU CUONG

The RAG Bravo change of command ceremony was more a public relations event for the president's nephew than a military transfer of command from one person to another. Due to the presence of the South Vietnamese Navy's chief of naval operations and the president's wife and sister, nearly every South Vietnamese flag and general officer within two hundred kilometers of Phu Cuong were in attendance.

Chang, who was being promoted and given the command of the RAG, was wearing his full dress white uniform, a copy of the French Navy's. He looked sharp, and his wife and children sitting in the front row smiled proudly. But he was grumpy and irritable, not having had a cigarette for over an hour.

Seated in the second row were Powell, Mondello, Theodore, Coburn, Robinson, and Cruz, all dressed in their whites. All wore several rows of medals except for Coburn, whose solitary National Defense Medal hung above his left breast pocket. But he was confident that would soon change. It was customary for a departing Vietnamese to recommend his counterpart for a decoration, and Coburn was sure that newly promoted Commander Toh had put him in for at least a Cross of Gallantry.

At the reception on the floating pier, Coburn congratulated Commander Toh and joked about the cold winter he would be facing in Newport at the Naval War College. Toh laughed and said he hoped that Coburn would visit him in Newport when he returned to the United States.

After taking another sip from his champagne glass, Toh told Coburn how much he appreciated his counsel and bravery. Then he added how sorry he was that he was not allowed to recommend him for a medal. Coburn kept the smile on his face and wasn't sure he heard Toh correctly.

"Not allowed, Trung Ta?" asked Coburn.

"Yes, I sincerely wanted to recognize your bravery, Lieutenant Coburn. But I was told by the highest authorities to not do so. I don't understand, but I must do what they say. You understand?"

"Of course, Trung Ta Toh. Medals are not important to me."

Coburn was trying to save face. His disappointment was combined with shock. *Who in the hell are these higher authorities, and why are they not letting this useless, spoiled piece of shit write me up for an award?*

"I hope you were able to recommend Robinson and Cruz for awards, Trung Ta. They do an outstanding job," said Coburn, fishing for information.

"Yes, of course. In fact, I was instructed to do so, although I was already intending to do that." Coburn was angry. He didn't want to keep on smiling and shaking hands in the sun with a bunch of pricks who didn't recognize his accomplishments and talent.

He walked over to Chang and congratulated him. Chang was the one person here he trusted.

"Need a cigarette, Thieu Ta?" asked Coburn.

"Yes, I snuck one half an hour ago when I went to the toilet, but I need another now," grumbled Chang. "So you will be doing things that no one can talk about, Dai Uy Coburn? Will I be on the river with you?"

"I'll be here, Thieu Ta Chang. I'm still living here. And I'm sure sometimes we will be on an operation together. But I'm your co van in title only. Chief Robinson will be taking my place. But I'll still be here."

Chang nodded solemnly. "So I understand. Chief Robinson and Cruz are very good men. Brave and smart. Very good. And what you will be doing you cannot tell me." He looked around for eavesdroppers and smiled. "I understand, Dai Uy, that you do not exist, and what you will do never happens. It must be magic."

It suddenly struck Coburn that the high level of security of his new assignment is what had stopped his recommendation for a medal from Toh. Special operators were rarely recognized in public awards ceremonies. Their recommendations for awards were probably classified. His anger dissipated.

"Yes, Thieu Ta Chang, I am magic."

* * *

The PBR crews walked down the ramps of the two big, twin-rotor CH-47 helicopters sitting on the clearing just upriver from the Phu Cuong bridge. An hour before, they had been standing on the banks of the Nha Be River southwest of Saigon, watching their fast fiberglass patrol boats being rigged with massive lifting straps. As the boat crews unloaded gear from the CH-47s, their CO, one of the navy lieutenants at the table at the classified meeting at MACV, recognized Coburn and walked up to him. A younger officer, a jaygee, was with him.

Three of the RAG boats, including the big monitor, were idling in the river. A ring of US soldiers was around the clearing. Although the boats and the soldiers were there to provide security, the clearing was probably the safest spot in III Corps. Nobody was looking for the enemy; they were all waiting for the arrival of the circus.

After shaking hands with the two PBR officers, Coburn led them to the riverbank, where Robinson and a Vietnamese sailor stood by the skimmer. Since his return from Saigon, Coburn had kept Robinson and Cruz at arm's length—he considered them insubordinate and traitors. Traitors to him personally.

For their part, Robinson and Cruz were deferential and polite and forced a conversation with Coburn after Ba Mei left the hootch to do some shopping. They explained that they knew he was doing some hush-hush work that was important, that they were to assume the actual responsibilities and authority as advisors to Chang, but that Coburn was the titular senior advisor and they'd still need his signature on reports and paperwork. They had also received orders to provide all assistance to Coburn without asking questions.

Coburn hated these two men. They had been recommended for medals by Gordon and Toh. Although he had no proof, he was certain they were leaking their own self-serving bullshit about him to Mondello and Powell. But he told them that he had strongly endorsed their taking over the senior advisor job and was very glad he was still living with them and working with them.

Loud, wop-wop beats of helicopter rotor blades preceded the arrival of the gigantic CH 54 Flying Crane helicopter. It looked like a monstrous locust carrying a dark green cradle from slings attached to its belly. The cradle was a PBR. As the helicopter approached, the Vietnamese sailor in the skimmer started the outboard motor, and three PBR crewmen and Robinson climbed aboard.

The giant insect hovered and lowered the PBR into the river in a lee provided by the three RAG boats. The downwash of its rotors formed whitecaps on the smooth river. As the slings came loose, the skimmer approached the drifting PBR and tied up to it. The crew clambered aboard, started its engines, and checked out the steering. Three more PBRs were delivered within the next hour and a half. The circus was over.

There were now four high-speed patrol boats on the Saigon River.

* * *

Neal handed Coburn a piece of paper across his desk. It said that two VC officers were operating out of a small rice and fishing hamlet on the Kinh Ho Bo tributary of the Saigon River. They had replaced a tax collector killed in an ambush by RAG Bravo several months earlier.

The two VCs were recruiters and operational planners for the VC provincial leader. In twelve days just before dawn, they would move on a sampan to an unknown location. Teller, the operations officer, was sitting next to Coburn. Mrs. Nguyen sat at her desk in the corner of the office, busy reading files and taking notes.

Neal said to Coburn, "This is from the same source that gave us the information on that VC tax collector your people ambushed and killed."

Coburn looked over his shoulder at Mrs. Nguyen and then back at Teller and Neal. He raised his eyebrows in question and pointed his thumb over his shoulder at her.

Neal smiled. "Yeah, I know this is NOFORN, but as far as we're concerned, Ba Nguyen is one of us. I trust her more than I trust myself. We can talk in front of her. Shit, she's the one who wrote this analysis and connected it to that other source that gave us the VC tax collector."

Hearing her name, Mrs. Nguyen looked up and met Coburn's eyes. She stared at him without expression. Then she looked at Neal and said, "Do you need me, Dai Uy Neal?"

"Of course I need you, Ba Nguyen. I couldn't run this place without you. But not now. Just ignore us."

Teller outlined an operation he and Neal had roughed out and wanted Coburn's input on. The major thought this a perfect mission for PRUs. The CIA had just brought in rubber boats with silenced outboard motors. Two PBRs would tow two of the boats to the mouth of the tributary at night. The PRUs would be in the boats with motors running and would drop off while the PBRs continued upstream as if on a patrol.

The PRUs would insert into the tributary, hide the rubber boats, then move into an ambush position. The two patrol boats would remain on the river for support, and if needed, emergency extraction. Coburn would go in with the PRUs, carrying the PRC 25. He'd initiate the ambush with a pop flare. Once the flare went off and the firing started, the PBRs would come up the tributary for support and extraction.

Coburn praised the plan and agreed that he should be the one with the PRUs. He was excited and happy, although he tried to maintain a calm, professional demeanor—a cool, combat-seasoned veteran. This was more like it, he thought. Fun and games with the spooks and gooks.

Teller said they'd have the final plan finished in two days and then would call a meeting of all the players.

Coburn hung around Neal's office, pretending to be looking at some maps on Mrs. Nguyen's desk. That intense stare she had given him earlier was pure passion. Perhaps it was time to make his move.

She ignored him, studying the papers and her notes. In Vietnamese he asked her what she was working on. In English she replied without looking up that she was preparing another report for Captain Neal and did not have much time to finish it. Again in Viennese, Coburn told her that it wasn't healthy to spend so much of her energy on this work. She needed to treat herself better, have some fun.

"Dai Uy Coburn, maybe I will, after this war is over."

"But I may be gone by then," he said with his most charming smile, trying to catch her eyes.

"You probably will be gone by then, Dai Uy. Please have a nice day," she said without looking up.

Big-titted prick tease, thought Coburn. Must be her period.

CHAPTER 31
PHU CUONG

Mrs. Nguyen was sitting across from the lacquer factory owner and Vo in the supply shed. They were discussing an NLF cell leader who operated out of the little hamlet on the Kinh Ho Bo tributary of the Saigon River. The hamlet had no name. It was a small collection of river fishermen and farmers. NLF officers frequently used the hamlet as a temporary head-quarters when in the area. Several months ago, two of the visiting officers were ambushed by the Southerners' river assault boat sailors. The ambushers obviously knew the details of the officers' travel plans.

According to Mrs. Nguyen, only the NLF cell leader would have been privy to that information. Since that ambush, several other reports had come into the ARVN division's G2 office, all about NLF movements and supply depots in the same area. ARVN troops had conducted several raids, capturing a cache of rice and medicine at the mouth of the tributary. Nonproductive but harassing search-and-destroy missions by the ARVN usually followed the arrival of visiting NLF officers.

An NVA political officer and an NLF liaison officer were scheduled to be in the hamlet in a few days. Both the ARVN

487

and Americans were aware of this visit but not the details. Mrs. Nguyen was worried about the NLF officers' safety. And now, so were Vo and Pham.

The three discussed whether the suspect cell leader had ever given any indications of disloyalty. To the contrary, they decided he had not. In fact he had served with the NLF for nearly a dozen years and was known for his bravery. During the Tet Offensive, he had kept a squad of ARVN pinned down so his men could safely retreat, and then he was captured, only to escape the next day. He lived in the hamlet with his wife and two small daughters.

"I will be meeting with the two visitors when they arrive at the hamlet," said Vo. "The fishermen usually leave the hamlet at dawn to tend their traps and nets. I've always sent our people out with them. I'll do the same with our friend from Hanoi and the liaison officer. But I want our cell leader to be told that the two will leave two days before they actually leave."

"Plant a false date and see what happens?" asked Pham.

"Exactly. Let's see what information gets to the intelligence office on this movement. And then let's see how they respond. If nothing happens, then he may not be the spy. If intelligence reports indicates the false date, or an ambush is set for the false date, then he most certainly is."

Ba Nguyen looked worried and asked, "If I receive intelligence of the planted date, then do we not let the fisherman set their traps that morning? If there is an ambush set for the officers, and innocent fishermen are taking their sampan to the river, they will be killed."

"Comrade Nguyen, you are right. If the Americans and Southerners set up an ambush and they think the fishermen are our officers, they will be killed. But if we tell the fishermen not to go out that morning, the intelligence people will know that we have infiltrated their operation planning," said Vo, pushing the thought of killing innocent fishermen out of his mind.

"This is the price of war, Comrade Nguyen," he added softly and covered her hand with his and then quickly removed it.

"And fishermen killed by the Southerners, as tragic as it is, turns more of the people against them," added Pham.

"If the cell leader is the spy, how shall we handle him?" asked Vo.

"You kill him, Comrade Vo," answered Pham as Ba Nguyen nodded her head in agreement.

CHAPTER 32
UPPER SAIGON RIVER

The two PBRs motored up the Saigon River, each towing a black rubber boat with a black outboard motor on the stern. The jaygee in charge of the patrol boat detachment was peering through the starlight scope mounted in the boat's bow, looking for the entrance to the Kinh Ho Bo tributary. Coburn—excited, happy, and anxious—stood next to him.

In the stern of both patrol boats were four PRUs, all Cambodian mercenaries. They were a ragtag bunch, an impression they liked and cultivated. Short, unshaven, and scarred, they were dressed in civilian clothes that ranged from pork pie hats to what at one time had been someone's brown-and-white golf shoes. They carried Swedish submachine guns and AK-47s with folding stocks. The PRUs sat on the deck, dozing or just staring into the darkness.

"Okay, it's coming up on the left about a hundred meters. Better get everyone in the FWBs," said the jaygee to Coburn without taking his eye from the scope.

"FWB?" asked Coburn.

"Fuckin' Wubber Boats, sir" answered the boat's coxswain over his shoulder.

Coburn gave a single click on his radio handset, which made the radio on the other PBR squawk, the signal for the PRUs to board the towed boat. He walked aft to the four in his PBR and told the leader that they needed to get aboard; the mouth of the tributary was ahead to the left.

Coburn's PBR kept its speed and moved closer to the left bank, and the other boat slowed down to an idle. The towline to the black rubber boat was let loose, and a PRU started the outboard. It made a quiet purring sound. The lead PBR increased speed and moved back into the middle of the river.

Within a few seconds, Coburn's FWB was in the tributary. He clicked his handset twice, and the idling PBR sped up and let its tow loose. The two black rubber boats with their cargo of eight PRUs and one American moved up the pitch-black Kinh Ho Bo. At the second bend in the tributary, they beached the rubber boats under a shelf of mangrove trees.

The nine men, with Coburn in the middle, moved silently along the tributary's bank and came to the next bend. The hamlet that housed the tax collectors and their sampan was a kilometer upstream. Without any orders being spoken, the PRUs took their ambush positions on the water's edge, with their leader and Coburn at the center. The ambush line followed the tributary bank, forming a V. It was a little after 0200. They planned to sit and wait for three and half hours.

On the Saigon River, the two PBRs continued a slow patrol upriver, although they expected to find nothing. Reversing course after two hours, they would be back at the tributary's mouth, idling quietly when the ambush began. If it did begin. Most ambush operations in Vietnam were boring, long waits culminating in absolutely nothing.

Phakdei was the leader of the PRU squad. He looked as ragtag as the others—wearing a golf jacket over a plaid shirt, baggy dress pants, shower shoes, and a gray canvas fedora with a Disneyland logo of Mickey Mouse on the crown. He had a deep scar on his left cheek. And he was missing his right thumb. His British-accented English was a startling contrast to his appearance.

492

It started to rain, and Coburn was convinced something had just crawled over his leg. The wet tributary bank stank of rotting vegetation and sewage from the hamlet. A mixture of rain, sweat, and insect repellant made his eyes sting and tear. He was miserable and started hoping that something would happen to compromise the ambush and they could get the hell out of this shit pile. Not having thought to bring a poncho, he was getting soaked. Coburn didn't even try to shelter the PRC 25 radio from the rain.

About an hour before dawn, Phakdei broke the silence and interrupted Coburn's fantasy of taking off Jean Miller's clothes and having sex with her in some clean, dry Waikiki hotel room.

In a low whisper, Phakdei asked, "Why are you here?"

"Here? This place?" replied Coburn. "Because I'm the one with the radio and the one who starts the operation."

"No, no. Why are you here in Vietnam?" asked the PRU leader. "I'm here because you pay me more money tonight than I can earn forever at home. Why are you here?"

"Shit, it's not for money, Phakdei. I get about fifty dollars a day. I'm here because it's my job. I'm a naval officer, and this is my job."

"You believe in what you're doing?"

Coburn looked at the Cambodian for a long time while he decided how to answer that question. Then he went into a quiet monologue of helping America's friends, patriotism, domino theory, and fighting for freedom and democracy.

"You think the South Vietnamese will win?" asked Phakdei. "You want that, Coburn?"

He couldn't care less what happened after he left this fucking place and these people. But Coburn knew he shouldn't say that.

"Of course I do, Phackdei. Why would I be sitting here? Why would the Vietnamese have asked me to come here?"

"You think Vietnamese like you? They like Americans?"

"Sure they do. Not the VC and Hanoi, but the average guy around here? Sure," he answered, believing what he was saying.

"Coburn. These people don't like you. They hate you. Not as much as they hate the French, but they hate you."

"Fuck no. No way."

"Let me ask you something, Coburn. Some young man in the North says goodbye to his family, knowing he'll probably never see them again. Then he walks down the Ho Chi Minh trail carrying a couple of mortar rounds or B-40s with ten of his comrades. By the time he gets to this place, maybe eight of his friends are dead because of malaria or B-52s.

"This young man comes down here and sits on the riverbank waiting for one of those patrol boats to go by. He sits there with dysentery and no food, and finally he sees one of those boats and shoots off his B-40. And misses. The patrol boat calls in an air strike and kills him. And while he's dying, another ten men say goodbye to their families and march down the trail."

"So what?" asked Coburn.

"In the South they take a young man, feed him well, put him in good uniforms, give him boots and an M-16, and train him and pay him. And then he goes to war in a helicopter, jumps out, and someone shoots at him. What's he do? He throws away his rifle, throws off his helmet, and runs away. So, Coburn, who do you think will win this war?"

Before Coburn could reply, Phakdei held up his hand for silence. The distant putt-putt of a sampan motor could be heard. Coburn's heart started pounding. The putt-putt didn't fade. The intelligence was correct. Two VC officers were heading downstream into the ambush. Coburn clicked his handset three times, telling the PBRs to stand by, the ambush would be starting soon.

"Coburn, something's wrong," whispered the PRU. "Too early, much too early. Much too early. Too much noise."

"What do you mean something's wrong? This is exactly what the intel said."

Coburn took the pop flare out of his pack, tore off the tape, and fitted the cap to the bottom of the flare. All he had to do was point the flare skyward and hit the cap with the palm of his hand.

"Don't start the ambush, Coburn, until we can see who's in the boat. We should try to stop them first. Don't shoot."

"Are you fucking nuts? Wait for them to get close enough to shoot the piss out of us? This is a fucking ambush, you idiot."

The sampan motor's noise was loud and getting louder. It had to be only fifty meters away, around the upstream bend. Coburn planned to shoot the flare as soon as it entered the top of the ambush V. The PRUs would open fire, the momentum of the sampan would bring it into the center of the killing zone, and the PBRs would come up the tributary.

The low shadow of the bow of the sampan rounded the bend and started down the V. As Coburn readied the flare, he could feel Phakdei's hand trying to restrain him. Shaking off the Cambodian's grip on his forearm, Coburn slammed the firing cap with the palm of his hand, and the flare shot up like a small skyrocket. The PRUs opened fire, and the flare popped into illumination. Coburn picked up his M-16 and emptied his magazine at the sampan.

The PBRs motored around the downstream bend as the firing stopped. Coburn yelled for some illumination. The lead patrol boat fired an illumination flare, bathing the killing zone in brilliant white light. One of the PBRs pulled alongside the listing sampan.

"Oh, Jesus fucking Christ. Shit!" yelled someone from the PBR.

They had ambushed and killed a young girl and a younger boy, her little brother, probably on their way out of the tributary to tend their family's fishnets.

CHAPTER 33
VIN HO BO TRIBUTARY

The cell leader's hut on the Kinh Ho Bo tributary was dimly lit by a small kerosene lantern. In the gloom squatted the cell leader, two visiting officers, and one of the members of the Military Affairs Committee, Comrade Vo. The officers had been operating out of the hut for nearly a week, their schedule spontaneous and seemingly at random. The locations were not known to anyone but themselves. The only information known for sure was that they would leave via sampan tomorrow at dawn. Comrade Vo had arrived earlier in the afternoon to debrief the officers and see them off in the morning.

"Let's all get some sleep, Comrades. You have a long journey in the morning," said the cell leader, pointing to the raised wood sleeping platform. His wife and children were asleep in the little room attached to the rear of the hut.

After a few minutes packing their papers and gear and checking their pistols and their lone rifle, the two travelers lay down and tried to sleep. The cell leader joined his family in the little room. Vo leaned against the center pole of the hut and shut his eyes. He knew he wouldn't sleep. Besides being accustomed to being awake during the night, his nerves and senses were alert.

With the first lightening of the sky in the east, Vo shook the shoulders of the two visiting officers and motioned them out of the hut. Lantern light flickered from two of the hamlet dwellings—fishermen getting ready to check their nets and traps. The three men walked to a sampan tied to a stake in the tributary bank, out of earshot of the sleeping cell leader.

"Comrades, you will not be leaving today. You will leave two days from now," said Vo. "The American intelligence office has been told that you are leaving today, and they will try to ambush you on the Kinh Ho Bo."

"Are you serious, Comrade Vo?" asked the NVA officer from Hanoi. "You know this for certain?"

"Yes, Comrade."

"But who would provide them that information? The only ones who know the date are us."

The cell leader walked out of his family's home. He peered around in the dark and then made out the forms of the men. He carried a kettle and some cups.

"There you three are. Early risers, huh? Here's some tea." The cell leader walked up to them and handed them each a teacup and poured tea.

"We can all go back to sleep, Comrade. There's been a change in schedule," said Vo.

"Change? We don't want them to travel during daylight, at least not until they reach the Saigon River," said the cell leader. It was too dark for Vo to see the man's face, but his voice had a new and strident timbre. "Comrades, you should go now. Right now. It's too dangerous to wait until the sun comes up."

"Don't worry about that. The schedule has been changed. They won't leave in the daylight." Vo's voice was flat, quiet, definite.

Two small figures came out of one of the lit huts, carrying some parcels. A woman's voice from inside the hut told them to hurry up and check the crab traps first, then the nets. The two shadows walked to a sampan beached on the bank and put their parcels in the bow. The smaller one climbed over the gunwale and sat near the little engine at the stern. He tinkered with the fuel tank and in a little boy's voice said it was okay to push the boat off the bank. The bigger one pushed on the bow and climbed into the front of the sampan. The engine putted to life, and they motored down the tributary, waving at the four men standing on the bank in the faint pre-dawn light.

"What's wrong, Comrade Cell Leader?" asked Vo. "You seem very nervous."

"I'm worried about those children, Comrade Vo. The river can be dangerous."

"They seem very skilled and comfortable to me. What could happen to them on a nice dawn like this?" Vo knew he was sending the two children to their deaths. Unless the information from Yung was wrong. But that was not likely. "Do you want to chase the children and bring them back?"

Saying nothing, the cell leader shrugged his shoulders and walked back to his home, leaving Vo and the two officers at the water's edge.

"Him? He's the spy?" asked the NVA officer incredulously.

"We will find out shortly, Comrade," answered Vo.

They stood on the bank, cold tea in cracked cups in their hands, the putt-putt of the sampan motor fading as it moved towards the Saigon River.

Down the tributary, a pop was followed by a whoosh and then white light and the staccato fire of automatic weapons. The firing stopped after a few minutes and was replaced by the sound of powerful diesel engines.

The cell leader looked up as Vo entered the doorway of the hut. Vo pointed his pistol and shot him in the face, startling the man's family awake.

The next day Captain Neal read an intelligence analysis from Ba Nguyen that their source of valuable intelligence was dead. His body was found by his family. And two children had died in a Phoenix ambush on the Kinh Ho Bo tributary.

CHAPTER 34
UPPER SAIGON RIVER

A month had passed since the killing of the two children in the sampan. Heavy rain beat down on two PBRs nosed into the Saigon River bank. It was the middle of the wet season. The boats had inserted SEALs several hours ago. A platoon of PRUs was traveling by foot to the village where they would meet the SEALs. Coburn was aboard the PBR with the officer in charge of the detachment monitoring the radio that had been silent since the SEALs disembarked. The patrol boats would stay in place until called to extract the SEALs and PRUs. As usual, Coburn had no idea how long that would be.

The glory and glamour he had expected with his assignment to work with the Phoenix program, the Provincial Reconnaissance Units, the special forces, and these patrol boats never occurred. Most of the operations consisted of sitting on his ass, miserable, tired, and bored. The only good thing was seeing Ba Nguyen in the intelligence office. But she was always too busy to talk to him.

Jean Miller wrote back after she got his bullshit letter, and her response might as well have been written on dry ice. She basically called him a shit and told him to fuck off. Too bad, her loss.

The worst part of his assignment was the realization that there would be no medals for him. The missions were classified and could not be acknowledged by the Department of Defense. To write him up for an award would be evidence that such operations had occurred. Even the text of his fitness report was going to be classified, although the grades and ranking would be available to the detailers and the selection boards.

Two thirds of the way through his tour in Vietnam, and Coburn was feeling fucked over and screwed. Powell and Mondello were always asking him why missions he was connected with were not successful, or worse, fucked up. The fact that none of it was his fault didn't seem to have much effect on them. Coburn was certain that Robinson and Cruz and probably McGruder and maybe even Chang were doing their best to make him look bad to NAFVORV.

Vernon gets killed and he gets awarded a bunch of medals. Vernon's senior enlisted, Chief Willits, tried to save his ass and failed, and even he gets a medal for that. Coburn worked himself up at least twice a day thinking how he was getting screwed not getting the recognition he deserved.

And finally, he wanted to get out of the country now, not in another 120 days. He wanted out of country, a cushy assignment like CO of some nice, cushy vessel or maybe graduate school and then a CO job. He spent many hours of boredom fantasizing and planning about getting a heroic but non-disfiguring wound, getting revenge on Robinson and Cruz, and being recognized for some heroic deed like Chief Willet's.

What could be better than getting some flesh wound while trying unsuccessfully to save Robinson's black ass?

A lightning flash brought Coburn out of his fantasy and back to sitting under the cockpit canopy on a patrol boat tied up to a tree on the stinking Saigon River at 0330 in a rainstorm. He wrapped his poncho tighter around himself and looked around.

Seated on the edge of the twin fifty-caliber machine gun tub was one of the PBR gunners. He had the watch while the others slept. Twenty meters down the bank sat the other PBR with another sailor on watch. Coburn thought how glad he was to be an officer. Trying to keep alert and dry in this shit was for the enlisted, not him. He lay back down on the cockpit deck, using his radio pack for a cushion.

From forward in the boat came a metallic click followed by a loud, dull thud and the shout "Grenade!"

Before Coburn could raise his head, an explosion peppered the boat with shrapnel and mud and the forward fifties opened up, shaking the boat and filling the rain soaked air with the smell of cordite and gun oil.

The firing stopped when the machine guns ran out of ammunition. The sailor on watch was seated behind the guns. The officer in charge was standing next to him, and two other sailors were climbing over the gunwales onto the riverbank. Coburn ran up and looked over the bow.

In the cone of light from the boat's spotlight lay four men ripped apart by and explosion and fifty-caliber rounds. Scattered near the shattered bodies were broken AK-47s and the remains of a claymore mine. The rain was washing their blood into the river.

On their way downriver the next morning, the OinC of the patrol boat detachment mentioned that he was putting the gunner in for a Navy Cross or, if that wouldn't fly, a Silver Star.

"Clark, that guy had the presence of mind to find that grenade and toss it back while screaming 'grenade' and then shooting off both fifties. He's a real hero. Saved our lives and the boat."

Although he voiced agreement, Coburn was overcome with jealousy and anger. If only he had been the guy who had been sitting up there and tossed the grenade back. Instead this dumbass, enlisted, hick, high-school dropout becomes a fucking hero.

"How are you going to write him up? You know, classification and all that?" he asked, hoping to derail the award recommendation.

"No problem, Clark. As far as the world knows, we were on patrol. I mean these are river patrol boats, and we're on the river, right?"

"Hey, good thinking. That'll work, huh?" answered Coburn. He turned, sat on the engine cover, and fantasized about a flesh wound and glory.

CHAPTER 35
CU CHI

The Military Affairs Committee members were discussing the increasing attention of the Americans and Southerners' Phoenix Program on the NLF infrastructure. NLF Commander Hoang had been following similar efforts for nearly eight years. This Phoenix Program, as far as he was concerned, was nothing new. It was the same CIA intelligence collection and exploitation but with a new name; same for the mercenaries they employed, these so-called counterterror teams or Provincial Reconnaissance Units.

The success and failure of the Phoenix Program varied throughout their area. Near the border between II and III Corps, the PRU were achieving tactical victories by wiping out a cell or disrupting a supply line. But these victories were often offset by civilian losses and distrust of the mercenaries and special forces. At the southern border between III and IV Corps, the PRUs had had some success infiltrating or destroying infrastructure and seemed to have turned into light infantry units for special operations forces.

Along the Saigon River corridor, the center of their area, the Phoenix Program was turning into a failure. Much of this was due to the program's reliance on the intelligence and operations coming out of Major Teller and Captain Neal's offices. This intelligence was manipulated by the advisory committee and Mrs. Nguyen.

Villages friendly to the Southerners were falsely identified by Mrs. Nguyen and the committee as NLF headquarters or staging areas. Villagers loyal to the Southern government were labeled as NLF cell chiefs, tax collectors, or spies for the NLF. Ammunition caches were said to be hidden in schools. These all became Phoenix Program targets, and before the PRU moved in, booby traps, mines and ambushes were put in place. The results were often a massacre of the friendly village, turning the survivors and neighboring villages into ardent NLF supporters.

Sensing the shifting sentiments, the Phoenix Program responded in kind. The PRU and even their American leaders would don the NLF fighters' garb of black pajamas and rubber-tire-soled sandals and attack a village or hamlet friendly to the NLF. Using AK-47 rifles, People's Republic of China-produced pistols and captured NLF grenades, they killed everyone. The only evidence of an attack were the dead bodies and livestock and a few deliberately discarded NLF rounds of ammunition and dud grenades. After a few days, the Saigon government reported that the NLF had viciously destroyed a peaceful hamlet of peasants, killing women and children as well as stealing livestock and burning crops.

Hoang said to Vo, "Well, Comrade, they seem to have learned your lesson of the value of a dead body, no matter who is the murderer."

* * *

Her breasts brushed against his chest as she leaned over to kiss him. Yung sat on the edge of the sleeping platform in the supply shed, naked, stretching her back. Vo ran his rough fingers lightly, gently down the curve of her spine. She turned and smiled at him, squeezed his hand, and stood up, looking for her clothes in the dim light.

Silently, the two dressed. She turned to him, kissed him good-bye, and went off to her home. Once the sun was down, he would leave the lacquer factory, walk north and then west to a spot on the river upstream of the Phu Cuong bridge, and be picked up in a sampan for a trip upriver to the village of Xom Dua. Vo was considering putting a supply depot and a weapons repair factory between the village and the tributary of the Saigon River that ran just north of it. He would stay there as long as it took to survey the area, probably two or three days, and come back to Phu Cuong and the feminine sanctuary of Yung.

ROT

CHAPTER 36
WORLD AIRWAYS CHARTER FLIGHT 442

The pilot announced they were an hour out of Saigon and would be starting their descent in thirty minutes. Coburn lifted the shade on the chartered DC-8's window and looked out on leaden clouds. The view matched his glum attitude and sour stomach. He was returning to the war from a week's R&R in Hong Kong. Nothing was going right. Everyone was trying to fuck him.

Jean Miller had called him a liar and a despicable scoundrel in her response to his letter. It seemed that Vernon's parents had asked Jean to attend the burial with full military honors at Arlington National Cemetery. Vernon's senior enlisted advisor, Chief Petty Officer Willits, at the family's request, escorted Vernon's body.

After the ceremony, Jean asked Willits to tell her how Vernon had died. She cried as Willits described his vain attempts to keep his officer alive. When she saw the tears in the man's eyes, she hugged him close. Later, she asked what Clark Coburn was doing during the ambush. Willits had never heard the name before.

The way he had treated Kelly Meredith was bad enough, Jean wrote. But to lie about the death of his friend for his own self-serving purposes was indefensible and despicable. She wished him nothing but the worst.

Coburn's initial reaction to Jean's letter was that Willits had a big mouth and should keep his nose out of other people's business. For sure Robinson and Cruz had a hand in feeding Willits bullshit about him. And Kelly and Jean were two gossiping bitches who would do whatever they could to shit on him.

Plans of spending a week pillowed between non-gook tits in an air-conditioned hotel room overlooking Waikiki were pretty well torpedoed. Thanks to Willits's meddling and vicious female gossip, Jean was no longer a target of opportunity. Betsy was too busy with her nose up some Madison Avenue draft dodger's asshole. And Kelly was out of the question. The three bitches had all screwed him over. And Ba Hung had never responded to an alcohol-fueled love letter proposal to meet in Hawaii.

Then there was the letter from his detailer, Lieutenant Commander Sperling. Coburn had opened it with happy anticipation of what his new orders would be. The happiness faded instantly with Sperling's phrase, "due to the needs of the navy."

A high-priority department head position on an amphib out of Norfolk was opening just as Coburn would be finishing his thirty day's leave after rotating out of Vietnam. According to the detailer's letter, the job was a good one with plenty of opportunity to excel. The long-range plan—assuming good "and improving" fitreps—was to have him screened for postgraduate school at the end of the amphib tour. In three years.

Three years of hauling jarhead marines around the Mediterranean or Guantanamo aboard a gator freighter was a prison sentence. And Norfolk was second only to Murmansk for lousy places to be stationed. This had to be the worst set of orders in the navy.

Coburn couldn't understand why this was happening to him. It made no sense. He had been picked to be an advisor over many officers senior to him. Admiral Benjamin had personally frocked him to lieutenant even though he had yet to be picked by the selection board. He was working on the Phoenix Program with all the spooks and mercenaries and CIA. Shit, he was a hot runner, top of his class, super officer. And he was serving a year in Dinkville, with all its stink.

He deserved to have better jobs than this. There had to be some. For sure, there was a lieutenant's command-at-sea spot available since Vernon was dead. He had been certain that was going to be offered to him. Mondello and Theodore must have stopped that. Those two were too chummy with the enlisted, especially Cruz and Robinson and McGruder. They were also buddies of Sperling. A bunch of lieutenant commanders afraid of a junior officer with more brains and talent were sabotaging him.

In the last paragraph of Sperling's letter was an option to leave the navy and become a civilian and join the reserves. But in the last sentence, Sperling wrote that he hoped Coburn would stay in. Fuck him, the lying sack of shit, thought Coburn.

No medals, nothing. And with the tight security of Phoenix, no one was going to learn about his courageous deeds. And then that insubordinate stubby spic Cruz comes up to him one night, takes the cigar out of his mouth, and tells him all polite and deferential how much he and Robinson are concerned about him and his smoking dope in the hootch.

If he could have, Coburn would have killed Cruz. This illiterate flange head was telling him, an officer, how to act. Coburn had kept these thoughts hidden and instead laughed it off, saying it wasn't him but the Vietnamese sailors who were smoking dope in the shelter between the hootch and the shower. It had been bothering him, too, and he'd be sure to talk to Chang about it in the morning. From then on, Coburn only lit up when out of sight and downwind.

The pilot announced that they were starting their descent and turned on the fasten seat belt sign.

* * *

A couple of weeks before flying to Hong Kong, Coburn took stock of where he was. After over nine months in-country, he had less than three months left. With a week R&R, a week turnover to whoever would replace him, and a week or so of debriefing and checking out in Saigon, he had maybe seventy days left in Phu Cuong running around the boonies. That should be enough time to turn things around.

First, he had to get out of those lousy orders to the amphib in Norfolk. He should be able to do that by messing with the schedule. If the job was that time sensitive, he'd make sure he wouldn't be available. Maybe catch a wound and a trip to the hospital. Nothing serious, but enough to delay him so that they'd find someone else to send to that shit barge. A leg wound in the fat part of the thigh like Marty Lender's would do nicely. And he'd get a Purple Heart out of it.

And he had to get even with Cruz and Robinson for ruining his reputation and career.

Then there were the medals and press release for the folks and pussy back home. Couple those together, get himself a good set of orders to San Diego, and see if he could bang Ba Hung. But how to do it all? And get himself out of this funk?

Coburn realized he needed a break. A real break. He put in for R&R and picked Hong Kong on the recommendation of the officer in charge of the PBR detachment. Civilized, inexpensive, good shopping, good food, good pussy.

With $1,200 in his pocket and wearing his clean, starched khakis for the first time in months, Coburn checked into the Sheraton in Kowloon. He spent hours shopping at the Royal Navy's China Fleet Club, Royal Rugs, Van Ziang tailors, and Jimmy Yip's jewelers. Evenings were long and boozy dinners at Jimmy's Kitchen, Landau's, and Gaddi's. Nights and mornings were spent with a beautiful Hong Kong woman he met the first night at the bar in Jimmy's Kitchen. They ate breakfast in the Sheraton overlooking the harbor or in the lobby of the Peninsula Hotel across the street.

He sent a carpet to his parents for their den, he had a suit and a dress blue uniform tailored for himself, and he bought a Seiko watch for his sister and a Rolex for himself. At Jimmy Yip's he bought a princess ring of gold and jade and a gaudy ring of glass, which he gave to his rented companion. The princess ring was for Ba Hung, whom he had every intention of seeing again.

The last night in Hong Kong was an orgy of liquor, food—including a flaming brandy dessert of fried ice cream called a Satellite—and crocodile tears from the Hong Kong woman who vowed she'd stay chaste until he returned to her. When Coburn took his seat on the Saigon-bound airplane, he was hung over, burping up vestiges of pickled onions and Satellite, and had about seventy-five dollars left in his wallet.

Between fitful naps on the flight, Coburn planned the rest of his time in-country.

* * *

The DC-8 returned the Hong Kong R&R troopers to the war. After picking up his bag, Coburn got in line at the cashier's booth to exchange his US dollars for MPCs. He passed his seventy-five dollars to the staff sergeant, who counted out seventy-five dollars in Military Payment Certificates and asked if he had been out of the country the previous Wednesday. Coburn said he had, and the noncom gave him a form with a stamp over a signature.

"Sir, we changed the MPCs Wednesday. Unannounced so the black marketers and the bar girls didn't get a heads-up." The US military, in an attempt to limit black market trading in MPCs and the hoarding of MPCs by Vietnamese civilians—mostly bar owners and prostitutes—would print and issue new MPCs. The date for the new MPCs was always a closely guarded secret. Only US forces were authorized to exchange their old MPCs for the new ones. The old MPCs now had no value. They were merely scraps of paper.

Coburn looked at the MPCs he had in his hand and noticed that they were all crisp and different colors than the old issue.

"Since you were out of the country and couldn't exchange your old MPCs for the new ones, this form will let you go to any paymaster or cashier and exchange any of the old MPCs. Without this form, the old MPCs are useless. Colored toilet paper."

Chief McGruder was waiting for Coburn as he walked out of the Tan Son Nhut terminal.

"Welcome back, Dai Uy. Cruz is coming down tomorrow morning, so I figured you'd stay overnight at the hootch and then go back with him. Ba Be's got a bunk room ready for you." McGruder tossed Coburn's bag into the back of the jeep and drove into the Saigon midday traffic, Coburn riding shotgun.

Bill Wilson, the intel officer, was sitting in for Mondello while the boss was out visiting RAG Alpha, Vernon's old assignment. After a brief chat about the splendor of Hong Kong pussy, Wilson went back to the pile of papers on his desk and Coburn borrowed a jeep and drove to the Continental Hotel, joining a journalist and a photographer he knew at a verandah table. After the MACV Five O'clock Follies—the daily official and sparsely attended press briefing of useless information—two more journalists joined them. He liked the camaraderie of these men. Scruffy, jaded, cynical, and smelly, they had no qualms about drinking too much or using drugs.

Coburn's stomach was still tender from the night before, so he uncharacteristically drank Bireley's orange soda. Passing on the Rex for a steak, he slurped some noodles from a stand across the street. Bored, he wandered into the Red Door.

"Where you been, Cluck?" It was the big-titted whore who had accused him of impotence the last time he saw her. She grabbed his arm, putting herself between him and several other girls looking for an early evening customer.

"You buy me Saigon tea?"

Coburn took a stool at the bar, and she sat next to him, pushing her thigh against his and rubbing her left boob on his arm. He ordered a 33 beer and nursed it as she let the phony cocktail sit in front of her untouched.

"How you been?" asked Coburn. She didn't look all that happy.

The whore told him that she just lost a lot of money. She had over a thousand dollars in MPCs, and then the US Army suddenly changed the money. Not knowing it was going to happen, she didn't have the time to find an American who would change the money for her. She even went to the army cashier, and he threatened to have her arrested by the White Rats since only US forces were allowed to possess MPCs. Now she was poor. No money. If he wanted to pay her in the new MPC, she'd sucky sucky his dick for cheap cheap.

"You still have the MPCs?" he asked.

"Sure, upstairs. No good now."

He looked at her, mulling it over in his mind.

"You give me your MPC. I can exchange them into new MPC and then into piasters for you. You don't want to have any MPCs in your possession."

"You no shit me? You do for me?" Her hand reached over to the inside of his thigh and then started stroking his crotch. "You do, we do long time tonight. Whatever you like. I love you no shit, Cluck."

"Whatever I want? I can take pictures of your pussy or you sucking my cock?"

"Whatever you like."

* * *

The next morning Coburn took his signed and stamped form and the whore's MPCs to the army cashier and received $1,100 worth of new MPCs. He stuffed the roll into his pocket and drove the jeep back to the RAG headquarters advisory hootch.

The whore sat at the front of the Red Door until dusk, waiting for him to come back with her money. She swore if she ever saw him again, she'd cut off his dick.

* * *

"Hi, John Paul Jones. How was R&R? Where'd you go?" Teller put a pile of reports on Ba Nguyen's desk in the intelligence office.

"Morning, Thieu Ta. Hong Kong. Ran out of money and Tums, so figured I'd better come back," answered Coburn with a smile. "Anything going on?"

"Been a little quiet for a change. The SEALs and Aussie special forces guys are conducting some PRU indoctrination and training for a couple of days starting today. Navy's sending two PBRs up there to join them. Nothing much, just training. You might want to watch."

"Where they doing this?"

"At the junction of the Saigon River and Thi Tanh River. That flat point here." Teller's index finger pointed to a spot on the map sitting on Ba Nguyen's reference table behind her desk. She glanced at the map and made a mental note to get that information to Vo since he was surveying possible depot sites a few kilometers downriver.

Coburn walked over to look at the map, although he knew the exact location of the junction. He just wanted to get close to Ba Nguyen, who continued to treat him like a leper.

"What kind of training they going to do?" he asked.

"Pretty much night ops. Insertion, ambush set up, extraction. And daytime surveillance and staying out of sight. Routine stuff."

A sense of excitement started Coburn's heart beating harder. This could be the golden opportunity.

"Major, I don't think there's much for me to pick up, but I was thinking that the two enlisted advisors at the RAG might find it worthwhile. If nothing else they'd get a little introduction to the PRUs and Phoenix. It's a little out of their pay grade, but do you think it would be okay if I take them up there tomorrow night in the skimmer so they can watch?"

Teller thought for a moment and said, "I don't see any problems with it. Do you, Bob?"

Captain Neal looked up from his writing and said, "Nope, seems like a good idea to me. Might be a little boring, but sure, go ahead. We'll let them know you'll be there tomorrow night."

* * *

Cruz and Robinson were out of the hootch when Coburn came back. Ba Mei was busy sewing VC flags in the bunkroom. Coburn took out the duffel he carried on operations and unlocked the gun cabinet. He took out an AK-47, a loaded banana-shaped magazine, a Chicom pistol, and a full clip of pistol ammunition and put them in the duffel. After locking the cabinet, he opened the gray steel supply cabinet and grabbed a handful of olive-drab compresses and bandages and put them in the duffel. He put a new battery in the PRC 25 and did a radio check with the TOC to test it.

He walked down to the pier, greeting several of the Vietnamese sailors with a smile and returning their salutes, then climbed aboard the skimmer. Coburn put his duffel in the never-used storage compartment beneath the driver's seat and sat down in the stern. He was excited. This was going to work out perfectly.

Back in the hootch he went through the mail and message traffic, keeping himself busy until Cruz and Robinson walked in.

"Hey, Dai Uy. How they hangin'?" asked Robinson.

"Pretty good, Chief. I've got something for you and Cruz for tomorrow night. Orders from the top want you to observe some of the spook training with me." He went on to explain that they would be taking the skimmer after dusk the next day and motoring up to the junction of the Saigon and Thi Tinh rivers. Once they got there, they'd just be observers.

"Sounds pretty good to me, Dai Uy," said Cruz. "When we coming back? Will we need rations?"

"Yeah, maybe not a bad idea to take with some C-rats. Let's figure we'll be back no later than late the next afternoon. Is the skimmer fueled up?"

"Yes sir, Cruz just did a tune-up on it. We can water ski up there if you want to," said Robinson.

"Not a bad idea, Chief, if we had any water skis."

CHAPTER 37
NORTH OF THE VILLAGE OF XONM DUA

Vo started walking toward the Saigon River at dusk. He had received information that the Americans were training mercenaries several kilometers up the river and that some of the American advisors to the Southerners' navy would be motoring up the Saigon River to observe.

Armed with that information, he timed his travels so that the American advisors would be past his pickup point when a fisherman's sampan would take him across the Saigon River. Reaching the pickup point, a small clearing on the Saigon River bank, Vo dropped his small pack in the shelter of thick foliage and sat down on the hard dirt to wait.

He awoke from a light sleep with a start. Two children from the little strategic hamlet just north of his hiding spot walked out of the shadows with a cloth-wrapped bundle.

Strategic hamlets were essentially South Vietnamese government relocation camps used to separate the populace from the NLF. This one, like many others, was filled with disgruntled peasants upset at having to leave their land and ancestral homes.

And like many others, this strategic hamlet supplied food to the nearby NLF troops.

Vo knew both of the children. Motioning them to be quiet, Vo opened the bundle of still-warm tapioca root and an aluminum container of cold tea. Hidden in the dense brush, the man and the two children silently ate the starchy root and drank the tea. At dawn, the children would return to the strategic hamlet.

* * *

Just after sunset, Coburn walked back to his bunkroom, checked the clip in his .45, and put a round in the chamber. Easing the hammer back, he put the pistol into its holster and buckled it around his waist. He looked around the room to make sure he hadn't forgotten anything, picked up his backpack, helmet, and flak vest, and walked into the hootch's main room. He unlocked the gun cabinet, took out his own, Robinson's, and Cruz's M-16s, and six magazines and quickly locked the cabinet.

Robinson walked out of the enlisted bunkroom, carrying his helmet, vest, and backpack, smiled at Coburn, and grabbed his rifle and two magazines. A few seconds later, Cruz came out and did the same. He had an unlit cigar in his mouth.

"Should be a pleasant ride tonight, huh, Dai Uy?" said Cruz. "I won't light this thing until after I check the fuel and oil. Don't need to learn that lesson again."

The three laughed, told Ba Mei they'd see her tomorrow afternoon, picked up an insulated water jug, a sack of C-rations and the PRC 25, and walked down to the pier. Cruz checked the motor while Robinson stowed the M 16s, backpacks, helmets, and vests.

"Cruz, how about you drive. I'm intending to nap, and I don't trust the chief to stay awake. That cigar will keep you from dozing off," said Coburn.

"Aye, aye, Dai Uy. I hear you about the chief. He's an old man, needs his sleep," said Cruz as he moved to the center console.

"Fine with me, youngsters. Shit, I haven't been on a field trip like this since grammar school. Wake me up if we get in a firefight and you guys can't handle it, please," said Robinson as he settled himself down on the pile of flak vests in the skimmer's bow.

"No firefights on this trip," said Coburn. "No Indians. This will be more relaxing than a bottle of Jack Daniels."

Cruz idled the skimmer up to the floating log boom protecting the bridge and just powered the skimmer up and over the boom, the propeller guard scraping over the logs. The ARVN guards waved down at them as they passed under the bridge and bumped over the upriver log boom. Clear of the bridge, Coburn picked up the handset of the PRC 25, did a radio check, and then reported their location to the TOC and gave their destination and an estimated time of arrival in about an hour and a half. Cruz lit his cigar, and Robinson walked back to the center console and leaned against it, facing aft so he could talk to Cruz and Coburn.

"Shit, Dai Uy, this is like old times. We haven't been out on the water together in, what, four, five months? Feels good," said Robinson.

Coburn was alive. He felt good. The kind of good he felt after a firefight or when he was calling in an airstrike or artillery or pulling the trigger and watching a chunk of a person disintegrate. His senses were sharp, he could feel his heart pounding. He just felt good.

"Yeah, I think it has been a couple of months, Chief. This spook stuff they handed me has kept me pretty busy and out of your hair," said Coburn. "Aren't you getting pretty short?"

"Let's put it this way, sir. I can sit on the edge of a dime and swing my legs. Do chin-ups on the bar stool rung. Trip on coffee stains. Twenty-eight days and a wake up, but who's counting?" said Robinson.

"Got your orders? Where you going?" asked Coburn.

Cruz butted in, "If there was any justice in this world, sir, his black ass would be a guest of the USA in a cell in Portsmouth Naval Prison for immoral turpitude."

"Look who's talking," laughed Robinson. "The only reason this fat-ass, cigar-smoking cocksucker isn't in jail is that he's extended here for another year because he thinks there's no extradition treaties between DC and Hanoi."

"No, seriously, Chief, where you going?" asked Coburn again.

"Pretty fat shore duty, sir. I guess the navy was dumb enough to select me for senior chief, and they needed an E8 gun and missile cocker on CINCPACFLT staff, so I'm headed for three years in Pearl Harbor. I'll have to learn to live with the wife and kids again."

"Hey, congratulations on the promotion. Senior Chief Robinson. That's got a nice sound to it." Inside Coburn could only think that Robinson was getting the kudos and the choice jobs while he was not. Well that was soon coming to an end.

"Thanks, Dai Uy. I appreciate that. You must be due for orders soon."

"Yeah, I'm under the three months left in-country mark. Got a letter from my detailer, and he mentioned some stuff, but nothing definite. Maybe get a command at sea. Maybe grad school and then command. I won't find out for a while."

The skimmer motored slowly up the middle of the Saigon River. At the bend that turned the river from a west to a nearly due-north direction, Coburn took the handset and again made a position report to the TOC. But he had not pressed the handset button. Only he and the two enlisted men heard the report.

Coburn was anxious. Excited. He was waiting for his opportunity. It had to happen.

Robinson went back to the bow and lay down on the flak vests and closed his eyes, hands folded over his chest. Within a minute, he was sound asleep. Coburn looked at the steady rise and fall of the big man's chest. Sailors could sleep anywhere, anytime.

Coburn found himself hyperventilating. With an effort he slowed his breathing and tried to calm himself.

The night was dark and clear, a half moon shining on a calm river. Coburn could make out the banks on either side. There were no lights from villages. The outboard motor purred loudly. Cruz's husky outline at the console was four feet in front of him. Coburn smelled the cigar.

Ahead and to the left, Coburn could see the clearing he had picked on the riverbank, just south of a little inlet. Time seem to be slowing down. The noise of the engine and the river slapping against the fiberglass hull got louder and louder. Coburn stood erect. He lifted the leather holster flap and took out the .45. The pistol felt good in his hand. Solid, clean, heavy, cold. Good. He looked down at his right hand, put his thumb on the hammer, and cocked it.

After taking a deep breath, holding it and then slowly letting it out, Coburn walked up behind Cruz, held the muzzle of the .45 a few inches from the base of the man's skull, and squeezed the trigger.

The gun barked, ferociously loud. The muzzle blast briefly wiped out Coburn's night vision. As if in time-lapse photography, he saw the top of Cruz's head disintegrate in an eruption of blood and brains and bones and hair. Warm, wet blood and tissue spattered the murderer's face and hands, soaking his uniform from the chest up. He could smell the cordite, cigar smoke, and brains. Cruz slumped forward onto the steering wheel, and the boat started a slow turn to the right.

Robinson had sat up and was yelling something, but Coburn's ears were ringing, and he couldn't make out the words. Robinson stood up, looked all around, and then walked quickly toward the dead man and Coburn.

Raising the .45 with his right hand and steadying it with his left, Coburn pointed the gun at Robinson and pulled the trigger rapidly four times, the gun bucking after each shot. Robinson crumbled on the deck in front of the console.

Pushing Cruz's body away from the steering wheel, Coburn pulled back on the engine throttle and let the boat idle. He walked around the console and looked at Robinson, who was alive but bleeding badly from his groin. The big man was lying on his side, mouth open, gasping in pain. As he had done with the NVA officer, Coburn put the .45 in Robinson's mouth and blew the back of his head off.

Out of the corner of his eye, Coburn noticed something glowing on the deck and realized it was Cruz's cigar. Holstering his pistol, Coburn reached down and picked it up, looked at it in the moonlight, brushed off some tooth fragments, and put it in his mouth.

Vo and the children heard the six pistol shots coming from the middle of the river. Motioning the children to stay put, he looked through the foliage and saw the small boat in the middle of the river. It picked up speed and seemed to be steering for the clearing in front of him.

Smoking the dead man's cigar, and with the wind drying the sweat and blood on his face, Coburn felt excited, happy, relieved. He steered the skimmer to the clearing and gunned the throttle to push the boat onto the riverbank. He secured the engine, jumped over the bow, and tied the boat to a scrubby tree trunk about five meters from where Vo and the children were hidden. Coburn stood in front of the boat, breathing deeply, feeling every cell in his body. Looking around the empty clearing, he smiled with his lips pursed around the cigar.

Coburn waded into the warm river water and climbed over the side of the boat. He wrestled into the PRC 25 shoulder straps, stepped over Cruz's corpse, and lifted the console seat and took out his duffel. Coburn slipped back over the side, waded back onto the clearing, and put the radio and the duffel down. He took out the AK-47, its magazine, the compresses, and bandages, and placed them on the dry ground. The Chicom pistol went into his pocket. Wading back into the river and reaching over the skimmer's side, he grabbed the M-16s and magazines and put them next to the radio.

Vo watched, not understanding what he was seeing and debating whether to move himself and the children away. He was unarmed, and he could see the American had several rifles as well as a sidearm. Staying put was best for the moment. Then he heard the sound of the fisherman's sampan.

The ringing in Coburn's ears had finally stopped, and he heard the sampan engine. Thinking rapidly, he realized it was probably some night fisherman or crabber. Then he smiled and spat out the cigar. This was indeed his lucky night. Now he'd have enemy bodies. He reached over and grabbed one of the M-16s, made sure the magazine was firmly seated, put a round in the chamber, and shifted the selector switch from safe to full automatic. He walked over to the skimmer, climbed in, put on his helmet and flak vest, and squatted behind the outboard motor to wait for the fisherman. The sampan motor grew louder. He could see the shadow of two people in a sampan coming across the river. Shit, they were headed for the clearing. He couldn't have planned it this well.

Vo was breathing deeply and rapidly, his heart racing. The sampan was his ferry across the river. If he warned off the sampan, the American would open fire on him and the children. If he didn't, the American might shoot the fisherman. Going against his instincts, Vo sat still, watching, with his hands over the children's mouths. They buried into his chest.

The sampan was heading right at the clearing. Giggling with his good fortune, Coburn lifted the M-16 to his shoulder and sighted down the barrel. The dinks were too stupid to realize the skimmer wasn't some fishing boat. God damn gook idiots are going to win me a Silver Star or Navy Cross and some pussy-filled job in San Diego or maybe DC. He opened fire on the sampan, spraying it until his magazine was empty, then loaded and emptied another magazine.

The sampan, its engine still running, ran up and onto the riverbank a few meters from the skimmer. A white-haired man, his conical straw hat askew, lay moaning on empty fish baskets, bone and meat dangling from what used to be his right arm. A smaller figure, which Coburn guessed was a woman, was lying on her stomach with her head over the gunwale, not moving.

Coburn walked over to the sampan, and after a little trial and error, shut off the tiny motor. He pulled out his .45 and emptied the rest of the clip into the old man and woman. Holstering the pistol, he walked back to the other M-16s and fired all the ammunition into the sampan and the two Vietnamese.

Slowly he walked back to the skimmer and with some difficulty, dragged Robinson's and Cruz's bodies onto the clearing in front of the skimmer. He turned them onto their backs, took the AK-47, and shot half the magazine into the corpses and the rest of the ammunition at the skimmer, making sure it was well holed.

Vo continued to watch, not understanding anything of what he was seeing. This was madness. This was beyond war. He hugged the children closer.

With a grin of satisfaction and a feeling of well-being, Coburn took the compresses and bandages and wrapped them around Robinson and Cruz's gaping wounds. He put Robinson's M-16 in the man's dead hands and picked up some of the spent cartridge casings and tossed them on the ground near the dead sailors. Stepping back, he admired his work. Robinson looked as if he had died fighting for his country. Then he did the same with Cruz, but twisted the body a little. He found the cigar stub and stuck it between what was left of Cruz's teeth and jawbone.

He pushed the sampan back into the water, waded in, and towed the slivered boat a few meters down the bank. Then he pushed it hard aground on the riverbank. The bodies in the boat needed no rearranging, he thought. He walked back up the clearing and grabbed the AK-47 and a handful of casings from the ground and placed the rifle in the remaining hand of the dead fisherman and sprinkled the casings over the bodies. Perfect, he thought. Just perfect. After he finished with the Chicom pistol, he'd give that to the old lady and call it a night.

Nearly giddy, Coburn walked around the clearing, picking up cartridges and sprinkling them near the bodies. Then he grabbed his duffel, tossed it back into the skimmer, and surveyed the battle scene he had created. Satisfied, he picked up the PRC 25 and walked back to the skimmer and sat at the console. He took the Chicom pistol out of his pocket and made sure there was no round in the chamber and the ammo clip was out.

Pushing the empty pistol's muzzle against the outside of his right thigh, Coburn considered the angle. Then he tried it against the inside of left thigh, right buttocks, outside right calf, inside left calf. He rehearsed pulling the trigger at each location, and finally decided that it felt most natural against the inside of his left thigh.

For the first time, he was nervous and anxious. This was going to hurt but not too bad. Like going to the dentist. He had his first aid kit, which contained a morphine syrette if it hurt too bad. It was worth it. A dust-off out of this shit hole, a Purple Heart, probably a Navy Cross, a stay in some nice, clean hospital between clean, white sheets and round-eyed nurses, a shortened tour in-country, and no way do they give a shit job to a wounded war hero.

He put the clip in the pistol and chambered a round. Then he keyed the PRC 25 radio and tried to make his voice sound as if he was out of breath.

"Break break TOC this is Crazy Razor, emergency, emergency, over."

The Tactical Operations Center replied immediately.

Coburn found he didn't need to make himself sound out of breath; the nervousness in his voice was good enough.

"Firefight coordinates 677155, east bank Saigon River. Fire suppressed. Three friendly WIA, including me. My enlisted badly hurt. Trying to keep them alive but don't know how long. I'm wounded in leg but stable. Need dust-off ASAP to get my men out of here. Shielding their bodies with mine. Repeat, need dust-off medevac ASAP. Two VC KIA that I know of. Over."

"Roger Crazy Razor, two PBRs in your area, headed your way with medic. Will be your location in one five. Hang in there, Crazy Razor. Can you give me names of other WIA? Over."

"Cruz. Robinson. Me. Over."

"Roger. Stay on this frequency. Hang in there."

"Will do. Out."

Coburn looked at the radio and decided he needed a finishing flourish. He stood the radio up on the console then shot it twice with the pistol, knocking it into the congealing blood on the skimmer's deck. Then he took the morphine curette from his first aid kit, and unscrewed the cap that protected the sharp needle. Sitting at the console with his eyes shut, he jammed the curette into the top of his left thigh, and squeezed the tube.

He opened his eyes, took a deep breath, and then another. Spreading his legs, he pointed the pistol at the meaty part at the inside back of his left thigh, took another deep breath, and then squeezed the trigger.

The pain was intense and excruciating. Unlike his rehearsal with the gun unloaded, when Coburn pulled the trigger this time, he dropped his hand a bit. The bullet left the muzzle and instead of passing through the fleshy part of his thigh, smashed directly into his femur, shattering the bone and severing the sciatic nerve. Bone and bullet fragments shredded his thigh and grazed an artery.

His ears felt plugged, as if he were underwater. His scalp prickled, and then all was quiet, dark.

Vo eased his grip on the children, not believing what he had seen.

CHAPTER 38
NORTH OF THE VILLAGE OF XONM DUA

The two patrol boats' bows settled onto the dark river as they lost speed. The coxswains steered loose figure eights, each boat covering the other with its machine guns. In the humid, black night, the only lights were the phosphorescence of their wakes, the green glow of the radar screen, and the red console dials. Barely audible over the radios' static, the engines thrummed at a low idle, the boats just making headway against the river current. The Saigon River's signature stink of rotting vegetation, sewage, and sulfur mixed with the diesel exhaust and the sailors' sweat.

The officer in charge pressed the button on the radio handset and raised the other boat. In a whisper turned raspy from too little sleep and too much smoke, he said, "It looks quiet. We're using the starlight scope, and nothing's moving. You see anything, over?"

"Just the skimmer and some sampan, nosed onto the bank. Over."

"Roger that. Let's put up some illumination. We'll put one above the south side of the clearing. Wait until ours is burning, and then you put one on the north side. I'll take us in about twenty meters to the left of the skimmer and go ashore with Nguyen and Doc. You see anything moving, open up, and we'll get flat. I don't care if it's a fucking cow, open up. Keep us covered. Over."

"Roger, illum north part of clearing and be ready to engage. Over."

"Keep the area lit as long as we're on the beach. I don't think this will take long. Out."

He ordered his coxswain to beach the boat on the riverbank. The order was a formality; the sailor was already steering to the shore. With a nod from the officer, the boat's gunner dropped an illumination round into the mortar tube.

A muffled whoosh was followed a few seconds later by a pop in the murky scud above. A faint sizzle, and then the clearing was bathed in a cold, sterile white. Low cloud bottoms reflected the light downward.

The other boat's mortar whooshed, and its illumination round popped. Now two white suns hung in the night sky from their parachutes.

"Okay, let's go," said the officer. There was no need to whisper. The two boats were clearly visible in the flares' light.

Nguyen was the Vietnamese scout and interpreter. A traitor to the Viet Cong and Hanoi, he had deserted to the chieu hoi amnesty and reeducation program. Now he was a member of the South Vietnamese military, assigned to the American river patrol squadron. Holding his M-16 rifle in one hand, he slid on his ass over the gunwale onto the riverbank. Doc, a US Navy hospital corpsman who was a foot taller than Nguyen, stepped over the boat's gunwales with his medical bag over his shoulder and his rifle at the ready in both hands.

Pointing to the portable radio, the officer said to the coxswain, "Give me the prick 25, you use the boat radio." Putting his hand on the helmet of the forward machine gunner, the officer said, "You open up if anything moves besides us." He shouldered the portable radio, grabbed his M-16, and stepped into the mud bank.

With their rifles at the ready, the three men looked around the clearing before taking another step. The skimmer belonged to the US advisors to the South Vietnamese Navy's River Assault Group Bravo. It was tied to a tree trunk, firmly beached on the riverbank. Two bodies in olive-drab uniforms lay a few meters in front of the skimmer. At the north end of the small clearing where a narrow tributary joined the Saigon River were two other bodies, sprawled in a sampan, conical hats of straw held onto their bodies by chin straps of braided fishing line.

Nguyen walked toward the skimmer, looked in, and then quickly climbed aboard.

"Trung Uy! Bac Si! Come quick! Hurry!" shouted Nguyen.

The two Americans ran over to find the Vietnamese bent over another body. In the brilliant illumination, the blood on the skimmer deck looked like thick, dark, maroon molasses. "He alive. Hurt bad."

"Jeez, Doc, that's Crazy Razor," said the officer.

Doc pushed Nguyen out of the way. "I got him. He's bleeding out. Leg's shot to shit. We're going to need a dust-off ASAP, sir."

"We can't get a helicopter in here." The young officer keyed this radio. "Come in and pick up a friendly WIA ASAP. Call in a medevac for that clearing across the river. Keep an eye open for a sucker ambush. Over."

"Roger. Calling in dust-off. Coming in alongside skimmer," answered the boat in mid-river. Its engines roared as the cox-swain opened the throttles.

As the corpsman worked to stop the bleeding, Nguyen and the officer helped load the unconscious American into the second patrol boat. Doc stayed with the wounded man, applying a tourniquet and inserting an IV needle as the boat backed off the mud bank.

The American and the Vietnamese walked around the clearing, taking inventory. The two men lying in front of the skimmer were dead, face up, their bodies pierced with bullet holes, parts of their heads blown away. Two M-16s, magazines empty, lay beside them. Brass bullet casings littered the area. Both men recognized what was left of the corpses' faces—they were the two US Navy enlisted advisors assigned to River Assault Group Bravo.

Nguyen walked back to the skimmer. Its fiberglass side was peppered with bullet holes. An M-16 and a pistol lay in the pool of congealed blood on the deck of the boat. Propped against the boat's steering console was a shattered PRC 25 radio.

Nguyen said, more to himself than to the officer, "Trung Uy, prick 25 no good, he couldn't use it."

The American walked back to the skimmer, looked at the radio, and shook his head. "Shit, Crazy Razor was probably out cold, he couldn't have used that radio even if it was working."

The two walked over to the sampan, where an elderly Vietnamese man and woman lay dead. Like the skimmer, the sampan and the bodies were riddled with bullet holes. An AK-47 assault rifle with a long, curved magazine, crab pots, fishing tackle, and the ubiquitous dented aluminum bowls of Vietnam lay in the sampan, covered with the old couple's blood.

"What do you think, Nguyen? VC? Ambush?"

"Trung Uy, this old man and woman. Probably go fishing for crab. I don't understand what I see. I don't understand gun."

"Yeah, this is a fucking mess. Just a fucking mess."

A medical evacuation helicopter was landing across the river. Doc sheltered the stretcher with his body from the rotor's dust storm. The radio squawked.

"Transferring WIA to chopper. Over."

"Roger. When you get done, relay to the boss that we've got four bodies including two USN and some weapons. Give him the details on Crazy Razor. I'm guessing they'll medevac him directly to Saigon. Then come back here."

"Roger that. Relay info and return to you. Doc confirms they're taking WIA directly to Saigon. Be there in about fifteen. Over."

The sun was rising above the flat Saigon River plain. The officer told his boats to stop firing illumination and ordered them to come to the clearing.

Using his Kodak Instamatic, the officer photographed the bodies, the skimmer, and the sampan. Then for the next hour, both boat crews loaded bodies and weapons into one boat and made a bridle for the other boat to tow the skimmer and the sampan back to the base at Phu Cuong.

Two small children and a man with a dirty face and filthy hands wearing what was at one time a white shirt, dirty gray shorts, rubber sandals, and a conical straw hat walked from the mangroves into the clearing. They stood there, not moving. Just watching.

Nguyen walked up to them. Neither the children nor the man moved. Their eyes were fixed on the old couple's bodies waiting to be loaded aboard the boat. Nguyen greeted the odd trio and asked if they knew who the Vietnamese couple were. The man looked at the ground, then at the American officer approaching, and said they were old people from the village across the river; they were going fishing for crabs. As they did every morning. They were grandparents.

Nguyen translated the officer's questions and the curt answers. Did the grandparents own guns? No. Were they VC? No. Where did the guns come from? I don't know. Were there VC or North Vietnamese in the area? No.

"Okay, Nguyen. Let's go back to base." The officer gave the man some C-ration cigarettes and gave the children small bars of soap with little cartoon characters and Vietnamese slogans extolling the virtues of cleanliness embedded in the soap surface. Neither the man nor the children said anything. They kept on staring at the dead fisherman and his wife.

The two patrol boats towing the bullet-riddled skimmer and the sampan returned to the base at Phu Cuong with the four bodies and the weapons. A sailor, nodding at the old couple's bodies, said to the officer, "Sir, if those two are VC, then Charlie must be really hurting, and we just might win this fucking war."

SEEKING

CHAPTER 39
SAIGON

"Pete, what the hell happened?" asked Captain Powell.

"Captain, I don't know very much," answered Mondello. "Here's what I do know for sure, sir. Coburn and the two enlisted advisors for RAG Bravo—Cruz and Robinson—were going to observe some Phoenix Program night training and indoctrination. In a secure area. They checked in with the TOC when they left Phu Cuong, and then about two hours later, Coburn called in for a dust-off, saying they had been in a firefight. PBRs found them. Cruz and Robinson dead. Vietnamese man and woman dead. Sampan shot up. Skimmer shot up. Radio shot up. Coburn out cold with his left leg hanging by a shred. AK-47 in the sampan with the dead man and woman. Chicom pistol in the skimmer. Helmets and flak vests in the skimmer except for Coburn, who was wearing his. Skimmer was tied to a tree trunk."

Theodore, sitting next to Mondello added, "Bill Wilson and I surveyed the scene the next morning sir. Talked to the TOC and the PBR OinC as well as the advisors to the ARVN in the area. Pete and I also talked to the army doc at the morgue. According to the TOC, Coburn called in and said both Robinson and Cruz were still alive, and he was shielding their bodies with his own.

There were compresses and bandages all over them, but the doc said he had never seen bodies this shot up and still in one piece. There was no way they could have been alive more than a few seconds after getting hit."

"So you think Coburn was shielding dead men?" asked Powell.

"I don't know, Captain. Something stinks."

"What do you mean, Jim?"

"First off, that area is probably more secure than a corn field in Iowa, sir. There has been no activity or even hints of VC or NVA movement in that area for months. And our intel is pretty good there. Second, while Cruz and Robinson were turned into hamburger meat, Coburn only had one wound, although it was a bad one. His helmet and flak jacket were clean, no blood, no shrapnel, no nothing. But his shirt was soaked with blood and guts but not his blood and guts. Third, there was a Chicom nine-millimeter pistol sitting in the skimmer, with nearly a full clip. How'd that get there? Fourth, why was the skimmer tied up? What was it doing there beached on the riverbank? It looks as if they got attacked on land, although the boat was full of blood. Why were they on land? And finally, the radio was destroyed by gunfire. Yet when Coburn asked for the dust-off, he said the fire was suppressed. Did they get hit again after he called?" Theodore looked at Mondello and raised an eyebrow.

"The oddest part, sir, are the Vietnamese dead," said Mondello. "According to the locals, a man and wife, both in their sixties or seventies. He's a fisherman, and she helps him. Lost a son who fought for the ARVN. Only two weapons, the AK-47 and that Chicom pistol that was in the skimmer. From what we could tell, only one magazine for the AK. Given the number of bullet holes in the skimmer and in Cruz and Robinson, that couple were remarkable marksmen. They made every bullet count. I guess it's possible, sir, but it sure doesn't make sense to me."

"Maybe there were more VC?" asked the Captain.

Theodore shook his head. "Bill Wilson and I looked at their bodies and the sampan. It seems as if every bullet Cruz, Coburn and Robinson had—six magazines of M-16—wound up in the old lady and man or in the sampan. Coburn's .45 was empty, and the casings were in the skimmer. It looks as if the firing was limited to the old couple and our guys, sir. That seems like a pretty weird match. Two grandparents against the three of them? Doesn't make sense to me."

"To me, too. Where's Coburn now?" asked Powell.

"He's been in Oaknoll Naval Hospital in Oakland for the last six weeks, sir," answered Mondello. "Chief McGruder saw him in the hospital in Saigon and talked to the docs. They had him pretty well doped up. According to McGruder, they got him stabilized and then amputated his left leg. No hopes of saving it. Once he was strong enough to travel, they medevaced him back to Oaknoll for further surgery and rehabilitation. He never really was coherent while he was here, sir. No chance to talk to him."

Powell nodded his head and looked at his desk for a few quiet moments. He got up, walked to the door, and asked the yeoman to bring in a pot of coffee and three cups. The three men sat silently, each lost in his own thoughts, waiting for the coffee.

After the yeoman left the pot and they poured themselves a cup, Powell broke the silence with a question. "What's the impact of this?"

Mondello spoke first. "If there's one Vietnamese navy unit that can operate without advisors, it's probably RAG Bravo. Unless their CO gets blown away or promoted out of the job, they're in good shape. We're expecting the senior advisor, a lieutenant, in-country next week, and Robinson's relief will be here the week after that, so we're covered. I recommend not bringing in another enlisted to fill Cruz's spot. Leave it vacant, sir."

"I agree with Pete, Captain," said Theodore.

"Okay, let's leave that billet open. What about Phoenix?" asked Powell.

Mondello and Theodore exchanged looks. Mondello nodded for Theodore to go ahead.

"Captain, Pete and I have been giving that a lot of thought. Neither of us likes the program or the CIA guys running it. As far as we can tell, it's a bunch of cowboys with no adult supervision. If there's anything positive happening, we can't measure it. In fact, from what I know of it, all we've done is scare the shit out of a lot of civilians. We've probably created more VC with the program. And frankly, sir, we don't have the expertise to participate in it."

"What do you mean by that, Jim?" asked the senior officer.

"We're not special warfare officers, Captain. We're not SEALS or UDT. All of our officers are surface ship drivers, surface line officers. I made a mistake in putting Coburn into that slot, sir. I was trying to put him into a place where we could use his talents and minimize his weak points, but it seems the opposite happened. A trained special warfare officer is what's needed."

"Listen, Jim, we all put him in that slot. You, me, Pete, and even the admiral chopped on that move," said Powell. "I'm going to recommend to the admiral that we just gap that position. Politics may force him to do otherwise, but let BUPERS find the properly trained person for the job."

Powell looked at his watch. "Let's grab some lunch and then meet with the admiral. We have to decide what we do about this Coburn thing."

Over lunch the three men talked about where they were being assigned next. Mondello, who had only a month left in-country, had been selected for promotion to commander and was being given command of a new Knox-class destroyer escort out of Long Beach. Theodore had two and a half months left and had a letter from the detailer that he was on his way to becoming executive officer of one of the big guided missile cruisers stationed in San Diego.

Both men were happy with their assignments. And they appreciated Powell's comments that they were being recognized for the fine jobs they were doing in Vietnam as well as all their hard work that went on before that. Powell was not the type to flatter.

As for Powell, the admiral had asked him to stay on for another two months, and then he would either be sent to be the chief of staff of the Seventh Fleet or commandant of midshipmen at the Naval Academy. The two younger men were impressed since both of those jobs were known for producing flag officers. Powell said he was looking forward to either job and that being selected for rear admiral would be a real honor. But having served in DC before and watching what the flag officers went through back there, he knew there was a lot more than privilege involved in being a flag officer.

After lunch they went into Vice Admiral Benjamin's office. He waved them to the conference table, called for another pot of coffee, and took the seat at the head of the table. Looking at the three officers, he smiled and shook his head.

"I just realized I'm losing all three of you in less than three months. Your replacements better be as good as you three have been, or I'll have your swinging dicks back here before you can kiss your wives hello." The three men all laughed at his remark.

They discussed at length the incident involving Coburn, Robinson, and Cruz, deleting the junior enlisted advisor position at RAG Bravo, and not filling the liaison position in the Phoenix program. The admiral agreed with their recommendations but said that the Phoenix program was coming out of Washington, and if he was pressured to fill it, he'd grab a SEAL from in-country.

"So, gentlemen, what do we have here with Coburn? At first glance, it looks as if he acted heroically. On second glance, it smells. So what do we have? A hero? A negligent loose cannon? Or something worse? Pete, you worked with him the most. What's your opinion of Coburn?"

"Admiral, Clark Coburn is charming, smart, and good looking, and I trust him as far as I can throw this table. A team player on the surface but strictly out for himself. And there's a part of him that, in my opinion, borders on the criminal."

"You mean shooting the chieu hoi and that prisoner, Pete?"

"Yes, sir. And I had reports from my counterpart, Commander Minh, of using drugs. The Vietnamese are pretty loose on that, so for it to come up through his chain of command seems pretty serious."

The admiral looked at Theodore. "Anything to add to that, Jim?"

"He's very quick witted, sir. Uses his sense of humor to good effect. But I received a very disturbing letter a few months ago from Chief Willits about him."

"Who's Willits?"

"Admiral, Chief Willits was Lieutenant Doug Vernon's senior enlisted advisor. He was with Doug when they got ambushed, and despite his own wounds, he got Doug to a medevac chopper. Doug's family requested that Willits escort the body and say a few words at the ceremony in Arlington. After the ceremony, Willits talked with Doug's fiancée. She wanted to know all the details of his death, what it was like in Vietnam, trying to fill in the blanks.

"It seems she had received a letter from Coburn claiming to have done what Willits did. When we were at school in Coronado, she had met Coburn. A very attractive young woman. She became very upset when Willits said Coburn wasn't there. The more he thought about it, the more upset Willits became. She kept in touch with Willits and said she was also very upset and wanted to tell Coburn's senior offices about what a 'scoundrel'— her words—he is. Willits told her to hold off and he'd write a letter."

"Art, you have anything to add?" asked the admiral of Captain Powell.

"I've talked to Coburn's previous CO from the DeKalb a few times about him, sir. Described him as smart, handsome, lazy, and always working the system looking for an advantage to replace hard work. Lots of unused potential. Good ship handler. Did a satisfactory job but an underachiever with a sense of entitlement. The little I've had to deal with him only confirms what you've heard from Pete and Jim. And, with me at least, he was not above twisting the truth."

Admiral Benjamin leaned back in chair and steepled his fingers, thinking. Then he sat up straight.

"The US military has had some real problems. Cancers. My Lai. Tet. Pueblo. I'm sure Walter Cronkite will be happy to have another mess to talk about. The navy doesn't need a Lieutenant Calley. What I see here ranges from an ambush that can't be explained to an idiotic land excursion to the outright murder of sailors and civilians. I don't know how that leg wound fits in. And the sole surviving character in this drama happens to be part of the Phoenix Program. Shit."

The admiral stopped talking and looked at each of the three men carefully. "Okay, here's what we're going to do. I want this incident investigated thoroughly, but not by the nincompoop army or MACV. Get Naval Investigative Service in here and put them on it. If NIS finds a crime, we charge and prosecute. I have a feeling they won't find much more than what we know now. Probably need to talk to the JAG back at CINCPAC. Have someone talk to Coburn when he's not drugged out. Give him all the legal rights he's entitled to, but I want someone to ask him what happened that night. You agree with this?"

The three men nodded, not saying anything.

"Also, I want Coburn out of the navy. That's certain to happen since he's lost a leg no matter what NIS comes up with. The thought of him with a navy disability pension makes me sick. I know we can't do anything about the Veteran's Administration benefits, but I'll be damned if he gets navy benefits."

Powell spoke up. "Admiral, we can't deprive him of what's legally his."

"Yeah, I know, Art. I'm just ranting. But you're getting the gist of my feelings, obviously."

"No doubt about that, Admiral."

"And finally, have Coburn mentally examined by the shrinks in Oaknoll. I don't want the navy responsible for letting a one-legged psychopath loose to prey on the population."

CHAPTER 40
OAKLAND, CALIFORNIA

Major Sidney Byrd, US Marine Corps, looked like a product of central casting or a recruiting poster model. Tall, fit, tan, his olive-drab uniform immaculate, the perfect dimple in his necktie, his shoes spit shined to where they looked like patent leather. He walked out of the hospital elevator, asked for directions at the nurses' station, and was directed to an empty office. He put his leather briefcase on the desk, took out a file and a pad of legal-size notepaper, and checked his wristwatch. One of the nurses came in with a paper cup of coffee, apologizing that she didn't know if he wanted cream and sugar. He smiled, said black was fine, and sipped the coffee, standing by the desk as he skimmed the file again.

Precisely on the hour, Lieutenant (Junior Grade) Clark Coburn, United States Naval Reserve was brought in by a nurse pushing his wheelchair. She closed the door as she left. Coburn was in light blue pajamas and blue robe with a slipper on his right—and only—foot. He was clean shaven but by military standards needed a haircut. Coburn was pale, almost white.

Major Byrd put down the file, walked around the desk, and put his hand out.

"Sid Byrd. COMNAVFORV has requested my boss, CINCPAC, to provide you with special counsel. I'm it."

Taking his hand, Coburn said, "Hi. Clark Coburn. What's a special counsel? Am I in the shits? You a lawyer?"

Major Byrd pulled the chair from behind the desk, put it next to the wheelchair, and sat down. "Yes, I'm a lawyer. I'm from the CINCPAC JAG office in Pearl Harbor."

"They sent you from Hawaii to this?" Coburn pointed out the window at the drizzly overcast Oakland weather. "Who'd you piss off?"

Major Byrd ignored the question and tapped the file. "Admiral Benjamin and my boss want to make sure you are given all the legal assistance you are entitled to under the Uniform Code of Military Justice—and more."

"What the fuck, Major? Am I under arrest or something? What did I do?" Coburn nervously licked his lips and found himself staring at the gold oak leaves on the marine's uniform.

"No, you're not under arrest. You have not been charged with any crime." Pointing with the file folder at what was left of Coburn's left leg, he asked, "How're you doing?"

"Fucking terrible is how I'm doing, sir. I shut my eyes in Vietnam and wake up here with my left leg gone. Toes that aren't there itch like crazy. Pain and surgery and more pain and more surgery. I'm still taking fucking painkillers, and now they've started me on rehab with some bitch of a physical therapist while they fit me with a wooden leg. That's how I'm doing, Major."

"You talked to Naval Investigative Service. Was there a JAG officer in attendance, advising you?"

"Yeah, some NIS civilian and a navy lieutenant JAG."

"What kind of advice did he give you?"

"The JAG? Not much. He said he was there to make sure I didn't incriminate myself or toss any legal rights down the shitter. I told him how could I incriminate myself if I hadn't committed any crime, and I'd answer the NIS guy's questions as best I could. That JAG officer said he advised against that. Y'know, he thought I shouldn't talk to the NIS guy. But I told him 'no sweat,' and I had no problem telling this guy whatever he wanted to know."

"Were you read your rights?"

"That Miranda thing? Not having to say anything, having an attorney stuff? Sure. The NIS guy said it, but hell, I had a JAG sitting there, and how could I incriminate myself if I didn't commit a crime?"

"What did he ask?"

"Oh, let's see...basically describe the night Robinson and Cruz got killed from when we left the base until I went unconscious. Which I did. Told him how we got ambushed by some dinks in sampans, firefight, trying to keep Robinson and Cruz alive, calling for a dust-off. You want me to go over it all again for you?"

"No. What did the NIS man say to you about why he was there?"

"Said he was investigating the 'incident,' as he called it. Didn't say much. Just took notes, had a portable tape recorder running, although the JAG guy said I could ask him to not do that, but I figure why not? Then the JAG tells me I was the focus of the investigation and to keep quiet. That's bullshit. The guy was talking to me because I was the only one who lived through that firefight."

"What did you think about the NIS interview?"

"I figure it must have been part of some award procedure. I'm guessing that when you get to the big medals like the Medal of Honor, Navy Cross—you know, those kind—they must do some sort of investigation, and he was doing that. I mean, Robinson and Cruz put up a big fight that night. Two heroes. Lost their lives."

"And you?"

"Well, I guess me, too. But I lost a leg, not my life," added Coburn in a quiet, deliberately quaking voice while looking at the floor in what he felt certain was a convincing show of modesty and sadness.

"I want to go over your file and situation, Lieutenant. Is your mind clear? You thinking okay?"

"Sure. I'm only taking aspirin or Tylenol or something now. Yeah, my mind's clear. I'm thinking okay. But my mind's also pissed at losing my leg. And two real good men. And no Medal of Honor hanging from my neck is going to give me my leg back."

Major Byrd stood up, put the desk chair behind the desk and sat down, the file open before him.

"Lieutenant, the investigation had nothing to do with awards. The investigation was ordered by COMNAVFORV—Admiral Benjamin—to determine if there may have been criminal activity that night. Activity such as the murder of civilians and military personnel, self-mutilation, and the issuance of and following of unlawful orders. And maybe more."

The blood drained out of Coburn's already pale face. His scalp tingled, his stomach fluttered, and he felt panic.

"Are you okay?" asked Major Byrd. "You don't look too good."

"I don't feel too good, Major," said Coburn in a genuinely weak voice.

Major Byrd got up and walked quickly to the nurses' station and brought back one of the nurses, who took Coburn's pulse and then his blood pressure.

"Looks as if you almost fainted," she said. "We'd better get you hydrated and flat for a while." She looked at the marine attorney, who nodded and followed her as she pushed Coburn to his room and helped him into bed.

"Can I talk to him this afternoon?" Major Byrd asked the nurse, who said if it was okay with Coburn it was fine with her. Coburn, his head against his pillow, nodded.

Coburn lay on his back in his hospital bed. He wanted to cry but wouldn't let himself. Why couldn't he ever get a break? Why did the world insist on shitting on him? Fucking navy was out to make a scapegoat out of him. Wasn't losing a leg bad enough? And who the fuck is this John Wayne grunt attorney nosing around?

He must have dozed off. Standing next to his bed was Major Byrd and the nurse. She took his blood pressure and pulse and smiled at him. "You up to getting in your wheelchair, or do you want to stay here?" she asked.

"Here," he said quietly. "Okay with you, Major?"

The attorney pulled up a chair and sat down next to Coburn's bed. The nurse cranked the bed so that Coburn was nearly sitting up. She walked out and closed the door, leaving the two men alone.

"Why they after me, sir? What the fuck did I do besides get my leg shot off and try to save my men?"

Major Byrd was silent for a while. Then he said, "Lieutenant, there are many inconsistencies in what you said happened and the physical evidence found at the scene. And this has led to suspicions and conjectures."

"Jesus. That's a fucking war over there. It's combat. Why the fuck are they wasting time investigating a fucking firefight? It's a war!" Coburn realized he was whining and shut up, frustrated and feeling persecuted.

"What kind of inconsistencies, sir?" he asked in quiet voice.

"There's the report from the ARVN G2 advisor at the time and his intelligent analyst," the attorney looked at his file, "a Captain Robert Neal and a Mrs. Nguyen, that the two Vietnamese KIA were not VC, but in fact a seventy-three-year-old fisherman and his seventy-year-old wife. They reported the area to have been quiet with no reported enemy activity for over two months. There was no evidence of any enemy weapons besides the one rifle and pistol found at the scene. Shell casings, vessel damage, and wounds indicate that all fire was confined to a single sampan, your boat, and the dead. There's nothing to support your claim that you were ambushed by multiple sampans."

"But they were there. Fucking big firefight."

"So you've claimed, Lieutenant." Major Byrd paused, waiting for a reply. He proceeded when Coburn remained silent.

"There's the question of how a sampan could ambush and stop a skimmer capable of 35 knots, a skimmer with intact engine, fuel, and working steering. Why were the American dead found on the land? Why was the boat tied to a tree? Why did you have blood on your uniform and face and in your hair but not on the outside of your flak vest and helmet? Why was there so much blood in the boat and so little near the two American bodies? And how did the Chicom pistol wind up in the skimmer, beneath your body? You called into the Tactical Operations Center supposedly wounded, but the doctors say you would have been unable to do so given the extent of your injuries."

Major Byrd closed the file. "I could go on, but let's stop it here. If you want to read the reports, they're in here. And there are also reports of your personal history before the incident, including shooting prisoners and illicit drug use."

"Christ Major, it's combat, it's war. Shit happens."

Major Byrd's face might have been made of stone. Then he sighed and looked down at the space on Coburn's bed where his left leg would have been and said, "Neal and this Mrs. Nguyen claim anecdotal information of an eyewitness to the events of that night who refuses to come forward. This person reported a skimmer landing at the clearing, a man tying up the boat and then taking two lifeless bodies from the boat and placing them on the land. This same man then opened fire, killing the fisherman and his wife, shooting weapons at the bodies and the sampan and the skimmer, then shooting himself. This supposed witness description of the event is the only thing that does not seem to be inconsistent."

"You don't believe me, do you sir? You think I killed my men and those gooks were civilians?"

"First off, it doesn't matter if I believe you or not. Secondly, it's my job to make sure your rights are protected, you get the best legal advice I can provide, and any proceedings against you follow the UCMJ and the Constitution of the United States. You are my client, not the Department of Defense or the navy. I will zealously defend you. I'm a damn fine lawyer, Lieutenant, and I'll give you the best counsel you can receive. But if you want different representation, I suggest you hire a civilian because you'll never get anyone better than me in uniform."

"But Major, you said I wasn't under arrest or being charged."

"That's right. Not yet. With all the inconsistencies and suspicions and circumstantial evidence the investigation has uncovered so far, a prosecution must still prove you guilty beyond all reasonable doubt. In my opinion, if you were tried with what they have now, they could prove you to be a person of questionable character and integrity, but whether or not they could prove you guilty of murder is probably less than fifty-fifty."

"Shit, I'm getting fucked," said Coburn.

"Not yet. But if they keep digging, you could be facing much worse odds. If they can find that witness or confirm his story, your odds get real lousy," said the marine.

"What can I do to get out of this, sir? Can I get out of it?"

"Taking the investigation further gets expensive in time and manpower, which NAVFORV can ill afford. A court-martial would attract the newspapers and television news reporters. This would fit right in with My Lai, Tet, and the Pueblo as examples of military incompetence. So I see three options for us."

"Us? Who besides me?" asked Coburn.

"'Us' is you and I, Lieutenant. First, if you actually did what that eyewitness claims—and I'm not saying you did—you could give a new statement, essentially confessing. We would do that only for the purpose of creating an insanity defense. But so far I think the psychiatrists and psychologists would call you sane. If we can't prevail with an insanity defense, you'll be facing life imprisonment, possibly a death sentence. Two, you stick with our story, NIS keeps digging, and they charge you and you go before a court martial. They'll have a tough time proving your guilt, but they just might succeed. If they can find that witness, they will succeed."

"So I can say I was nuts and live with a bunch of mental cases for the rest of my life, or I can stick by what happened and maybe go to Leavenworth for the rest of my life? That's a great fucking choice, Major. This isn't fair."

"It wasn't very fair for Robinson, Cruz, and the fishermen."

"You don't like your client, do you, Major?" asked Coburn.

"Whether I like you or not doesn't matter, Lieutenant. I represent you and counsel you to the best of my abilities, Lieutenant," said Major Byrd in a low voice.

"Yeah, I hope so, Major. What's my third choice? Cut off my other leg?"

"I've been approached by counsel for the navy with an offer. He knows a trial will be long and a media circus with an uncertain chance of conviction. And having NIS dig further may not bring up much more since the only available witnesses are you and two little kids who only heard the battle and didn't see much other than the medevac. And everything is clouded by the fog of war, which also may be our best defense. So he proposes that you resign your commission upon discharge from the hospital, waive all future navy benefits, particularly a disability retirement, hold the US Government harmless, and take a general discharge. You still keep all your veteran's benefits, GI bill, Veteran's disability payments, that sort of stuff. If you do that, they close the file."

The marine thought for a moment and added, "And you'd better hope that the Vietnamese government doesn't come after you. Although given the situation, I don't think that'll happen."

Coburn and Major Byrd talked for another hour, then Coburn read through the file of reports.

* * *

Early that evening, Major Byrd called CINCPAC headquarters and asked for the navy JAG officer he had met with before flying to Oakland.

"Steve? Hi, it's Sid Byrd. Coburn took the deal. He's signed the waiver and accepts a general discharge per the agreement."

After listening for a few seconds, Major Byrd said, "Yes, Coburn's getting away with murder."

THE WALL

CHAPTER 41
NOVEMBER 12, 2012
WASHINGTON DC

"Good afternoon, sir, Doctor."
The driver helped the ambassador and his wife into the back seat of the armored luxury SUV. From the driver's seat he looked into his rearview mirror at the white-haired diplomat and his graying wife.

"Where to, sir? Back to the embassy?"

"Not yet," said Vo. "In all my time here, I have never seen the Vietnam Veterans Memorial. Please take us there."

A DC policeman halted traffic. "The Wall, sir?" asked the driver as he pulled away from the front of the Hyatt Regency Hotel.

"Yes, that's right, the Wall," said Vo as he reached across and put his hand on his wife's. "After all these good-bye parties and testimonials, I need a real change."

"Yes, sir. Tomorrow morning I take you to the airport, and then you're on your way home, sir. You must be excited."

"We are indeed excited," answered Ngoc. "These years in DC have been wonderful, but it's time to go home. See our children and grandchildren. There's a new little girl we haven't even seen yet."

"Mr. Ambassador, you're retiring, right? What will you do to keep busy?"

Vo chuckled. "I'm afraid that will not be a problem. Dr. Tram here has a long list for me. The American Secretary of State told me she calls such lists 'honey do' lists."

Ngoc punched Vo playfully on his arm. "Don't listen to him. The only thing on my list is for him to enjoy himself and relax. After almost forty-five years of sacrifice and dedication to his country, it's now his turn."

The driver smiled and said, "Madame Doctor, I agree with you. But we will miss the ambassador very much. And what will we do without our favorite embassy physician?"

"You will, first, not get sick. But if you do, you will see my very able replacement."

The embassy car turned onto Henry Bacon Drive.

* * *

Coburn had been to Washington, DC, several times since the Vietnam Veterans Memorial was completed nearly thirty years ago. He had intended to visit the Wall each time, but for whatever reasons he never did.

He was in DC to attend his niece's wedding. With an entire day to kill before his flight back to St. Louis, he took up the offer of a nephew to play tourist and visit the Smithsonian and the Wall.

Holding on to his niece-in-law's arm, he crossed the street, not noticing the black SUV with diplomatic plates that had stopped for him. He limped as he walked.

A year ago the Department of Veterans Affairs fitted him with a new prosthetic leg, a high-technology, lightweight contraption of titanium and carbon graphite, a byproduct of sending troops to Iraq and Afghanistan. His leg-swinging limp of over forty years was still prominent, but he found himself more mobile and less susceptible to fatigue. A year ago he'd have been exhausted half-way through the Aerospace Museum.

There were only a few people standing at the long, black marble slabs in the cold late afternoon rain. A handsome, well-dressed Asian couple and a well-built Asian man in his thirties, all wearing dark raincoats and carrying umbrellas, were walking toward the Wall, the young man a short distance behind the older couple.

* * *

Without saying anything, the driver stopped walking at the edge of the walk. He scanned the area, then looked at the ambassador and his wife, then continued his scan. The young man wore an earpiece and lapel microphone and carried a semi-automatic pistol in his shoulder holster.

The only people he could see were the ambassador and his wife, a man with a limp, a younger couple, and a docent handing out brochures, tracing paper, and graphite to rub on the tracing paper.

"What are you looking for, dear?" asked Ngoc, holding her husband's arm as they walked slowly down the path, the face of the Wall.

"I don't know what I'm looking for, Ngoc. I don't even really know why I wanted to see this before we went back home. But look at this. Just look at this." He stopped and waved his hand, shaking drops off the umbrella.

"What do we have here? How many? Sixty thousand names? All dead, killed in their youth. For what, Ngoc? This is a forest of dead men. At least they could get all the names on these marble slabs." Again, he waved the umbrella at the Wall. "What would we have needed? Five kilometers of marble slab. And we still wouldn't have all those who died."

She held onto his arm tight and put her head on his shoulder. "You thinking of Ky, dear?"

"Ky? Yes. And many others."

He thought of Ninh, his school friend Le who died in his wheelchair, his middle brother, an old fisherman and his wife, a mother and her hair-lipped child, a traitor, two little children going to tend their fishing nets. Yung and their unborn child. And many others.

* * *

Coburn walked the length of the Wall and then back to the alphabetical list of names and wall locations. The docent handed him a pencil, several rectangular sheets of paper, and a graphite bar.

"These are so you can take a rubbing of the names," she said. "You must know some of these." She walked down the path and picked up some wilted flowers at the base of one of the slabs.

Coburn looked up Orlando Cruz, Mathew Geralds, Charles Robinson, and Douglas Vernon. He wrote down the marble slab and line locations of their names, then walked down the path, looking for the names. The only people on the walk were the docent, his nephew and wife, and the Asian couple.

"You know some of these names, Uncle Clark?" asked his nephew, who with his wife had walked up to him. Coburn was at the slab with Robinson's name on it. At the bottom of the slab, someone had placed a Combat Infantryman Badge, an Army Commendation Medal, a Purple Heart Medal, and sergeant stripes. There were similar objects along the base of many of the slabs, including photographs, religious pictures, and poems.

"Yes, I do. Too many," answered Coburn. He wasn't going to make any rubbings of the names.

Coburn looked at a small object at the bottom of a slab. He recognized an olive-drab Timex watch with a nylon strap and nudged it with the toe of the shoe on his prosthetic leg.

"Uncle Clark, I've never heard you talk about your time in Vietnam. You see much action?"

"Yes, I did. But I was in special forces. You know, like the SEALs. We couldn't talk about it. Still can't. You wouldn't want to hear about it anyway. War is hell." Coburn pressed his lips and put on what he assumed was a bitter face.

"Get any medals?"

"I was awarded a lot. But medals don't mean anything. So I refused them all. Just pieces of metal and fancy cloth."

"I didn't know that. You lost your leg and turned down the medals. That's really something. Must have been an interesting transition from SEAL to selling insurance."

"I was tired of war and killing," said Coburn. Then he laughed. "And the insurance business let me afford your two ex-aunts."

The three laughed. His nephew's wife reminded him of Jean Miller.

Ngoc and Vo were walking near them when they laughed. She turned and stared at the three, finding the laughter and smiling cruelly out of place. Her husband's face was like stone, lips pressed together grimly. His eyes were locked on the tall man with the young couple.

Coburn's gaze met Vo's. He stared at the man's face. What the fuck's the matter with this Chinaman, thought Coburn. What's his fucking problem? Does he know me? Unless he's some waiter at Uncle Chin's in St. Louis, I sure don't know his yellow ass. Fuck him.

Vo adjusted the umbrella to better cover Ngoc, his sleeve sliding back from his wrist. Coburn noticed a brass bracelet, sparking a momentary, odd, indefinable, vague bit of memory that he immediately ignored.

Coburn turned away from Vo and wrapped his arm around his nephew's wife. "What say I take you two for a drink or a cup of hot coffee before we return the rental car to the airport?"

* * *

The SUV drove slowly through the rain up Twentieth Street on the way to the embassy. Vo was quiet. Ngoc reached over and put his hand in her lap.

"Vo, did you know that man? Had you met him before?"

561

"No, dear, I never met him. But there was something about him...I don't know how to say it...disturbing about him. Like a person who has rotted from the inside. I don't know..." Vo let his words die.

After a few minutes, he sighed deeply, looked out at the traffic and the rain, then put his arm around his wife's shoulder and pressed her tightly against him.

"I'm tired of this. It's been long. But tomorrow we go home. And the first thing I want to do when we get there is hug and kiss my new granddaughter."

GLOSSARY

I, II, III, IV Corps: Military divisions of South Vietnam, each a US Army or USMC area of operation. I Corps's northern border was the DMZ, II Corps covered the center of South Vietnam, and II and IV Corps were the most southern.

33, Ba Muoi Ba: A popular Vietnamese brand of beer.

Amphib: Amphibious, referring to a ship or base dedicated to amphibious operations. A ship used to land or support landings of US Marine Corps on hostile shores.

AO: Area of operations. MACV had divided South Vietnam into chunks of geography and assigned these AOs to various military units. These units—usually US Army and ARVN divisions, all commanded by two-star generals—were responsible for all military operations in their AOs.

Ao dai: A traditional Vietnamese female garb, a full-length, tight-fitting, silk tunic split from the hip down worn over long pants.

ARVN: Army of the Republic of Vietnam.

B-40: A rocket-propelled grenade used by VC and NVA.

Ba: Misses, ma'am, title for mature woman. Feminine equivalent of Ong.

Balboa, Oaknoll: Balboa Naval Medical Center and Oaknoll Naval Medical Center. Large navy hospitals in San Diego and Oakland, California.

Bac Si: Doctor.

Binh Tram: A way stop encampment on the Ho Chi Minh trail.

Bravo Zulu, BZ: Well done, good job, nice work.

Buddha stick: A marijuana cigar tied with cotton twine that has been soaked in opiates or LSD.

BUPERS: The US Navy's Bureau of Personnel.

Butter Bar: A US Army second lieutenant.

BOQ: Bachelor Officers Quarters, lodging for single and unaccompanied married officers.

C-4: A stable and easy-to-use explosive.

Cafe sua: Strong, espresso-like coffee floated atop sweetened condensed milk.

Calley: The principal US Army officer involved in the My Lai massacre. See My Lai Massacre.

Charlie: VC.

Chicom: Chinese communist.

Chief, Chief Petty Officer, CPO: The most senior of US Navy enlisted ranks. The three levels of CPO: Chief Petty Officer, Senior Chief Petty Officer, and Master Chief Petty Officer.

Chieu hoi: The South Vietnamese government's program of VC/NVA defection. Also the term to describe the defectors who were interrogated, trained, or indoctrinated and who then often worked for Southern and allied forces as "Kit Carson" scouts or interpreters. Kit Carson scouts were used as reconnaissance and intelligence scouts for US military units.

Chin chin: A drinking game where a glass of liquor is drained while everyone chants "chin chin."

CINCPAC: Commander in Chief, Pacific. Four-star officer in charge of entire Pacific land, air, and sea forces.

Civvies: Civilian clothes, as opposed to a military uniform.

Claymore: A command-detonated, directional mine that sprays heavy buckshot.

Co van: Advisor.

Cobra: A dedicated attack helicopter, as opposed to the multipurpose Huey.

Commanding Officer, CO, Charley Oscar: The officer in command of a commissioned military unit such as a navy ship or aircraft squadron, or an army or marine corps company. Referred to in the navy as "Captain," "Skipper," or "the Old Man," no matter what rank. Senior to an Officer in Charge.

CONUS: Continental United States, the US minus Alaska and Hawaii.

Crew Served Weapon: An infantry weapon that requires more than one person to transport and operate such as a recoilless rifle, heavy machinegun, or mortar.

Cum Shaw: Bartered goods and services.

Dai Uy : Vietnamese rank equivalent to US Army, Air Force, and Marine Corps captain or US Navy lieutenant.

Dai Ta: Vietnamese rank equivalent to US Army, Air Force, and Marine Corps colonel or US Navy captain.

Detailer: A US Navy officer assigned to BUPERS responsible for the assignment of personnel.

Di di: Run quickly. Move quickly.

Di di mau: Run like hell.

Dink: Pejorative term for Vietnamese.

Dust-off: Helicopter medevac.

Executive Officer, Exec, XO: The officer second in rank and seniority to the commanding officer of a unit.

FAC: Forward Air Controller

Fitrep: Fitness report by a senior officer, usually a commanding officer, on a junior officer in the senior's command. Fitreps are important in determining assignments and selection for promotion to higher ranks.

G2: Intelligence department.

G3: Operations department.

GAZ: Soviet bloc and Chinese military vehicle.

Geedunk: Snack shop.

Gook: See Dink.

Gator Freighter: See amphib. "Gator" refers to alligator, which can move from sea to shore.

H&I,, Harassment and interdiction: The firing of ordnance into an area where all were considered enemy combatants in the hopes of disrupting logistics and operations, as well as killing the enemy. HE: High explosives.

Ho Chi Minh Sandals: Sandals made from truck tire tread soles and inner tube rubber straps.

Ho Chi Minh Trail: Logistics routes from North Vietnam through Laos, Cambodia, and South Vietnam used to supply VC/NLF and NVA forces. The North Vietnamese referred to the trail as the Truong Son Strategic Supply Route.

Honeywell: Hand-cranked grenade launcher manufactured by the Honeywell Corporation.

Hootch: Quarters hut.

Illum: Illumination.

Intel: Military intelligence, G2.

JAG: Judge Advocate General, the uniformed attorneys in the military.

Jaygee, jg: US Navy rank of lieutenant (junior grade), equivalent of US Army, US Air Force, and US Marine Corps first lieutenant.

Junior Officer, JO: Junior ranks of US Navy commissioned and warrant officers, usually referring to ensign and lieutenant (junior grade) but sometimes extended to lieutenant.

KIA: Killed in action.

Landline: Telephone, as opposed to radio communications.

LBFM: Little brown fucking machine, a term referring to an Asian prostitute, usually Filipina.

MACV, Military Assistance Command, Vietnam: Senior over-riding military command in Vietnam, commanded by a US Army four-star general.

Medevac: Medical evacuation of wounded and ill.

MPC: Military Payment Certificate, scrip used in place of US dollars for in-country purchases by US military personnel. MPCs were an attempt to control the flow of black-market goods and currency.

My Lai Massacre: The mass destruction of the village and residents of My Lai by a unit of the US Army on March 16, 1968.

Naval Supply Center, NSC: Major US Navy logistics center.

National Liberation Front, NLF: Viet Cong.

NAVFORV, Naval Forces Vietnam: All US Naval forces operating in and around Vietnam. Commanded by a vice admiral–three stars—whose title was Commander Naval Forces Vietnam or COMNAVFORV.

NIS: Naval Investigative Service, the internal investigators of the US Navy.

NOFORN: No foreign. Distribution of information or material limited only to US citizens.

Non Commissioned Officer, NCO, noncom: Military enlisted ranks from E4 through E9. In the Navy this corresponds to third-class petty officer through master chief petty officer.

North Vietnamese Army, NVA: American term for the regular Army of North Vietnam, as opposed to the NLF or Viet Cong.

Number one: Vietnamese term for good, excellent.

Number ten: Vietnamese term for bad, lousy.

Officer in Charge, OinC: The senior officer in charge of a unit or detachment. OinC reports to a commanding officer.

Officer of the Deck, OOD: Officer authorized by the commanding officer to control the movement of the vessel or operation of a naval unit.

OCS, Officer Candidate School: School that trains candidates for commissioning as officers. Training usually consists of four months before commissioning, with additional training following. Navy graduates are usually commissioned in the reserves as USNR, as opposed to USN.

Ong: Mister, sir. The title for an adult man. Masculine equivalent of Ba.

Ops: Operations, G3.

PACFLT: Pacific fleet, commanded by a four-star admiral.

Pueblo Incident: The capture and imprisonment of the crew of the USS Pueblo, a US Navy intelligence-gathering ship, by the North Korean Navy on January 23, 1968.

PCOD, Pussy Cutoff Date: Last day to have sex to allow time for venereal disease to be diagnosed, treated, and cured before returning home. Six weeks before end of tour.

Pogue: Military person in a safe, rear echelon job.

PBR, River Patrol Boat: Fiberglass-hulled boat used by US Navy for riverine patrols. Made famous in the movie *Apocalypse Now*.

People's Army of Vietnam: NVA.

Pho: Noodle soup.

Phoenix Program: CIA-administered pacification and counterinsurgency program aimed at destroying the infrastructure of the VC/NLF organization in South Vietnam.

PRC 25, Prick 25: Portable, two-way radio.

Provincial Reconnaissance Unit, PRU: Special counterinsurgency military forces composed of mercenaries and special operations personnel as part of the Phoenix Program.

Psyops: Psychological operations, as opposed to armed combat operations.

Punji stick: A sharpened bamboo stick dipped in feces and planted as a booby trap by the VC.

RAG: River Assault Group.

R&R: Rest and recreation, a vacation from the combat zone.

Round eye: Caucasian woman.

Ruff-Puff, RF/PF: Regional and provincial governments' military forces in South Vietnam.

Scuttlebutt: Rumor.

SERE: Training in Survival, Evasion, Resistance, and Escape, ending in a mock POW camp.

Skivvy: Underwear.

Skivvy joint: Brothel or pickup bar.

Slick: The UH-1H helicopter, used for transportation and command and control.

Slope, slope head: Pejorative terms for Asians.

Smoke: Colored smoke grenade used for identification and location.

Snoopy: A US Air Force gunship, also called Puff the Magic Dragon.

SNA, Senior Naval Advisor: An advisor to a South Vietnamese Navy unit whose counterpart is that unit's CO.

Swift Boat, PCF: An aluminum-hulled, high-speed coastal patrol craft.

Spooks: Intelligence personnel, spies, and personnel on classified and covert missions.

Tactical Operations Center, TOC: A centralized communication center for combat operations.

Tet Offensive: A NLF/VC and NVA major military campaign launched at the start of Tet, the lunar new year holidays, on January 31, 1968. Although a tactical defeat for the communists, the Tet offensive marked the turning point of the war. US and South Vietnamese forces were caught by surprise. US public opinion turned against the war from that point forward.

Thieu Ta: Vietnamese rank equivalent to US Army, Air Force, and Marine Corps major or US Navy lieutenant commander.

Tin Can: A destroyer or destroyer escort.

Trung Ta: Vietnamese rank equivalent to US Army, Air Force, and Marine Corps lieutenant colonel or US Navy commander.

Trung Uy: Vietnamese rank equivalent to US Army, Air Force, and Marine Corps first lieutenant or US Navy lieutenant (junior grade).

Truong Son Strategic Supply Route: The Ho Chi Minh Trail.

UCMJ: The Uniform Code of Military Justice, the United States military legal code.

USNR: The United States Naval Reserve, as opposed to the "regular Navy" or United States Navy. Reserve officers normally serve under contract while regular officers serve at the pleasure of the president.

Viet Cong, VC: Southern Vietnamese members of the National Liberation Front. Titular Vietnamese communist.

WESTPAC: Western Pacific.

White Mice, White Rats: South Vietnamese national policemen, usually dressed in uniforms with white shirts.

WIA: Wounded in action.

Willy Peter: White phosphorous.

Xyclo: A motorized rickshaw.

NAMED CHARACTERS

Note: The first name in a Vietnamese name is the family name, and the last name is the given name. For example, in Tran Vo, Tran is the family name. It is common to use the given name with a title, such as Ong Vo or Lieutenant Vo. Using only the given name without a title is reserved for those closest and intimate.

Ba Be: RAG advisory group headquarters' hootch maid.

Vice Admiral Daniel Benjamin, USN: Commander, Naval Forces, Vietnam.

Major Sidney Byrd, USMC: JAG counsel to Coburn.

Lieutenant (later Lieutenant Commander) Le Binh Chang, South Vietnamese Navy: XO of RAG Bravo and Coburn's acting counterpart, promoted to CO of RAG Bravo.

Crazy Razor: Coburn's radio call sign.

Lieutenant (Junior Grade) Clark Coburn, USNR: Senior Naval Advisor to RAG Bravo and then Phoenix Program liaison.

Betsy Cooke: Girlfriend of Coburn, college student, then assistant magazine editor.

Engineman First Class Orlando Cruz, USN: Enlisted Naval Advisor to RAG Bravo.

Yeoman First Class Robert Culpepper, USN: Enlisted administrative assistant to Admiral Benjamin and Captain Powell.

Lieutenant Mathew Geralds, Supply Corps, USN: Supply Officer on USS DeKalb, Coburn's roommate on DeKalb and later assigned to NSC Saigon.

Lieutenant Arnold Gordon, USN: Senior Naval Advisor to RAG Bravo relived by Coburn.

Captain Peggy Griffith, US Army: Nurse.

Lo Anh Hoang: VC/NLF District Commander.

Ba Hung: Counterinsurgency course Vietnamese language instructor.

Lieutenant Trung Hoa Ky, People's Army of Vietnam: Assistant basic training platoon leader to Vo, comrade of Vo, member of Transportation Group Detachment South, People's Army of Vietnam.

Thieu Van Le: Disabled veteran of the People's Army of Vietnam, high school classmate of Vo.

Lieutenant Martin Lender, USN: Counterinsurgency course instructor, previously served as an advisor to South Vietnamese Navy.

Hospital Corpsman Chief Petty Officer Donald McGruder, USN: Medical advisor to Vietnamese RAG headquarters' medical officer, Mondello's staff corpsman.

Ba Mei: RAG Bravo advisory group hootch maid.

Kelly Meredith, RN: San Diego nurse.

Jean Miller: Vernon's girlfriend.

Commander Tam Minh, South Vietnamese Navy: Commander, South Vietnamese Navy River Assault Groups, Mondello's counterpart.

Lieutenant Commander Peter Mondello, USN: Senior Naval Advisor to South Viennese Navy Commander, River Assault Groups.

Captain Robert Neal, US Army: Intelligence advisor to ARVN division G2.

Quanh Ahn Ngoc: Medical student and girlfriend of Vo.

Nguyen Hao Yung: Intelligence analyst in ARVN G2 office, VC/NLF member.

Sergeant Khan Cao Nguyet, People's Army of Vietnam: Female administrative assistant to General Ong.

Lieutenant Thu Hai Ninh, People's Army of Vietnam: Company Commander in basic training, comrade of Vo, member of Transportation Group Detachment South, People's Army of Vietnam.

Senior Colonel (later General) Nguyen Sy Ong, People's Army of Vietnam: Transportation Group Commander, People's Army of Vietnam.

Phakdei: Cambodian mercenary PRU platoon leader.

Senior Instructor Tuc Son Pham, People's Army of Vietnam: One-armed basic training senior instructor.

Canh Chien Pham: Lacquer factory owner in Phu Cuong, VC/NLF communications and liaison agent.

Captain Arthur Powell, USN: NAVFORV chief of staff.

Gunner's Mate Chief Petty Officer Charles Robinson, USN: Senior enlisted naval advisor to RAG Bravo.

Lieutenant Commander Harrison Sperling, USN: US Navy Surface Junior Officer Detailer.

Major David Teller, US Army: Operations advisor to ARVN division G3.

Lieutenant Commander James Theodore, USN: Counterinsurgency course classmate of Coburn and class senior student, NAVFORV assistant to Powell for naval advisory effort.

Nguyen Tri Thieu: Professor of Economics, Hanoi Polytechnic University.

Lieutenant Commander (later Commander) Nguyen Van Toh, South Vietnamese Navy: CO of RAG Bravo until transferred to Naval War College in Newport, Rhode Island. Nephew of the President of South Vietnam.

Tran Van Tra: Head of the National Liberation Front.

Lieutenant (Junior Grade) (later Lieutenant) Douglas Vernon, USN: Counterinsurgency course classmate of Coburn, Senior Naval Advisor to RAG Alpha.

Lieutenant Tran Vo, People's Army of Vietnam: North Vietnamese logistician and economist, leader of Transportation Group Detachment South, People's Army of Vietnam.

Machinist Mate Senior Chief Petty officer Francis Willits, USN: Senior enlisted naval advisor to RAG Alpha.

Lieutenant (Junior Grade) (later Lieutenant) William Wilson, USN: Advisor to RAG headquarters intelligence officer, Mondello's intelligence officer.

About the Author

Kenneth Levin is a decorated combat veteran of the war in Vietnam. Blindness forced his retirement from the US Navy with the rank of commander. A student of the war, he completed several drafts of *Crazy Razor* then traveled to Hanoi, Hoi An, and Cu Chi where he interviewed VC and NVA veterans and their children. He incorporated their experiences in the final draft of *Crazy Razor*. Originally from Chicago, he holds degrees from Washington University in St. Louis and the US Naval Postgraduate School in Monterey, California. He and his wife Eileen live in Oakland, California

16345232R00313

Made in the USA
Lexington, KY
20 July 2012